‖‖‖‖‖‖‖‖‖‖‖‖‖‖‖‖‖‖‖‖‖‖‖‖

D0683369

THE "PATTON" OF THE GERMAN ARMY
VS.
"THE LAST KNIGHT"

A chivalrous gentleman of the old school known as "The Last Knight," Gerd von Runstedt was the German Army's oldest active general. Disapproving of Nazism and other modern nonsense, he preferred cavalry to tanks—and had little faith in the lightning panzer warfare proposed for the drive through France.

Opposed to him was youthful, iconoclastic Heinz Guderian, an ex-rifleman and transport specialist who had been called the "Patton" of the German Army, who had earned his spurs in the Polish *blitzkrieg*—and who believed that a spearhead of motorized armor was the only weapon to break through to the Channel.

As the war hung in the balance, one or the other of these two powerful men had to give. . .

THE GERMAN ARMY
1933-1945
Volume II: CONQUEST
By Matthew Cooper

ZEBRA BOOKS
KENSINGTON PUBLISHING CORP.

ZEBRA BOOKS

are published by

KENSINGTON PUBLISHING CORP.
21 East 40th Street
New York, N.Y. 10016

Copyright © 1978 by Cooper and Lucas, Ltd.

All rights reserved. No part of this book may be reproduced in any form or by any means without the prior written consent of the Publisher, excepting brief quotes used in reviews.

First Printing: May, 1979

Printed in the United States of America

Introduction

*Things and actions are what they are, and the conse-
quences of them will be what they will be: why, then,
should we desire to be deceived?*
BISHOP JOSEPH BUTLER
1692–1752

'My hands are done for, and have been ever since the
beginning of December. The little finger of my left hand
is missing and—what's even worse—the three middle
fingers of my right one are frozen. I can only hold my
mug with my thumb and little finger. I'm pretty hopeless;
only when a man has lost any fingers does he see how
much he needs them for the very smallest jobs. The best
thing I can do with the finger is to shoot with it. My hands
are finished. After all, even if I'm not fit for anything
else, I can't go on shooting for the rest of my life.' Thus,
in January 1943, an anonymous German soldier wrote of
his condition during the battle of Stalingrad; it is not
known whether he survived, but it was unlikely. His
suffering was not unique. In the German Army alone, in
the five and a half years of the Second World War, more

than 2,500,000 soldiers were killed and 5,000,000 wounded in the pursuit of an empty cause.

Although no further direct mention of the suffering of individual fighting soldiers will be made, it is as well to remember from the outset that this, in the final analysis, is what this book is all about. For the political and military failure of the German Army, both in the corridors of power and on the field of battle in the years from 1933 to 1945, had one result: the unnecessary death of two and a half million of its men, and untold suffering for countless others. For the world at large, the victim of Hitler's aggression, this was a cause for great relief; for the German Army, it was a tragedy.

The Army of the Third Reich was a failure. Certainly, it won many victories: it conquered Poland in twenty-seven days, Denmark in one, Norway in twenty-three, Holland in five, Belgium in eighteen, France in thirty-nine, Yugoslavia in twelve, and Greece in twenty-one. In the vast spaces of the Soviet Union and the North African desert, although final success was to elude it, its feats have remained remarkable to this day. Indeed, the myth quickly developed that the German Army of the Second World War was an excellent fighting machine, one of history's best, and that its defeat was mainly, even solely, due to Hitler burdening it with tasks far beyond its material resources. But this is to mistake appearance for reality; from the beginning there were evident beneath the façade of easy victory the seeds of later defeat, both in the headquarters of the high commands and on the field of battle. The first transient victories should not obscure this. The German Army was the prisoner of its heritage, both political and military, from which it never succeeded in breaking free. Had it not been for one man—Adolf Hitler—this need not have been so disastrous, for contemporary foreign armies were, after all,

4

suffering the same disability. But the moment this dictator entered the European scene as Führer of the Third German Reich, the fate of the Army was sealed, and an irreversible destiny appears to have determined its descent to ultimate failure.

To understand the reasons for this failure, this book concentrates on two themes: the relationship between Hitler and the senior generals, and the strategic development of the Army. It is argued, firstly, that in their political relationship with Hitler, the generals were largely innocent of the blame that has so often been laid at their door, but that, at the same time, they inexcusably surrendered up their military responsibility and, knowingly, allowed an ungifted amateur to gain operational control of the Army, pervert its strategy and lead it to disaster; and, secondly, that the commonly accepted idea of the German Army having been well-equipped and well-trained, and having practised a revolutionary form of warfare known as *Blitzkrieg*, is a myth. Throughout, I have attempted to look at the ideas and events of 1933 to 1945 as the Army leaders themselves would have seen them, rather than as historians have tended to understand them with the advantage of hindsight. Thirty years after the end of the Second World War we may be able to see clearly where, from the beginning of his dictatorship, Hitler was leading Germany; from the relative security of contemporary western society, we find it easy to condemn all those who condoned or ignored the evils of National Socialism; and, having seen the potential of modern weapons, we believe that we discern their use in a revolutionary strategy during the early years of the war. But are we right to expect the German generals to have done so? I think not. Their background, their heritage of political and strategic thought, was very different from ours, as was the society and age in which they lived. Only when this is realised, do the failures of the German Army

5

under Adolf Hitler become understandable; and only when these failures are recognised, do we see how fortunate were its enemies. It is easy to believe that it was not the Germans who won the early campaigns, but the Allies who lost them, just as it was not the Allies who finally won the war, but the Germans who lost it. For the failings of the German Army under Hitler may we all be thankful; without them, the world today would be a far different place.

Those looking for a detailed, chronological account of the many campaigns undertaken by the German Army from 1939 to 1945 will be disappointed. This, they can find elsewhere. Here, I deal solely with the themes outlined above. In Part One, the reader will find portrayed the political relations between Hitler and the Army leaders from 1933 to 1939; in Part Two, the strategic basis of the Army until 1939 is analysed; in Part Three, the political and military developments in the years of victory are described, covering the campaigns in Poland, Norway, western Europe, the Balkans and the Soviet Union until early 1942; and, in Part Four, the events of the years of defeat are dealt with, showing how the German Army failed to gain victory in the Mediterranean, the east and the west, and how Hitler gained final, total, control over its operation.

This book may be likened, although, alas, not too closely, to the broad brush-sweeps of the Impressionist painters rather than to the detail of the Pre-Raphaelites. It attempts to provide for all readers, whether specialist or general, a fresh interpretation of the fortunes of the German Army from 1933 to 1945, so long overdue for revaluation; but, within the physical constraints of one book, much has had to be left out. Some may believe that my choice of subjects has been at fault, and that important aspects have been omitted; others may think that my selection of facts and quotations has been too subjective, designed only to support my own view of events. Perhaps; but, from the beginning, Napoleon's admonition was always with me: 'It is easier for the ordinary historian to build upon suppositions and to weave hypotheses together than to tell a simple story and stick to the facts. But man, and especially the historian, is all vanity; he must give full rein to his imagination, and he must hold the reader's interest, even if truth be sacrificed in the process.' Whether I have avoided this pitfall, the reader alone can judge.

No man is an island, and no author is entire in himself. The writing of this book owes much to many. Foremost among them is Miss Elaine Austin, who has given much time to reading and correcting the manuscript; her knowledge of the English language and her patience have been invaluable. Lady Liddell Hart, whose hospitality I shall always remember with gratitude, has been of great help in allowing me to work in her husband's library and among his papers; this has been of inestimable value. I should also like to thank James Lucas of the Imperial War Museum, who has been of considerable help in many ways. My editor, Michael Stevens, together with Graeme Wright, has patiently given his great experience to the production of this book; they have my warmest appreciation. Others who have made valuable contributions are Dr. Anthony Clayton, of the Royal Military Academy, Sandhurst, Anthony Shadrake, of King's College, London, Terry Charman, of the Imperial War Museum, Paul Silk, of the House of Commons, Douglas Dales, Miss Elizabeth Malone-Lee, Nigel Carnelley, John Calder, Otto Kuhn and Herr L. Klein, who has been to many institutions in Germany on my behalf. Particular thanks must also go to David Henson, who occasionally let me work! Then there is the army of women who typed the manuscript: Miss Beatrix Hawkins, Miss Susan

Banks, Mrs. Annabelle Egremont, Miss Jane Howard, Miss Ann Power, Mrs. Diana Faires, and, last but not least, Miss Julia Burn; to them all, my thanks. I should also like to express my gratitude to Brian L. Davis for the loan from his collection of the uniform and helmet for the jacket, and to all those at Macdonald and Jane's who have put so much effort into producing this book. Mention must also be made of institutions that I have used: the Library of the House of Commons, the Library of King's College, London, the War Office Library, the Department of Documents and the Library of the Imperial War Museum, and the Public Record Office. Again, may I express my gratitude to all who have helped me.

Matthew Cooper
LONDON, JUNE 1977

The
Years of Victory

Thou hast chosen war.
That will happen which will happen,
and what is to be we know not.
God alone knows.

GHENGHIS KHAN

1

Poland

All units have to maintain the initiative against the foe by quick action and ruthless attacks.
GENERAL JOHANNES BLASKOWITZ

On 1 September 1939, the High Command of the Wehrmacht announced: 'By order of the Führer and Supreme Commander, the German Armed Forces have taken over the active defence of the Reich. In fulfilment of their commission to withstand the Polish menace, troops of the German Army early today launched a counter-attack. At the same time, squadrons of the Air Force started for Poland in order to crush Poland's military objectives.'[1] Twenty-four days later, OKW was able to report: 'The campaign in Poland is at an end. In a consecutive series of destructive battles . . . the Polish Army, numbering several millions, was defeated, imprisoned, or dispersed. Not a single one of the Polish active or reserve divisions, not one of her independent brigades etc. escaped this fate.'[2] A decisive victory indeed, and one gained at the cost of only 10,572 German servicemen killed, 30,322 wounded, and 3,409 missing—some three per cent of the total force engaged. But such an achievement should not obscure two fundamental truths of the Polish campaign: that against an enemy as deficient in the military art as the Poles then were, the invaders were bound to win; and that the German Army gave no demonstration of *Blitzkrieg*, but practised, instead, a traditional form of war, *Vernichtungsgedanke*. From the outset, the armoured idea was still-born.

It is difficult to conceive just how any force could have benefited more from the weaknesses and mistakes of its enemy than the Germany Army did from those of the Poles in 1939. In peacetime the Polish Army consisted of some thirty infantry divisions, one cavalry division, and eleven cavalry brigades—a force which could be doubled on mobilisation. Although well-trained, and aggressive, the Polish soldiers were armed mainly with equipment from the 1914–18 War; they possessed little motorised transport and only a few companies of tanks, amounting to no more than 225 machines in all. Indeed, in modern military equipment and tactical thought, the Poles were alarmingly deficient; they possessed only a few, obsolete aircraft and anti-tank and anti-aircraft guns, and continued to maintain their belief in the efficiency of the cavalry charge and the attack *a l'outrance*.

Even more important than this was the nature of the disposition of these forces to meet the expected German attack. The Poles shared a common border of some 3,000 miles with the Reich and German-occupied Czechoslovakia, the western half of their country being surrounded on three sides by German territory. The terrain of this salient was flat and, except for the river Vistula and its tributaries, possessed few natural obstacles and even fewer fortifications to hinder an invader, especially if the attack was in the dry season.

11

Furthermore, the traditionally bad relations between Poland and the Soviet Union compelled the Poles to divide their limited military resources between both their eastern and western frontiers. The Polish generals could do nothing to alter this. However, they made the situation worse by deploying their forces along the border of the western salient, directly between the German 'jaws.' Because of their intention to defend the main industrial zone, and because of their need to cover the mobilisation of the reserve, their active units were arranged west of the Vistula and near to the frontier, with a concentration in, or near, the Corridor, dangerously positioned between East and West Prussia. The Polish High Command were aware of the problems presented by these dispositions, but relied on their mobilisation being as rapid as that of the Germans, on a continuous line of defence to check any attack, and on an early French offensive against the western frontier of the Reich to deflect, or halt, the invasion. Such were the miscalculations that ensured the rapid defeat of the Poles in 1939: with these handicaps, not even a well-equipped, modern army would have possessed a good chance of victory against the Germans.

The Polish dispositions gave an immense advantage to the German Army High Command. Had the Poles massed well behind the frontier, possibly behind the Vistula, the initial German onslaught would have struck air and exhausted itself before meeting the enemy; its logistical system would have been severely overstrained by the great distances involved; the campaign would have been considerably lengthened, and its outcome less assured. As it was, OKH was offered a guarantee of a speedy victory. Not only could it undertake a grand encirclement to destroy the mass of the enemy army in one quick, decisive blow, but the relatively short distances involved west of the Vistula would ensure that the supply system need not be over-strained. The proximity of good railheads to western Poland was an added advantage, for they were positioned exactly at the proposed assembly areas, and thus facilitated the stockpiling of supplies. Furthermore, the length of time necessary for mobilisation was shortened decisively for the Germans by their 'Wave' system, which enabled them to undertake a surprise attack with their active forces before the Poles could mobilise their reserves. Moreover, the Poles initiated their mobilisation only on 30 August, two days before the invasion, whereas the Germans had begun five days earlier, on the 25th.

Such were the fundamentals on which the Army's plan for the invasion of Poland were based. The document that detailed them was Deployment Plan White, dated 15 June 1939, which, although under the signature of von Brauchitsch, was the result of the combined efforts of the General Staff and the army group planning staffs. The officers most closely associated with it were Halder, General Karl-Heinrich von Stülpnagel, Chief of Operations, Colonel Hans von Greiffenberg, Head of the Operations Section, and General Kurt von Tippelskirch, Chief of the Intelligence Section. The German plan was simple and direct:

'The object of the operation is to destroy the Polish Armed Forces. The political leadership demands that the war should be begun by heavy surprise blows and lead to quick success. The intention is to prevent a regular mobilisation and concentration of the Polish Army by a surprise invasion of Polish territory and to destroy the mass of the Polish Army west of the Vistula-Narev line by a concentric attack from Silesia on the one side and from Pomerania-East Prussia on the other.'[3]

13

To achieve this, the Germans divided their forces into two army groups—North and South. Two armies, the 3rd under von Küchler and the 4th under von Kluge, formed Army Group North (630,000 men), under von Bock, and these would advance across the Polish Corridor between East and West Prussia and strike south towards Warsaw. Three armies, the 8th under Blaskowitz, the 10th under von Reichenau, and the 14th under List, composed Army Group South (882,000 men), under von Rundstedt, and would strike north, also towards the Polish capital. There, the two arms of the pincer would meet; the final and decisive battle would be fought on the rear of the Poles, with their path of retreat blocked. To ensure that no large enemy forces succeeded in escaping over the Vistula into eastern Poland, thereby frustrating the whole design and possibly endangering the German flanks, two more thrusts, one from the north and the other from the south, would move out behind the river and its tributaries. The Polish forces, therefore, would be caught in a grand, double encirclement; destruction would be total. This was pure *Vernichtungsgedanke*; the German General Staff had represented faithfully the strategic principles of their great master, von Schlieffen.

The force of fifty-two divisions, 1,512,000 men, that marched into Poland on 1 September was the flower of the German Army. It consisted of all fourteen mechanised divisions (as well as an ad-hoc armoured unit, *Panzerverband Kempf*), twenty-three infantry divisions of the First Wave, five of the Second, and nine of the Third, together with one mountain division and one cavalry brigade. These were reinforced later during the fighting by two more infantry divisions of the First Wave, three of the Fourth, and two mountain divisions. Seventy per cent of the force that took part in the campaign were active formations of adequately trained soldiers; the reserve divisions (seventeen out of the final total of fifty-nine) acted mainly as army or army group reserves. Good units though the majority were, however, the thirty-nine infantry divisions that crossed the border on the first day of the war lacked adequate motor transport, and were dependent on some 197,000 horses, which required enough fodder each day to fill 135 railway trucks. It proved impossible to provide each infantry division with enough food for the horses to travel more than 120 miles, with rations for more than ten days in the field, or with ammunition for more than one issue—i.e. 90 rounds per infantryman, 3,750 rounds per machine-gun, and 300 rounds per artillery piece. In comparison, the mechanised formations were given enough petrol and oil to carry them 450 miles, and, because their fuel was of high efficiency in relation to its bulk, further supplies could be delivered quickly by air transport (a Junkers 52 was capable of carrying some 10,000 lb). But the mass of the invasion army had no such freedom from logistical restraints; it was closely dependent on the efficient use, and the speedy extension, of the railheads and on the umbilical cord of supply transport between the trains and the advancing troops. Thus, it became dangerous to prolong operations, or to advance far beyond the termination of good railways. The longer the Army remained in the field, the more it became dependent on regular and adequate supply and reinforcement. For the Germans, time was, as it always had been, the essence of military operations.

The outcome of the campaign in Poland was decided in four days; by the seventh, Halder even began to prepare plans for the transfer of divisions to the west; and by the eighteenth all was effectively over. Seldom have military operations gone so nearly to plan as this one: the great mass of the Polish forces was trapped before it could retreat across the Vistula, and by the seventeenth day the outer pincer behind the great river had closed. On that day, too, the armies of the Soviet Union crossed Poland's eastern frontier. From that point, all that was left for the German forces to do was to complete the destruction of the remaining fortifications, which included the city of Warsaw. The Polish capital capitulated on the 27th, and the very next day the guns fell silent throughout the shattered and humiliated country.

The Armed Forces had lived up to the highest expectations. On 5 October a grateful Führer announced to his soldiers: '. . . you have fulfilled the task allotted to you. You have fought bravely and courageously.'[4] Comparisons were made with the old imperial armies, and these, however romantic, were not far off the mark. Decisive manoeuvre and encirclement had characterised the campaign on the ground. Much was made of the battle of the Bzura, the largest, self-contained action of the campaign, a giant battle of encirclement in the bend of the Vistula near Warsaw, which ended with the capture of some 170,000 Polish soldiers and the complete destruction of the Poznan Group, the only major part of the Polish Army that still remained intact and dangerous by 10 September. The traditional German strategy of *Vernichtungsgedanke* had resulted in the largest encirclement battle of annihilation in history until that date. Many more, and greater, were to follow. The dominant force in the campaign had been the infantry divisions, which formed roughly seventy-five per cent of all formations taking part. In its report on 24 September, OKW gave them the major accolade:

'German infantry formations added one more to their list of triumphs. Their achievements on the march and their endurance of hardships were as great as their achievements on the battlefield. Their courage in attack was supplemented by indomitable

16

and stubborn powers of resistance which no crisis could daunt. Their overwhelming powers of attack were supported by their comrades in arms. Heavy and light artillery lent them valuable assistance. Thanks to their intervention and to the work of the engineers, the fortified frontier positions of the Poles were successfully bombarded, stormed, or overrun in the shortest possible time and the enemy annihilated in a subsequent irresistible pursuit.'[5]

The mechanised forces, by comparison, were assigned second place: 'Armoured and motorised units, cavalry, anti-tank defence, and reconnoitring detachments with their magnificent *cooperation* [author's italics] more than fulfilled the expectations placed in them.'[6]

Because of the Polish dispositions, the area in which the German Army fought was relatively small. Many Polish divisions were encircled within fifty miles of the frontier, and only a few German formations were forced to cover more than 200 miles. Supply, therefore, did not become a problem, nor did the physical deterioration of the foot-bound infantry. Indeed, the marching achievements of the infantry divisions of the First Wave were remarkable, reaching standards expected of veterans. Distances of twenty miles a day were not unknown, and this compares not at all unfavourably with the average of the best performances of the mechanised divisions, which was around twenty-two. It is, perhaps, interesting that von Manstein, while recognising that 'A vital factor in the speed of . . . success was the unorthodox [*sic*] use of big, self-sufficient tank formations supported by a far superior Air Force,' nevertheless believed that what was decisive was the 'spirit' of the ordinary German fighting soldiers and their staffs: 'In the German Wehrmacht it had been found possible, with the help of new means of warfare, to *reacquire* [author's italics] the true art of leadership in mobile operations . . . right down to the most junior NCO or infantryman, and in this lay the reason for our success.'[7]

What, then, of the armoured and motorised infantry divisions, which, on 1 September, formed some twenty-eight per cent of the invasion force? The mechanised units were distributed along the 1,000 mile front, positioned among the armies in groupings no bigger than corps. Four motorised corps were instituted: XIX, under Guderian, with 4th Army, and XIV, under von Wieter-sheim, XV under Hoth, and XVI, under Hoepner, all with 10th Army, the one that was to bear the hardest fighting. At the same time *Panzerverband Kempf* and 5th Panzer Division were each given to an infantry corps; 1st Light Division was held in 10th Army's reserve; 10th Panzer was sent to Army Group North's reserve; and 4th Light and 2nd Panzer were grouped with a mountain division in an ordinary corps. The principle of concentration, so earnestly advocated by Guderian, had been disregarded. This was partially corrected shortly after the opening of the campaign, with the formation of XXII (motorised) Corps under von Kleist in 14th Army, composed of 2nd and 5th Panzer and 4th Light, but it still came nowhere near Guderian's ideal. After the war, he wrote to Liddell Hart: 'Concerning the strategy of the panzer forces, I always proposed deep thrusts operating independently of the infantry corps—and never clung with panzer forces to the flank of infantry armies. It is clear, however, that independent operations of panzer troops cannot be too far-reaching if the general disposes of only a small body of them. One or two divisions cannot execute independent operations as well as a panzer army.'[8] The composition of the motorised corps likewise proved to be unsatisfactory; XVI Corps included within its order of battle two infantry divisions, and XIV and XV Corps were composed entirely of light or of motorised infantry divisions.

The campaign was to see no use of the principles of the armoured idea. Certainly, the panzer and motorised divisions played an important role in the ground operations, spearheading three out of the five armies involved, and, certainly, the new concept found tactical expression in Hoepner's corps' advance to Warsaw which covered 140 miles in seven days, in Guderian's long thrust with one motorised and two panzer divisions, which, on one day, managed fifty miles in twelve hours; and in von Thoma's infiltration of some fifty miles by night, through undefended, but thickly wooded, hilly country, to turn the Polish flank at the important Jablunka pass. But there it ended. At every point throughout the campaign the actions of the mechanised forces were subordinated to the strategy of encirclement, and, for most of the time, the movements of the individual units were closely coordinated with those of the mass of the infantry armies to which they were attached. As Liddell Hart recognised: 'The German advance might have travelled still faster but for a lingering conventional tendency to check the mobile forces from driving far ahead of the infantry masses that were backing them up.'[9] The OKH Deployment Directive of 15 June 1939 saw the employment of the mechanised forces only in relation to the movement of the army as a whole. As an example, it stated:'It is the task of 10th Army with its three motorised corps using to their fullest capacities the mobility of the mechanised troops, and *in collaboration with* [author's italics] the driving power of armoured formations, to thrust across . . . to reach the Vistula without delay. . . .'[10] Thus, the role of the panzer forces was to spearhead the general advance by the whole army, not to mount any independent action. The OKH plan continued: 'This will lead to the elimination of dispersed enemy units, and the non-motorised detach-

19

ments, will be brought forward as quickly as possible to guard the flank and the rear of the far-advanced mechanised troops.'[11] In other words, all efforts would be made to protect the flanks of the advance: a sound, traditional military principle basic to *Vernichtungsgedanke*.

During the campaign, the handling of the armoured forces left much to be desired. For example, after the successful conclusion to the battle for the Danzig Corridor, the future employment orders issued by OKH for Guderian's motorised corps stipulated that it was to be kept in close attendance of 3rd Army and held back in cooperation with the infantry divisions. Fear of French intervention in the west caused the High Command to prevent any deep easterly penetration. Despite protests from Guderian and von Bock, the General Staff refused to lift their restrictions, and only after it was clear that Army Group South was not achieving the desired occupation of Warsaw was the northerly mechanised force allowed to undertake a strategic envelopment southwards towards Brest-Litovsk, more than a hundred miles east of the Polish capital. Even then, the OKH envisaged the role of XIX Corps as being merely to protect the flank of Army Group North and to make it possible to resume von Bock's advance into southern Poland without delay. Fear of enemy action against the flanks of the advance, fear which was to prove so disastrous to German prospects in the west in 1940 and in the Soviet Union in 1941, was present from the beginning of the war.

Throughout, the employment of the mechanised units revealed the idea prevalent among the senior army and army group commanders that they were intended solely to ease the advance and to support the activities of the infantry. Many were the occasions of direct cooperation between infantry and panzer. An instance of this was on 15 September, when the headquarters of 10th Army directed an infantry corps to establish a bridgehead over the Bzura to enable a motorised corps to continue the advance on the other side. Motorised divisions were often incorporated within infantry corps (for example, 10th Panzer was attached to XXI [infantry] Corps for a short period). On 15 September, von Bock even decided to divide XIX Corps into two so that it could undertake two separate tasks in conjunction with infantry formations; Guderian reacted strongly against this, but it was only on the conclusion of the campaign that the proposal was dropped. And there were a number of tactical failures in the employment of tanks. The abortive attack on the Mlawa's fortifications on the first day of the campaign, and the foolish attempt to occupy a well-defended Warsaw, in which as many as fifty-seven tanks were destroyed, are the most extreme examples, but others exist, such as a panzer division in Guderian's XIX Corps running out of fuel on only the second day of the advance.

Thus, any strategic exploitation of the armoured idea was still-born. The paralysis of command and the breakdown of morale were not made the ultimate aim of the operational employment of the German ground and air forces, and were only incidental by-products of the traditional manoeuvres of rapid encirclement and of the supporting activities of the flying artillery of the Luftwaffe, both of which had as their purpose the physical destruction of the enemy troops. Such was the *Vernichtungsgedanke* of the Polish campaign.

2

Military Impotence

'The time has come for action—but what action?'
GENERAL FRANZ HALDER
Chief of the General Staff, 1938–42

For the Army High Command, the Second World War opened very differently from the First. In 1914, the Chief of the General Staff had become automatically one of the most important personages of the state; on his abilities had rested the fortunes of the nation at war. In this, he did but follow a distinguished tradition; just as it had been von Moltke the elder and not Wilhelm I who had defeated Austria in 1866 and France in 1870, so it was von Moltke the younger, supported by the ghost of von Schlieffen, and not Wilhelm II who was responsible for the destruction of France and Russia in 1914. And in 1916, it was two generals, von Hindenburg and Ludendorff, who took over the entire war direction of the German Reich from the Kaiser and the politicians. Twenty-three years later, in 1939, the contrast could hardly have been greater. On the fourth day of the war, the Law for the Defence of the Reich was passed, specifically limiting the executive power of the Army Commander-in-Chief to the operational control of his Army, and, furthermore, leaving the definition of that limit to Adolf Hitler, in his role of Commander-in-Chief of the Wehrmacht. Any influence over the wider aspects of war policy was firmly denied to the Army.

Such a law, although of course unwelcome to the generals, merely confirmed the whole style of Hitler's dictatorship from 1938 onwards, and it occasioned little comment. War policy was, after all, a legitimate area of concern for the politicians, and during the Polish campaign it had appeared as if Hitler would limit himself to this sphere of activity and not interfere with the Army's direction of ground operations. The plan of invasion had been drawn up by the General Staff, and, although Hitler had given his agreement to it, he had not interfered in its operational precepts; the Supreme Commander had limited himself merely to planning, to the smallest detail, the attack on a bridge at Dirschau. On the third day of war the Supreme Commander boarded a train, the 'Führer Special,' taking with him Keitel and Jodl (men who had contributed nothing to the operational planning of the invasion), their aides, and the liaison officers of the Army and Air Force, as well as his Party associates, 'and set off in a vaguely easterly direction with no definite destination.'[1] Hitler and his OKW chiefs spent their time visiting army and corps headquarters, and met von Brauchitsch only on two occasions. The Supreme Commander took little direct interest in the operational conduct of the Army, limiting his supervision of events to expressions of opinion and exchanges of view. Nor did the OKW act; Halder noted in his diary on 24 August: 'OKW will not interfere in the conduct of operations. OKH will report directly to the

Führer.'[2] Hitler's recommendation to increase the force in East Prussia and his intervention in the conduct of von Blaskowitz's 8th Army did not take the form of definite orders, not did they incur the displeasure of the Army High Command, while his decision to raze Warsaw by bombing, rather than to reduce it by seige, was more in the nature of a political move than a military one. The one man above all others in whose hands lay the direction of operations, the Chief of the General Staff, never even once spoke on the telephone during the entire campaign to Hitler, Keitel, Jodl, or von Vormann, the Army liaison officer on the train.

Such a state of affairs well-suited the Army. No interference from Hitler, or from his bureau, the OKW, or from the Air Force, which was acting primarily in support of the ground forces, left the Army as the dominant service and the unquestioned supreme director of military operations. However, not all was as the generals wished. During the Polish campaign, Halder had noted: 'Strict separation between the political (OKW) and military establishment (OKH) has proved a great drawback. OKH ought to have exact knowledge of the political line and of its possible variations. Otherwise, no planned action on our own responsibility is possible. OKH must not be left at the mercy of the vagaries of politics, else the Army will lose confidence.'[3] This was prophetic, for at the conclusion of one of the most successful campaigns in German history, Hitler struck yet one more blow at the Army's autonomy, this time the most serious in the political-military relationship of the Third Reich. Its importance, so often overlooked, can hardly be exaggerated; it is at this point that the moral culpability of the generals is first brought into question.

On 25 September, the day when Hitler was flying over the Polish battlefields, Halder entered in his diary the simple sentence: 'Information from Warlimont about the Führer's intention to attack the west.'[4] This was the first indication the Army leaders had been given that Hitler had any idea of taking direct military action against France. Two days later, on the day Warsaw fell, the Führer summoned his service commanders to the Reich Chancellery, where he informed them of his decision to 'attack in the west as soon as possible, since the Franco-British Army is not yet prepared.'[5] He even set the date: 12 November. And on 9 October Hitler issued 'Directive No. 6 for the Conduct of the War,' which opened: 'Should it become evident in the near future that England, and, under her influence, France also, are not disposed to bring the war to an end, I have decided, without further loss of time, to go over to the offensive. . . . An offensive will be planned on the northern flank of the West Front, through Luxembourg, Belgium, and Holland. . . .'[6] In such a manner was the Army committed to a new campaign, with neither its prior knowledge nor its consent. The Army leaders were dismayed, certain that defeat or, at best, stalemate was the only prospect for such a venture. Seldom, if ever, in the history of warfare has a campaign that was to be won so decisively been entered with such reluctance by the victorious generals as that waged by the Germans in Flanders and France in May 1940.

Until that time, the Army High Command had not considered the west as a future battleground. The war was being fought in Poland, and, although France and Britain had intervened, there were no signs that these countries were prepared to take the offensive. In the final analysis, would the Men of Munich take action at all? Certainly, the generals feared the results of an Allied attack while the bulk of the German Army was occupied in the east, but they had been quite prepared to leave a force in the west of only some forty low-standard divisions sheltering behind the much-vaunted West Wall, fortifications which were, in reality, by no means impenetrable and only partly complete. Moreover, Hitler had previously given no indication that he was intending to invade the west once Poland was reduced to ruins. Indeed, his first War Directive, issued on 31 August, contained the statement '. . . it is important to leave the responsibility for opening hostilities unmistakably to England and France,'[7] and on 19 September he had declared in a speech: 'I have neither toward England nor France any war claims, nor has the German nation. . . .'[8] The Army, therefore, acted accordingly. As early as 10 September Halder had begun forming his ideas about 'position warfare' in the west, and on the 24th von Stülpnagel had prepared a detailed memorandum in which he advised against attacking the French defences until the spring of 1942. Von Brauchitsch and Halder therefore resolved to conduct the war, at least for the foreseeable future, on a defensive basis; von Stülpnagel held it advisable not even to question Hitler on the matter; and Von Leeb, commander on the Western Front and a leading expert in defensive strategy, submitted a report which confirmed the Army High Command's attitude. The General Staff even went so far as to draw up an order for the partial demobilisation of the Army, although this was withheld from issue at the intervention of Keitel. Then, in late September, came the bombshell: Germany would, indeed, attack in the west, and only some six weeks would be allowed for preparation. It was, as von Leeb recorded, 'insane.'

The Army chiefs' objections to launching the invasion of the west were many and reasonable, and were shared even by Göring. The remarkably successful campaign in Poland, they argued, could not be held as assurance for a future German victory against France and Britain. Halder noted in his diary: 'The technique of the Polish campaign [was] no recipe for the west. No good against a well-knit army.'[9] In contrast with the Poles, the French were generally supposed to possess the largest and strongest army on the continent of Europe, one, furthermore, which was by then fully mobilised, deployed behind the redoubtable Maginot Line, and prepared for an enemy attack. Time, the vital element in strategy, had been lost by the Germans; surprise was gone, and the year so far-advanced that good weather and ground conditions, so important for the conduct of operations, were most unlikely. Nor was the German Army prepared for an onslaught in the west: the deficiencies in supplies and equipment, especially in mechanisation, were acute; the four light divisions were about to undergo transformation into panzer formations, a lengthy process; the refitting of the armoured units which had been in Poland would not be complete for some time; and the number of fully trained men under arms was still not sufficient for such a speedy extension of the war, especially one that, in the generals' opinion, would probably lead to a costly stalemate. On 8 October, the Quartermaster-General submitted to Halder a gloomy report, of which the latter noted: 'Ammunition: We have enough for an operation with about one-third of our divisions, for fourteen combat days, then we shall have a reserve of fourteen more combat days. Current production of ammunition: one combat day for one-third of our divisions.'[10]

Moreover, the Army leaders were disturbed by Hitler's proposals for the violation of neutral Holland and Belgium, with all its unacceptable international consequences. Keitel recorded:

'Quite apart from their [the senior generals'] daunting recollections of the First World War, and the strength of the formidable Maginot Line against which there were then virtually no weapons of destruction, they considered that the Army was as yet not capable of launching any fresh assault after its eastern campaign, without a pause to recover, to regroup and remobilise, to finish its training, and to complete its re-equipping. Particular doubts were expressed about winter warfare, with the fog and rain, the short days and the long nights that made mobile warfare virtually impossible. In addition, the fact that the French had not exploited either the good weather or the weakness of our western defences earlier, could only lead us to conclude that they did not really want to fight, and that any attack we might launch would only foul up the prospects of peace talks—probably making them impossible. It was clear to us that the Maginot Line would oblige us to press our attack through northern France, Luxembourg, and Belgium, and possibly even through Holland, with all the consequences we had suffered in the 1914–18 war.'[11]

The decision to attack the west was Hitler's and Hitler's alone. He received advice from only one. Warlimont wrote:

'No one can say on what day the Supreme Commander reached the decision to take the offensive in the west or what influenced him to do so. One thing is quite clear: the Commander-in-Chief of the Army was the man most intimately involved; yet when von Brauchitsch appeared on the train on the 9th and again on 12 September, on the first occasion spending no fewer than two hours alone with Hitler, the latter breathed not a word to him of his intentions. . . . It is also clear that no other senior officer was consulted before the decision was made, in spite of the fact that it was tantamount to no less than a decision to embark on a second World War. . . . Even . . . the Chief of the OKW, the "sole adviser in Wehrmacht matters," had not been told by Hitler but had learnt of it through one of his aides!'[12]

At the time, von Manstein remembered: 'What horrified me was my realisation of the extent to which OKH's status had declined . . . [and] this just after it had conducted one of the most brilliant campaigns in German history!'[13] For Hitler's decision had marked a fundamental departure from what had gone before. Although the Führer had become accustomed to completely disregarding the views of his military advisers, he had hitherto confined this to the political sphere. Now, however, as von Manstein argued:

'. . . the position was quite different. It is true, of course, that the question of how the war should be continued after the defeat of Poland was a matter of *over-all war policy* which ultimately had to be decided by Hitler as the Head of State and Commander-in-Chief of the Wehrmacht. However, if the solution were to be a land offensive in the west, this must depend entirely on *how, when* and *whether* the Army would be able to tackle the task. In these three respects the primacy of the Army leadership was inalienable. Yet in all three Hitler confronted the High Command of the Army with a fait accompli. . . . Without any previous consultation with the Commander-in-Chief, he not only ordered offensive measures in the west, but even decided on the timing and method to be adopted. . . . The Commander-in-Chief of the Army was to be left with merely the technical execution of an operation on which he had deliberately not been consulted and for which, in autumn 1939 at all events, he could certainly not guarantee any prospect of decisive success.'[14]

By his decision, Hitler had extended significantly the process he began in 1938. The Army's operational autonomy was now not only threatened, it was breached. Warlimont recognised this:

All he [Hitler] was interested in was to reinforce his position in the military field, as in all others, as the man having sole power of command; he did not want expert, responsible advice because, from the Army at any rate, that might sometimes imply opposition and warnings. . . . Instead he was determined to have "unquestioned authority downwards." He decided that during the forthcoming campaign the Commander-in-Chief of the Army should be tied to the same location as Supreme Headquarters and accompanied only by his Chief of Staff and a reduced staff; his real reason was to achieve more rapidly and more surely his object of concentrating power in his own hands, to reduce the General Staff of the Army to the level of an executive mechanism for his decisions and orders. . . .'[15]

Von Manstein moralised: 'Hitler had now taken over the functions which Schlieffen believed could at best be performed in our age by a triumvirate of king, statesman, and warlord. Now he had also usurped the role of the warlord. But had the "drop of Samuel's anointing oil," which Schlieffen considered indispensable for at least one of the triumvirs, really fallen on his head?'[16]

* * *

Faced with such a fundamental threat to their position, the reaction of the Army leaders should have been vigorous, for Hitler's intention struck at the very basis of their responsibility to both the nation and the Army. Although war might be the continuation of politics by other means, the conduct of warfare is most certainly not the conduct of politics by other means; Hitler's decision was not one simply of national policy, when it would have been the statesman, and not the soldier, who was accountable to the people for its validity; rather, it was one which directly involved military operational planning and execution, the, till-then, exclusive preserve of the highly-trained group of men at the Army High Command. In this sphere of activity, the senior officers were not to be confined by any narrow concept of unquestioning obedience to the Head of State; instead, they possessed a greater duty to the nation they served and to the troops they led. On the quality of their professional judgement lay the success or failure of their country at war, the well-being and prosperity of their fellow citizens, and the lives and welfare of their soldiers. No oath to Hitler could override this. He might have the prerogative of declaring war, but it was they who had to direct the military movements consequent upon his decision. Such a responsibility, the preserve of a professional Army Commander-in-Chief, could not be taken over by a politician and an amateur, even though he might be the constitutional 'Supreme Commander,' especially by one who was so mesmerised by the power of his own intuition that he completely disregarded the military implications of his actions. To allow this to happen would, indeed, be a criminal abnegation of duty on the part of the generals.

The opposition from the military leaders to Hitler's plan for the invasion of the west was immediate. Even the Chief of the OKW could perceive the hazards of his Führer's intentions. Keitel records: '. . . the result was the first

31

serious crisis of confidence between Hitler and myself . . . when I publicly told him what I thought, as I was bound to do, Hitler violently accused me of obstructing him and conspiring with his generals against his plans . . . he began to insult me and repeated the very offensive accusation that I was fostering an opposition group against him among the generals.'[17] If this were the case with Keitel, how much more so was it with Hitler's other military 'advisors'? On 4 October, Jodl told Halder that a 'very severe crisis is in the making' and that the Führer was 'bitter because the soldiers do not obey him.'[18] And certainly the opposition from von Reichenau was extremely disheartening. Hearing that the attack would proceed through Belgium and Holland, von Reichenau, already disillusioned with events, had declared that such a step would be 'veritably criminal'[19] and proceeded to commit himself to its prevention. Characteristically, von Reichenau's opposition was an individual act, unhampered by any ties with organised groups. He was one of the very few to stand up openly and sharply against the Führer, man to man, first on 30 October, then on the 31st, and again on 1st and 3 November. His most disheartening attempt was made on 5 November, when he realised that all was futile: his Führer's mind was fixed and closely resembled a stone wall, unassailable by argument, logical or otherwise. Subvert opposition was von Reichenau's only alternative, and he unhesitatingly adopted that attitude. The next day, the 6th, he met Goerdeler, revealing to him Hitler's plans and suggesting that Germany's enemies be informed of them. Von Reichenau hoped that Hitler would thus be persuaded to abandon his idea if the advantage of surprise could be shown to have been lost. By the 9th von Reichenau's message was on the way to London. Similarly, Warlimont attempted to induce King Leopold III of the Belgians to make an offer of mediation that the Führer would find difficult to refuse. How successful the Deputy Chief of the OKW Operations Staff was, it is impossible to say, but on 8 November the Dutch and Belgian monarchs offered their services of mediation to the belligerent powers.

In the Army High Command all was confusion. The Führer's decision found no favour with either von Brauchitsch or Halder, who were both shaken and unnerved by the situation in which they found themselves. As the days passed, the prospects for a successful attack became increasingly more distant. On 29 September, for example, General Thomas presented a brilliant analysis which revealed the inadequacies of the armament and raw material programme, foremost among which was a shortage of 600,000 tons of steel per month. Nine days later, on 8 October, Colonel Wagner, Chief Quartermaster, submitted a report which argued that the present state of munitions ruled out an offensive for some time to come; supply was enough for only one-third of the available divisions over a period of fourteen days in the field. Other reports reaching the General Staff indicated that the fighting spirit of the troops in Poland had not, in fact, been as promising as initial impressions had indicated; that training and morale in the Replacement Army were not good; that the divisions of the Third Wave could be counted on to hold their positions only if the enemy did not mount a heavy attack; that the divisions of the Fourth Wave needed considerable further training before they would be of any use for even defensive warfare; that only five armoured divisions would be ready to take the field by the middle of November; and that the French artillery was far superior to that of the Germans. Beck, who managed to see most of this information, predicted that an offensive would be turned into a stalemate after a loss of some 400,000 men killed.

By mid-October, von Brauchitsch and Halder had come to an agreement as to what must be done. Of the three choices with which they were faced—to obey orders, to await events, or to attempt a revolt—they chose the second, which would enable them to promote every argument in the cause of peace. Of the two men, von Brauchitsch was set most firmly against the idea of bringing down the régime, believing this to be a negative solution which would expose his country to the enemy. He hoped that it would be possible to dissuade Hitler of his decision, and he may have counted on the weather making it impossible to carry out the offensive until the following spring, by which time a means might have been found to end the war by a political compromise. Halder, on the other hand, was more undecided, and, as subsequent events showed, was inclined to support the idea of a military coup if he and his chief achieved nothing with their chosen option. Such, indeed, was to be the case. Von Brauchitsch made no headway in his representation to the Führer. On 11 October, for example, Halder recorded in his diary: 'Result of conference of the Army Commander with the Führer: Hopeless.'[20] The climax of the Bendlerstrasse's official opposition to Hitler came on 5 November, the day set for deciding to unleash the offensive on the 12th. Von Brauchitsch held a fatal meeting with the Führer, which von Manstein believed caused 'an irreparable breach between Hitler and the generals.'[21] The Army Commander began by reading out a memorandum summarising all his reasons against the venture in the west. Many cogent, thoroughly sensible arguments were advanced, all incontrovertible, but they included one that served to undermine completely the worth of the others. Von Brauchitsch made the mistake of criticising the performance of the infantry during the Polish campaign, accusing it of being over-cautious and insufficiently aggressive. Moreover, he went on, discipline had become exceedingly lax. Whatever the truth, or otherwise, of these assertions, they proved fatal to the Army Commander. Keitel, who was present, recorded:

'After the Commander-in-Chief had finished speaking, the Führer jumped up in a rage and shouted that it was quite incomprehensible to him that just because of a little lack of discipline a Commander-in-Chief should condemn his own Army and run it down. . . . he left the room, slamming the door behind him, leaving all of us just standing there. . . . It was plain to me that this signalled the break with von Brauchitsch and that what little confidence there had been between them was finally shattered.'[22]

Von Manstein realised the tactical error made by the Army Commander: 'By raising such objections in the presence of Hitler, a dictator whose self-esteem was already inflated, von Brauchitsch attained precisely the opposite of what he intended. Disregarding all von Brauchitsch's factual arguments, Hitler took umbrage at the criticism he had presumed to direct against his—Hitler's own—achievements [the creation of the new Wehrmacht].'[23] The Army Commander came out of Hitler's chamber 'chalk white and with twisted countenance.'[24] It was the end of the official opposition.

As indicated by von Reichenau's and Warlimont's individual efforts, the subversive opposition to Hitler had been developing apace since the outbreak of war. The first to plan decisive action was General von Hammerstein, the Army Commander-in-Chief in 1933, who, on 7 September, had taken command of Army Detachment A, an ad hoc force formed for the defence of the West Wall.

He spent his few weeks in active command attempting to lure Hitler to his headquarters at Cologne, there, as he later put it, 'to render him harmless once and for all—and even without judicial proceedings.'[25] But the Führer did not get within pistol-shot range of his would-be killer, and in late September von Hammerstein was transferred to the deputy command of Wehrkeis VIII, and then was soon retired.

However, the idea of killing Hitler did not end with the former Army Commander, and during October, whether, and, if so, how to manage the deed became the most widely discussed subject in opposition circles. Halder, even before the evident failure of von Brauchitsch's attempt to make Hitler see reason, began to carry a pistol in his pocket whenever he visited the Reich Chancellery but, as he confessed later, he could not 'as a human being and a Christian . . . shoot down an unarmed man.'[26] Nonetheless, he took steps to prepare for a coup: he concentrated troops within easy reach of Berlin and ordered one Lieutenant-Colonel Groscurth, a member of the Abwehr group, to institute a working party, under the general direction of von Stülpnagel, to draw up a blueprint for the overthrow of the government. Fervent preparations were also made by the other Abwehr resisters, foremost among whom was Oster, in alliance with Beck. By the beginning of November the conspiracy, which had its contacts reaching even into the Vatican, had advanced so far that Halder had committed himself to lead a coup on the 5th of that month, the day of the fatal meeting between Hitler and von Brauchitsch. He had made only one qualification: no action would be taken if the Army Commander succeeded in persuading the dictator to abandon his plans.

The support of the Chief of the General Staff, the second most influential officer in the Army, was essential to the whole conspiracy. Apart from von Brauchitsch, he was the only person in the German Army who could command general support and provide the leadership required for such momentous action. The pressures on this one man were immense. Looking back after the war, Halder felt that at that time he had been faced with two alternatives:

'Resignation—the way Beck went—or treacherous murder. In the making of a German officer there are deep and earnest inhibitions against the idea of shooting down an unarmed man. . . . The German Army did not grow up in the Balkans where regicide is always recurring in history. We are not professional revolutionists. Against this speaks the predominantly conservative attitude in which we grew up. I ask my critics, who are still very numerous, what should I have done, i.e. what must I have prevented? Start a hopeless coup for which the time was not ripe, or become a treacherous murderer as a German staff officer, as a top representative of the German General Staff, who would act not only for his own person but as representative of the German tradition? I say honestly, for that I was not fitted, that I have learnt. The idea that was at stake was clear to me. To burden it in the first stage with a political murder, of that as a German officer I was not capable.'[27]

But there was more to it than that. There were very severe practical implications in what Halder was preparing himself to do. Here was he, the Chief of the Army General Staff, proposing a most momentous act—the overthrow, during wartime, of the nation's legally constituted Head of State. The risks to Germany, let alone to the Army, were considerable; failure would be disastrous. Therefore, he had to be quite sure of success.

The responsibility was his; history and the nation would judge him accordingly. Was Halder certain of getting the military support he so earnestly required? The Commander-in-Chief of the Army had set his face firmly against any conspiracy; the Commander-in-Chief of the Replacement Army, Fromm, had studiously fostered a non-commital attitude; and of the three army group commanders, von Rundstedt, von Bock, and von Leeb, only the last had promised to follow unreservedly any action Halder might take. Just as disturbing was the state of the Army; the war had made the conspirators position infinitely more difficult. The mass of soldiers knew nothing of their Führer other than the considerable successes under his rule. The campaign in Poland had resulted in a stunning victory, and there was no comprehension of the defeat that might so easily result from a November offensive in the west. Indeed, few had knowledge even of the possibility of that offensive. Only failure would turn the men against Hitler, and this they had yet to experience. Moreover, mobilisation had meant a further dilution of the officer corps and a massive intake of National Socialist indoctrinated youth, giddy with the Reich's victory. Even so resourceful a conspirator as von Witzleben was fearful of the officers 'drunk with Hitler,' and had no idea whether, in a crisis, the soldiery would be influenced more by 'the general who attempted a coup or the troop officer babbling Nazi slogans.'[28]

In view of such weighty considerations, it is a matter of some remark that Halder did in fact commit himself to action on the part of the conspirators. It was a decision requiring much courage, and yet one taken with many reservations. 'What if?' must continually have occupied his mind. The strain told, and by the fatal day, 5 November, his nerves were at breaking-point. At times he seemed on the verge of collapse. Little was needed to shake his resolve, and this Hitler unwittingly provided during his stormy interview with von Brauchitsch. During his tirade against the Army Commander, the dictator had screamed that he knew all about the 'spirit of Zossen' and was determined to crush it. Zossen was the wartime location of the Army High Command, and the spirit referred to was one of defeatism and cowardice. But relayed to Halder, this phrase carried a terrifying significance: Hitler knew all about the plot against him and was prepared to take action. Halder's, by now, finely balanced nerves snapped. All was lost; the conspiracy must be ended immediately, the evidence destroyed. On his return to Zossen, he unhesitatingly took the necessary action. The incriminating plans for the régime's overthrow were consigned to the fire, and all attempts by the other conspirators failed to goad the Chief of the General Staff into renewed action. Two days later, on the 7th, the weather succeeded where the generals had failed, and the western invasion was postponed, to be reconsidered daily until the middle of January, when, on the 16th, it was positively deferred until the spring.

Without the support of the Chief of the General Staff, and without the certainty of backing from the troops, the military opposition had no hope of executing a successful coup. Even the assassination of Hitler by a lone gunman was dismissed as impracticable. Oster described it as 'an act of insanity' with no more than 'one chance in a hundred. You cannot see Hitler alone. And in the anteroom in the presence of adjutants, orderlies, and visitors you would hardly get a chance to shoot.'[29] The risks involved in using a pistol or a bomb were out of all proportion to the chances of success. But what was left? The plans at Zossen had been consigned to the flames; the armoured divisions that had been kept near Berlin were transferred to the west; opposition officers who had been manoeuvred into key positions were being moved to other posts; and, as the weeks passed, the Army leaders' ideas of a putsch receded as their hopes for success in the west grew. By 7 January, after a trip to the front, Halder could record that he envisaged a series of 'really great successes.'[30] Day by day German military preparedness became more imposing, and by mid-January the prospects of a spring offensive had developed from poor to good. As a result, all further attempts to spur von Brauchitsch and Halder into action met with failure, and even the so-called 'X Report,' which stated that the Pope was prepared to act as an intermediary provided the National Socialist régime was removed, had no effect. Von Brauchitsch admitted after the war: 'The whole thing was plain high treason. . . . Why should I have taken such action? It would have been action against the German people. Let us be honest . . . . The German people were all for Hitler.'[31]

By 6 November, therefore, official military opposition to Hitler's decision to invade the west was over, and the underground conspiracy was effectively rendered impotent, and the Army leadership had resigned itself to carrying out the Führer's orders. Von Brauchitsch had not the personal resources with which to continue to oppose Hitler, as a conversation he held on 16 November testifies: 'But what should I do? . . . None of my generals will speak with me. . . . Will they follow me? . . . I do not know what I should do. . . . Will we again see each other alive?'[32] Halder, likewise, was so nervous and unconvinced of the success of a putsch, that his resolve, once shaken, could not be resurrected. Thus, by default, Hitler was allowed to dominate. Impervious to the formidable array of military arguments, he stuck to his intention; his only concession was to postpone the date of the attack–and then simply because of the weather, over which even the Führer of the Greater

German Reich had no control. His resentment of the OKH grew, as also did his suspicion, and, after the 5th, he would not allow the Army to present the daily weather forecasts. Instead, he created a special Reporting Group headed by a top Luftwaffe meteorologist, and went so far as to prohibit the Army weather expert from attending the daily weather briefings. Even then, in case the Luftwaffe relied on meteorological information supplied by the Army officer he was invariably asked for the origin of his sources, and Hitler was always inclined to downgrade its importance. The Führer was also suspicious that the Army High Command was the source of the leak of information about the impending offensive, when it did in fact come, separately, from von Reichenau and the OKW Abwehr section.

The confrontation with von Brauchitsch on 5 November marked the final irreconcilable breach between Hitler and the Army leaders. Goebbels, Göring, and Ley, the Reich Labour Service Chief, also entered the fray. Guderian records the series of lectures organised by the first two, in which 'an almost identical train of thought was apparent, as follows: "The Luftwaffe generals . . . are entirely reliable; the admirals can be trusted to follow the Hitlerite line; but the Party cannot place unconditional trust in the good faith of the Army generals."'[33] The climax of this campaign came on 23 November, when Hitler addressed senior officers of the Wehrmacht in the imposing surroundings of the Reich Chancellery. His determination to attack was reaffirmed: 'My decision is unchangeable. . . . Breach of the neutrality of Belgium and Holland is meaningless. . . . I consider it is possible to end the war only be means of an attack.'[34] For the rest, as von Manstein put it, 'his speech constituted a massive attack not only on OKH but on the generals of the Army as a whole, whom he accused of constantly obstructing his boldness and enterprise.'[35] In one part of his speech,

the Führer referred back to von Brauchitsch's blunder of
5 November: 'If the leadership in national life always had
the courage expected of the infantryman, there would be
no setbacks. When supreme commanders, as in 1914,
already begin to have nervous breakdowns, what can one
ask of the simple rifleman? . . . With the German soldier
I can do everything if he is well led.'[36] And in the early
evening Hitler called back von Brauchitsch and Halder to
lecture them further on the 'spirit of Zossen.' The Army
Commander tendered his resignation; it was rejected.
Not for nothing did Halder note in his diary that this was
a 'day of crisis.'[37] OKH was finally intimidated; Hitler's
disillusion irreversible.

Among the rest of the audience, reaction to Hitler's
open condemnation of 23 November was mixed. Some,
such as General Hermann Hoth, found the occasion
inspiring, but others were profoundly depressed at the
criticisms voiced. Only a very few took matters further.
One, Guderian, managed to see the Führer. He told him: 'I
have since talked to a number of generals. They have all
expressed their astonishment and indignation that so
outspoken a distrust of themselves should exist among
the leading personalities of the government, despite the
fact that they have only recently proved their ability and
risked their lives for Germany in the Polish campaign. . . .'[38] For twenty minutes Hitler listened to him
without interruption and then, on Guderian's conclusion, placed the blame entirely on von Brauchitsch's
shoulders: 'It's a question of the Army Commander-in-
Chief.' Replacements were suggested to Hitler, but none
was found acceptable. Von Reichenau, for example, was
'quite out of the question.'[39] Then the dictator began a
long tirade against his military advisers, beginning with
the trouble von Fritsch and Beck had caused him over
rearmament and ending with the difference of opinion
over the offensive in the west. The interview was then

concluded, and Guderian retired 'deeply depressed'[40] by the insight he had gained.

Hitler and his Party leaders were not the only men to range themselves against the Army command; the chiefs of the OKW did so, too. Keitel, for all his early misgivings, withdrew into silence and, along with his deputy, stood firmly behind the Supreme Commander and his decision. Jodl firmly rejected OKH's arguments, noting in his diary for 18 October: 'Even though we may act one hundred per cent contrary to the doctrine of the General Staff, we shall win this war because we have better troops, better armament, stronger nerves, and decisive leadership which knows where it is going.'[41] Warlimont, by now thoroughly disillusioned with the situation at OKW, wrote that Keitel and Jodl 'were the men who, when Blomberg departed, had worried and fought for a unified command of the Wehrmacht; yet now their actions were a major factor in destroying its solidarity.'[42] Friction between OKH and OKW mounted, the former resentful at what it considered to be unwarranted and unsound interference, the latter annoyed at what it believed to be hide-bound conservatism and lack of faith in the Führer. Indeed, the position had become extremely difficult for the Army High Command.

Hitler's decision when and how to attack the west had signalled his intention to take over command of the Army himself. As Warlimont argued:

'If this was in fact his intention he ought at the same time to have taken over OKH or the General Staff of the Army, as being by far the most effective command organisation in the Wehrmacht, and have cut OKW out of these questions. . . . it would have provided the best possible core for the

Supreme Headquarters which was in process of forming, and it would have given the Army General Staff the position which it merited. The procedure adopted by Hitler in encroaching on the preserves of the Army was exactly the opposite. . . . Jodl . . . clearly looked on this development as a considerable step forward in the process of cutting the Army staff down to size . . . and [seized] every opportunity to push himself into the chair of command of the Army. The door was now wide open to those "irresponsible backstairs influences" against which Beck had warned.'[43]

Thus did the OKW begin to supplant the OKH. Hitler did not meet von Brauchitsch to discuss matters pertaining to the Army from 5 November to, at the earliest, 18 January the following year—an impossible situation for any service chief. The Army Commander possessed no automatic right of direct access to the Führer, appearing only when he was summoned. In his place came Keitel and, more important, Jodl. At the meetings where the daily situation reports were presented, Jodl became the principal reporting officer and no representative of the Army was allowed to attend; and when, on 21 October, the time came for the Army to present its intentions for Operation Yellow, the attack in the west, it was Keitel, and not von Brauchitsch, who did so (the Army Commander staying away to indicate his disagreement with the plan). Hitler's comments and alterations were then relayed back to OKH. In such a manner did the planning for the western offensive proceed, the OKW becoming the official channel for the Supreme Commander's intentions, the Army Command waiting on its every instruction—and all this despite the fact that the Wehrmacht Operations Staff had neither the manpower nor the resources, nor the cooperation from the other services, required to undertake efficiently such important work. Moreover, communication between OKW and OKH was poor; Warlimont noted that although 'Jodl always treated Halder outwardly with all military courtesy . . . his diary shows that only once during these eight or nine months did he have any prolonged discussion with him. Equally, there was only one meeting between Jodl and Halder's principal subordinate, General von Stülpnagel, and this took place only after an agreement on improved cooperation had been reached between Keitel and Halder.'[44] Even the words used by Hitler and his OKW chiefs when addressing the Army Command, either verbally or in writing, indicated a complete disregard for its prerogatives. At one point Jodl went so far as to propose names for appointments to senior Army commands. It was not for nothing that Warlimont wrote that OKW 'had a tendency to take over responsibility for the operational plans and measures of the Army General Staff, or even . . . to cut the Army out altogether and take over the Army's job.'[45] Warlimont's words found true expression in the planning and direction of the invasions of Norway and Denmark. Here, for the first time, but not the last, OKH was totally eclipsed by OKW. Hitler had taken full operational control.

Hitler had not intended to go to war with Norway and Denmark—they were small, neutral countries posing no threat to the security of the Reich—but by the spring of 1940 several developments had made the occupation of Norway imperative. First, in November 1939, the Soviet Union had attacked Finland and there were fears that, under the pretext of aiding the Finns, the Allies might violate Norwegian neutrality and attack Germany's northern flank. Second, Norway was vital to the traffic in iron ore between Sweden and Germany, and any enemy occupation of that country would seriously disrupt the

Reich's war production. Lastly, the Navy was pressing for bases beyond the North Sea so as to attack the Atlantic sea-lanes, and Admiral Raeder stressed the suitability of the Norwegian fiords and ports. The final decision to invade was taken on 19 February, following hard on the British Navy's daring raid on the *Graf Spee's* auxiliary supply ship, the *Altmark*, then stationed in Norwegian territorial waters. The inclusion of Denmark in the plan appears to have been due to the desire both to reinforce the security of the Baltic and to gain valuable advanced fighter bases for an extension of the Luftwaffe's defence network. The invasion of the two countries duly took place on 9 April; Denmark fell in a day, Norway in a month, at a cost to the Armed Forces of 1,317 killed, 2,375 missing, and 1,604 wounded. The infallibility of the Führer's judgement, and the success of his ventures, then appeared to be established beyond all reasonable doubt.

For the Army Command, however, although nine of its divisions, two of its corps headquarters, and an assortment of supporting units, including a rifle brigade and a tank battalion, took part in the battle and acquitted themselves well, the campaign was a disaster. It was excluded from all advance knowledge and planning of the operation, as well as the direction of its own troops. Hitler, through OKW, took direct control. Thus was reached the logical conclusion to the events of January-February 1938.

Hitler never set out his reasons for deliberately excluding OKH from any influence over *Weserübung* (Exercise Weser), the code designation of the operation, but they were clear enough. As Warlimont recorded: 'This had been the first attempt on the part of the dictator to subordinate the organisation for command and leadership of an operation in war to his own personal ambition and thirst for political prestige.'[46] In the pursuit of this, there was no place for the Army Command. On 13 December 1939 Hitler had ordered that 'investigations on how to seize Norway should be conducted by a very restricted staff group'[47] at OKW; by the middle of January, its study, an outline plan for the occupation of Norway, had been completed, to be further developed by a working staff headed by a Luftwaffe general, with a naval officer as chief of staff and an operations officer from the Army. Hitler rejected this arrangement, and required that the staff should be organised on the basis of equality for the three services, and be under the overall command of the Chief of OKW. On the 27th the Führer issued an OKW directive to the three service commanders, stating that the operations in the north would be carried out 'under my immediate and personal influence.'[48]

However, the operations staff at OKW were quite incapable, in numbers, organisation, and experience, to undertake the planning for such a complicated combined operation as 'Weser.' On 19 February Jodl reached the conclusion that rapid results could be achieved only by a properly organised headquarters with the necessary resources: in other words, an Army command under the guidance of the Army General Staff. Warlimont wrote:

'At last after all this vacillation, the Army had . . . become the central factor in this undertaking. OKW did not, however, turn to the Commander-in-Chief of the Army who, in view of the special nature of the operation, would undoubtedly have detailed at least an army group or army headquarters for the job; instead they acted entirely on their own and detailed a corps headquarters, i.e. the lowest level of command organisation which could possibly have been considered. . . . Jodl and the Head of the Personnel Section saw in this an opportunity to present themselves as new-style officers on the Hitler model, as opposed to the ordinary run of Army officers, by proposing the *man* who in their view was most suitable for the job irrespective of his *rank*. OKH was merely told that "the Führer wishes to speak to General von Falkenhorst since he is an expert on Finland." This form of words was used to conceal Hitler's real intentions. . . . He [Falkenhorst] and XXI Corps headquarters [now nominated Group XXI], into which was incorporated the previous Special Staff, then set to work, still in close cooperation with Section L; this produced the extraordinary picture that the Supreme Commander relied for all matters concerning the participation of the Army in the Norwegian operation not on the Army General Staff, but on a corps headquarters, and the latter under OKW was responsible for overall command of the operation!'[49]

On 21 February, the day when von Falkenhorst presented himself to the Führer, Halder noted angrily in his diary: 'Not a single word has passed between the Führer and the Commander-in-Chief of the Army on this subject [the projected invasion]; this must be put on record for the history of the war. I shall make a point of noting down the first time the subject is broached.'[50] That date was to be 2 March, at a meeting between Keitel and von Brauchitsch, when the former presented OKW's demand for seven divisions, a motorised brigade and sundry other units, a requirement that had already been worked out with Fromm, Commander of the Replacement Army, behind OKH's back. Jodl recorded that the reaction of the Army leaders was furious.

Furious they might have been, but compared with Göring and the Luftwaffe commanders they were mildness itself. In an unconvincing justification of their

48

actions, OKW had announced that 'Headquarters XXI Corps is to be placed under OKW in order to avoid difficulties with the Luftwaffe,'[51] and a few days later they subordinated the Air Force units to von Falkenhorst. Göring, his pride injured and his prerogatives endangered, would have none of this; after a short, sharp battle it was decided that the Luftwaffe formations would receive their orders from the Luftwaffe High Command, to which organisation all requests for air support would have to be addressed. The Army, on the other hand, gained no such concession, and, moreover, did not demand one. Not one point in its favour was conceded by Hitler and the OKW, who until the conclusion of the campaign maintained their determination to be directly responsible for command. The OKH lamely acquiesced. As a result, 'the Commander-in-Chief of the Army was pushed completely out into the cold; for instance, he was not even summoned to attend Hitler's final conference on 2 April with the Commanders-in-Chief and General von Falkenhorst.... Yet he raised no objections.'[52]

In such a manner did full operational control of a major operation fall to one man and his staff antipathetic to the interests of the Army. During its execution the Führer took close interest in all that went on and, as Jodl wrote, insisted 'on giving orders on every detail.'[53] But how did this man, whose proudest boast was that he possessed an intuitive appreciation of the situation in complete disregard to 'General Staff defeatism,'[54] cope for the first time with the rigours of military high command? Warlimont, who was close to him that April, remembered that the periods of crisis during the campaign produced in him 'a spectacle of pitiable weakness lasting more than a week,'[55] and that had it not been for Jodl, who rose to the occasion, events might have taken a somewhat different turn. Warlimont remembers a visit to the Reich Chancellery when he saw the Führer—the Supreme Commander—siting 'hunched on a chair in the corner, unnoticed and staring in front of him, a picture of brooding gloom. He appeared to be waiting for some new piece of news which would save the situation, and in order not to lose a moment intended to take it on the same telephone line as his Chief of Operations Staff. I turned away in order not to have to look at so undignified a picture.'[56] Field-Marshal Lord Wavell once wrote that 'The first essential of a general is the quality of robustness, the ability to withstand the shocks of war';[57] Hitler lacked that, even from the beginning.

The crisis of nerves had begun on 14 April, when it was realised that General Eduard Dietl and his 3rd Mountain Division were cut off in the Norwegian port of Narvik, and that ten destroyers, an entire group, had been lost there. Jodl noted that 'Hitler became terribly agitated,'[58] and Halder wrote: 'General von Brauchitsch returns from a meeting with the Führer. Result: it is not thought possible to hold Narvik. "We have had bad luck" (Hitler's words).'[59] Hitler's first reaction was that Narvik should be abandoned and Dietl's men be made to fight their way southwards down the coast to Trondheim, an idea which Jodl rejected emphatically. The tension mounted. On the 17th the Chief of OKW Operations Staff wrote: 'Further argument regarding the orders to be given to the Narvik group. Every unfavourable piece of information makes the Führer fear the worst.'[60] To this was added controversy over the civilian administration of occupied Norway, which, on the 19th, caused Keitel to turn his back on his Führer and walk out of the room. Jodl's diary entry for the day included: 'We are once more facing complete chaos in the command system. Hitler insists on giving orders in every detail; any coordinated work by the existing military command set-up is impossible.'[61] Furthermore, when operations began to turn out badly, Hitler, for the first time, exhibited his propensity to blame everyone but himself, and during the Narvik battle he criticised the Navy for not having taken energetic action. It was a story often repeated. As events proved, Jodl was correct in his handling of the situation; the campaign was won in spite of Hitler's amateurish interventions. But, as Warlimont pointed out, it should always be remembered that had Hitler had his way, Narvik, the decisive point of the operation, would have been evacuated needlessly after only a few days, and the entire operation might well have foundered. Such a man was the Supreme Commander.

The Army leaders had lost the battle for control over ground operations. It had been an easy victory for Hitler. To the generals' political impotence was now added a far more serious charge: command impotence. From this time on, the fate of the individual soldier, of the various formations that composed the Army, and, consequently, of the entire German nation, rested on shoulders ill-suited to bear it. The senior generals had abdicated their own heavy responsibility with an acquiescence that defies justification. Not one of them resigned; not one acted decisively to prevent such a dangerous transfer of power. The judgement of history must surely be that expressed by a German, Helmut Lindemann, who wrote in 1949:

'It is astonishing that the generals always speak only of their military duty toward their superiors but not of their duty to the soldiers entrusted to them, most of whom were the flower of the people. One can certainly not require anyone to kill the tyrant, if his conscience forbids him to do so. But must one not require of these men that they expend the same care and scrupulousness on the life of every single man among their subordinates? The reproach of not having prevented the slaughter of many hundreds of thousands of German soldiers must weigh heavily on the conscience of every single German general.'[62]

3

The West—The Plans

*'Better rashness than inertia; better a mistake than
hesitation.'*
DIE TRUPPENFÜHRUNG

As was consistent with Hitler's adoption of responsibility for the operational employment of the Army, the
first plan drawn up by OKH for the invasion of the west
followed closely the three guidelines laid down by the
Supreme Commander. These were stipulated clearly in
Hitler's 'Directive No. 6 for the Conduct of the War,'
dated 9 October 1939. First, that the offensive be carried
out 'without further loss of time' (before Christmas and
preferably on 12 November); second, that it take place
'on the northern flank of the Western Front, through
Luxembourg, Belgium and Holland'; and third, that its
purpose 'be to defeat as much as possible of the French
Army and of the forces of the Allies fighting on their side,
and at the same time to win as much territory as possible
in Holland, Belgium, and northern France, to serve as a

53

base for the successful prosecution of the air and sea war against England and as a wide protective area for the economically vital Ruhr.'[1] This was confirmed subsequently by other directives, in particular No. 10, issued in February 1940, which included the following: 'The objective . . . is to deny Holland and Belgium to the English by swiftly occupying them; to defeat, by an attack through Belgium and Luxembourg territory, the largest possible forces of the Anglo-French Army, and thereby to pave the way for the destruction of the military strength of the enemy.'[2]

Within these imposed limits, the original OKH plan was adequate, despite the barrage of adverse comment that it has received since the war, not only from historians but also from German generals, including, astonishingly, Halder himself. One fact, arising directly out of Hitler's specifications, should be remembered: the plan was not one aimed at the occupation of the whole of France; it was one with a limited territorial objective— the acquisition of Holland, Belgium, and northern France only. Thus, although it had some superficial similarities with the famous Schlieffen Plan carried out in 1914 (both were based on an advance through Belgium and both placed the main effort on the right wing), there was no intention of any vast encircling movement extending up to the Swiss border that would end in the total downfall of the French. Indeed, the OKW minutes for 27 September 1939 reveal that: 'From the very beginning it is the Führer's idea not to repeat the Schlieffen plan but to attack . . . through Belgium and Luxembourg under strong protection of the southern flank, and to gain the Channel Coast.'[3] Fundamentally, the plan lacked any far-reaching strategic conception; all future movements were left completely unspecified.

The OKH plan for *Fall Gelb* (Operation Yellow) was dated 19 October 1939. Its preamble reflected the

Führer's directive: its intention was 'to defeat the largest possible element of the French and Allied armies and simultaneously to gain as much territory as possible in Holland, Belgium, and northern France as a basis for successful air and sea operations against England and as a broad protective zone for the Ruhr.'[4] The main objective of the initial attack was to secure central Belgium by means of a large pincer operation around Liège, with the main weight in the north. Then, the three armies (37 divisions), comprising Army Group B, were to concentrate north and south of Brussels so as to continue the offensive westwards without delay. In the second phase of the attack a thrust would be directed at Ghent and Bruges. The task of Army Group A (27 divisions) to the south would be to guard Army Group B's left flank. Meanwhile Holland would be occupied in a separate operation by Army Detachment N (North), a small force of three divisions. No attack would be made on the Maginot Line. A total of seventy-six divisions would take part in the operation, including those of the reserve. This plan, however, was a hasty improvisation, and when von Brauchitsch and Halder were summoned by Hitler on 25 October to discuss the coming offensive, they were clearly dissatisfied with it. They knew, for example, that it lacked organisational depth and made no provision for adequate reserves. Halder saw little purpose for Army Detachment N, and doubted whether it would be able to continue an advance to Amsterdam if the Dutch flooded the approaches. He also favoured a stronger concentration of motorised forces in the direction of Ghent (north of Liège) so as to carry out an encirclement manoeuvre more effectively. At the meeting with the Führer, no firm conclusions were reached, but Hitler strenuously advocated a concentration of the attack south of Liège in order to break through in a westerly direction. This meant that the operational *Schwerpunkt* (the decisive point) would be in the centre of the German front, and any hope of a wide-flanking manoeuvre, such as hoped for by Halder, would be out of the question. Hitler's somewhat vague reasoning was that, because the most important task was not to occupy the Belgian-French coast but to defeat large sections of the enemy forces, there should be a breakthrough both north and south of Liège. Further meetings took place on the 27th and 28th, when Hitler again advanced his proposal with such force that it might be regarded as a fourth stipulation to add to the three already advanced in Directive No. 6. On the 29th, a revised OKH plan was issued giving effect to the Supreme Commander's new instruction.

The second version of Operation Yellow reflected Hitler's new intent. Its preamble was reworded to read: 'All available forces will be committed with the intention of bringing to battle on north French and Belgian soil as many sections of the French Army and its allies as possible. This will create favourable conditions for the further conduct of the war against England and France on land and in the air.'[5] The principal changes were the avoidance of Holland, except for the so-called 'Maastricht appendix,' a narrow strip of land between Belgium and Germany (this was at Halder's suggestion, which had found favour with Hitler) and, most important of all, the placing of the centre of gravity of the invasion south of Liège rather than to the north. Army Detachment N was disbanded; Army Group B, under von Bock, was enlarged to forty-two divisions (four armies) and directed to drive north and south of Liège westwards to the coast; Army Group A, under von Rundstedt, with twenty-three divisions (two armies) was given the task of attacking through the Ardennes corner of southern Belgium, crossing the Meuse and continuing in the direction of Reims-Amiens, while at the same time providing flank cover for von Bock's army group; Army Group C under von Leeb, with twenty divisions, was left to tie down the enemy forces in the Maginot Line. The total force, with ten divisions in reserve, was ninety-five divisions. Thus, the original plan, which had aimed at the encirclement of the Allied northern flank, had been altered to one that relied on a frontal attack on both sides of Liège. In von Manstein's words, the operational intention 'might best be expressed by saying that the Anglo-French elements we expected to meet in Belgium were to be floored by a (powerful) straight right, while our (weaker) left fist covered up. The territorial objective was the Channel coastline. What would follow this first punch we were not told.'[6] Such a plan was hardly imaginative, nor was it in line with the German strategic tradition of decisive encirclement ending with the total destruction of the enemy; it was, however, the result of Hitler's interference in, and dominance of, operational planning.

The second OKH plan met with instant opposition from all quarters of the Wehrmacht; even Hitler was not satisfied with it. Göring and his commanders were dismayed that Holland was not to be occupied, arguing that this not only enabled England to take possession of the Dutch airfields and thereby threaten western Germany, but that it denied to the Luftwaffe important bases for the future conduct of the war. Thus, in reaction, Hitler's Directive No. 8, issued on 20 November 1939, stated that: 'Contrary to earlier directives, all measures planned against Holland may be taken without special orders when the general offensive opens.'[7] At the end of January 1940 a revised OKH version of the plan specifically provided for the fast occupation of Holland, and detailed an army for the assignment. But more fundamental than the question of Holland was the criticism that both versions of the plan were too limited in their objectives and would not result in any decisive success. The leading proponents of this argument were von Rundstedt and his chief of staff, von Manstein, strongly supported by men such as Guderian. Their fight to have their ideas accepted lasted from the end of October until mid-February, and lost none of its intensity with the passage of time.

The argument advanced by von Rundstedt and von Manstein was simple. As they saw it, the fundamental shortcoming of the existing OKH plan 'according to Hitler' was that it would lead to a frontal encounter between the German and enemy forces in Belgium; this would allow the Allies to retreat back to the Somme in northern France and, while the German attack might be able to secure the Channel coast, the Allied armies would still remain intact on a line from Sedan to the Somme estuary. A strong enemy counter-attack north-eastwards into the weak hinge of the German line centred on the northerly end of the Maginot Line might well result in the bottling-up of German forces in Belgium. Furthermore, the plan lacked the decisive advantage of strategic surprise. Allied commanders had anticipated that, in order to avoid the Maginot Line, the Germans would be forced to turn the barrier by means of an advance through Holland and Belgium, and then proceed to attack northern France to gain control of the Channel and North Sea coastline. From the outbreak of war, it had been clear that Allied deployment had been determined by anticipation of such a threat. In short, the two men believed that the plan possessed little chance of achieving a decisive victory in the German tradition, and that it was positively dangerous to German prospects. In its place von Rundstedt and von Manstein proposed moving the *Schwerpunkt* of the assault to the south, where it would be faced by relatively weak enemy forces. There, a strong Army Group A (with three armies and two strong armoured corps) would launch a surprise attack through the Ardennes, cross the Meuse at Sedan, cut through northern France to the coast below the Somme, and then encircle the Allied forces that had already been drawn into central Belgium to meet a subsidiary attack there from Army Group B. Also, a strong southern wing would be better able to check any French counter-attack from the south-east. To achieve all this, Army Group A would have to be reinforced to three armies, including a high proportion of the mechanised units. As von Rundstedt wrote in a letter to von Brauchitsch on 31 October, which marked the opening round of the 'battle,' the success of the whole operation depended 'on whether it will be possible completely to defeat and annihilate the enemy forces north of the Somme, not merely to push back their front line.' Therefore 'the main effort of the whole operation . . . must be on the southern wing.'[8] In the succeeding three months, the Army High Command was to be kept constantly aware of this alternative plan for the operation, one that was contrary to Hitler's intention, but which was nevertheless true to the German strategic tradition.

For a long time, the proposals emanating from Army Group A met with nothing but scepticism from OKH. It should be remembered that, while von Rundstedt and von Manstein were advocating their proposals, the Supreme Commander and the Army Command were preparing for the offensive which, until its firm postponement in mid-January, was never more than two weeks away. Under such pressure it is difficult to change in its entirety an intricate operational plan, involving vast numbers of troops, as well as supplies and communications on a considerable scale. Moreover, the new idea called for a massive, wide-ranging sweep on the part of Army Group A which required not only good weather and good ground, but also a sufficient number of mechanised troops with which to spearhead the advance; none of these could be relied on until the spring of 1940.

These dangers were minimised in the existing plan, but emphasised by the von Rundstedt-von Manstein variant. Halder foresaw other difficulties. First, the enemy intentions were not known, and there was no guarantee that their northern forces would advance into Belgium as anticipated (indeed, the Allies had no such plan until mid-November); second, there were immense logistical difficulties to any major advance through the Ardennes to the coast—one of the advantages of the OKH plan was that it placed the main effort where there were adequate roads and railways to support a major attack; and, in view of the strength of the Allies and, until early 1940 at least, the relative weakness of the Germans, a daring plan dependent on one manoeuvre, which sought total victory at the risk of total defeat, was not acceptable—the existing plan at least avoided the risk of putting all eggs into one basket. But, most important of all, the new proposals were not in accord with the Führer's stated conditions.

For his part, Hitler failed to comprehend immediately the possibilities of a southern sweep. Ironically, when meeting his Army leaders on 25 October, the Supreme Commander had asked whether it would be possible to do exactly what Army Group A proposed a few days later, namely to envelop Belgium and the enemy forces from the south, by means of a drive through the Ardennes westward and then north-westward. However, he immediately expressed his own doubts about the project, asked OKH to examine its potential, and then felt disinclined to pursue the matter when it was rejected by the Army Command. From that time on, Hitler rather fumblingly moved towards the idea that an attack through the Ardennes by way of Sedan might be advantageous, but, typically, he did not pursue this to its logical conclusion—that the main weight of the attack should be placed there from the outset—and this despite the fact that, at least from 27 November, he was aware of Army Group A's proposals. Nevertheless, he remained dissatisfied with the plan of 29 October, as did everyone else, although it met all his requirements. The day after it was issued, Jodl noted in his diary: 'The Führer comes with a new idea about having one armoured and one motorised division attack Sedan via Arlon.'[9] By 11 November this proposal had matured sufficiently for OKH to order: 'The Führer has now decreed: on the southern wing . . . a third group of mobile troops will be formed [the other two were with Army Group B, detailed to attack north and south of Liège] and will advance in the direction of Sedan.'[10] A third version of the OKH plan was accordingly issued on 15 November. The idea that the *Schwerpunkt* might be shifted to the south gained momentum, and in Directive No. 8, dated 20 November, Hitler announced that: 'All precautions will be taken to enable the main weight of attack to be switched from Army Group B to Army Group A should the disposition of enemy forces at any time suggest that Army Group A could achieve greater success.'[11] This was the state in which Operation Yellow remained until 16 January, when it was definitely postponed until the spring. A fourth edition issued on 20 January did not differ materially from its predecessor. The concessions towards the southern attack continued to be totally inadequate: the one armoured formation placed there, Guderian's XIX Army Corps, was not made strong enough to exploit any success by advancing to the Channel, and the main weight of the attack remained with von Bock in Belgium, to be changed only if he ran into difficulties during the operation. However, Hitler was still subject to nagging doubts about the plan. Jodl, a staunch opponent of any *Schwerpunkt* in the south, recorded in his diary for 13 February: Führer 'says most of the gun-armed tanks have been expended on places which are not decisive. The

61

armoured divisions with 4th Army [south of Liege] can do little in areas where there are obstructions and fortifications. They will come to a standstill on the Meuse, if not before, and will have to be withdrawn. . . . They should be concentrated in the direction of Sedan, where the enemy does not expect our main thrust.'[12]

It was at this point, in mid-February, that a number of events occurred to produce the new, and final, version of Operation Yellow. First, the forced landing in Belgium on 10 January of an aircraft carrying a staff officer with papers relating to the OKH plan produced doubt as to how much the Allies now knew of the German intentions; second, the postponement of the operation of 16 January owing to the weather, to the incident on the 10th, and to the obvious lack of surprise; and, third, OKH, dubious of its own plan and apprehensive of enemy preparations, had held map exercises at each of the army group headquarters for a ten-day period in the first half of February, and these had revealed that the present disposition of forces would result in a loss of time and opportunities in the event of an offensive.

Von Brauchitsch and Halder were at last convinced of the soundness of Army Group A's proposals and drew up new plans accordingly. Indeed, so convinced was OKH, by then, of the importance of the southern *Schwerpunkt* that it produced an outline of operations which was considerably more drastic, relying upon a greater concentration of force, than anything ever proposed by von Rundstedt and von Manstein: the line between Army Groups A and B was moved northwards; 4th Army, the strongest of von Bock's four armies, was transferred to von Rundstedt, as also were most of the mechanised formations, which were to be concentrated for a grand assault across the Meuse north of Sedan; 2nd Army was brought down, also from Army Group B, ready to be deployed in Army Group A's sector as soon as the front was broadened in attack. The Channel coast south of the Somme estuary and the Allied rear were the new objectives. To carry out this plan, the relative strengths of Army Groups A and B were reversed: von Bock was left with two armies and twenty-nine divisions, while von Rundstedt was given four armies and forty-five divisions, including three-quarters of the mechanised units. This plan left open the question of the future employment of Army Group A once it had reached the coast, but at least it laid the basis for the realisation of von Schlieffen's aim of strategy—a battle of annihilation on a reversed front. The new proposals were presented by von Brauchitsch and Halder to Hitler on 18 February, the day after the Führer, at a dinner, had heard from von Manstein of his ideas. They were approved unreservedly. On the 24th, the final OKH orders for Operation Yellow were issued. The controversy was over; tradition had triumphed.

The OKH plan for Operation Yellow which had finally evolved was audacious; it relied on surprise action followed by fast, decisive maneouvre ending in the destruction of the enemy forces. It was not, however, a plan which took any cognisance of the armoured idea—indeed, its precepts were based on ideas entirely alien to that new concept. Von Rundstedt's advance, in particular, was to be spearheaded by strong mechanised forces, but that, in itself, was no revolutionary innovation. As in Poland, Germany's armoured and motorised infantry divisions were to be tied to the armies they led, dependent for their movement on the directions emanating from army, army group and, ultimately, from Führer headquarters in accordance with traditional concepts of strategy, not on the potential for exploitation offered them by the enemy's positions and by their own power of velocity. The nearest the OKH plan of 24 February came to recognising the revolutionary value of the mechanised troops was the vague sentence: '. . . strong motorised forces are to push forward.'[13] This was not even as advanced as the thinking exhibited in the much-derided plan of 29 November 1939, which was expressed thus: 'With the release of the motorised forces for the advance, their leadership must be separated from that of the infantry divisions which are following.'[14] For the future, the armour enthusiasts might search in vain for such a far-sighted sentence to be included in any Army operational plan. Never again were the mechanised forces to be given so much independence, even in theory. The final version of Operation Yellow restrained itself to the following:

'Strong motorised forces are to push forward in close formation in front of the Army Group [A] towards the Meuse sector Dinant-Sedan. Their task is to rout the enemy forces brought up to southern Belgium and Luxembourg, and to gain a foothold on the western bank of the Meuse, thus creating favourable preliminary conditions for the further-ing of the attack in a westerly direction [by the rest of the Army Group!]. . . . The 12th Army will break through the Belgian border fortifications on both sides of the Bastogne and, closely following the fast moving units which will go forward ahead of them, force a crossing of the Meuse. . . .'[15]

Dry phrases of OKH operational directives apart, what of the senior commanders in whose hands lay the ultimate direction of the mechanised forces? Did they understand the potential within their grasp? Were they favourably disposed to the implications of handling armour? Hitler certainly was not. Although he found the power and the success of his panzer divisions fascinating, the evolution of Operation Yellow reveals him as having no conception of the operational needs of the armoured force. At first, not only was he fully prepared to dissipate its limited strength into three widely spaced groups (by his decision of 11 November), but he was also ignorant of the limitations of such a force: for example, one army corps alone, with its two panzer divisions, one motorised infantry division, and two motorised infantry regiments, would have been quite unable to exploit any success it might have had in crossing the Meuse. Furthermore, it was clear from the OKH directive of 20 January 1940, that, in common with his Army leaders, Hitler envisaged the task of the formation as merely supporting the infantry armies. It included such phrases as: 'The task of the group will be . . . to lighten the task of 12th and 16th Armies . . . [and to create] a favourable situation for the subsequent phases of the operation. . . .'[16] On 21 January, Hitler told Halder that 'The armour whose strength is in the attack, must be closely supported by the infantry.'[17]

The commander of Army Group A, Gerd von Rundstedt, was a soldier of the old school. Widely respected throughout the German Army, and even by Hitler until the end of the war, he was known as 'the last knight.' Born in 1875 von Rundstedt was the Army's oldest serving general and, in his prime, one of Germany's most capable commanders. Chivalrous, modest, kind, humane, conscious of his subordinates' opinions and interests, he was a symbol of the old army and believed firmly in the ideal of 'duty' and in his oath of allegiance. Distasteful of National Socialism and its protagonists, he stood apart from politics in the tradition of the officer corps. He possessed a fine strategic sense, the heritage of von Moltke and von Schlieffen, and instinctively preferred cavalry to armour; confident in his own abilities and capable of understanding complicated situations in a moment, he was as forthright in expressing his military opinion as he was reserved politically. Von Rundstedt's views on the final plan of campaign accorded closely with Hitler's. As soon as it appeared that OKH would accept his, and von Manstein's, ideas, he began to worry about using armour to spearhead the attack. In his subsequent preparations for the offensive there is no impression that he understood the implications of the fact that seven panzer divisions would lead his attack; as before, he continually laid stress on a 'relentless forward drive by *all* formations.'[18] Furthermore, von Rundstedt was at that time without von Manstein, who, on 1 February, had been transferred to command an infantry corps, a long overdue field promotion.

In his place came General Georg von Sodenstern, an able General Staff officer but one who possessed no appreciation of the armoured idea. He was horrified by the prospect of using armoured forces even in the relatively limited way envisaged in the OKH plan; and, with the full approval of von Rundstedt and von Mellenthin, the army group's Chief of Operations, he expressed these fears in a memorandum to Halder, dated 5 March 1940:

> 'I have serious objections to the use of armoured and motorised forces ahead of the front line of the attacking armies. These mobile forces can have a strong effect on morale, because of their speed and heavy armament, and yet, quite apart from my basic opinion that they should be held back as operational reserves to force a decision after the enemy front has been broken [this was the role envisaged for the cavalry in the First World War], I fear that they will be unable to carry out the task allotted to them in the imminent operation.'[19]

Von Sodenstern then proceeded to list the reasons for his assertion. There was little chance of achieving surprise, he argued, and this, combined with the French fortifications, mines, and armoured forces, would ensure the exhaustion of the German attackers. 'The panzer divisions, therefore, will reach the Meuse sector, where their task really begins, with weakened fighting strength and so late that the enemy will have taken all the necessary defensive measures. The limited mobility of the heavy artillery, and that of a great number of vehicles which are usually to be found in a panzer division, must likewise be indicated in this connexion.'[20] He also feared that enemy air attack would immobilise the panzer divisions, and he was convinced that the Meuse would be so well defended that the Germans would not be able to withstand the pressure even if they managed to force a bridgehead. He continued: '. . . the panzer forces would be exhausted and need to be thoroughly refreshed before being sent in for their most important task—an operational breakthrough in a westerly or south-westerly direction.'[21] Von Sodenstern concluded that the Meuse crossing had to be forced by the infantry. 'Above all, we must have at our disposal after the breakthrough a motorised army which can be sent in for the decisive attack. This army will really spread panic among the approaching enemy reserves and the civil population and will create an effect which, I am firmly convinced, would be lacking in face of the Meuse defence.'[22] But he envisaged this advance not in terms of a deep armoured penetration, but as a fast, well-coordinated attack in which the infantry formations would play a major part. The panzer divisions would be strictly subordinated to higher control from army headquarters:

'I should, however, like to force this breakthrough with the 12th Army reinforced as in the case of 4th

67

Army, by one or two panzer divisions, so that we could send the motorised divisions through the breach, followed by panzer divisions, which would in the meantime be subordinated to the 12th Army—and, if the occasion arises, to the 4th Army. This method would take most advantage of the possibilities that may be offered beyond all expectations to the armoured forces on the Meuse, only with the difference that the conduct of operations would be in the hands of the army [headquarters], which could synchronise the movements of the armoured forces with those of the infantry. The infantry could then really follow up closely . . . and the exploitation of any armoured success in gaining a bridgehead would be ensured.'[23]

The other army group commanders held similar views. The man in charge of Army Group B, Feodor von Bock, was, like von Rundstedt, an aristocrat, an officer of the old school, and an excellent soldier. Ambitious, sarcastic, and obsessed by good manners, von Bock was noted for his eloquence and skill in conversation, and, among friends, for his dislike of the Reich's new political creed. Possessing a good traditional strategic and tactical understanding, he was energetic and elastic enough despite his years (he was born in 1880) to comprehend at least a part of the potential offered by the armoured force. In this he was aided by his readiness to take risks. However the mass of the armour was not to be placed under him for the invasion.

Born in 1876, the commander of Army Group C, Wilhelm von Leeb, was a descendant of a Bavarian Catholic family that had sent many sons into the Army. Of an ascetic, reserved and taciturn personality, he was very religious and rejected totally the philosophy of National Socialism. Politically, however, he was inhibited by the traditional sense of *'Uberparteilichkeit'* that permeated the old officer corps. His strategic abilities were well known, and he was an expert in defensive warfare, which suited the exactitude and thoroughness with which he approached military problems.

One other general of importance was the commander of 4th Army under whose command was to come the panzer group which spearheaded Army Group A's advance. Gunther von Kluge was born in 1882. In common with most other senior generals, he disliked National Socialism but did nothing about it. Energetic, ambitious, intolerant of half-measures and compromise, von Kluge had no time for the armoured idea or for its adherents. The enmity between him and Guderian was to become legendary. He enjoyed soldiering, and could often be found with the troops in battle. Although he was not generally liked, von Kluge was respected for the quickness of his decisions, his initiative in the field, his grasp of tactics and the authority with which he conducted his commands.

Such were the men in whose hands the final direction of the mechanised formations lay. Their attitude may be summed up by von Leeb who, although as commander of Army Group C possessed no armoured units under his control, wrote: 'The arguments that our mobile and armoured forces succeeded in Poland are fallacious. Not only are armoured forces dependent on the weather, but the French and the British are both equipped with armoured units and anti-tank weapons, whilst the excellence of the French Army and its commanders must not be underestimated. We cannot expect our armoured forces to maintain the same tempo here as in Poland.'[24] These men, who represented the established thinking of the great mass of the German Army, had no thought that they were being unusually conservative in their outlook; after all, they were embarking on a plan of campaign which would be as audacious as it would be decisive, and they were relying on surprise, speed, and daring manoeuvre to defeat a numerically far superior enemy. Furthermore, they believed that they were prepared to use their new mechanised and air forces to spearhead such an offensive in a manner unlike that of their more militarily hide-bound enemies. This was a feeling expressed by Halder, who wrote in reply to von Sodenstern's memorandum: 'The task the German Army faces is very difficult. In view of the given terrain and the opposing forces (especially artillery), it cannot be carried out by methods to which we became accustomed in the last war. We must use extraordinary methods and bear the risk connected with them.'[25]

But this was not enough; the generals had failed to realise the potential that the situation presented. They had already concentrated three-quarters of Germany's armoured strength, by far the largest assembly of tanks ever known, at the decisive point opposite the weakest area in the Allied line, and had put them in a position to take the fullest advantage of the enemy's main dispositions to the north. Furthermore, the Allied forces facing them were restricted by rigid conceptions of war, ill-suited to the flexible response needed to combat well-directed mechanised forces. Could not the German leadership have exploited this to the full? The requirements were simple: the greatest possible concentration of the mechanised units, which included transferring to Army Group A the few divisions 'dissipated' in the Army Group B; a determined attack by these units through the Ardennes, across the Meuse and westwards on to the coast. Command paralysis would bring victory, and a northern swing would then ensure the encirclement of the disorganised, demoralised enemy armies before they could escape across the Channel.

But speed and independence of action had to be the

fundamentals on which all else was based. The mechanised forces should not be hampered by the slower speed of the infantry; the momentum of the panzers, supported by aircraft, must not be made dependent on the infantryman's feet. The armour enthusiasts agreed that the mass of the army had to follow at all possible speed in order to consolidate the success achieved by the armour, but argued that its slower movement should not for one moment be allowed to dictate the pace of events. Organised velocity was the key to victory. The panzer generals, however, had no chance of their proposals being accepted. Guderian wrote: 'My . . . task was to persuade my superiors and equally the men under my command that my ideas were correct and thus to achieve freedom of decision from above and confident collaboration from below. The former endeavour was only partially successful, the latter much more so.'[26] So exhausting was this struggle, that Guderian had to be granted leave in the second half of March to recover his health. He later recorded despondently: 'After years of hard struggle, I had succeeded in putting my theories into practice before the other armies had arrived at the same conclusions. The advance we had made in the organisation and employment of tanks was the primary factor on which my belief in our forthcoming success was based. Even in 1940 this belief was shared by scarely anybody in the German Army.'[27]

The battle for the armoured idea came to be centred around the crossing of the Meuse. This was the decisive point in the campaign: a disaster here, and Army Group A's operation would be ruined almost before it began. The traditionalists saw it as the role of the mechanised forces to dash ahead from the border and throw themselves across the river, there to form a bridgehead and await the advance of the rest of the army. Halder wrote in reply to von Sodenstern:

'A normal advance to the Meuse and a frontal attack on this section offers no sound prospects . . . I do not consider it important that the first wave of panzer divisions should reach the Meuse in full fighting strength, but that they should attempt to gain a hold on the western bank of the Meuse quickly and with adequate forces, which will be decisive for further employment. They will be relieved by the second and third armoured waves and by the infantry divisions, which will be brought up quickly and in strength. I do not fail to appreciate that these advanced units on the west bank of the Meuse would be in great danger for some hours. . . . It is not expected that the first armoured forces that gain a foothold across the Meuse will have a direct strategic effect. The area they have reached they will clear by attacks in different directions and with changing tactical objectives, until they are relieved by the infantry divisions. Only when infantry units in sufficient strength have a firm hold on the area necessary for manoeuvring on the west bank of the Meuse can the question arise of the concentration of still service-able armoured forces for strategic operation. . . . I believe that the consolidation of an attack over the Meuse needs so many days, if only to arrange ammunition and supply. . . . '[28]

This, too, was the view of Army Group A. On 6 March, Halder wrote: 'Phone talk with von Sodenstern; order of army group on operations of armour west of the Meuse. No distant objectives, only capture of bridgeheads (it seems that the army group has caught on to our ideas).'[29]

The armour enthusiasts, however, were far less worried at what happened before, or during, the actual crossing of the Meuse; they were concerned at what was to take place afterwards. In direct contradiction to the wishes of their superiors, they wanted to plunge forward towards the coast immediately, without waiting for the infantry to come up and consolidate the ground won. Guderian remembered the struggle with his superiors:

'. . . I proposed [on 7 February] that on the fifth day of the campaign an attack be made with strong armoured and motorised forces to force a crossing of the Meuse near Sedan with the objective of achieving a breakthrough which would then be expanded towards Amiens. . . . Halder, who was present, pronounced these ideas "senseless." He envisaged . . . a "unified attack" would be launched, which could not be mounted before the ninth or tenth day of the campaign. He called this "a properly marshalled attack in mass." I contradicted him strongly and repeated that the essential was that we use all the available limited offensive power of our armour in one surprise blow at one decisive point: to drive a wedge so deep and wide that we need not worry about our flanks; and then immediately to exploit any successes gained without bothering to wait for the infantry corps.'[30]

A week later, on the 14th, the same subject came under study, and Guderian, together with his fellow corps commander, von Wietersheim, became so depressed at the tone of the senior generals that they declared that under the circumstances they could have 'no confidence in the leadership of the operation.' Guderian added: 'The situation became even tenser when it became clear that not even Generaloberst von Rundstedt had any clear idea about the potentialities of tanks, and declared himself in favor of the more cautious solution. Now was the time when we needed Manstein.'[31] Halder knew of the despondency of the armoured enthusiasts; his diary for the 14th revealed that 'Guderian and von Wietersheim plainly show a lack of confidence in success. Guderian has lost confidence—the whole tank operation is planned wrong.'[32] But the controversy over the Meuse crossing was not to be resolved before the opening of the campaign. Both sides adhered to von Moltke's precept that 'no operational plan extends with any certainty beyond the first encounter with the main body of the enemy.'[33] Of this, the panzer leaders intended to make the fullest use. Guderian had told Hitler on 15 March: 'Unless I receive orders to the contrary, I intend on the next day to continue my advance westwards. . . . In my opinion the correct course is to drive past Amiens to the English Channel.'[34] Two days later, Halder observed that Hitler had 'reserved decision on further moves after the crossing of the Meuse.'[35]

Two final points concerning the disposition and command of the mechanised forces should be noted. First, the armoured divisions were distributed throughout the invasion force in a manner that left much to be desired. Army Group B was allocated three such formations, almost one-third of the total, much to the discontent of Guderian and others. They argued that this limited armoured support would have been of far greater value to the *Schwerpunkt* in the south. Furthermore, they were distributed singly to two army corps and one army reserve, only one of them being grouped with a motorised infantry division. Of the seven other panzer divisions, all in Army Group A, one came within II Army Corps, with two infantry divisions, and another within XV Army Corps, with an infantry division of the Second Wave as its partner. The remaining five, half the total, together with three motorised infantry divisions, were within a panzer group of three motorised army corps, XIV, XIX, and XLI, and formed the only satisfactory grouping of mechanised forces. Initially this did not come under the control of any infantry army commander but of Army Group A headquarters itself—in other words, it began the campaign subordinated only to von Rundstedt, and independent of the three army commanders. The question of the command of the panzer group was, however, more contentious. The most obvious candidate for the post was Guderian, whose experience was considerably greater than any of his fellow corps commanders. He was, however, outranked by a number of others, including von Wietersheim and a certain von Kleist, and, although the question of rank could have been solved in Guderian's favour, OKH preferred not to do so. Instead, Ewald von Kleist was chosen, and on 29 February approved by Hitler. Although an able general, who had commanded armour in Poland (XXII Corps), von Kleist was widely regarded as one of the old school in tactical as well as in political matters, and until that time, as Guderian acidly recorded, 'had not shown himself particularly well disposed to the armoured force.'[36]

Nor was the state of the German Army in general, and the invasion force in particular, conducive to the proper conduct of panzer operations of any type, let alone to the deep, demanding thrust of the armoured idea. Poland, which had seen ten per cent, 218, of the German tanks that took part destroyed in action, had proved beyond doubt that the PzKw I was obsolete, and that the PzKw II was effective only in a reconnaissance role. Yet on 1 April 1940, two-thirds of the Army's total tank strength was composed of these vehicles; of 3,381 machines, 1,062 were PzKw Is, 1,086 PzKw IIs, 243 PzKw I command tanks, 329 PzKw IIIs, and only 380 PzKw IVs, the tank that had impressed the panzer experts so greatly in Poland. Within their order of battle, the Germans were forced to include 143 PzKw 35(t)s and 238 PzKw 38(t)s, light Czech tanks which mounted two variants of underpowered 3.7cm anti-tank guns. For the invasion, 2,574 tanks were assembled, and of these the 349 PzKw IIIs and 278 PzKw IVs composed roughly one-seventh and one-ninth of the total; the rest, threequarters of the force, were made up of 523 PzKw Is, 955 PzKw IIs, 135 command tanks, 106 PzKw 35(t)s, and 228 PzKw 38(t)s. The lack of adequate mobility and protection for the tanks' supporting units, especially the infantry, had, on occasions, caused serious trouble in Poland, for it hindered the essential cooperation of all arms on which the fortunes of the panzer division heavily depended. Experience had proved what Guderian and his associates had argued for so long: that without infantry to support or even at times to spearhead the attack, without anti-tank guns to ward off enemy armour, without artillery to soften-up strong points, without engineers to provide passage across obstacles, and without the supply columns to bring up the all-important fuel, ammunition, and spare-parts, neither the tank nor the panzer division could operate effectively. But little was done to provide the tracked armoured transport so urgently required to produce the combination of maximum fire-power concentrated at one point, the high speed across sometimes rough country, and the complete flexibility of response to enemy action that was demanded by the rapid, ever-changing thrusting movements of armoured warfare. By May 1940, the only improvement since the outbreak of war in the provision of tracked transport and self-propelled carriages within the panzer force lay in the increasing numbers of SdKfz 251 armoured personnel-carriers for the infantry, and these were still so few in number that they appear to have been sufficient to equip only a few rifle companies. Thus, the reliance of the mechanised divisions on four-wheeled transport was as great as ever before, transport which, in the Polish campaign, had experienced a temporary breakdown rate of as high as fifty percent at any one time. Moreover, the mounting of the Czech 4.7cm anti-tank gun on the PzKw I chassis, to form the first *Panzerjäger* (self-propelled anti-tank gun) to enter German service, appears to have been used, again in limited numbers, by anti-tank units not of the panzer but of the infantry divisions.

The only substantial improvement in the state of the panzer arm lay in the conversion of the four light divisions into full armoured formations. The campaign in Poland had shown that these light divisions, with a single tank battalion, possessed little staying-power in sustained operations; but, with the infusion of Czech tanks, it became possible to reorganise them into panzer divisions, thus bringing the total of such formations to ten. However, these new divisions had fewer tanks than the old; Panzer Divisions 1–5 and 10 each possessed four battalions and a total of some 300 tanks, whereas Panzer Divisions 6 and 8 each had only three battalions and 210 tanks and Panzer Divisions 7 and 9, two battalions and 150 tanks. Thus the offensive capacity and endurance of the units within the panzer arm were far from uniform. In addition, the initial six armoured divisions benefited by acquiring extra motorised infantry from the motorised infantry divisions, each of which shed one of its regiments, their three-regiment organisation having proved too unwieldy.

Weak though the panzer arm might have been, the position in which the rest of the Army found itself was even worse: it was little short of chronic. The winter and spring of 1940 were, for the Germans, a time of crisis in motorisation: not only were the Reich's factories not producing enough motor transport for the Army's requirements, but the Army was not even receiving its fair share of the little that was being produced. By early

February only 4,000 of the total production of 12,000 trucks per quarter went to the Armed Forces as a whole; of these, 2,500-2,600 were supposed to be sent to the Army. In fact, the Army was receiving only about 1,000 trucks per quarter—less than one per cent of its entire stocks—not enough to replace its normal losses through wear, let alone to build up a reserve to cover future losses in battle. Little hope of forming a stock for the forthcoming operation remained, because the civilian economy had already been deprived of 16,000 trucks; of these, 2,800 had gone to the Replacement Army, 5,000 to equip newly-activated units, 5,000 to replace others under repair, and 3,200 to supply existing shortages. On 4 February Halder noted: 'We have now about 120,000 trucks, with shortages reported from the field of 2,668.'[37] Even including those under repair, the Army was some 5,000 below authorised strength—a situation made even worse by the fact that many of the existing vehicles were too old to take part in combat conditions. Halder believed this meant that the Army 'cannot pull through in any operation . . . if we allow . . . two per cent [some 2,400 trucks] for the normal monthly loss (not including combat casualties), which is the normal rate, new production will cover only half that loss. The consequence is a continuous drain on our truck strength, impairing the operational efficiency of our forces.'[38] The situation was further exacerbated by the nature of vehicle production which, instead of concentrating on one or two standard types, was spread throughout a multiplicity of designs. This not only caused a relatively slow output, but also impaired efficiency in the field. The shortage was never to be overcome: indeed, it worsened as time went on and new designs and foreign vehicles were introduced.

The High Command was faced with an impossible situation. Any increase in truck production would be limited owing to rubber and steel shortages, and no more than 4,000 vehicles a quarter for all three services was counted on. Little hope could be held that Hitler would allow the Army's share of new trucks to increase, especially in face of strong opposition from Göring. The remaining resources of vehicles in the civilian economy could be tapped, and would provide a temporary solution, but within seven months normal wear alone would have cancelled out their effect. And the stocks in occupied areas, especially in the Protectorate of Bohemia and Moravia, would be insufficient to bring about any marked alleviation. By the end of April, of the 16,000 new trucks demanded by the Army, more than one quarter had not been delivered. The only permanent solution that the Chief of the Army General Staff saw lay in a de-motorisation programme, which would increase the already heavy German dependence on horse-drawn transport: 'the most important thing . . . is to start at once procuring [horse-drawn] vehicles, harness, etc., without wasting a long time for computations and conferences.'[39]

Thus, as the German Army prepared for a modern, mobile campaign against an enemy possessing large numbers of vehicles (the British Expeditionary Force, for example, was completely mechanised), it began to increase its already considerable reliance on horses. They were used wherever it was considered tactically possible to do so, although this required greater numbers of men to care for, and guide, them. They were sent especially to supply and rearward services of infantry divisions. Despite all efforts, the situation had not altered significantly by the time of the invasion. On 8 May it was established that the worst equipped divisions were lacking more than ten per cent of their establishment of vehicles. As late as March, Guderian was so appalled by the state of the motorisation of his panzer divisions that he declared that he could take no responsibility for their performance in action, and during the campaign these élite formations of the German Army were forced to rely on captured vehicles for their continued action in the field. There was no doubt that in May 1940 the German Army was incapable of undertaking anything but a short campaign, and, as Halder realised, if the fighting continued for long, 'it would be necessary to call a pause in operations in view of the impossibility [of obtaining] . . . replacement for all material losses.'[40]

Shortages made little impression on Hitler, who counted strength in terms of numbers of men and divisions rather than in quality and quantity of equipment. Thus, numerical growth continued despite the lack of resources to supply even the already existing units. The further expansion of the German Army had been decided on even before the outbreak of war. In mid-August 1939, Hitler had ordered five divisions of the Fifth Wave to be raised, and this was duly done in September, bringing the total number of divisions in the German Army to 108. In the following months until May 1940, another forty-three infantry divisions were formed: four of the Sixth Wave; thirteen of the Seventh; ten of the Eighth; nine *Landesschützen* divisions of the Ninth; and four fortification divisions. To this was added three divisions to the Second Wave and one to the Third. The grand total was now 153 divisions, for the cavalry brigade was also enlarged to divisional status. Those formations of the Fifth to Eighth Waves were organised similarly to the divisions of the First Wave, but with certain differences in equipment: Fifth and Sixth Wave divisions, for example, were equipped with Czech weapons and material, possessed no infantry guns, and only eight medium mortars. The Ninth Wave divisions were intended only for occupation and guard duties, and as such were poorly armed, as were the four fortification divisions. Immediately before the invasion of the west, orders were given for the formation of a further twelve divisions, nine of the Tenth Wave and three mountain divisions, but of these only one mountain division was ready before the end of the campaign. Thus, by May 1940, the future German Army was to consist of 144 infantry divisions of all types, six mountain divisions, one cavalry division, four motorised infantry divisions, and ten armoured divisions, making a grand total of 165, an increase of sixty-two over the number upon mobilisation. In March the strength of the Field Army, including the armed SS, was 3,300,000 men, and for the forthcoming campaign, 88 *Marsch* (Replacement) battalions from the Replacement Army were made ready, some 80,000 men in all.

The consequences of this sixty per cent expansion (which takes no account of the increase in the SS-VT formations) were detrimental. All the newly raised units faced severe shortages in equipment, and it was not possible to improve the inadequate equipment of the already established units. The critical position of the Army's motorisation has already been noted, but that of weapons and munitions was little better. Between 1 September 1939 and 1 April 1940, only 567,700 rifles, 21,100 machine-guns, 1,630 anti-tank guns, 2,172 mortars, 394 light and 55 heavy infantry guns, 536 10.5cm and 281 15cm field howitzers, and 102 21cm mortars had been added to the Army's stocks—on average only a ten per cent increase in armament.

However, the months since the outbreak of war had seen some improvements in the quality of troops within the mobilised divisions. On the whole, only the motorised and First Wave divisions had taken part in the campaign in Poland, and so the others, which were either concentrated along the quiet western frontier or assembled in training areas, had been able to improve the training of their men and to embark on the replacement of unfit personnel, in particular the First World War veterans who had been mobilised in default of younger trained reservists. By the end of the winter, several hundred thousand veterans were transferred to the service troops or other suitable units. Just as important was the battle experience gained by those units who had fought in Poland. These amounted to half the Field Army as it was then composed, and formed the great majority of those active divisions on which the offensive power of the Wehrmacht so greatly depended. Further sources for recruitment were available after September 1939 by the establishment of two new *Wehrkreise* in the annexed territory of the east and the expansion of another (East Prussia), followed by the creation of military areas in the Protectorate in Bohemia and Moravia and in the General-Government of Poland.

At the outbreak of war, the SS-VT also underwent considerable expansion. On 17 August 1938, the Führer issued a decree which, in the event of an emergency, provided for the reinforcement of the armed SS with the SS *Totenkopfverbände* (the Death's Head units, the concentration camp guards). In October 1939 this was put into effect, three *Totenkopf* infantry regiments forming the *Totenkopf* Division. Other *Totenkopf* personnel entered the *Polizei* Division, formed on Hitler's order of 18 September 1939 mainly from members of the *Ordnungspolizei*, which, although not nominally a part of the SS-VT, came under SS control. At the same time, the three SS-VT regiments—*Deutschland, Germania,* and *Der Führer*—were brought together to form the SS *Verfügungs division*. These SS divisions were larger than their Army counterparts, averaging some 21,000 men each. Hitler's guard regiment, the *Leibstandarte* SS, was reinforced with further infantry and, especially, artillery units, but otherwise remained untouched by this reorganisation. Thus, at the beginning of the campaign in the west, the SS-VT could put in the field two motorised infantry divisions *(Verfügungs* and *Totenkopf)*, one division *(Polizei)* the equivalent of the Second Wave Army formations, and one strong motorised infantry regiment *(Leibstandarte);* some 70,000 men, which, together with thirteen other *Totenkopf* infantry regiments, two *Totenkopf* cavalry regiments, replacements in training, and headquarters personnel, brought the total strength of the armed SS in May 1940 to some 125,000 soldiers.

For the campaign in the west, the German Army High Command disposed its invasion force into three army groups, seven armies, and ninety-three divisions (including those of the armed SS), a number which, if the OKH reserve were taken into account, would be increased to 135 divisions and one brigade. Only sixteen were fully motorised, two-seventeenths of the total. The two army groups, A and B, on whose endeavours lay the success or failure of the plan, were composed of seventy-four divisions, fifteen, roughly one-fifth, of which were mechanised, ten of them panzer formations. Army Group A, entrusted with the vital breakthrough was made up of three armies, the 4th, 12th, and 16th, and a reserve; a total of forty-five divisions composed of twenty-two First Wave, one mountain, eight Second Wave, one Third Wave, and three Fourth Wave infantry divisions, and three motorised infantry and seven armoured divisions. Army Group B was smaller, only twenty-nine divisions in two armies, the 18th and 6th, and a reserve—ten First Wave (including one air-landing division), one Second Wave, six Third Wave, five Fourth Wave, one cavalry, two motorised infantry, and three armoured divisions. Army Group C, because of its secondary, static role, was given only nineteen infantry divisions, none of which were First Wave; four were Second Wave, two Third Wave, five Fourth Wave, and four Fifth Wave, and four fortification divisions, divided into two armies, the 1st and 7th, a reserve. The OKH Reserve was composed of forty-two infantry divisions (three First Wave and twenty-four from the Fifth to Eighth Waves) and one motorised infantry brigade. Furthermore, the Luftwaffe fielded two fully mobile Flak corps to aid the fast-moving units of 6th and 4th Armies (Panzer Group Kleist and II Army Corps). These Flak corps each included ninety-six 8.8cm anti-aircraft guns which could be used in an anti-tank role. For duty in the east, the Germans could find only ten low-grade infantry divisions; for Norway, only seven (including two mountain divisions); and for Denmark, one.

The greatest advantage the Germans possessed over their enemies in the west lay not in their own strength but in the weakness of their enemies. This was not, however, a numerical weakness. Ranged against the 135 German divisions in May 1940 were ten Dutch infantry divisions, twenty-three Belgian infantry divisions, nine British infantry divisions, and seventy-seven infantry, five cavalry, three light armoured, and three armoured French divisions, a total of 130 plus a large number of supporting units. Against 2,574 tanks, the Allies could field some 3,600 of at least equal calibre. In artillery, too, they possessed a decided advantage, with 11,500 pieces compared with 7,700. A total of 2,760,000 Germans faced 3,740,000 enemy soldiers, an unequal contest, especially when it is remembered that an attacking force is usually held to need a numerical superiority of three to one to be successful. Only in aircraft, of which they marshalled 1,200 fighters and 1,300 bombers, were the Germans markedly superior to their opponents. However, they had been brought up in the tradition that victory did not necessarily belong to the big battalions; strategic considerations could alter the balance conclusively against the numerically superior, but qualitatively inferior, enemy.

It was not that the Allies possessed worse equipment than the Germans, or less of it—neither proposition would be true. It was that they based their strategic and tactical concepts on the mistaken lessons of the deadlock of the First World War, and not on any tradition of decisive manoeuvre, let alone on the revolutionary implications of the indirect approach. The French, the Dutch, and the Belgians based their strategy on linear defence and mass attack, on fire-power rather than manoeuvre, and on a slow, organised, and 'safe' method of advance. For the French, lulled into a sense of false security behind their Maginot Line, this was especially serious. Their *Instructions for Tactical Employment of Large Units* stipulated: 'The infantry is charged with the principal mission in combat. Protected and accompanied by its own fires and by those of the artillery, perhaps preceded and supported by tanks, aviation, etc, it conquers the ground, occupies it, organises it, and holds it.'[41] Tanks were relegated to a purely supporting role; most of them were dispersed among the infantry divisions, and the few armoured divisions were scattered along the whole front. The British, although on 10 May they had no fully armoured division in France, nevertheless had some 600 tanks, half of them dispersed throughout the infantry formations and the other half massed in an unbalanced, inflexible armoured formation with too few motorised infantry to accompany them. Furthermore, the British and French armies had suffered from twenty years of neglect by parsimonious governments, and from the derision of people who blindly rejected the very possibility of war. As a result, they lacked that aggressive self-confidence so necessary for success.

The lamentable condition of the strategic and tactical thought of the Allies was made considerably more serious by the plan on which they based all their calculations to counter the expected German invasion. It could not have suited their enemy better. The Allied dispositions counted on the main thrust coming through the Belgian plain, as the original German plan had envisaged; there was no thought that the Germans might launch their *Schwerpunkt* through the Ardennes to the south. Although this was the most important point in their defences, being the hinge between the Maginot Line and the Allied northern forces, it was at the same time their weakest. Because of the wooded, hilly nature of the terrain, with its narrow, winding roads, the Allied generals believed that the Ardennes were impassable to a large army, especially a motorised one. Therefore they placed only nine divisions to face what was, unbeknown to them, the mass of the invasion force, forty-five divisions in all. The actual mechanics of the Allied plan further assisted the Germans, for they required that, once the invader set foot on Belgian soil, the British and French forces in the north would move forward sixty miles into Belgium to the Dyle river, there to form a continuous defensive front from Antwerp to the Maginot Line. Thus, while the best of the Allied armies moved into Belgium to counter Army Group B, the main German thrust, undertaken by Army Group A, began to develop from the Ardennes. Not only would the Allied move expose the southern flank of their northern armies, but it would facilitate the German thrust to the Channel and the vast, decisive encirclement of the French and British in Belgium. The state of Germany's enemies in May 1940 bore out fully the truth of Sun Tzu's saying: 'To secure ourselves from defeat lies in our hands, but the opportunity of defeating the enemy is provided by the enemy himself.'

4

The West—The Campaign

Strategy is the art of making use of time and space. I am less chary of the latter than of the former. Space we can recover, lost time never.

NAPOLEON

At 5.35 a.m. on 10 May 1940, the German Army and Air Force attacked along the Western Front: 135 divisions, supported by 2,750 aircraft, moved against Holland, Belgium, and France. In Holland, 4,500 parachutists and 12,000 troops of an air-landing division were sent in to seize vital bridges and aerodromes and to dominate the centre of political and military leadership, The Hague, while an armoured division sped to their assistance and an army of ten divisions moved in to crush all resistance. In five days the battle for Holland was over. Against Belgium, the opening of the campaign was just as spectacular: 500 airborne troops were used to capture two bridges over the Albert Canal and the fortress of Eben Emael, which not only guarded the bridges over the wide, unfordable River Meuse, but controlled the approaches to the heart of Belgium. The invading army of fourteen infantry divisions then burst into the Belgian plains beyond. By the 15th, the Allies' position there was rendered hopeless; on the 27th, Belgium capitulated, and 500,000 troops laid down their arms.

But it was to the south that the decisive stroke was mounted. On the 10th, the spearheads of the forty-five divisions of Army Group A struck at the Ardennes, on the 13th they crossed the Meuse, and, by the evening of the 20th, the furthermost unit had reached the coast; the Allied forces had been cut in two, and more than fifty Allied divisions in Belgium faced total annihilation. By 4 June, the battle was over: the Allies had lost fifty per cent of their forces on the Continent, and more than seventy-five per cent of their best equipment. The flower of the French Army was behind wire, the majority of the British humiliated and back in Britain. On the 5th, began the final destruction of France: Paris was occupied on the 14th; on the 22nd, the German terms for an armistice was accepted, and at 1.35 p.m. 25 June firing ceased. Hitler ordered that throughout the Reich the bells be rung for seven days in celebration of victory.

The campaign in the west had lasted just forty-six days and had been decided, effectively, within ten. A German Army had defeated a highly rated enemy, superior both in numbers and equipment; the defensive, so long believed to have been the strongest form of war, had been shattered by a decisive attack in which manoeuvre and organisation counted for far more than men and weapons. The speed and decisiveness of the German victors had stunned and impressed their enemies. Typical of the contemporary reactions was that of a staff officer with the Commander-in-Chief of the British Air Force in France; in his diary he made the following entry for 19 May: 'News that the panzers are in Amiens. This is like some ridiculous nightmare. . . . The Germans have taken every risk—criminally foolish risks—and they have got away with it. . . . The French General Staff have been paralysed by this unorthodox war of movement. The fluid conditions prevailing are not dealt with in the textbooks and the 1914 brains of the French Generals responsible for formulating the plans of the Allied armies are incapable of functioning in this new and astonishing lay-out.' A few days earlier he had written: 'It is the cooperation between the dive-bombers and the armoured divisions that is winning the war for Germany.'[1]

From such beginnings evolved the myth of *Blitzkrieg*. It is easy to understand why the misconception rose in relation to the campaign in Flanders and France, which had been fast, furious, and decisive, and in which modern weapons had been prominent. The exploits of the panzer divisions were considered remarkable, and it proved easy to construe them to be the result of a revolutionary, coherent system of warfare practised with supreme efficiency. General Fuller, for example, easily fell prey to this illusion. Writing in 1961, he described the exploits of Guderian's corps as *'Blitzkrieg in excelsis.'* His account was as follows:

'On 10 May, the attack was launched; on the 11th French advanced troops in the Ardennes were hounded westward; on the 12th Guderian stormed and took Bouillon, and before nightfall two of his divisions occupied the eastern bank of the Meuse at Sedan, while Reinhardt's corps closed in on Monthermé, and Rommel's division was at Houx. On the 13th, under cover of dive-bomber attacks, the Meuse was crossed and bridged, and by nightfall the village of Chémery, eight miles south of Sedan, was in German hands. On the night of 14th–15th, against Guderian's violent protests, the advance was halted by Kleist. Early on the 16th it was resumed, to be halted again on the 17th. From then on it became a race for the English Channel. On the 18th St. Quentin was reached; on the 19th the Canal de Nord, between Douai and Péronne, was crossed, and on the 20th Montreuil, Doullers, Amiens, and Abbevillle were occupied. The whole stretch of country between the Scarpe and Somme rivers was now in German hands; the British lines of communication were cut, and the way to the Channel ports opened. In eleven days the Germans had advanced 220 miles: such was *Blitzkrieg. . . .*'[2]

Liddell Hart went even further when he described the battle of France as 'one of history's most striking examples of the decisive effect of a new idea, carried out by a dynamic executant.'[3]

But the campaign was no such thing. It has already been shown that the German plan was firmly based on the traditional concept of *Vernichtungsgedanke*, in which decisive manoeuvre and encirclement by the whole attacking force, supported by the Luftwaffe's dive-bombers, were predominent; the proposals for deep, unsupported thrusts by mechanised formations, were not only actively discouraged, they were positively feared. At the outset the armour enthusiasts possessed only two advantages over the traditionalists: their major role as the 'cutting edge' of Army Group A's scythe-cut, and the freedom given to them in accordance with von Moltke's dictum that no operational plan should extend beyond the first clash with the main enemy forces. But could they exploit this, and, forging ahead from the slower infantry armies, conduct their operations according to the precepts of the armoured idea? The chances were not good. The test would come not during the advance to the Meuse, but at its crossing, and from the moment the breakout from the bridgehead began.

As the German advance into Belgium drew the Allies' attention, together with the bulk of their armoured forces, to the north, the decisive stroke was being mounted in the south. As the parachute and air-landing forces spearheading Army Group B dropped on to an unsuspecting enemy, the tanks and infantry of Army Group A quietly crossed the Luxembourg and southern Belgian borders and moved into the seventy-mile stretch of hills, streams, and forests known as the Ardennes. Flinging aside weak opposition, they emerged from that 'impassable' tract of country, crossed into France, and reached the Meuse by the fourth day of the campaign. Surprise was total. Every mile the Allies' northern armies had moved into northern Belgium was a minor victory for the Germans. Not only had the Allies failed to stop the advance of von Bock's forces, but, and more important, they had exposed more and more of their flank and rear to von Rundstedt. The German plan was working; but the greatest obstacle was yet to be overcome: the crossing of the Meuse. All depended on gaining the open country on the other side, where speedy manoeuvre would bring total victory. A halt on the Meuse, even for a few days, could prove damaging to the prospects for success. Time lost to the Germans would be time gained by the Allies, time in which to recover their balance, strengthen their defences, and switch the point of their main effort to the south. Had a counter-stroke then been possible against the advancing panzer spearheads, even if it were not particularly successful, the effect on the ever-fearful German Command would have been stunning, and might well have have served to paralyse the advance. Indeed, even before the Meuse was reached, the Germans were showing some nervousness.

As Guderian wrote to Liddell Hart after the war:

'A stroke from the direction of Montmedy [to the
south] towards Kleist's left, perhaps would have
caused more trouble to the German Command.
When, during 11 May 1940, Kleist got the news
that French cavalry tried to advance from that
direction, he immediately gave orders that 10th
Panzer Division—my left wing division—was to be
stopped and turned against the enemy. This order,
if followed, would have made nearly impracticable
that attack on Sedan and an early breakthrough. I
therefore ordered . . . 10th Panzer Division to
continue [its] march towards Sedan on a way
several kilometres north of his previous route,
asking General von Kleist to safeguard my left by
the units of Wiersheim's army corps and infantry
units following behind.'[4]

And on 12 May, Halder noted in his diary: 'Group Kleist
believes that the armour could have advanced faster if
they had not to wait for the infantry to close up. Attacks
should have been accompanied by armoured infantry
brigades.'[5]

To the lasting credit of the generals of Army Group A,
the paramount importance of the Meuse crossing was
recognised. Von Blumentritt, the Operations Officer of
the advancing army group, wrote:

'According to plan, the infantry corps were to
attack the Meuse and force a passage for the
subsequent crossing of the armoured corps. But
this would have occupied nearly a week while the
infantry corps were coming up, taking up their
positions and making their preparations. Previous
to the assault the whole of the artillery would have

had to get into position *en masse* and take steps to ensure an ample supply of ammunition. Then the second miracle occurred [the first had been the weakness of the Allied air forces]. Receiving word that the panzer divisions were already in position on the heights of the Meuse north of Sedan, not only Kleist and I, but . . . Rundstedt drove forward to see them. From there we drove down to the Meuse—where the panzer engineers were already working on a bridge. Here and there a few French machine-guns were firing from small, ludicrous concrete emplacements on the west banks of the Meuse. That was all. We simply could not grasp this miracle—and feared that it was a French ruse. But in fact the dreaded Meuse position was almost non-existent, and only weakly defended. Then the panzer-race across the river began.'[6]

At 4.00 p.m. on 13 May, the first soldiers of Guderian's corps crossed the Muse, just west of Sedan, and by nightfall of the following day the bridgehead had been extended to ten miles. On the 15th the last line of defence was broken; the way to the Channel lay open. The question then was: would the military leaders follow the daring precedent they had established on the Meuse? On the answer to that lay the prospects for total victory.

However, 15 May, the day on which the advance to the Channel began, saw the Germans revert to traditional military principles; from the moment the tanks started to move west, the whole character of the future attack was set. Caution replaced daring. The progress of the mechanised forces was to be governed as much by the fears, hesitation, and conservatism of the senior generals as by the dash and brilliance of the panzer leaders. Guderian later wrote bitterly: 'The High Command's influence on my actions was merely restrictive throughout.'[7] On the morning of the 15th, although Army Group A's war diary specified von Rundstedt's intention that there should be no 'shackling' of the mechanised forces, which must be 'given every opportunity to gain ground to the west,' it also recorded that the Kleist group was placed under the command of 12th Army in order to 'bring coordination between the movement of the motorised forces and the infantry divisions.'[8] A 'loose rein' was the term he used to describe the tactical control to be exercised over the armour; Guderian and his fellows wished to be rid of the harness altogether. The evening of the 15th was to witness the first warning tug on the reins, an irritation for the panzer enthusiasts which boded ill for the future. In the daylight hours the French rearward line of defence had finally collapsed, and, although no one knew it, it had been the last occasion on which von Kleist's group was to meet any solid opposition in its race for the Channel. But that evening there came an order from panzer group headquarters to halt the advance and consolidate the bridgehead. For Guderian this must have been a disheartening moment, for it seemed that Halder's idea of a 'properly marshalled attack in mass' would now be enforced. Guderian later recorded:

'I would not, and could not, put up with this order, as it meant forfeiting surprise and all our initial success. I therefore telephoned the Chief of Staff of the panzer group, Colonel Zeitzler, and getting no satisfaction I then telephoned General von Kleist himself to get the order cancelled. The exchange of views became very lively. . . . At last Kleist agreed to permit a continuation of the advance for another twenty-four hours in order to widen the bridgehead sufficiently to allow the infantry corps to follow us.'[9]

Guderian plunged on. The next day, the 16th, Halder began his diary entry with the exultant words: 'Our breakthrough wedge is developing in a positively classical manner. West of the Meuse our advance is sweeping on. Enemy armoured counter-attacks are being smashed in its path. The marching performance of the infantry is superb (5th Division and 1st Mountain Division).'[10] By nightfall, Guderian's and Reinhardt's units were over fifty miles west of Sedan. But however pleased Halder or Guderian might have been at the victories up to that time, there were others who saw the momentum of the attack, the cause of such success, as threatening the outcome of the campaign. As early as the 15th von Rundstedt was expressing his fears thus:

'For the first time the question has arisen whether it may not become necessary to halt temporarily the mechanised forces on the Oise [some seventy miles from Sedan]. . . . the enemy is in no circumstances to be allowed to achieve any kind of success, even if it be only a local success, on the Aisne or, later, in the Loire region [some sixty miles from the Meuse]. This would have a more detrimental effect on operations as a whole than would a temporary slowing-down of our motorised forces.'[11]

Early the next day, von Rundstedt ordered, by telephone, that a general tightening-up of the army group's formations was to take place: only advanced units were to be allowed to pass the line Beaumont-Hirson-Montcornet-Gruignicourt [forty miles from Sedan], then the furthermost limit of the offensive, although bridge-heads could be seized, but not exploited, over the Oise, some thirty miles distant. The southern flank was to be covered as the armies closed up, and all infantry formations would be moved forward at the greatest possible speed. The army group's war diary contained the following entry for the 16th:

> 'Army group headquarters have no doubt that, if motorised forces were to continue their push in advance of 12th Army, they would probably be able to cross the Oise between Guise and la Fère without difficulty. Their commanding officers are convinced of this and would like to act accordingly, especially Generals Guderian and von Kleist. But looking at operations as a whole, the risk involved does not appear to be justified. The extended flank between la Fère and Rethel [forty-five miles] is too sensitive, especially in the Laon area. The southern flank is simply inviting an enemy attack. . . . If the spearheads of the attack are temporarily halted, it will be possible to effect a certain stiffening of the threatened flank within twenty-four hours.'[12]

That evening, when he visited the army group headquarters, von Brauchitsch endorsed von Rundstedt's decision that no formations should pass the Oise and Sambre without specific authorisation. Consequently, early in the morning of the 17th, von Kleist ordered Guderian to halt; the eager corps commander had already pushed too far. Guderian was astonished. Later he remembered: 'After the wonderful success on 16 May it did not occur to me that my superiors might still be thinking on the same lines as before. . . .'[13] Von Kleist flew in at 7.00 a.m. to inform Guderian of the decision, and a violent quarrel ensued, terminating with the panzer group commander accepting his subordinate's offer of resignation. Later that day General List, commander of 12th Army, arrived to pour oil on the troubled waters. He explained that the order to halt had come from OKH and must be obeyed, but that army group headquarters had given permission for a reconnaissance in force to be carried out, although Guderian's corps headquarters would be required to remain exactly where it then was. That evening the panzer divisions moved again, Guderian laying a wire from his stationary corps headquarters to his new and mobile 'advanced headquarters,' and interpreting his 'reconnaissance in force' as loosely as was possible. As early as 9.00 a.m. on the 18th, his 2nd Panzer Division had reached St. Quentin, ten miles beyond the Oise, the town that was specified in von Rundstedt's order to be the objective for that day.

Von Kleist later claimed that the direction to halt had come from Hitler, and, although no documentary evidence appears to exist which corroborates this assertion, certainly the atmosphere at Führer headquarters was conducive to such an order. Hitler was fully aware of the importance of Army Group A's thrust, even to the extent of ordering, on the 16th, that the three panzer divisions of Army Group B be transferred to the south. However, his concern for the *Schwerpunkt* also included fear. Siewert, von Brauchitsch's personal assistant, recorded: 'The Führer was nervous about the risk that the main French armies might strike westward, and wanted to wait until a large number of infantry divisions had been brought up to provide flank cover along the Aisne [the southern flank of the advance].'[14] At midday on the 17th, while von Kleist's panzers were halted, Hitler told von Brauchitsch that 'he considered the principal danger to be in the south.'[15] At 1.30 p.m., Army Group A received an order from the Army Commander-in-Chief urging a strong defence of the Aisne (the southern flank of the advance). By 3.00 p.m., the Supreme Commander was at von Rundstedt's headquarters, only to have his anxieties confirmed. The army group's war diary reported Hitler as saying: 'At the moment, decision depends not so much on a rapid thrust to the Channel, as on the ability to secure as quickly as possible an absolutely sound defence on the Aisne in the Laon area and, later, on the Somme; the motorised forces at present employed there will thus be made available for such a thrust. All measures taken must be based on this, even if it involves a temporary delay in the advance to the west.'[16] That evening Halder wrote despondently: 'Rather an unpleasant day. The Führer is terribly nervous. Frightened by his own success, he is afraid to take any chance and so would rather pull the reins on us. Puts forward the excuse that it is all because of his concern for the left flank. Keitel's telephone calls to the army groups, on behalf of the Führer, and the Führer's personal visit to army groups have caused only bewilderment and doubts.'[17] The only man to remain calm was Halder himself, who believed that the French on the southern flank were 'too weak to attack at this time.'[18] But even his confidence might have been disastrously misplaced had he been able to exert any influence on the campaign; instead of continuing the attack west, towards the coast, he favoured a grand movement in a south-westerly direction towards Compiègne, with the possibility of subsequently wheeling south-east past Paris to take the Maginot Line in the rear. So much for the Channel!

The next day, the 18th when Guderian's tanks were entering St. Quentin, an atmosphere of near crisis still bedevilled the German Command. Jodl wrote in his diary: 'It has been a day of high tension. OKH has not carried out the instruction to build up the southern flank as rapidly as possible... . The Army Commander-in-Chief and General Halder were summoned at once and given the most explicit orders to take the necessary measures.'[19] Jodl then interfered directly with the Army's operations and signalled that: '1st Mountain Division and the rear elements of 4th Army to turn south.'[20]

Keitel, for his part, flew to von Rundstedt to impress on him the urgency of his Führer's orders. The same day Halder noted:

'They have a completely different view in the Führer headquarters. The Führer is full of an incomprehensible fear about the southern flank. He rages and shouts that we are doing the best to ruin the entire operation and are running the risk of defeat. He entirely refuses to carry on the operation westwards, let alone south-west, and still clings to the plan of a north-western drive. This is the subject of a most unpleasant discussion . . . between the Führer on the one side and von Brauchitsch and myself on the other. A directive was issued on this occasion which is a confirmation in writing of our conversation which took place at 10.00 a.m. Conversations between the Army Commander-in-Chief and Generaloberst von Rundstedt, and my conversation with Salmuth, produced the effects the Führer desired (sharp switch of forward divisions to the south-west, main body of motorised forces to be ready to move to the west).'[21]

Thus, on the 17th and 18th, despite the agitations of Guderian in the field and Halder at OKH, the idea of a 'properly marshalled attack in mass,' with the armoured divisions as the cutting edge and with a coordinated defensive line to the south, came to dominate over the urgently expressed desire to push ahead with the panzers at all possible speed.

So strong was the control now exerted over operations by Führer Headquarters that Halder was forced to wring from Hitler his approval for further advance on the part of Army Group A's mechanised forces. At midday on the

18th Halder had become most concerned that the Allies were trying to form a defensive line between Valenciennes-Cambrai-St. Quentin-la Fère, across the intended western path of the German advance. Although he knew that some elements of Guderian's command had reached these points, he was also well aware that they consisted of a 'reconnaissance in force' and not a full attack. The Chief of the General Staff therefore concluded that 'we must punch through this new line before it has a chance to consolidate'[22] and that this would require far stronger forces than were permitted. Preliminary orders were issued to that effect, and Halder went to the Führer for permission to launch the attack the following morning, the 19th. This Hitler gave, but, as Halder noted, 'in an atmosphere of bad feeling and in a form calculated to give the outside world the impression that it is a plan conceived by the OKW.'[23] Concession though this was, it amounted to very little, for already by the late evening of the 18th Guderian's advanced units had nearly reached the Oise at Péronne (still as part of his 'reconnaissance,' and some eighteen miles as the crow flies from St. Quentin), and the new orders specified that the corps advance units should push on to 'capture a bridgehead over the Canal du Nord [two miles from Péronne] and advance towards the line Le Mesril-Clery.'[24] This meant that the ground to be gained on the 19th would be, at most, only five miles. Furthermore the OKH order issued to Army Group A on the evening of the 18th stressed that 'The dangers of separation must be avoided.'[25] If Guderian's advance was no longer to be classified a 'reconnaissance in force,' it was certainly an attack held in tight reins.

On 19 May Guderian's corps went only to the line Cambrai-Péronne-Ham. That evening, the orders for the next day's movements came in; Guderian recorded that 'the corps at last received its freedom of movement once again.'[26] Objectives were set: Amiens, some twenty-eight miles from Péronne, where a bridgehead was to be established on the south bank of the Somme, and, more ambitiously, Abbeville, also on the Somme, fifty miles from Péronne and only fourteen from the sea. By midday on the 20th the objective at Amiens had been reached, and by 7.00 p.m. (Army Group A war diary gave the time as 9.00 p.m.) Abbeville was in German hands. At midnight one battalion of the 2nd Panzer Division reached the Atlantic coast.

The 20th was, understandably, a day of great elation. Halder and von Brauchitsch were more than content with Guderian's achievement, and Hitler, according to Jodl, was 'beside himself with joy' and even talked 'in words of highest appreciation of the German Army and its leadership.'[27] But it was at the same time a day of some confusion. The predicament of the German Command was considerable: its troops were at the coast and the Allied forces were cut in two, certainly, but what of the future? Which way should Army Group A now turn— north to effect the battle of annihilation so favored by von Rundstedt and von Manstein, or south-west to begin a vast encirclement up against the rear of the Maginot Line, as proposed by Halder, and, it seems, concurred with by von Brauchitsch? To add to this dilemma, there was the intense disquiet felt not only about the vulnerability of the southern flank, but also about the possibility of concerted Allied action coming from the north against the extended German line. The day previously, there had been great concern at OKW about Franco-British armoured attacks from Belgium, and, early on the 20th, Halder, although confident about the chance of holding off such threats, had expressed his fear of large Allied forces escaping to the south in front of von Kleist's panzer group. (Even the advance to the coast that night cannot have completely allayed his fears, as the front from Péronne to the sea was then only sparsely held.) The result of all this was that, on the 21st, the day Lord Gort, the British commander, became convinced that the BEF had to evacuate to England through the Channel ports, Guderian's panzers lay idle; no orders were forthcoming because no decision had been reached.

The 21st, then, was marked not by any further startling German advance behind the undefended flank and rear of the northern Allied armies; rather it was dominated by a British counter-attack at Arras in the evening against the northern-most armoured spearhead of Army Group A—Rommel's 7th Panzer Division, a unit of Hoth's panzer group—which succeeded in penetrating ten miles into the German line. This was regarded as the fulfilment of German fears—fears that had already been increased by the attack from the south by the French 4th Armoured Division under de Gaulle on the 19th, which had penetrated to within a mile of Guderian's advanced headquarters before being repulsed. Of the Arras affair, von Rundstedt recalled that it was 'a critical moment. . . . For a short time we feared that our armoured divisions would be cut off before the infantry divisions could come up to support them.'[28] Although the attack was delivered by only a relatively small force, with just two battalions of tanks, and although it was brought to a halt, this incident, together with Rommel's consequent failure to capture the town of Arras, had a profound psychological effect on the German command. Rommel believed himself to have been fighting against 'hundreds of enemy tanks,'[29] and XIX Corps' war diary recorded that the British counter-attack had 'apparently created nervousness throughout the entire [Kleist] group area.'[30] Hitler became extremely worried by the lack of infantry divisions in the vital forward areas, and remained in the map room until 1.30 a.m. the following morning. The Army Command felt forced to issue an order stating that 'the question of an attack by Army Group A in a northerly direction will only arise when the infantry divisions have gained possession of the high ground north-west of Arras.'[31]

The British counter-attack at Arras had its effect on the major event of the 21st: the decision to continue the German attack northwards, with the capture of the Channel ports as the objective. In the evening, any idea of a south-westerly attack having been rendered unthinkable by the Arras counter-attack, OKH issued its order for von Kleist's group to proceed to Boulogne and Calais, the latter being some fifty miles as the crow flies from Guderian's stationary tanks. But fear of another counter-attack similar to that at Arras caused the army group to hold back Hoth's units, and Reinhardt, commander of XXXXI Corps, felt it necessary to deploy a division eastwards as a precaution against any further counter-attacks. But most damaging to German interests was von Kleist's decision to weaken XIX Corps. Guderian explained the situation:

'I wanted the 10th Panzer Division to advance on Dunkirk ... the 1st Panzer Division to move on Calais and the 2nd on Boulogne. But I had to abandon this plan since the 10th Panzer Division was withdrawn by an order of the panzer group dated 22 May, and was held back as panzer group reserve [to cover any Allied threat from the south]. So when the advance began on the 22nd, the only divisions I commanded were the 1st and 2nd Panzer. My request that I be allowed to continue in control of all three of my divisions in order quickly to capture the Channel ports was unfortunately refused. As a result the immediate move of the 10th Panzer Division on Dunkirk could not now be carried out.'[32]

103

Furthermore, units of the 1st and 2nd Panzer Divisions had to be left behind to hold the Somme bridgehead until they were relieved. Thus was missed the first opportunity to cut the Allies' only means of escape. The push to Dunkirk was inhibited from the outset.

The attack by Guderian's depleted corps was to be renewed at 8.00 a.m. on the 22nd, but still it was dogged by the near paralysis that had gripped the German command after Arras. At the same time as the tanks were moving out, von Rundstedt ordered that, until the situation at Arras had been cleared up, the Kleist group should not push on to Calais or Boulogne; the OKH order was to be disregarded. However, although Arras was not to fall until the evening of the next day, von Rundstedt soon thought better of his decision. The war diary of XIX Corps noted that 'for reasons unknown . . . the attack on Boulogne was only authorised by group at 12.40 p.m. on the 22nd. For about five hours 1st and 2nd Panzer Divisions were standing inactive on the Amache.'[33] Such was Guderian's impatience, though, that he had sent his 2nd Panzer towards Boulogne half an hour earlier, at 12.10 p.m., without waiting for orders. By the middle of the afternoon the outskirts of the town had been reached, but it was only after some thirty-six hours had elapsed that Boulogne fell to the Germans. Calais held out even longer, and it was not until the evening of the 26th that it capitulated. The XIX Corps' war diary entry of the 23rd ended with the comment: 'Corps' view is that it would have been opportune and possible to carry out its three tasks (Aa Canal [halfway between Calais and Dunkirk], Calais, Boulogne) quickly and decisively, if, on the 22nd, its total forces, i.e. all three divisions, had advanced northward from the Somme area in one united surprise strike.'[34] Time lost by the panzers was time gained by the enemy, time in which to organise defences and stiffen the resolve to fight.

On 22 May, while Guderian's divisions were battling towards Boulogne and Calais, Hitler was busily concerning himself with future operations. A quick look at his deliberations will serve to illustrate how he, and other German commanders, viewed the use of mechanised forces. His decisions have been left to posterity in a pencilled memorandum, unsigned, but dated 22 May 1940 and addressed to, and initialled by, Keitel. It ran:

'Führer's wishes. Free motorised divisions as fast as possible by [using] infantry divisions—the nearest ones that you can lay hands on. Panzer divisions forward—take them out of flank protection actions and defensive battles. Only motorised formations still come forward into [battle] at the right time. They will therefore be freed from rear flank protection tasks. They will support and free the most forward armoured formations. . . . Throw forward, without delay, at least forward motorised units of infantry who are advancing to the west in forced marches. . . .'[35]

These points were probably used by the Chief of OKW when he was sent by Hitler to Army Group A to impress on von Rundstedt and his staff Hitler's desire to commit all Hoth's motorised troops on both sides of Arras and in the westward area towards the sea, while von Kleist's units on the Somme front were to be replaced as quickly as possible by the infantry divisions. In other words, the Führer wanted to relieve the mechanised forces from protection and defensive duties, and concentrate them in the spearhead so as to further the army group's advance. But this formed no indication of any sudden acceptance by Hitler of Guderian's ideas; the Keitel memorandum can be seen only in relation to Hitler's misgivings over the handling of the panzer forces exhibited during the whole campaign. Certainly, the Führer wanted fast, powerful advances by armoured spearheads, but then so did the majority of Germany's generals; what he, in common with most of the senior officers, believed were also necessary were properly constructed, secure flanks. Those would be made possible only through a coordinated attack in which the mechanised units were not allowed independence of action, but, instead, were kept in contact with the infantry. This attitude he had made clear repeatedly over the previous week. In simple terms, the form of offensive envisaged by the Supreme Commander, and also by the senior generals, was a series of moves in which the mechanised units punched their way through enemy territory and one by one fell out of the advance in order to form a continuous, secure flank extending back from the point unit to the rear of the whole army group. Meanwhile, the infantry formations would follow their faster partners with all possible speed and relieve them of their flank-guarding role, thereby allowing the motorised units to regroup and begin the attack once again. During the invasion of the Soviet Union in 1941 this method came to be known as the 'panzer raid.' In effect, the advance degenerated from the armour enthusiasts' ideal of a swift, deep thrust, ending only with the defeat of the enemy, into a succession of short, sharp jumps, with a pause between each for regrouping. Swift though this method of war was, compared with that of the enemy, it fell far short of Guderian's theories. The organised velocity of the armoured idea gave place to the initially powerful, but ever-fading, punches of the modernised *Vernichtungsgedanke.*

The dawn of 23 May witnessed the initial phase of the move on the last remaining port left open to the escaping British: Dunkirk. During the previous day, von Kleist had released 10th Panzer Division from it reserve duties, and Guderian had quickly sent it against Calais so as to relieve 1st Panzer for the attack against Dunkirk. At 10.00 a.m. on the 23rd, so his orders read, the 1st Panzer would move towards 'its objective via Gravelines.'[36] Despite meeting strong resistance, the attack continued well, and on the 24th the Aa Canal, just fifteen miles from the port, was crossed. The British reckoned that Dunkirk would fall the next day, before the main body of the BEF had managed to embark. But then, on the 24th, came the order to halt; the tanks, once again, stopped dead in their tracks and the Luftwaffe took over the entire responsibility for the fall of the port. The ground attack did not resume until the 27th, by which time the British defences had been considerably improved. Dunkirk itself did not fall until 4 June, too late: the bulk of the BEF had got back to England.

The famous 'halt order,' which saved the British Army, has been a subject of much controversy. Where did the blame lie—with Hitler, the Army Command or von Rundstedt? If the fateful decision to stop the panzers outside Dunkirk is regarded as an isolated, untypical, incident of the campaign, then the answer is difficult to find. If, however, it is seen as the culmination of the fears, hesitations, and failings of the previous nine days, it becomes readily understandable. Coordination of force, and security of flanks, had been basic to the German advance so far; and on 24 May, just as they were on the verge of one of the most decisive battles of annihilation in history, Hitler and his generals chose to behave exactly as they had done for the past fourteen days. They saw no reason why they should act against their tradition.

On 23 May, von Rundstedt and his senior commanders were worried men. Certainly, they believed that, by the evening, the position of the Allies in the north was hopeless, and that there no longer existed any real urgency to their operations. But other matters, which had dogged the advance of the army group after the crossing of the Meuse, troubled them. The five armies of Army Group A were extended over some 260 miles, a huge area with widely separated fronts to secure; its ten armoured divisions were spaced far apart—the 3rd, 4th, 5th, and 7th were near Arras, the 6th and 8th were opposite Aire, the 1st at Gravelines, the 2nd and 10th at Boulogne and Calais respectively, and the 9th near the Somme. Furthermore these forces, the vital spearhead of the German Army, had suffered heavily yet would soon be needed for the forthcoming offensive into the south of France. On the morning of the 23rd von Kleist informed von Kluge, and, through him, von Rundstedt, that his group had suffered heavy losses in men and equipment, and that tank casualties amounted to more than fifty per cent. Furthermore, his much-weakened group was expected to safeguard the Somme front, establish strong bridgeheads across that river, take Boulogne and Calais, secure the territory between them, and deploy over a thirty-five-mile front for an attack in the direction of Dunkirk-Ypres. This was just not possible, he remonstrated; reinforcements and regrouping must precede any determined attack in whatever direction. Halder, who heard of von Kleist's misgivings, took an opposite view and commented that a final supreme effort should be made; the crisis would be over in forty-eight hours. The Hoth group, too, had suffered much; its XXXIX Corps' war diary noted on the 24th: 'Casualties for each armoured division [5th and 7th], approximately 50 officers and 1,500 NCOs and men, killed or wounded; armour, approximately thirty per cent. Owing to frequent encounters with enemy tanks, weapon losses are heavy—particularly machine-guns in infantry regiments.'[37]

Von Rundstedt, too, on the 23rd was of the opinion that a halt was necessary. He feared concerted action by the Allied forces to the north and south; he believed it vital that the armoured units be closed up and the northern flank consolidated immediately; and he felt that, because the southern flank was not yet secure and the ports of Boulogne and Calais had not yet fallen, the advanced units of von Kleist's and Hoth's Groups should only hold the Aa Canal line, and not attempt to cross it. At around 6.00 p.m., von Kluge, commander of 4th Army which now contained both panzer groups, received from von Rundstedt a directive along these lines, and he, in turn, issued an order to the effect that 'in the main, Hoth group will halt tomorrow; Kleist group will also halt, thereby clarifying the situation and closing up.'[38] Von Kluge had himself already told his chief that the troops 'would be glad if they could close up tomorrow'[39] (the 24th), and his army's war diary confirmed his eagerness to halt 4th Army, 'in the main, tomorrow in accordance with Generaloberst von Rundstedt's order.'[40] Once again, the armour was to be closed up and the flanks secured before the attack was allowed to continue.

One final development on the 23rd was to prove of immense significance for the morrow. For the first time in the campaign, the Luftwaffe Commander exerted his influence. Warlimont related the story:

'. . . late in the afternoon of 23 May, Göring was sitting at a heavy oak table beside his train . . . when the news arrived that the enemy in Flanders was almost surrounded. Göring reacted in a flash. Banging his great fist on the table, he shouted: ''This is a wonderful opportunity for the Luftwaffe. I must speak to the Führer at once. . . .'' In the telephone conversation that followed, he used every sort of language to persuade Hitler that this

109

was a unique opportunity for his Air Force. If the Führer would give the order that this operation was to be left to the Luftwaffe alone, he would give an unconditional assurance that he would annihilate the remnants of the enemy; all he wanted, he said, was a free run; in other words, the tanks must be withdrawn sufficiently far from the western side of the pocket to ensure that they were not in danger from our own bombing. Hitler was as quick as Göring to approve this plan without further consideration. Jeschonnek [the Luftwaffe Chief of Staff] and Jodl rapidly fixed the details, including the withdrawal of certain armoured units and the exact timing for the start of the air attack.'[41]

The reasons for Hitler's accession to Göring's forceful request are not hard to understand: the Führer was as worried as anyone about the extended flanks of Army Group A and the possibility of strong Allied counter-attacks. Arras had proved a salutary lesson. Further-more, as well as safeguarding the Army by allowing its units time to regroup and rest, Hitler could ensure that his very own Luftwaffe, the special creation of National Socialism, would be allowed the glory of the final decision of the campaign in which, until then, the achievements of the ground forces had necessarily played the chief part. Possibly, too, he was concerned that the watery terrain of the surrounding country was unsuitable for armoured operations. Consequently, strengthened in his new resolve, Hitler made prepara-tions to visit Army Group A on the 24th.

The morning of 24 May saw only a very limited advance, and even that was against the letter of von Rundstedt's order, which was to halt at the Aa Canal and not cross it. However, it was consciously limited by the spirit of that order. To the south of Dunkirk, Reinhardt's corps fought to secure its bridgehead over the River Aa at St. Omer, and, to the west, Guderian's 1st Panzer crossed the canal and established three bridgeheads. Both then halted, having achieved only the consolidation of a favourable position from which to continue the attack when, and if, it was ordered.

As von Kleist's group was making its final move forward, Hitler arrived at von Rundstedt's headquarters. The army group's war diary noted:

'At 11.30 a.m. the Führer arrives and receives a summary of the situation from the Commander of the army group. He completely agrees with the opinion that the infantry should attack east of Arras while the motorised units should be held on the line Lens-Béthune-Aire-St. Omer-Gravelines in order to "catch" the enemy who are being pushed back by Army Group B. He gives it added emphasis by stating that it is necessary to conserve the tank units for the coming operations and that a further narrowing of the pocket would result in an extremely undesirable restriction of Luftwaffe operations. . . .'[42]

Jodl, who had accompanied Hitler, wrote that day: 'He is very happy about the measures of the army group, which fit in entirely with his ideas.'[43] After Hitler had left, von Rundstedt issued an order at 12.31 p.m., which read: 'By the Führer's orders . . . the general line Lens-Béthune-Aire-St. Omer-Gravelines (Canal line) will *not* be passed.'[44] Late that day Hitler gave further substance to his decision that the panzers should halt. His Directive No. 13 stated: 'The task of the Luffwaffe will be to break all enemy resistance on the part of the surrounded forces, to prevent the escape of the English forces across the Channel. . . .'[45]

The only men of influence in the German Armed Forces who, at the time, strongly opposed von Rundstedt's decision and Hitler's order were Guderian, who confessed himself to be 'utterly speechless,'[46] von Brauchitsch, although lamely, and Halder. On the morning of the 24th, the Chief of the General Staff had been confident of victory: 'The situation continues to develop favourably, even though the progress of our infantry units in the direction of Arras is taking time. But as, for the moment at least, there is no danger south of the Somme, I do not regard this as disturbing. We needn't rate the enemy's powers of resistance very high, except for local fighting. Things will take their own time; we must be patient and let them develop.'[47] But in the evening he was to comment gloomily: 'The left wing, consisting of armoured and mechanised forces, which has no enemy before it [there were some, but few and relatively disorganised] will thus be stopped dead in its tracks on the direct orders of the Führer. Finishing off the encircled enemy army is to be left to the Luftwaffe!'[48] That night Halder and his aide, Colonel von Greiffenberg, attempted to impose OKH's terms, instead of Hitler's, on the battle. In the very early hours of the 25th they sent a wireless order to both Army Groups A and B which read: 'Further to OKH's instructions of 24th May, the continuation of the attack up to the line Dunkirk-Cassel-Estaires-Armentières-Ypres-Ostend is permissible. Accordingly, the space reserved for Luftwaffe operations is correspondingly reduced.'[49] Although Army Group B agreed with this order, its arrival at Army Group A was far from welcome. On receiving it, at 12.45 a.m., von Blumentritt, von Rundstedt's Operations Officer, wrote across it: 'By order of the Commander and Chief of Staff, *not* passed on to 4th Army, as the Führer has delegated control to the Commander of the army group.'[50] In the war diary the following entry was made:

'The Commander . . . considers that, even if their further advance is extremely desirable, it is in any case urgently necessary for the motorised groups to close up.'[51] So was the OKH disregarded by its own field units; such was Hitler's achievement in reducing its authority.

On the morning of 25 May, the Army High Command made one more effort to persuade Hitler to change his mind. Halder recorded in his diary:

'The day begins once again with unpleasant arguments between von Brauchitsch and the Führer concerning the future course of the battle of encirclement. I had envisaged the battle going as follows: Army Group B [with only twenty-one infantry divisions left to it] would mount a heavy frontal assault on the enemy, which would make a planned withdrawal, with the aim merely of tying them down. Army Group A [by then composed of seventy divisions, including all the panzer formations], meeting a beaten enemy, would tackle it from the rear and bring about the decision. This was to be achieved by means of the motorised troops. Now the political leadership gets the idea of transferring the final battle from Flanders to northern France. In order to disguise this political aim it is explained that the Flanders terrain with its numerous wterways is unsuitable for tanks. The tanks of the other motorised troops, therefore, had to be halted after reaching the line St. Omer-Béthune. In other words the position is reversed. I wanted Army Group A to be the hammer and B to be the anvil. Now B is made the hammer and A the anvil. Since B is faced with an organised front [and was also by far the weaker of the two] this will cost a lot of blood and take a long time. Another thing, the Air Force on which hopes were pinned is completely dependent on the weather. Because of these differences of opinion, a tug-of-war has developed which is more wearying to the nerves than the whole organisation of the campaign itself.'[52]

Of the same meeting Jodl noted: 'In the morning the Commander-in-Chief of the Army arrives and asks permission for the tanks and motorised divisions to come down from the heights of Vimy-St. Omer-Gravelines onto the plains towards the east. The Führer is against, and leaves the decision to Army Group A. They turn it down for the time being since the tanks must have time to recover in order to be ready for the tasks in the south. . . .'[53] Such was the divergence of views within the German Command. During the day Hitler's order of the 24th was confirmed by telephone, and then passed on to the 4th Army: 'By the Führer's orders . . . the north-western wing (Hoth and Kleist groups) will hold the favourable defensive line Lens-Béthune-Aire-St. Omer-Gravelines, and allow the enemy to attack it. This line may be crossed only on express instructions from Army Group headquarters. The principal thing now is to husband the armoured formations for later and more important tasks.'[54] By the evening, 4th Army was able to report: 'The motorised groups remained—as ordered—along the canal and have closed up.'[55] The army group's war diary concluded with satisfaction: 'The battle in northern France is approaching its conclusion. There is no further possibility of any crisis except perhaps of a local nature. The task of Army Group A can be considered to have been completed in the main.'[56]

The 26th dawned, and the tanks were still motionless overlooking Dunkirk. Halder wrote despairingly in his first diary entry for the day:

'No change in the situation. Von Bock, suffering

114

losses, is pushing slowly ahead. . . . Our armoured and mechanised forces are standing motionless on the heights of Béthune and St. Omer as though they were rooted to the ground. On orders from above, they are not allowed to attack. At this rate, it can take weeks to clear up the cauldron, and that will be very damaging to our prestige and hamper future plans. All through the morning the Army Commander-in-Chief is very nervous. I can fully sympathise with him for these orders from the top just make no sense. In one area [Bock's army group] they call for a head-on attack against a front retiring in an orderly fashion and still possessing its striking power, and elsewhere they freeze the troops to the spot when the enemy rear could be cut into any time you wanted to attack.'[57]

But he concluded hopefully: 'Von Rundstedt, too, is clearly not hanging on any longer and has gone forward to Hoth and Kleist in order to get thing clear for the further advance of the mobile formations.'[58]

Even as Halder was penning these lines, the Führer himself was expressing considerable disquiet at the situation at Dunkirk, and at midday a telephone call from Führer headquarters notified OKH that Hitler had authorised the left wing to be moved to within artillery range of the town. This was followed by a summons to von Brauchitsch to attend upon the Supreme Commander. Jodl recorded the meeting: '18th and 6th Armies [Army Group B] are making only slow progress and II Corps in the south is meeting very stiff resistance. The Führer therefore agrees to a forward thrust from the west by panzer groups and infantry divisions in the direction of Tournai-Cassel-Dunkirk. . . .'[59] Halder noted that the Army Commander returned 'beaming' from this meeting at 2.30 p.m. 'At last the Führer has given permission to move on Dunkirk in order to prevent further evacuations.'[60] At 3.30 p.m., OKH issued orders accordingly. But the earliest the attack could resume was that night, and most units were not committed to battle for some sixteen hours. As Guderian pointed out, 'by then it was too late to achieve a great victory.'[61]

The organised opposition, with which the German ground attack now had to contend, was considerable. The War Diary of XXXIX Corps of the Hoth Group gave the reason for this: 'As foreseen, the enforced two-day halt on the southern bank of the canal produced two results on 27 May: first, the troops suffered considerable casualties when attacking across the la Bassée Canal, now stubbornly defended by the enemy; second, there was no longer time to intercept effectively the stream of French and English troops escaping westward from the Lille area towards the Channel.'[62] XXXXI Corps recorded on the 27th that 'At every position heavy fighting has developed. . . . In consequence, the corps has been unable to make any notable headway to the east or north-east. Casualties in personnel and equipment are grievous. The enemy are fighting tenaciously and, to the last man, remain at their posts.'[63] This was a new experience for the Germans in the campaign; time wasted by the Germans had been time gained by the Allies, a consequence which was in direct contradiction to the precepts of the armoured idea. Continued movement was essential, if only to keep the enemy off-balance and prevent him from organising a coherent defence. Now it was possible for Reinhardt's XXXXI Corps war diary to record that 'when engaged against enemy troops stubbornly defending a partly fortified held position, and particularly barricaded villages, the panzer division is not so suitable because it does not command sufficient infantry forces and because tanks made good targets for numbers of emplaced anti-tank weapons.'[64] Moreover, heavy rain

116

had fallen on the 26th and 27th, and had rendered the marshy Flanders countryside around Dunkirk unsuitable for motorised units. On the 28th Guderian was forced to the conclusion that 'The infantry forces of this army [the 18th of Army Group B which was approaching from the east] are more suitable than tanks for fighting in this kind of country, and the task of closing the gap on the coast can therefore be left to them.'[65] Furthermore, in view of the forthcoming operations in the southern half of France, Guderian felt it was necessary to conserve his divisions, which had now only fifty per cent of their armoured strength, and not to pursue this 'useless sacrifice of our best troops.' Von Kleist agreed with this, and that same night, seven days before Dunkirk was to fall, orders were issued for the withdrawal and replacement of the XIX Corps. This was nothing less than a confession of failure on the part of the panzer leaders; the traditionalists had succeeded in imposing their conditions upon the battle.

The *Vernichtungsgedanke* that had been fought out in the first twenty-one days of the campaign in the west was, by any standards, an outstanding military achievement. On 4 June, OKW issued an official communiqué:

'The great battle of Flanders and Artois is over. It will go down in military history as the greatest battle of annihilation of all time. . . . The full extent of our victory in Holland, Belgium, and northern France can be gauged by the enemy's losses and the volume of booty captured. French, British, Belgian, and Dutch losses in terms of prisoners are in the region of 1,200,000 men. To these must be added the figure, not yet known, of killed, drowned, and wounded. The arms and equipment of some seventy-five to eighty divisions . . . have been destroyed or captured. . . . By comparison with these figures, and in view of the scale of our success, the Wehrmacht's losses from 10 May to 1 June seem trivial: 10,252 officers, NCOs, and men killed, 8,463 missing . . . 42,523 wounded. . . . Since our adversaries persist in refusing peace, the fight will continue until they are destroyed utterly.'[66]

The Allies had lost sixty-one divisions, well over half their order of battle and the best they possessed, and three quarters of their most modern equipment. Facing the victorious Germans in the rest of France were only forty-nine divisions, many of them inadequately trained and armed, and, at most, only 200 tanks. That afternoon of the 4th, Winston Churchill for the first time publicly admitted the possibility of Germany dominating the continent of Europe.

Overwhelming though the German victory might have been, it was not decisive. On 30 May, Halder noted in his diary:

'He [von Brauchitsch] is angry, because the effects of the mistakes forced on us by OKW . . . are beginning to be felt now. We lost time and so the pocket with the French and British in it was sealed later than it could have been. Worse, the pocket would have been closed at the coast if only our armour had not been held back. As it is, the bad weather grounded our Air Force, and we must now stand by and watch countless thousands of the enemy get away to England right under our noses.'[67]

Some 366,000 troops, nearly a third of them Belgian and French, had been evacuated by the British from the

Channel ports, principally from Dunkirk, to provide the Allies with the nucleus of an army with which to continue the war. Before the panzers had halted on the 24th, Churchill believed it would be lucky if as many as 45,000 soldiers managed to escape.

The reason for this failure on the part of the German Army was simple. It arose out of the unanimous lack of appreciation on the part of the German command of the potential of the new weapon in its armoury: the armoured force. Had Guderian and his commanders been released from the strict control imposed on them from above, had they been allowed to pursue the advance as they alone thought fit, and not been shackled to the mass of the army group, had the liberating idea of 'organised velocity' predominated over the paralysing fear of exposed flanks, then the fate of the Allied troops in the north might well have been sealed, and an important victory turned into a total one. In the attack to the Channel, Army Group A's spearheads advanced an average of only twenty-two miles a day (the distance being measured as the crow flies) for ten days (including 17 May, when they were halted on orders for some twelve hours), a relatively slow rate considering that the last significant opposition was passed on the 15th, that the average top speed of German tanks was 25 mph, and that on the last day, the 20th, no fewer than fifty-six miles were covered by Guderian's troops. Because of the delays imposed from above on the 21st (through indecision) and on the 24th, 25th, and 26th (through considered policy), Army Group A's foremost unit advanced, on average, only nine miles per day from 22 May to 1 June. From 10 May until the 29th, when it was withdrawn from the front, Guderian's XIX Corps, as a result of the higher command's actions, was stationary for some 100 hours of the 700 it was in the field. The fears expressed by Hitler and von Rundstedt of enemy threats on the flanks were at no time proved to be justified, and the single counter-attack with any measurable success, that at Arras on the 21st, was mounted with only a small force and was never near to effecting any dislocation of the German advance. When Guderian reached the seaboard late on the 20th, there was nothing to prevent a strike eastwards up the coast at the undefended Allied rear. But the Germans proved incapable of exploiting the priceless opportunity then presented to them; consequently the events from 21 May to 4 June were for them a significant failure. The only obstacle to total victory lay not in the Allied opposition, which was, at first, negligible, or in the nature of the ground to be covered, which, before the rains, was quite adequate for any unopposed advance; it lay in the minds of the German commanders. Tradition had stifled revolution, and had ensured failure.

Even while Operation Yellow was in its initial stages, the General Staff, quite properly, was working on plans for the second, and final, phase of the destruction of France. On 21 May, the day after Guderian's troops reached the coast, the plan, known as *Fall Rot* (Operation Red) was presented to the Führer by Halder. Based on the doctrine of encirclement, OKH's proposal envisaged an attack along a broad front which spanned the 220 miles of Army Group A's line of advance to the coast, along the Aisne and Somme rivers, and a further 200 miles along the Maginot Line and the Upper Rhine. The main thrust with nearly all the armour was to be launched west of Paris and a further attack would take place to the east. A few days later another advance would be initiated over the Upper Rhine and a secondary attack thrown against the Maginot Line near Saarbrücken. The object would be to surround and destroy the enemy forces in the Plateau de Langres south-west of Paris. Hitler, however, had other ideas; his main dissension from the OKH plan was that he wanted the bulk of the mechanised forces, and therefore the main attack, to bypass Paris on the east side. On the 31st, the final, amended OKH plan for Operation Red was issued. On 5 June, Army Group B was to attack both sides of Paris and make for the Seine; on 9 June, Army Group A was to launch its offensive, the *Schwerpunkt* of the operation, and advance east of Paris south-west through Rheims; about a week later, Army Group C was to battle its way through the Maginot Line and the Upper Rhine. The three forces would converge and, as intended originally, the great battle of annihilation would take place on the Plateau de Langres and within the bend of the Maginot Line.

The strongest part of the invasion force was Army Group B, with thirty-six infantry divisions (of which eighteen were First Wave, five Second Wave, and a mountain division), one cavalry division, four motorised infantry divisions, two motorised infantry brigades, and six panzer divisions—a total of forty-seven divisions, two brigades. Army Group A, although it was to undertake the main thrust, possessed two fewer divisions and fewer mechanised troops. Of its forty-five divisions, thirty-nine were infantry (fourteen First Wave and seven Second Wave), two were motorised infantry, and four were panzer. Both army groups had three armies, B, the 4th, 6th, and 9th, and A, the 2nd, 12th, and 16th. 18th Army, of four divisions, was to remain in the Dunkirk area for the time being. Army Group C, as befitted its secondary role, had only twenty-four infantry divisions, none of which were First Wave and only three Second Wave. OKH Reserve consisted of twenty-two infantry divisions, bringing the total in the west to 142. Only seven were left in the east, and a further seven in Norway. The mechanised units were organised into two groups, each of two corps. One group, under Guderian, spearheaded Army Group A, the other, under von Kleist,

Army Group B, and one motorised Army Corps, the XV, under Hoth, was also attached to B.

Once again, the German operation was planned in accordance with traditional military precepts: decisive manoeuvre resulting in encirclement was the means to the physical destruction of the enemy. The OKH deployment order of 31 May contained no sign of any application of the armoured idea, and it made no mention of independent panzer groups which, although they were themselves the size and importance of armies, were to be subordinated to army control (Guderian to List's 12th Army, von Kleist to von Reichenau's 6th Army, and Hoth's corps to von Kluge's 4th Army.) This control was to be rigidly maintained from the outset; for example, despite all Guderian's protests to the contrary, List persisted in giving the infantry corps the task of crossing the Aisne river and canal and establishing bridgeheads before the armour was released for the breakthrough. Apparently the lesson of the Meuse had not been understood; the panzers were relegated to a secondary role for the second time in the campaign (the first had been during the final advance on Dunkirk).

Although the German plan for Operation Red was unexceptional, the preparations for the final destruction of France were quite remarkable. For example, Guderian's 1st and 2nd Panzer Divisions had covered the 300-mile sweep to Dunkirk, and had then followed that by a further 200 miles to reach their starting positions for 'Red.' No wonder Guderian could record that 'Signs of extreme fatigue on the part of the troops and of wear of their vehicles began to be apparent.'[68] The troop and supply movements required for this change of front were extremely complex but, on the whole, were undertaken with high efficiency. Kesseling, commander of Luftflotte 2, later wrote: 'Anyone who watched from the air and on the ground, as I did, von Kleist's and Guderian's panzers swing round from the northern manoeuvre toward the Channel and drive south and south-east to the Somme and the Aisne, could not repress a surge of pride at the flexibility and skill of the German Army Command and the state of training of the troops.'[69]

Against this force, the remnant of the Allied armies were all but powerless. The new French commander, Weygand, faced the impossible task of defending central and southern France with an army inferior both in numbers and equipment, and with its forty-nine divisions extended from the Channel to the Maginot Line over a front of nearly 250 miles. He attempted to organise a defence in depth, a checker-board of centres of resistance based on villages, towns, and forests from which counter-attacks could be launched, continual jabs at the enemy thrusts designed to bring the German advance to a halt. But against the two hammer blows, first from the Somme and then from the Aisne, the French could do little.

At 4.00 a.m. on 5 June, the Germans began the final destruction of France. After a short artillery barrage, units of Army Group B moved forward to their first main objective—the Seine. By the 9th the river was reached, in the very early morning by Hoth's mechanised corps, and roughly twelve hours later on the left by von Manstein's infantry corps. This was a remarkable achievement, not so much for the armour as for the infantry, who had advanced, while fighting, seventy-five miles in fewer than five days. By the 22nd, von Manstein's corps had covered no less than 300 miles on foot. The rest of the campaign closely followed this precedent: fast armoured advances rivalled by equally remarkable infantry manoeuvres. Indeed, Guderian recorded of his own advance with irritation: 'Our progress was made more difficult through confusion that arose from the impetuous advance of the infantry following behind us. The infantry units . . . in some cases . . . had caught up with the panzer units which were fighting their way forward. . . . Both arms of service wanted "to be there." '71 Another infantry unit, the XXVI Army Corps, under General Wodrig, achieved an average enemy.'70 One panzer commander, von Mellenthin, remembered that the troops of the 197th Division 'gladly submitted to tramping thirty-five miles a day as everyone wanted "to be there." '71 Another infantry unit the XXVI Army Corps, under General Wodrig, achieved an average rate of advance of twenty-one miles a day between 12 and 19 June from the Seine near Romilly to Moulins in the south. Such rates compared favourably with the movements of the mechanised formations such as Guderian's group, which daily averaged some forty miles.

Afterwards, as the coordinated attack increasingly took on the form of an unopposed pursuit into southern France, and as the German armies fanned out across the width of the country, the motorised and infantry components of the armies were each given different tasks, so that the infantrymen were no longer limited to following in the wake of the panzers but were instead given roles independent of the progress of the armour. For example, on 14 June, the day Paris fell, Army Group B sent its motorised forces westward to occupy the Normandy and Brittany peninsulas, while its infantry corps moved down to the south and south-west of France. Between Hoth on the Atlantic coastline and von Kleist and Guderian in Champagne, a distance of some 270 miles, there was not a single German tank to be seen, and yet the advance there continued unhesitatingly. The comment of von Bechtolsheim, the operations chief of 6th Army, concerning the earlier campaign in Flanders, was again appropriate: 'Even after the panzer group had been taken away, events proved that infantry attack was still possible without tank support—thanks to the way that the infantry had been trained, to well-controlled supporting fire, and to infiltration tactics. Widely dispersed threats create openings for concentrated thrusts.'[72]

Just as in Operation Yellow, so the handling of the mechanised forces by the higher commands in 'Red' left much to be desired. At the outset, von Kleist's group suffered the first failure experienced by German armour; its attacks north of Paris made slow progress, and on 8 June it was decided to pull it out of the line, remove it from von Reichenau's 6th Army (this was the second time this army had witnessed the removal of its armour), and attach it to 9th Army on the extreme left of von Bock's army group, near to Guderian. The cause of von Kleist's failure was simple: his troops had been thrown against the most heavily defended sector of the French front guarding their capital city, one that was relatively well-organised and of a fair depth. Furthermore, von Reichenau had gone against von Kleist's wishes and had split the two corps for a pincer stroke rather than concentrating their strength for a single *Schwerpunkt*. Thus, the armour was neither concentrated nor committed against the weakest point of the enemy, but instead was divided and sent against the strongest part of his line in an attack which was properly the province of the German infantry if, indeed, it should have been made at all. To the east, where Army Group A lay, the offensive opened on the 9th, and immediately Guderian's formation ran into trouble. The infantry of List's army failed to cross the Aisne at Rethel, where the armour was concentrated in preparation, and it was until late that night that elements of a panzer division managed to cross the river at another point gained by the infantry. At 6.30 a.m. on the 10th, Guderian began the advance that should have started some twenty-four hours earlier—

and it might well have done so had he been able to influence the planning of the operation.

During the victorious surge from the Aisne to the Marne, from there to the Swiss border and then up towards the Maginot Line, Guderian was dogged by command failures from above. The confusion resulting from the intermingling of the rapidly advancing infantry with the panzers has already been alluded to; nothing was done to alleviate it, despite the several protests made by Guderian to 12th Army headquarters. Further complications arose from the orders that continually came to the panzer group; despite the intentions of OKH to pursue Operation Red to its logical conclusion—the destruction of the enemy forces in the field—Hitler insisted on imposing his own conditions on the course of the battle. Although France's imminent fall was ensured, the Führer perversely insisted that it was necessary to secure Lorraine so as to deprive the French of their armaments industry. On 6 June, Halder wrote in desperation:

'The Führer thinks that changing the direction of the offensive [to the west], as proposed by me, is still too hazardous at this time. He wants to play absolutely safe. First, he would like to have a sure hold on the Lorraine iron-ore basin, so as to deprive France of her armament resources. After that, he believes it would be time to consider a drive in a westerly direction, probably having in mind a strong wing at the coast (4th Army). Here we have the same old story again. On top, there just isn't a spark of the spirit that would dare putting high stakes on a single throw. Instead, everything is done in a cheap piecemeal fashion, but with the air that we don't have to rush at all.'[73]

On the 10th, the Chief of the General Staff wrote: 'One could cry if it were not such a farce. What I recommended a few days ago is now being dispensed piecemeal and haltingly as the producers of his supreme generalship.'[74] And three days later, Halder recorded: 'Führer headquarters now is slowly seeing the point of the recommendation made by me as early as 5 June, to the effect that the swing south-west should be made in the area east of Paris. . . . One could laugh about all this if that system did not always obstruct efficient work.'[75] Finally, on 19 June, Halder wrote:

'Some days ago I tried desperately hard to get permission to commit the armour and motorised infantry divisions on Kleist's right wing. At that time the plan was directly vetoed at top level. Now, after those forces have been racing off in a south-easterly direction for several days, and not meeting organised resistance, they have to be reversed and ordered in a north-westerly direction. It is indeed an effort to keep calm in the face of such amateurish tinkering with the business of directing military affairs.'[76]

If the confusion at OKH was great, in the field it was greater. Fortunately for the Germans, every resistance was so weak and disorganised that their own misconduct of affairs proved not to be too dangerous. Guderian recorded:

'From now on [12 June], the panzer group received every day many mutually contradictory orders, some ordering a swing towards the east, others a continuation of the advance southward. First of all Verdun [to the east] was to be taken by means of a surprise attack, then the southward advance was to go, then we were to swing east on St. Mihiel, then again we were to move south once more. Reinhardt's corps was the one that suffered from all this vacillation: I kept Schmidt's corps on a steady course southwards, so that at least half of my panzer group was assured of continuity of purpose.'[77]

However, despite such deficiencies in the conduct of the advance, the second campaign in France went astonishingly well for the Germans. Apart from the check of von Kleist's group, everything proceeded very much as planned. On both sides of Paris the advance continued rapidly, so that, on 12 June, Weygand felt that he had no alternative but to inform the President of the Council of Ministers, M. Reynaud, that further resistance was useless and that an armistice should be sought; if not, 'chaos will take hold of the armies as it has already taken hold of the civilian population.'[78] On the 10th, Italy had entered the war on the side of the Third Reich, and on the 14th the Germans marched through Paris for the second time in seventy years. Their flanks turned, the French were dispersed to the west, shattered in the centre, and pushed up against their Maginot Line in the east. This line, upon which such hopes had been placed before the war, had already been pierced by Army Group C. There, between von Leeb's infantry and von Rundstedt's motorised formations, the final battle of annihilation took place; some 500,000 men were taken prisoner on 22 June, the day of the French acceptance of the armistice terms. Hostilities ended on the 25th, and Hitler announced to a jubilant nation: 'After fighting valiantly for six weeks, our troops have brought the war in the west to an end against a courageous enemy. Their heroic deeds will go down in history as the most glorious victory of all time.'[79] Holland, Belgium, and France had been conquered, Britain had been humiliated, and all at a cost to the Germans of 27,074 dead, 18,384 missing, and 111,034 wounded.

5

Decisions

I make decisions; I need men who obey.
ADOLF HITLER
1940

On 19 July, in celebration of Germany's great victory in the west, Hitler handed out honours by the handful to his soldiers. In doing so, he created twelve field-marshalls—von Brauchitsch, Keitel, von Rundstedt, von Bock, von Leeb, List, von Kluge, von Witzleben, and von Reichenau, in order of seniority, and three from the Air Force, Milch, Kesselring, and Sperrle—nineteen colonel-generals—among them Halder, Fromm, von Kleist, Guderian, Hoth, and Falkenhorst—and seven generals—foremost being Jodl and Dietl. Above them all came Göring, glorying in the new title of *Reichsmarschall des Grossdeutschen Reiches*. With these ranks went generous gifts of money, to allow the recipients to live as their new exalted positions demanded.

Never before in the history of the German Army had

there been such a profusion of high ranks (throughout the First World War, for example, only five generals had been elevated to field-marshals). As a result, many felt that their quality and prestige had thereby been debased. Von Manstein recorded:

'Hitherto (apart from a few field-marshals nominated by Wilhelm II in peacetime) one needed to have led a campaign in person, to have won a battle or taken a fortress to qualify for this dignity. . . . Yet now he was creating a dozen simultaneously. They included . . . the Chief of OKW, who had held neither a command nor the post of a Chief of Staff. Another was the Under-Secretary of State for the Luftwaffe [Milch], who, valuable as his feats of organisation had been, really could not be ranked on a par with the Commander-in-Chief of the Army.'[1]

Whether Hitler deliberately intended to cheapen military rank is unknown, but he must have been aware of the deliberate slight to von Brauchitsch and to the Army by raising Göring above all other generals, and by making the Luftwaffe Commander the sole recipient of the Grand Cross of the Knights' Cross, Germany's highest military decoration.

Awarded with high but meaningless ranks they might have been; fêted the generals certainly were not. During the First World War, victorious commanders had been accorded the status of national figures, and a man like von Hindenburg had been venerated equally with the Kaiser; now, it was Hitler the crowds greeted as the conquering hero, not the generals. Von Brauchitsch and Halder sought to reverse this position, to regain for themselves and for the officer corps the prestige of former days, aware as they were of their relative anonymity in the German nation. But Hitler, jealous of his glory, did all he could to frustrate their design; Halder recorded of von Brauchitsch in early September that he was 'very bitter about the obstacles put in his way whenever he wants to reach the public.'[2] Only a chosen few, such as Guderian or, more spectacularly, Dietl, the 'hero of Narvik,' were to be publicly recognised as men who were brilliant field-commanders. In the area of strategy and in the direction of the Reich's war effort, which were the special province of the Führer, no one was to detract from his aura of genius and omnipotence; powerless anonymity was the lot of the Army's leadership.

The victory ceremony in the Reichstag on 19 July was symbolic of the relationship between Hitler and the military. The generals might sit in the balcony, glittering with gold braid and medals, all smiles and back-patting as they received their promotions, but it was one man, clad in a simple uniform of field-grey, who held the attention of the gathering, and of the nation: Hitler. His speech was not one of a Head of State gratefully thanking the authors of his country's victory; it was one of a Supreme Commander graciously acknowledging the help given to him by his assistants, an acknowledgement which served only to increase his own stature as a military leader. The plan for the downfall of France—had it not been his? The brave order for the attack—had he not given it? And the successful outcome of the campaign—had it not been due to his direction? To Keitel and Jodl, picked out for special praise, he accorded the role of playing 'the chief part in the realisation of *my* plans and ideas.'[3] The Army High Command and General Staff were thus pictured as mere automatons of their Führer's will. Bombast it might have been, but it nevertheless contained much truth. His interference in, and dictation of, the plans for Operation Yellow have already been described, as has also his continual interference in von Rundstedt's advance to the Channel. On one occasion, on the fateful 23 May, Hitler had even countermanded an order from the Army Commander-in-Chief, this being described by Halder as 'a new crisis of confidence.'[4] Indeed, during the campaign, Hitler's involvement with the direction of the ground manoeuvres had become compulsive. Keitel wrote flatteringly that 'the Führer liked to immerse himself in every detail of the practical execution of his ideas, so wide was the sweep of his unparalleled inventiveness. . . . there was no end to his questioning, intervening, and sifting of facts, until with his fantastic imagination he was satisfied that the last loophole had been plugged.'[5]

Others held a different view. Warlimont noted:

'Between the campaigns in Poland and Norway the habit had grown up of trying to run the battle in detail from the [Führer] headquarters, and the system had been tried out on a small scale in Norway. This dangerous game now continued, in spite of all Halder's warnings and in spite of the facts that we were now faced with a formidable enemy and were dealing with a rapidly changing situation. Diffuse discussion led to opinions, opinions to decisions and decisions to written directives or even direct intervention in dispositions already ordered by some military headquarters; although OKH was within a stone's throw, this was generally done without any previous reference to them. The best the Army leaders could expect was occasionally to be summoned to a briefing for some special reason but, just as in the preparatory period, they found themselves faced with preconceived ideas which only tiresome and time-wasting argument could alter. . . . There was therefore very soon an atmosphere of tension between these two neighbouring high-level headquarters. But on the side of the OKW stood Hitler, dominating everything, impatient and suspicious; he had no idea of time and space and refused to wait and let things develop; at the decisive moment, as in the case of Narvik, he would take fright at the boldness of his own decisions and then abdicate his authority and allow the situation to develop uncontrolled. Close at his side stood Keitel who, as always, considered his sole duty to be to support Hitler. . . . Jodl's influence was even greater. He . . . now seemed determined to ensure that the "Führer's genius" should win the day against the "indiscipline of the generals"; he did not appear to realise that the "pusillanimity" which he had previously ascribed to the General Staff had now become Hitler's sole prerogative.'[6]

Whatever the defects of Hitler's military leadership, after France one thing was clear: it was he, and he alone, who led the German Army. The victory in the west had confirmed his position as a military commander superior to his generals, the crowning triumph to a process that had begun in 1936 with the reoccupation of the Rhineland. The deterioration in the status of the Army High Command was thus taken one stage further; the victory of the German soldier in the field had been yet another defeat for the German general at home. The stunned submission of the Army commanders was even more complete than after the Czechoslovak affair, and they were more than content to leave decisions of peace and war to their Führer. Even the formerly sceptical Army Quartermaster-General, Eduard Wagner, could write: 'And wherein lies the secret of this victory? Indeed, in the enormous dynamism of the Führer . . . without his will it would never have come to pass.'[7]

From July to December 1940, the Army High Command was ordered to plan no less than seven operations: the invasion of England, the capture of the Azores, Canary, and Cape Verde islands, the occupation of Greece, the defence of the Finnish nickel mines, the protection of the Romanian oilfields, the support of the Italians in North Africa, and the attack against the Soviet Union. Yet throughout this period the Army leaders were not once called on to offer their advice to the Führer. As Wagner admitted, grand strategy was a subject 'of which we understand nothing, and which the Führer conducts quite alone, without any assistance, even from Göring.'[8] In July, the most important month, von Brauchitsch met Hitler on only two occasions, and between August and the end of December met him only once a month, while Halder, in the same six months, saw his Führer just eight times, and in October not at all. Hitler simply made his pronouncements, and delayed his final decisions if he so wished; the generals merely waited and obeyed. Unfortunately for the German Army, and for the Third Reich, the result was a grand strategy that was vacillating, wrong-headed, and disastrous in the long run.

Apart from the overriding importance of the proposed attack on the Soviet Union, the decision whether or not to invade Great Britain, the operation code-named *Seelöwe* (Sea-Lion), was certainly the most crucial of the period. Victory in the west had brought the Germans to the decisive turning-point of the war; in nine months they had defeated the Poles, overrun Norway and Denmark, crushed the Dutch, Belgians, and French, and forced the British to withdraw ignominiously from the Continent. Of Europe, only a part of Scandinavia, Italy, the Balkans, the Iberian peninsula, and the Soviet Union lay outside the Reich's domination, and these countries were either neutral or pro-German. Her Army exhausted, her alliances broken, Great Britain possessed only her fleet, her Channel, a far-off empire and an outnumbered air force with which to face Hitler's triumphant war-machine on an unbroken front extending from Narvik in the north to the Gironde in the south. It was an unequal struggle, and Halder had every reason for noting in his diary on 22 June 1940 that, if she continued to resist single-handed, 'the war will lead to Britain's destruction.'[9] In the summer and early autumn of 1940 Hitler held within his grasp the prize fervently sought by so many European conquerors: the conquest of Great Britain. The initiative was his, but he failed to exploit it. A year later, with Britain victorious in the air, secure round her shores, and intransigent in her aims, Hitler's attention was engrossed elsewhere—in the vast expanses of the east. The war had taken the course that in just three years was to lead to the downfall of the Third Reich.

In this momentous decision—to leave an undefeated island-fortress in the rear—and to turn instead on the Soviet Union, the German Army, which had wielded such immense influence over the course of the previous world conflict, took no part. At this, the most crucial juncture of the war, Germany's senior generals, her highest military professionals, could only say to Hitler: 'Command, and we will follow.' Advice, there was none.

From the Army's point of view, the failure to embark on the invasion of Britain represented a significant setback. Faced as it was by innumerable difficulties, foremost among which was the inadequacy of the Reich's naval resources, it is debatable whether the invasion ever possessed a reasonable chance of success. However, this is not at issue here (the question is, in any case, purely hypothetical); what is of considerable importance is the

135

fact that the Army, alone of the three services, wanted 'Sea-Lion' to take place, and, moreover, was optimistic about its outcome. Yet in spite of this, its hopes and aspirations counted for nought in the final decision. Then, only two things mattered: Hitler's attitude, and the outcome of the Luftwaffe's performance in the skies over southern England.

Apart from a number of half-hearted service studies, the first time the idea of the invasion was contemplated as an act of policy was during a conversation between Hitler and Raeder on 21 May 1940, the day after Guderian's tanks had reached the Channel coast. But there was no attempt to prepare for a seaborne invasion after the victorious conclusion of Operation Yellow; not one voice was raised in protest at the concentration, for Operation Red, of 136 German divisions to defeat a demoralised, weak enemy less than half their size, instead of holding back certain divisions for the training of an amphibious invasion force. The question appeared to have been laid to rest on the issue of a Führer directive on 14 June, Halder noting in his diary the next day that the 'Luftwaffe and Navy alone will be carrying on the war against Britain.'[10] Then, on 25 June, Hitler unexpectedly informed the OKW Operations Staff that in a few days he wished to see studies for an invasion. From then on, the idea of a seaborne assault took shape: on 2 July an OKW directive declared that the Supreme Commander had decided an invasion might be possible, provided that air superiority could be achieved, and ordered the three services to draw up plans accordingly. On the 13th von Brauchitsch and Halder presented their proposals to Hitler, the first time they had seen him to discuss the affair; and on the 16th the Führer issued a directive 'On preparations for a landing operation against England,' which stipulated: 'The Commanders-in-Chief will lead their forces, under my orders.'[11] Then, seven weeks after the Germans had reached the Channel, preparations began apace. Inter-service rivalries and lack of communication intensified, and by late August a compromise plan had been resolved, giving the Army a landing force and a landing area it believed inadequate, and the Navy a responsibility for transport which it feared to be too great. The Luftwaffe, engrossed in its private war with the RAF, gave little consideration to the matter. On 6 August Halder had noted: 'We have here the paradoxical situation where the Navy is full of apprehension, the Air Force is very reluctant to tackle a mission which at the outset is exclusively its own—and OKW, which for once has a real combined operation to direct, just plays dead. The only driving force in the whole situation comes from us. But alone we can't swing it.'[12]

The Army had embarked enthusiastically on its preparations, von Brauchitsch regarding the whole operation a little optimistically as a 'large-scale river crossing'[13] and believing the entire operation would be concluded in a month. On 17 July, the diarist of the Naval Operations Directorate recorded: 'It appears that OKH, which a short time ago strongly opposed such an operation, has now put aside all its doubts and regards the operation as entirely practicable. . . .'[14] Indeed, the General Staff considered it of decisive importance. Even after 'Sea-Lion' had been postponed, Halder continued to regard the invasion as the surest way to hit England, and when the Army turned to move east, the senior generals were plagued by nagging doubts about the military propriety of leaving in their rear an undefeated Britain that was daily getting stronger. However, their thoughts had no effect on the supreme warlord. At no time did a hesitant Hitler commit himself irrevocably to the invasion, making it clear from the outset that it was to be undertaken only after certain conditions had been met (most important being the victory of the Luftwaffe), and then only if necessary. In such a state of indecision were the plans and deployments for 'Sea-Lion' undertaken: on 31 July the target date of mid-August was delayed a month to 17 September, and the final decision was put off until the results of the Luftwaffe's attack on the RAF were known; on 7 September, when the German Air Force's new mission, the complete destruction of London's docks, industries, and supplies, was announced, Hitler declared that his pronouncement on 'Sea-Lion' would depend on its outcome; on the 17th, when it was apparent that the RAF was, at the very least, surviving its desperate fight, OKW issued orders to postpone the invasion indefinitely, with options kept open for October; on 12 October, after the admitted failure of the air offensive, 'Sea-Lion' was further postponed, with the possibility of reopening it in the spring of 1941; and, on 5 December, Hitler told von Brauchitsch that the operation should be left out of the Army's considerations. On 2 March 1942, the idea of invasion was finally discarded altogether.

If the delays in the operation had been frustrating to the Army's leaders, its effective abandonment in October was a blow. But as the Army had partaken not at all in the strategic decision whether or not to invade, its enthusiasm for the operation had counted for nothing. In July, the month in which the idea and initial plans were formulated—the month, therefore, in which it was crucial to win the argument and force Hitler to commit himself to firm action—von Brauchitsch and Halder had seen Hitler only three times in all: the first, on the 13th—to present him with the OKH invasion plan, which he accepted—degenerated into an opportunity for the Führer to lecture the Chief of the General Staff on the political situation from the military angle; the second, on the 21st, was held in the presence of the service chiefs, and again Hitler regaled his audience with his view of world politics, brought up the question of attacking the Soviet Union, and pointed out the naval difficulties involved in 'Sea-Lion,' while von Brauchitsch could only express his optimism; and at the third, on 31 July, when Hitler announced his decision to invade the Soviet Union and listened to Raeder's recommendation for a postponement of 'Sea-Lion' until the following spring, it appears that the Army Commander and his Chief of Staff said absolutely nothing concerning the operation. At no time did von Brauchitsch have an informal conversation with his Supreme Commander, as, for example, Raeder did, and no attempt was made to submit a written memorandum on the subject. The generals confined themselves in Hitler's presence to the technical details of the operation; its strategic desirability they left to their own counsels.

Thus, the military made no attempt to counter Hitler's fears about the invasion and effect him with their enthusiasm for the idea. The Führer considered that the risks were too great, and agreed with Raeder that the invasion should be undertaken only as a last resort, carried out against an enemy already broken by blockade and air attack. A reversal on the beaches of England's south coast, although it would not have been unacceptably injurious militarily, he considered to be unthinkable politically. Any outcome other than total victory might seriously impair his personal prestige, and that he was careful to preserve above all else. Furthermore, the Army failed to challenge his assertion that the amphibious assault had to await the Luftwaffe's dominance of the skies over Britain, an idea which von Manstein later described as 'an error of leadership.'[15] Had 'Sea-Lion' been conceived not as a mopping-up operation after a successful air attack over all south-east England, but as a major offensive for conquering Britain in which each of the three services was to play an equally crucial role, then the Luftwaffe would have joined battle with the RAF over the Channel and the beaches immediately before, and during, the landings. The operational conditions would have put the German planes on a more equal operational footing with the British, and might well have led to victory in the air and, consequently, over the sea and on the land. Certainly, once ashore, the German force would have faced relatively weak opposition from the British Army. But OKH suggested nothing; it would advise only on Hitler's request, and this he did not make. At the crucial time, no attempt was made to influence Germany's war policy. Instead, Hitler's instability of purpose, his search for easy solutions, and his military naïvety were allowed to dominate unchallenged.

Nor did the Army leaders take any part in initiating, or influencing, the other grand-strategic decisions of 1940, the most important of which, apart from the invasion of the USSR, was the extension of the war against Great Britain to the periphery of Europe. The British Empire was seen as the prize, and Gibraltar and Suez especially were considered to be the immediate aims. Their occupation would seal off the Mediterranean, enabling the Reich to seize the spoils of the Near East, above all, the oil. The generals were not averse to such a course of action; von Brauchitsch even advocated limited support of the forthcoming Italian offensive on Egypt to Hitler during the conference on 31 July, to which the Führer replied that the proposal should be studied. Further pressure for some move in the Mediterranean came from OKW and the Navy. In memoranda issued in January, March, and June, Jodl had proposed such a move, and in two private meetings with Hitler in September, Raeder supported the idea. Hitler was at last persuaded. On 27 September he concluded a tripartite pact with Italy and Japan, and then proceeded to broaden the coalition by attempting to secure the adherence of Spain and Vichy France, both of which would be valuable as a springboard for any attack in the Mediterranean area. In this, however, he was to fail. But, not to be put off, on 4 November he outlined his plans to the military commanders: he had decided not to send troops to Libya until the Italians had advanced further into Egypt, but instead—with the help of Spain—Gibraltar, the Canary Islands, and the Cape Verde Islands would be taken (in Operation 'Felix') and the Mediterranean closed to the British. Even Portugal might have to be occupied to deny the Iberian peninsula to the enemy. These decisions Hitler confirmed in his Directive No. 18, issued eight days later. The OKH, which had already surveyed the situation of Gilbraltar, immediately began to draw up plans for 'Felix,' and to elaborate its ideas on the future aid to Italy in North Africa. On 5 December, the day von Brauchitsch was informed that 'Sea-Lion' must be left out of his calculations, Hitler stipulated that 'Felix' should take place not later than 10 January 1941.

Then came a setback. The British counter-attacked in the desert and pushed the Italians back at lightning speed; Spain refused to enter the war on the side of Germany. Thus, on the 10th December, OKW issued an order stating that 'Felix' was abandoned, and on the same day Hitler dictated his Directive No. 19, which proposed that Vichy France should be occupied, the western Mediterranean crossed, and French North Africa taken. This was the only decision of the many taken in those months that was directly influenced by the Army High Command. It was the product of a visit to Keitel by Halder on the 8th, and Hitler's approval of the OKH's draft plans on the 9th. The Führer did, however, reserve to himself 'the right to decide how this operation will be carried out.'[16] Ironically, the occupation of Vichy France, code-named 'Attila,' never took place, for it was

141

overtaken by events. On 31 December the German military attaché in Rome telegraphed Halder to inform him that the Italians in North Africa were completely defeated; it was then obvious that the Italian forces were in danger of collapsing. On 8-9 January 1941, Hitler held a military conference at which he stressed the importance of getting immediate aid to the Italians before Libya was overrun. This was to be seen as a stop-gap measure before the Axis offensive was resumed there in late 1942. 'Attila,' therefore, was superseded by *Sonnenblume* (Sunflower), the operation to send covering forces to hold Tripolitania, although it was kept under review in case of any trouble from the Vichy government. Directive No. 22 of 11 January confirmed these decisions. Such was the genesis of the famous North African campaign.

At the same time as Hitler was planning his moves against the British Empire in the Mediterranean, he was also forced to consider action in the Balkans. On 28 October 1940, Mussolini, much against Hitler's desires, launched his invasion of Greece. It was an inept military operation, soon to go wrong. In retaliation the British occupied the islands of Crete and Lemnos, the latter providing them with an advanced air base from which they could invade the Balkans and bomb the Romanian oil fields so vital to Germany's oil supply. Thus, the Balkans were brought sharply to the attention of Hitler and to the Army High Command. At his conference of 4 November, when he announced his decision to occupy Gibraltar, the Führer also ordered that the Romanian oilfields be protected. He requested that plans should be drawn up for an invasion of Greece to be undertaken from the German bases in Romania and Bulgaria (code-named 'Marita') so as to enable the Luftwaffe to attack targets in the eastern Mediterranean, especially Crete and Lemnos. These requirements he confirmed in his

Directive No. 18 of 12 November. On 5 December, Hitler set the date for 'Marita' for early March, although the final decision as whether or not to undertake it was left open. A few days later, as the British were sweeping up the Libyan desert, the Greeks sent the Italians in Albania reelinig back. On 13 December, Directive No. 20 was issued, reaffirming the importance placed on 'Marita' and stipulating the conditions on which it was to be undertaken. A month later, on 9 January 1941, at the Führer conference, Hitler ordered that the troops for 'Marita' be ready for the offensive no later than 26 March, one month later than OKH wanted. And on 11 January, the Führer's Directive No. 22, entitled 'German support for battles in the Mediterranean area,' announced assistance to the Italians in Tripolitania, at the same time as a rescue operation to aid the Italians in Albania, under the code-name *Alpenveilchen* (Alpine Violet). On 17 February, predictions of bad weather in the Balkans caused a postponement of the starting date for 'Marita' until 2 April, but in spite of this hitch preparations proceeded apace. By the third week of February, the Germans had massed 680,000 men in Romania, and on the night of the 28th, in pursuance of an agreement signed twenty days earlier, troops of the 12th Army crossed the Danube and took up strategic positions in Bulgaria, which then joined the Tripartite Pact. Yugoslavia followed; on 25 March Prince-Regent Paul allied his country with the Germans and Italians. The way was open for the invasion of Greece on 1 April.

Then came the Yugoslav coup. During the night of 26–27 March, the government of Prince-Regent Paul was overthrown and the agreement with Germany repudiated. Hitler's calculations had gone awry; the dictator erupted into one of his wildest rages. On the 27th he decided 'to annihilate Yugoslavia,'[17] and issued Directive No. 25 which linked the invasion of that country with operation 'Marita.' It laid down fairly detailed orders for the military moves, based on a plan known as Operation Twenty-Five drawn up by Halder and von Brauchitsch and presented to him that same afternoon. On the 29th, military cooperation between Germany and Hungarian forces was agreed on, and on 3 April Hitler's Directive No. 26 laid down guidelines for 'cooperation with our allies in the Balkans.'[18] At dawn on 6 April the German Army fell on Yugoslavia and Greece, and in three weeks all was over.

Four grand strategic decisions were taken in the year following the fall of France in June 1940. All were bound inextricably one with another; all had considerable influence on the course of the war; and all contributed in some measure to Germany's final defeat. But one was of such crucial importance that it completely overshadowed the rest. Whether or not to invade Great Britain, to become involved in North Africa, or to occupy the Balkans were, indeed, full of significance for the future; but whether or not to attack the Soviet Union was crucial. By his decision to launch the invasion, Hitler committed the German nation to a life-or-death struggle in which total defeat was the only alternative to total victory. All now would depend on the quality of the advice received from the military leaders, and on the capacity of the Führer to accept it. Should either of these conditions not prevail, disaster would result.

As was by now the accepted practice, it was Hitler alone who made the decision to move eastwards. On 21 July 1940, two days after his victory speech in the Reichstag, Hitler announced to his assembled Wehrmacht chiefs that he was considering an attack on the Soviet Union. The momentous declaration he approached cautiously, presenting it as a measure made necessary by Stalin's 'flirtation' with Great Britain. A plan for the invasion was proposed—by whom it is not known precisely—the aim of which Halder recorded as: 'the defeat of the Russian army, or the capture of at least as much Russia territory as necessary to prevent enemy air attacks against Berlin and the Silesian industrial areas. It would be desirable to advance far enough to attack the most important Russian centres with our Air Force.'[19] Victory would be achieved that autumn by, at most, 100 divisions.

No doubt the response expected by the Führer was, at the very least, one of scepticism, similar to that which had greeted his proposals for the military reoccupation of the Rhineland, the annexations of Austria and Czechoslovakia, and the attack on the west. But von Brauchitsch said not a word against the new proposition. The reasons for this change of attitude were two: practical and political. The Army leaders viewed the Soviet Union, its leaders and its ideology, with a mixture of suspicion and contempt; they fully agreed with Beck, who warned that it might become 'a serious or, under certain circumstances, a deadly danger.'[20] The generals were keen to end the traditional Salvonic rivalry for the domination of Eastern Europe, and constantly expressed their fears as to the future expansionist intentions of Stalin's Soviet Union, which, even if they did not actually conflict with Germany on purely territorial questions, nevertheless posed a threat to the Reich's supremacy in Europe. Economic and psychological subversion were also considered a real risk. Therefore, after the fall of France, the attention of OKH had become ever increasingly focused on the Soviet Union, for sound grand-strategic reasons. Divisions were transferred to the east, and on 25 June it was ordered that twenty-four, including six panzer and three motorised infantry, be sent there and placed under the command of von Küchler for 'special military tasks.' It was specified that they should not '*openly* [author's italics] reveal a hostile attitude.'[21] At the beginning of July, Halder had warned that, apart from Great Britain, the other major problem still left for the Army was the delivery of 'a military blow at Russia which will force her to recognise Germany's dominant role in Europe.'[22]

However, it was not until 13 July that the OKH received the necessary impetus for the preparation of a detailed plan of action against the Soviet Union. Until then, the projected invasion of England had occupied the attentions of the generals, and probably would have continued to do so had not Hitler dropped certain hints in conversation with von Brauchitsch. Halder recorded in his diary for that day: 'The question in the forefront of the Führer's mind is why England is still unwilling to make peace; like us, he thinks that the answer is that England still has some hope of action on the part of Russia.' The Army Commander thereupon asked his Chief of the General Staff to take this problem into account so that 'OKH shall not be caught unprepared.'[23] Thus the practical merged with the political; not only did the Army leaders believe it was militarily necessary to prepare for a conflict against the Soviet Union, they also saw it as the means by which they could regain some of their influence with Hitler. Instead of pessimism, they would exude optimism; in place of doubts, they would present plans. Their Führer would have no cause to mistrust or to humiliate them; rather he would be grateful for the whole-hearted assistance given to him by the Army. Such were the considerations that lay behind OKH's initial zeal for the new foreign adventure. As a result, when on 21 July Hitler broached the subject of an eastern invasion, the Army leaders had already begun the planning of such an operation.

Shortly after the conference, Hitler asked for a memorandum on the subject from OKW; it returned the verdict that an autumn attack was totally impracticable. Hitler then decided on a campaign with a more ambitious objective—the total extinction of the Soviet Union—and a later starting date: spring 1941. This, Hitler believed, was the first and last date on which sufficient forces could safely be concentrated for an attack on such a vast scale. Any earlier, the Wehrmacht would not be ready, and the weather would be unsuitable; any later, the peak of operational efficiency would be passed and the strength of the German forces, compared with that of their enemies, would be on the wane. May 1941 was the date on which the destruction of Bolshevism was to begin.

But the Army leaders, although they were convinced of the need some day to deal with the Soviet Union—and, moreover, that Germany was capable of doing so—now, once again, became concerned at Hitler's intentions. They thought that he failed to appreciate the true priority of the Reich's grand-strategic objectives. Although they remained confident of the Army's ability to defeat the USSR, they came to doubt the wisdom of attempting it at that time. In their opinion, the invasion of the Soviet Union should be contemplated only after Britain had been subdued. Indeed, on 30 July, von Brauchitsch and Halder had come to the conclusion that an attack on Russia in 1941, as an alternative to action against England, could be positively dangerous. The latest intelligence reports had revealed that Red Army strength was significantly greater than previously thought, while the head of Army signals, General Fellgiebel, had said that preparation of communication-networks simultaneously for both the east and for 'Sea-Lion' was impossible. Furthermore, pessimistic reports were being received about Italian chances in the North African desert. Such factors made the Army leaders realise that, instead of starting a war on two fronts, it was better for the time being to remain friendly with the Soviet Union, which showed no immediate signs of hostility, and to concentrate on attacking Great Britain and her empire with all the resources at Germany's disposal. History had shown that a defiant Britain, with her fleet intact and her empire around her, was the greatest of dangers to a Continental power; this was especially true at that time, when she had an air force capable of striking deep into the Reich's territory. Moreover, the Russians might even be induced to cooperate with the Reich, especially in connexion with their desired expansion towards the Persian Gulf. Britain before the Soviet Union, therefore, was the generals' programme of conquest. Halder noted on 30 July: 'The question whether, if a decision cannot be enforced against England and the danger exists that England allies herself with Russia, we should first wage against Russia the ensuing two-front war, must be met with the answer that we should do better to keep friendship with Russia. A visit to Stalin would be advisable. . . . We could hit the English decisively in the Mediterranean [and] drive them out of Asia. . . .'[24] Even Jodl believed that, if economic circumstances made it necessary to choose between the two courses of action, then the invasion of England should take precedence; the attack on the USSR 'could be postponed because it is not a dire necessity for the victory over Britain.'[25]

Hitler, however, did not share the views of his military advisers: he was not even aware of them. As far as can be seen from the records, only twice, on 5 and 9 December, did any representative of OKH even tentatively broach the subject, and then the first occasion was restricted merely to questioning the Luftwaffe's capacity to undertake a war on two fronts, and not the Army's. Perhaps the military leaders realised that any hesitation on their part, especially coming as it did after their unrestrained enthusiasm at the Führer conference on 21 July, would have brought into the open, once again, Hitler's mistrust and contempt for his generals, something they dare not risk. All appearance of vacillation was carefully avoided; the Army proceeded to be merely the silent executor of its Supreme Commander's will.

And so, from 21 July 1940, only eight days after the plans for 'Sea-Lion' had been approved, there began the process by which the defeat of Britain was relegated by Hitler to a lower priority than the attack on the Soviet Union. By the end of July, the Führer's mind was becoming set on dealing with Russia in the spring of 1941. From this time on, the defeat of Britain was not made a condition to the invasion of the Soviet Union, although, until the invasion, operations against 'Perfidious Albion' would continue with every hope of success. Indeed, it now became, for a short while, imperative to defeat Britain as soon as possible. On 26 July, the preparations for a landing were placed above 'Priority No. 1' of the Reich's economic objectives, and on 31 July the final decision to launch an air offensive was taken. However, failure in the skies over south England, together with Hitler's continuing doubts about the feasibility of a seaborne invasion, led to the fight in the west being relegated to the status of a side-show compared with the preparations for the move east. On 31 August, the landing ceased to have top priority in the Reich's allocation of resources; on 17 September 'Sea-Lion' was postponed indefinitely; and by the end of the month it was clear that the air offensive had been unsuccessful. Not that Hitler worried; he reasoned that Britain would still be there when he would have finished with the Soviet Union by the middle of the autumn of 1941. He did not see that his decision to turn eastwards involved a war on two fronts—the traditional German nightmare. After all, by the time the Bolshevik Empire had been destroyed, Britain would still be far from able to launch an invasion of the Continent; she would remain merely an irritation, one which an increase in U-boat production and a strengthening of the Reich's anti-aircraft defences would go far to alleviate.

Such were the thoughts behind the process of decision to invade the Soviet Union, a process that began on 21 July and ended on 18 December. On 31 July, at a conference with his military leaders, Hitler stated his belief that a decisive victory could be achieved only by the defeat of Britain, but that this might be brought about by the elimination of the Soviet Union, which, together with the neutralisation of the United States by the power of Japan, would end all hope for the little island. Halder's cryptic notes on Hitler's remarks state: 'Russia must be defeated in the course of this struggle. Spring 1941.'[26] Preparations were ordered to begin. On 28 September, Hitler issued a major directive which confirmed his orders for the preparation of the attack and for the increase in the size of the Army necessary for such an operation. On 12 November, Directive No. 18 declared: 'Political discussions for the purpose of clarifying Russia's attitude in the immediate future have already begun. Regardless of the outcome of these conversations, all preparations for the east for which verbal orders have already been given will be continued. Further directives will follow on this subject as soon as the basic operational plan of the Army has been submitted to me and approved.'[27]

After conversations with Molotov, the Soviet Foreign Minister, during the next few days, it became clear that any hope of a German-Soviet coalition against Britain was still-born. At the Führer conference of 5 December, it was clear that Hitler took it for granted that an attack on the Soviet Union would take place in spring 1941. 'Sea-Lion' was 'no longer possible';[28] the Mediterranean excursion (Operation Felix, the occupation of Gibraltar) would begin as soon as events allowed; and the preparations for the occupation of Greece (Operation Marita) were to continue. Apart from von Brauchitsch's feeble questioning, already mentioned, of the Luftwaffe's capacity to cope with such an extension of the war, no general openly doubted the wisdom of the Führer's proposed course; Halder did not even mention his fear that 'Marita' might delay the opening of the attack in the east. Instead, the Chief of the Army General Staff dutifully presented OKH's operational plan for the invasion of the Soviet Union.

It was not until 9 December that any member of OKH summed up enough courage to tackle Hitler specifically on the absolute necessity for defeating Great Britain. Halder, when called to discuss with Hitler the situation in the Mediterranean, stressed the need to concentrate on the invasion of England and to counter any strengthening of the enemy's position in North Africa or any formation of a Balkan front. Nothing, however, was said about postponing the eastern campaign, and Hitler merely expressed agreement with the Chief of the General Staff. No good came of Halder's attempt; it came far too late. The Führer's opinion had been set rigid for four months. On 18 December, he issued his Directive No. 21 for the conduct of the war. It left no doubt as to his attitude: 'The German Armed Forces must be prepared, even before the conclusion of the war against England, to crush Soviet Russia in a rapid campaign. The Army will have to employ all available formations to this end, with the reservation that occupied territories must be insured against surprise attacks. . . . Preparations [long-term ones] . . . will be concluded by 15 May 1941.'[29]

Nevertheless, OKH, as if unable to comprehend reality, was still unwilling to believe the seriousness of

Hitler's intentions. Von Brauchitsch, for example, asked the Führer's Army adjutant to establish whether Hitler really intended to resort to force, or was merely bluffing. The generals' disquiet over Britain grew even more marked. In July, when they had first thought of the plans for the attack eastwards, the British were a weak enemy daily expecting invasion; by December they had successfully defeated a concerted attack by the Luftwaffe; they had bombed targets within the Reich throughout the autumn; they had inflicted serious reverses on Italy, both at sea and in North Africa; and, by their defiance, they had discouraged Spain from entering the war on the side of the Axis and had encouraged an independent attitude in the leadership of Vichy France, an independence which had even necessitated German plans for the occupation of Vichy. Thus, the OKH leaders clung stubbornly to Operation Sea-Lion, even though the conditions in which it might have been possible had passed, and Hitler had stated categorically that it was not now part of his policy. Göring and Raeder, too, although they recognised the strength of the Führer's determination, were opposed to the attack on Russia. Göring's protest was unlikely to have been strong, but Raeder's was unequivocal. On 27 December, he told Hitler that it was vital to recognise that the prime task should be the fight against Britain, to which assertion he received the same old reply: this could not be achieved until the Soviet Union had been defeated; only then could production priorities be switched from the Army to the other two services, and a seaborne invasion seriously contemplated. The Grand Admiral then realised that all further argument was completely useless. Once again, Hitler had decided on his course of action alone, and the few uncoordinated, desultory attempts to deflect him from it came to naught.

The disquiet of the generals continued to grow. On 28

January 1941, a conference between Halder and the senior administrators of the Army and Luftwaffe placed emphasis on the purely practical difficulties of any invasion in the east. Most important were the strains that would be imposed on the supply system, due in large part to enemy demolition and to the difference in gauge between the German and Soviet railways. Deficiencies in stocks of fuel and tyres, too, were disturbing, for they would restrict severely the ability of the already insufficient motor transport to provide adequate logistic support for the invasion force. That evening Halder noted gloomily in his diary:

'The purpose [of the operation] is not clear. We do not strike at the British, and our economic potential will not be improved. The risk in the west should not be underestimated. It is even possible that Italy might collapse after losing her colonies [at this time the Germans were not in North Africa] and we find ourselves with a southern front through Spain, Italy, and Greece. If we are then committed against Russia, our position will become increasingly difficult.'[30]

The next day, at a luncheon attended by von Brauchitsch, Halder, and the three commanders of the army groups designated for the invasion, all expressed considerable doubt about the grand-strategic position of the Reich. One of them, von Bock, observed, 'Brauchitsch gives a picture of the situation which does not please me,'[31] and expressed his doubts as to whether the Red Army would be destroyed west of the Dvina-Dnepr line before it retreated virtually intact into the vast interior of the Soviet Union. Halder conceded 'that it might well turn out differently'[32] to what had been planned. Three days later, on 1 February, von Bock, a bold man, raised some of his objections with the Führer himself. Although he agreed that the Soviets would be defeated if they were made to give battle, he wondered whether they could be forced to make peace. Hitler answered that he was sure that, once Leningrad, Moscow, and the Ukraine had been captured, further resistance would be impossible. And if it were, he continued, 'I am happy that our war production is equal to any demand. We have such an abundance of material that we had to reconvert some of our war plants [to civilian production]. The Armed Forces now have more manpower than at the beginning of the war, and our economy is in an excellent condition.'[33] When the severe shortages that were then facing the Army are taken into consideration, the extent to which Hitler had already lost his grip on reality is clear.

Had the generals pressed home their doubts, the Führer might have wavered from his plan, for Hitler himself was then suffering from a growing anxiety that all was not well. On 18 December, Engel, his Army adjutant, noted: 'The Führer doesn't yet know himself how things should go. He is constantly preoccupied with mistrust towards his military leaders, uncertain over the Russians' strength and disappointed at the toughness of the British.'[34] He now began to fear attacks on the flanks of the proposed advance, and he doubted the encouraging reports he had received on the weakness of the Soviet war industry. He also expressed concern at any future British attack in Norway, especially in the light of their successful raid on the Lofoten Islands in early March, and worried about their possible support for the Russians through Murmansk, the Arctic port. In March, he wondered whether the *coup d'état* in Yugoslavia would strengthen the British influence in the Balkans. The Army leaders, however, did nothing to increase Hitler's self-induced doubts; von Bock's was a lone voice in questioning the wisdom of the plan. On 3 February, at a meeting with the Führer, Halder made no mention of the immense logistical problems; instead, he merely outlined a number of the difficulties, and then proceeded to explain how they could be overcome. Likewise, the General Staff's study of the possibility that the Pripyat Marsh might become a point of Soviet resistance in the centre of the German advance, presented to Hitler on 1 March, contained no cause for concern, declaring that only cavalry divisions and other enemy units up to regimental strength could operate there at all effectively. Moreover, when Hitler demanded that security along the coastline of Europe should be increased, thereby dissipating the Army's already limited strength, von Brauchitsch made no attempt to point out that this would weaken unduly the already minimal force committed to the east. Thus, once again, the Reich embarked on a course of action by the will of the Führer and by the default of the generals.

Left: The PzKw II, a stop-gap, training tank of which 2,000 were built. Although production ended in July 1942, the machine was used in a reconnaissance role until late 1944. *Below:* The PzKw III, intended to be Germany's main battle tank, armed with a 3.7cm gun. No less than 5,644 of these tanks, of all variants, were produced, some 5,000 being destroyed in action.

Above: The horse-drawn supply column so basic to the operation of the German Field Army. Here in the Soviet Union in 1941, wagons bring up rations to the front-line troops. *Below:* The PzKw IV, the panzer force's support-tank, armed with a short-barrelled 7.5cm gun. By 1944 the PzKw IV, with heavier armour and a more powerful gun, had become Germany's main tank, and by the end of the war 7,350 had been produced.

Left: Hitler at the Front in Poland. *Below:* Infantry and tanks in attack, Poland 1939.

Above: Obsolete equipment: old armoured cars dating from the early 1920's during the Polish campaign. *Below:* German infantrymen taking cover during the opening phase of Operation White, September 1939. The machine gun is the MG 34 in a heavy support role.

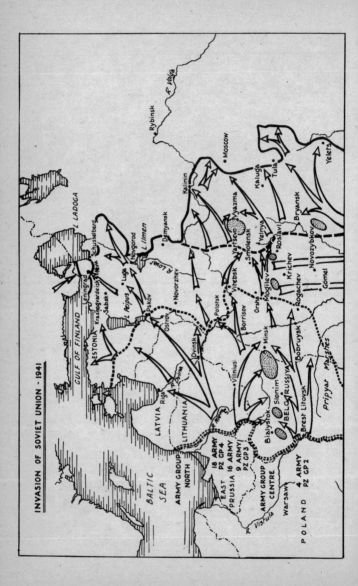

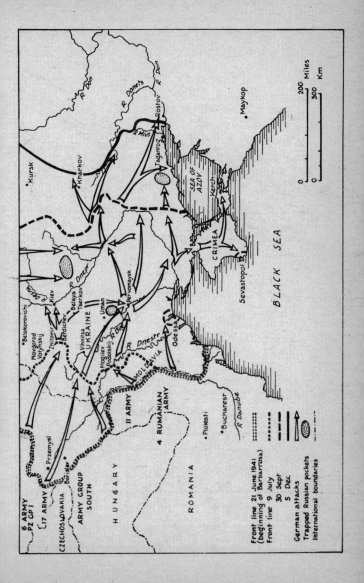

Front line 21 June 1941
(beginning of Barbarossa)

Front line 9 July
30 Sept
5 Dec

German attacks

Trapped Russian pockets

International boundaries

Above: A 15cm heavy infantry gun in action on the Polish plains. *Below:* German cavalry; these cavalrymen are probably engaged in reconnaissance duties, for which they were used in Poland.

Above left: Hitler takes the salute during the victory parade in Warsaw on 5th October 1939. *Above right:* The Chief of the General Staff, General Franz Halder, and the Commander-in-Chief of the Army, Walter von Brauchitsch, studying a map of Europe during the planning of the invasion of the west. *Left:* Tanks and infantry advance during the invasion of Norway, the first campaign conducted by the Wehrmacht High Command. *Opposite top:* Operation Yellow begins: infantrymen of Army Group B move, under cover of smoke, towards the enemy, May 1940. *Opposite bottom:* Crossing the Meuse under fire.

Opposite top: **Tanks of Army Group A at the beginning of the advance to the Channel. The leading machine is a PzKw 35 (t) captured Czech model.** *Opposite bottom:* **Infantry in the attack, securing the flanks of Army Group A's thrust.** *Top:* **French prisoners surrendering.** *Left:* **A pioneer of Army Group C storming the Maginot line, June 1940.**

Top right: Field Marshal Gerd von Rundstedt, the Army's most senior general and an able army group commander. *Top left:* Field Marshal Ewald von Kleist, who, as a general, was responsible for the armoured drive to the Channel in 1940. *Bottom right:* Field Marshal von Leeb. *Bottom left:* Field Marshal von Bock.

6

'Barbarossa'—The Plans

The Russian colossus will be proved to be a pig's bladder; prick it, and it will burst.
GENERAL ALFRED JODL
Chief of Operations, OKW

The military planning for the invasion of the Soviet Union had preceded by almost three weeks Hitler's decision to attack. On 3 July 1940, Halder had asked Colonel von Greiffenberg, of the Operations Branch of the Army General Staff, to study 'the requirements of a military intervention which will compel Russia to recognize Germany's dominant position in Europe.'[1] This was a somewhat vague order of reference, but on 21 July Hitler made it more specific. Halder's notes on the conference include the following:

'German assembly will take at least four to six weeks. Object: to crush the Russian Army, or slice as much Russian territory as is necessary to bar

156

enemy air raids on Berlin and the Silesian industries. It is desirable to penetrate far enough to enable our Air Force to smash Russia's strategic areas. . . . Political aims: Ukrainian State, Federation of Baltic States, White Russia—Finland. . . . Strength required: 80 to 100 divisions; Russia has 50 to 75 . . . divisions.'[2]

The Romanian oilfields were also to be protected. At the 31 July Führer conference, Hitler confirmed these objectives, and, according to Halder, added:

'The object is the destruction of Russian man-power. The operation will be divided into three sections: first thrust to Kiev and secure flank protection on the Dnepr. Luftwaffe will destroy river crossings [and ?] Odessa; second thrust to Baltic States and drive on Moscow; finally, link up of northern and southern wings [presumably east of Moscow]. Successively: limited drive on the Baku oilfields [in the Caucasus].'[3]

All this would be achieved with 120 divisions.

Such were the specifications given to OKH by the Supreme Commander. The geographical objectives of the over-all advance met with little or no dissension; but the actual strategy of the invasion, the 'lines of thrust,' were by no means generally acceptable. On 26 July, after a briefing with Colonel Kinzel, of the Foreign Armies, East, Branch of the General Staff, Halder noted: 'The best chances of success lie in an operation in the direction of Moscow with flank on the Baltic Sea, which, subsequently by a drive from the north, compels the Russian concentrations in the Ukraine and on the Black Sea to accept battle on an inverted front.'[4] This bold scythe-cut, so reminiscent of von Schlieffen, might well have resulted in the greatest encirclement battle of history; whether it would have been successful is another matter. Certainly, other members of the General Staff, some of whom wanted a strong attack in the south, advised caution, and Halder agreed to defer his final decision.

On 29 July, Halder gave to General Erich Marcks, Chief of Staff to 18th Army then in the east, the special task of planning the invasion of the Soviet Union; by 1 August his plan was ready. In it, Marcks rejected the idea of a single thrust, making instead proposals corresponding closely, although unwittingly, with Hitler's specifications of the previous day. Marcks envisaged the campaign in two phases: in the first, the Germans would seek to encircle and destroy the main Soviet armies close to the frontier; in the second, the most valuable industrial areas of European Russia would be occupied—Leningrad, Moscow, and the Donets Basin of the Ukraine—and a line Archangel-Gorkiy-Rostov achieved. Two operational groups, one directed at Moscow, the other at Kiev, would be employed. Halder, while accepting the basic premises of Marcks's plan, pointed out 'that Operational Group Kiev, based on Romanian territory, is treading on very insecure political ground, and . . . that the extension of the operations of the Moscow Group into the Baltic States should be treated as a subsidiary action which must not detract from the main thrust of Moscow.'[5] Because of the economic, political, and military importance of the Soviet capital, Halder argued, it was there that the Red Army was likely to make its final stand. As the most vital aspect of the campaign was to destroy the Red Army, it was therefore necessary to concentrate the main German effort of the second, or 'pursuit,' phase on Moscow, thereby relegating the drives on Leningrad and the Donets Basin to subsidiary, flanking operations.

With this in mind, Marcks produced his final plan on 5

August. The methods by which the objectives would be attained were conditioned by four factors: the strength and disposition of the Soviet forces, as estimated by German intelligence; the geographical feature of the Pripyat Marsh, a vast area of swampland, 150 miles in width from north to south and over 300 miles in length, which lay in the centre of the proposed front; the proximity to the Soviet border of the Romanian oilfields, so important to the German war economy; and the unreliability of the Balkan countries of Hungary and Romania as military allies, at least in the initial stages of the operation. Because Marck's operational proposals distilled much of the contemporary thought among the German leadership as to the aims and methods of any attack in the east, and because it provides a base by which to evaluate the future development of the invasion plan, it is worth quoting fairly extensively from its pages.

Marcks began his appreciation with a definition of the operational aims:

'The purpose of the campaign is to strike the Russian Armed Forces and to make Russia incapable of entering the war as an opponent of Germany in the forseeable future. In order to protect Germany against Russian bombers, Russia must be occupied to the line lower Don-central Volga-north Dnepr. The main centres of the Russian war economy lie in the food and raw-material producing areas of the Ukraine and Donets Basin and in the armament industries of Moscow and Leningrad. The eastern industrial regions are not yet productive enough. *Of these areas, Moscow constitutes the economic, political, and spiritual centre of the USSR. Its capture would destroy the coordination of the Russian state* [author's italics].'

Marcks continued with an appreciation of the terrain of the 'War Zone,' and pointed out that the Pripyat Marsh divided the frontier zone into two separate operational areas. He then proceeded to deal with enemy intentions, foremost among which he envisaged 'a Russian breakthrough into Romania . . . in order to deprive us of oil. At the very least, strong air attacks on the Romanian oilfields must be expected.' Marcks then made an important distinction between the proposed operation and Napoleon's 1812 campaign, which had ended in disaster: '. . . the Russians cannot avoid a decision as they did in 1812. Modern armed forces of 100 divisions cannot abandon their sources of supply. It is expected that the Russian Army will stand to do battle in a defensive position protecting greater Russia and the eastern Ukraine.' He gave the strength of the Red Army as 151 infantry divisions, 32 cavalry divisions, and 38 motorised brigades, of which 96, 23, and 28 respectively were ranged against Germany. These were 'almost evenly divided south and north of the Pripyat Marsh, with a reserve around Moscow. This form of distribution can also be expected in the event of a war with Germany.' The Soviet armoured strength was negligible, and there was little doubt as to the general weakness of the army as a whole. 'Because the Russians no longer possess the superiority of numbers they had in the World War [I], it is more likely that once the long, extended line of their forces has been broken through, they will be unable to concentrate, or to coordinate counter-measures. Fighting in isolated battles, they will soon succumb to the superiority of the German troops and leadership.' Against such a weak force, he anticipated that the Germans could field 110 infantry and mountain divisions, 12 motorised infantry divisions, 24 panzer divisions, and a cavalry division—a total of 147.

Because of the size of the future combat zone, and

because of its division by the Pripyat Marsh, Marcks saw that 'a decision will not be achieved in a single battle. . . . Initially, it will be necessary to divide, and advance against the two main parts of the Russian Army separately, with the object of uniting later for an operation to reach the other side of the great forest region [before Moscow, of which the Pripyat Marsh formed the southern part].' Concerning the operational intentions, Marcks was clear: there would be two thrusts, one, the more important, by Army Group North, to Moscow, the other, by Army Group South, into the Ukraine. 'The main force of the German Army will strike that part of the Russian Army in northern Russia and will take Moscow [700 miles from the border]. . . . South of the Pripyat Marsh, weaker forces [based in Galizia and southern Poland] will prevent the advance of the enemy southern group towards Romania by an attack towards Kiev and the middle Dnepr [less than 350 miles from the border]. They will also prepare for subsequent cooperation with the main forces east of the Dnepr . . . either towards Kharkov or north-eastwards.' Marcks proceeded to describe in more detail the role of the northern force:

'The main purpose of the offensive is to strike and destroy the mass of the Russian northern group before, within, and east of the forest area, by means of a direct thrust towards Moscow. Then from Moscow and north Russia it will turn southwards, and, in cooperation with the German southern group, conquer the Ukraine and finally reach the line Rostov-Gorkiy-Archangel. To cover the north flank of this operation, a special force will be directed across the lower Dvina towards Pskov and Leningrad [500 miles from the border].'[6]

A strong reserve, almost one-third of the total invasion

force, would be brought into action as the width of the combat zone increased with the depth of the advance, thereby solving the strategic problem of the relationship of force to space.

The next development in the planning of the operation came on 3 September, with the appointment of General von Paulus as Deputy Chief of the General Staff. Straightway he was given the task of coordinating the planning for the forthcoming operation. By 17 September he had evolved a plan based on Marcks's ideas, but containing several variations. Von Paulus had created a third army group, largely by reducing the size of Marcks's reserve, thereby providing for three independent major thrusts in the place of two—Army Group North to Leningrad, Army Group Centre to Moscow, and Army Group South to Kiev. In the south, greater emphasis was placed on an attack on Kiev from Romania in conjunction with the more northerly movement from southern Poland. However, Moscow still remained the primary objective. This became clear when, in November and December, von Paulus held a General Staff war-game to test the plan. Although it was shown that the diverging advances of the three army groups would create dangerous gaps to the north-west and south-west of Moscow, the importance of the Soviet capital was such that it was decided that the two other army groups should deal with these gaps, thereby allowing Army Group Centre to continue its attack unhindered; Army Groups North and South were to converge on the flanks of Army Group Centre for the final advance on Moscow. Halder then confirmed that the capture of Leningrad and the Don Basin, beyond Kharkov, 'would depend on the progress of the general offensive against Moscow.'[7]

At the same time as OKH was working on its plan, the chiefs of staff of the three army groups then in existence, A, B and C, were ordered to undertake their own studies.

Each of them reaffirmed the prime importance of Moscow as an objective; two, Generals Brennecke and von Salmuth, produced plans similar to that of von Paulus. The other, General von Sodenstern, who was extremely pessimistic about the outcome of such an invasion, however conducted, went further. Instead of first destroying the Red Army, he advocated immediate and fast advances on Moscow, Leningrad, and Kharkov with the aim of crippling the Soviet leadership. The main weight of the attack would, initially, be concentrated on the northern and southern wings, which would then converge and meet east of the Pripyat Marsh, from where they would drive on to Moscow, their flanks being covered by subsidiary thrusts north and south. Von Sodenstern, however, had no influence on OKH's deliberations, apart, perhaps, from reassuring them of their intention to push on to Moscow.

On 5 December von Brauchitsch and Halder presented the draft of their plan to Hitler. They must have been well-content with the product, for few had expressed doubts as to its operational practicability, and, moreover, it was clear that its aims were close to those stipulated by the Führer on 31 July. They little expected his dissent; nonetheless, it came. Halder noted Hitler's remarks, of which the most important were:

'What matters most is to prevent the enemy from falling back before our onslaught; maximum objective: occupation of an area which will render the capital [Berlin] safe from air attacks. After attainment of this objective, combined operations to destroy the sources of enemy war potential (armaments industries, mines, oilfields); aim of campaign: crushing of Russian manpower; no groups capable of recuperation must be allowed to escape. . . . make the southern group strong. The

Russians must be beaten this side of the Dnepr. . . .
cut off the Baltic area. . . . By striking with strong
wings north and south of the Pripyat Marsh we
must split the Russian front and encircle the enemy
in separate pockets (similar to Poland); these two
wings must be fast and strong; *Moscow is of no great
importance* [author's italics].'[8]

Thus the fundamental principle on which the Army's
plan was based, that the attainment of the Soviet capital
should be the main objective, was reversed.

Exactly why Hitler decided on such a major alteration
to the OKH's plan has never been clear, but it seems to
have been due to a number of reasons; political,
economic, and strategic. No doubt he was anxious, for
political and psychological reasons, to capture Leningrad, the cradle of Bolshevism, and to occupy the
Ukraine (and the Caucasus), the economic power-house
of the Soviet Union, for the considerable material gains
that would accrue to the Reich and be denied to the
Soviets. Possibly, too, he feared to tread the same path as
Napoleon's ill-fated expedition, which secured Moscow
but allowed the Russian Army to remain intact.
However, these considerations aside, Hitler's decision
was also based on what he considered to be sound
strategic sense. He believed that the primary objective of
destroying the Soviet forces would be best achieved not
by the three thrusts advocated by the Army, but by two
large flanking operations, one to the north, the other to
the south. Furthermore, he felt that capture of the Baltic
ports would ease considerably the logistic difficulties of
such a campaign. It might well have been that Hitler was
influenced by the study, dated 15 September 1940, of
Lieutenant-Colonel von Lossberg of the OKW. Although
he had stated that the 'commitment of the main weight'
was to be in the direction of Moscow, von Lossberg

nevertheless proposed that it might be necessary to turn forces from the main thrust 'to the north . . . possibly east of the Dvina [some 230 miles from the border], in order to cut off the Russians facing the north wing.'[9]

However, Hitler arrived at his conclusion, one thing is clear: in his Directive No. 21, dated 18 December, he stated unequivocally:

'In the theatre of operations . . . the main weight of the attack will be delivered in the northern area. Two army groups will be employed here. The more southerly of these two army groups (in the centre of the whole front) will have the task of advancing . . . from the area about and north of Warsaw, and routing the enemy forces in White Russia. This will make it possible for strong mobile forces to advance northwards and, in conjunction with the northern army group operating out of East Prussia in the general direction of Leningrad, to destroy the enemy forces operating in the Baltic area. Only after the fulfilment of this first essential task, which must include the occupation of Leningrad and Kronstadt, will the attack be continued with the intention of occupying Moscow, an important centre of communications and of the armaments industry. Only a surprisingly rapid collapse of Russian resistance could justify the simultaneous pursuit of both objectives.'[10]

This he confirmed on 9 January, telling von Brauchitsch that the invasion 'should on no account turn into a frontal pushing back of the Russians. . . . The most important task is the swift envelopment of the Baltic area; thus the right flank of the German forces thrusting north of the Pripyat Marsh must be made especially strong. The aims of the operation must be the destruction of the Russian Army, the seizure of the most important industrial areas and the destruction of the remaining [ones]. . . . in addition the Baku area must be occupied.'[11] Warlimont's comment was: 'So with a stroke of the pen, a new concept of the main lines of the campaign against Russia was substituted for that which the OKH had worked out as a result of months of painstaking examination and cross-checking from all angles by the best military brains available.'[12] And, just as he had radically altered the nature of the plan, so Hitler gave it a new title. Until then, OKW had used the code-name 'Fritz' and OKH, 'Otto'; on 18 December the dictator declared that he had adopted the code-name 'Barbarossa,' the nickname of the Emperor Frederick I, who, according to legend, would one day return to aid Germany in her hour of need.

The Army leaders said not a word to the Führer about his fundamental change in the emphasis of their plan. There was no protest on 5 December, nor subsequently. Indeed, on 3 February 1941 Halder even agreed with Hitler on the necessity to occupy the Baltic coast as soon as possible so as to provide a secure supply base for future operations. With the exception of the Baku oilfields, Hitler's priorities were duly incorporated into the OKH's deployment directive of 31 January 1941—and this despite the fact that the generals continued to regard Moscow as the main objective. Probably because of their dismal record in remonstrating with the Führer, von Brauchitsch and Halder preferred to pass by the question of Moscow or Leningrad for the time being and wait until the campaign was under way before making their final choice, when events would, they hoped, dictate the correct course. A conspiracy of silence descended on the subject. Warlimont remembered: 'It later became known that their reasoning was that, in time, the course of the campaign would compel even

Hitler to go back to the original Army concept. This was to a certain extent taking the easy way out and it proved to be no more than self-deception.'[13]

The field commanders, who noted the vagueness with which OKH treated this crucial aspect of the plan, remonstrated with the planners about the contradiction that was clearly evident in the deployment directive. Certainly, its intentions accorded with those of the Führer. It declared unequivocally that 'Both Army Groups [North and Centre] will destroy the enemy formations in the Baltic area,' and said that only if this, together with the occupation of Leningrad, was achieved unexpectedly quickly, could 'the abandonment of the turning movement [northwards by Army Group Centre] and an immediate thrust towards Moscow . . . be considered.'[14] However, the operational guidelines it then proceeded to lay down were not in accordance with the achievement of this end. Had OKH's intention indeed been to concentrate on Leningrad, the best path to be taken by that part of Army Group Centre required to cooperate with von Leeb's force would have been to turn northwards once the Dvina River had been crossed west of Vitebsk. Instead, the deployment directive laid down that the main thrust of all elements in Army Group Centre should be towards Minsk and Smolensk, eastwards on the direct route to Moscow. Only after Smolensk had been taken would any move north-west be undertaken at a point beyond the terrain best suited for it. Indeed, nowhere did the OKH directive specify any lines of advance for Army Group Centre to assist Army Group North; it limited itself to the vaguest of references to such an operation. Perhaps this was in line with the General Staff's dictum that no plan should specify exact action after the first phase of an operation; but perhaps, too, it was indicative of something more: the attempted deception of Hitler by OKH. Thus the Army leaders satisfied Hitler's desire with such vague wording as:

'. . . Army Group Centre will commit strong mobile
forces . . . to force a breakthrough towards Smolensk. This will permit the turning of strong
formations to the north in order to cooperate with
Army Group North. . . . It [Army Group Centre]
will quickly win the area around Smolensk . . . and
so achieve the prerequisites for cooperation between strong elements of its mobile troops and
Army Group North. . . . At the appropriate time
the OKH will order powerful mobile forces from
Army Group Centre advancing on Smolensk to
cooperate with Army Group North.'[15]

Thus, both the time and the place of the move away from
Moscow to Leningrad would be determined by OKH, as
also would the strength of the force to be so diverted.
Moreover, the Army leaders declined to make any
detailed planning for the establishment of a supply base
on the Baltic, believing, as they did, that the campaign
would be over before this was necessary. Events, they
were sure, would lead them to Moscow; even Hitler, they
argued, could not withstand for long such obvious
military realities.

In spite of all their efforts to keep their intention
hidden from the Führer, however, Hitler sensed their
doubts about his plan. In December 1940 Engel, Hitler's
Army Adjutant, had told von Brauchitsch of the
Führer's nagging mistrust of the generals, a mistrust
that was evident in his continual emphasis on the
necessity for speedy, decisive action against the Soviet
Union. On 9 January 1941 he reminded the Army leaders
of the need for bold encircling operations that would
destroy the enemy, and on 3 February, when he accepted
the OKH's operational plan for the invasion, he lectured

them thus: 'It is important to destroy the greater part of the enemy, not just to make them run. This will be achieved only by occupying the areas on the flanks with the strongest forces, while standing fast in the centre, and then outmanoeuvring the enemy in the centre from the flanks.' The quick capture of Leningrad, he argued, was vital 'if the Russians succeeded in conducting a large-scale withdrawal to a new defensive line further east.'[16] This theme he returned to at the military conference of 17 March, when he described the capture of Moscow as 'completely irrelevant.'[17]

At the same conference of 17 March Hitler made a further significant alteration to the operational plan of the OKH. Both the Führer and the Army leaders were disturbed by the numerical inadequacy of the German forces available for 'Barbarossa,' especially in view of the dissipation of units along the European coastline, in North Africa, and in the Balkans. Halder believed the solution lay in a greater use of the armies of Romania, Slovakia, and Hungary in the south, and by allocating reserve divisions to the north. Hitler, however, would have none of this; instead, he amended the operational plan. The Romanians, he believed, lacked offensive capability; the Slovaks were best suited to occupation duties; and the Hungarians were unreliable, for they had no cause to attack the Soviet Union. Thus, he concluded, economy of force would be the only answer to the problem. As the Baltic coast was the paramount objective, no weakening of Army Groups North and Centre was possible; the Ukraine, however, was different. Using the argument that it was wrong to attack everywhere, Hitler abandoned the idea of a double envelopment to be undertaken by Army Group South, ordering instead a single main thrust north of the Carpathians towards Kiev and down the Dnepr. The German force to the south in Romania was to be reduced and relegated to a purely defensive role, safeguarding the vital Ploiesti oil-fields. Moreover, he rejected the Army's proposition that the Pripyat Marsh was an obstacle to movement, and argued that armies could progress through it. Thus, a coherent, advancing front could be maintained between Army Group Centre and Army Group South from the beginning, thereby rendering unnecessary the dispersion of forces from the south northwards, or from the north southwards, to counter any danger from the Pripyat area.

As if to emphasise his amateur's approach towards military strategy, on the same day that Hitler announced his decision to economise on force in the south, he confirmed his intention to dissipate it in the north, the area he had so long declared was vital to the whole operation. On 17 March he ordered that the garrison in northern Norway should be reinforced with two or three divisions from the west, at an expense of formations needed in Finnish Lapland for the attack on Leningrad from the north. (Finland was but 150 miles from the city.)

As had by then become the accepted form, not a word of protest or of question at Hitler's interference came from the Army leaders. Halder was critical of the decision to end the double envelopment, but no hint of this was evident at the conference. Engel noted that there was only 'cheerful agreement between the Commander-in-Chief and the Chief of the General Staff and Hitler over the deployment plan and concentrations of force.'[18] Only von Rundstedt, commander-designate of Army Group South, expressed any misgivings to Hitler. On 30 March he had heard from his Führer that 'the endless expanse of the space necessitates . . . the massive concentration of . . . forces,' and that 'the fate of major German formations may not be made dependent on the staying power of Romanian formations.'[19] Von Rundstedt could not disagree with this, but he pointed out that, unless the large enemy troop concentrations were, at the very least, pinned down by attacks along the Carpathian sector, they might prove a considerable threat to the right flank of his thrust to Kiev. Hitler remained unmoved. As Warlimont noted:

'This and other interventions by Hitler in operational matters had an increasingly disturbing effect on the whole basis of the operational plan for the east, and Halder's diary shows clearly with what grumbling and distaste they were received. The effects of the Supreme Commander's determination to play the role of great war leader can be seen by the very great difficulties encountered in the advance of Army Group South during the first weeks of the campaign.'[20]

The final plan for 'Barbarossa' was as follows. The task of the Wehrmacht was 'to defeat Soviet Russia in a quick campaign'; the Army's operations would be conducted so that 'the mass of the Russian Army in western Russia will be destroyed. . . . The withdrawal of elements left intact into the depth of Russian space will be prevented.' For this to be achieved, it was assumed that 'the Russians will accept battle west of the Dnepr and Dvina at least with strong parts of their forces.' The intention of the Germany Army was 'by means of swift and deep thrusts . . . to tear open the front of the mass of the Russian Army which, it is anticipated, will be in western Russia. The enemy groups separated by these penetrations will then be destroyed.' The invasion force would be divided into three army groups, North, Centre, and South. Army Group North was to attack 'from East Prussia in the general direction of Leningrad'; Army Group Centre was to advance from northern German-occupied Poland 'to force a breakthrough towards Smolensk.' Then, these two army groups would together 'destroy the enemy formations in the Baltic area.' Army Group South was to advance from southern Poland and move through Kiev to the great bend of the lower Dnepr. After the attainment of the objectives in northern Russia, 'freedom of movement for further tasks' would be assured, 'perhaps in cooperation with the German forces in southern Russia.'[21] Only then would Moscow become an objective. The role of the Luftwaffe was, firstly, to gain command of the air and, secondly, to support the ground operations. The Navy would operate in the Baltic, primarily to prevent enemy forces from breaking out of that sea; once Leningrad had been taken, and the Soviet fleet eliminated, it would safeguard the supply of the north wing of the Army. On the flanks, Finland and Romania would give assistance at the appropriate time.

The force allocated for 'Barbarossa' was divided into three army groups. Army Group North, the smallest, was commanded by von Leeb and comprised two armies—the 16th, under Busch (eight divisions), and the 18th, under von Küchler (seven divisions)—and one panzer group—the 4th, under Hoepner (eight divisions, of which three were panzer and three motorised infantry); these, together with the three infantry and three security divisions in reserve, made a total of twenty-nine divisions. Two more OKH reserve infantry divisions were stationed behind the army group's front. Army Group Centre, the strongest force, was under von Bock, and consisted of two armies—the 4th, under von Kluge (fourteen divisions, of which two were security divisions), and the 9th, under Strauss (nine divisions of which one was a security division)—together with two panzer groups—the 2nd, under Guderian (fifteen divisions, of which five were panzer, three motorised infantry, and one cavalry, plus a strong motorised infantry regiment), and the 3rd, under Hoth (eleven divisions, of which four were panzer and three motorised infantry); these, with the one division in reserve, made a total of fifty divisions. OKH disposed of a further six divisions behind the army group's front. Army Group South, commanded by von Rundstedt, was made up of three armies—the 17th, under von Stülpnagel (thirteen divisions, of which one was a mountain and two security divisions), the 6th, under von Reichenau (six divisions, of which one was a security division), and the 11th, under von Schobert (seven divisions), and one panzer group—the 1st, under von Kleist (fourteen divisions, of which five were panzer and three were motorised infantry regiment); these, together with the reserve of one division, comprised forty-one divisions. The OKH held another six divisions in reserve behind the army group's front, one of which was a mountain division. Thus, on 22 June 1941 the invasion force had a total of seven armies and four panzer groups made up of 134 divisions, of which seventeen were panzer, thirteen motorised infantry, one cavalry, four mountain, and nine security. To this must be added fourteen Romanian and twenty-one Finnish divisions. Moreover, OKH had allocated a further twelve divisions to be used in the east, two of which were panzer and one motorised infantry. Four divisions, two of which were mountain and one mountain motorised, were in Finland. For the forthcoming conflict, Hitler committed no fewer than 3,050,000 soldiers to the field, supported by 7,184 artillery pieces.

An impressive array of military might, but the total German strength for the invasion, including the OKH reserve not yet moved to the east, was, in terms of numbers of divisions, only fifteen more than that committed to the attack on the west in 1940 (150 and 135 respectively). The area in which the armies were to be deployed under the 'Barbarossa' plan was roughly one million square miles, whereas the whole area conquered between 10 May and 25 June 1940 was around 50,000 square miles—one twentieth the size. Moreover, although the number of mechanised divisions in the invasion force had more than doubled, from fifteen in May 1940 to thirty-two in June 1941, the number of tanks had increased by just under a third, from 2,574 to 3,332 (758 machines in all). Clearly, the Germans would have to rely more than ever before on their superior skill. Of the importance of the mechanised units in the forthcoming campaign, all were agreed: a panzer group would lead every main thrust. But here unanimity ended, and, once again, the battle of theories was evident, with the traditional emerging an easy victor over the revolutionary.

The men responsible for drawing up Operation Barbarossa were all, with one exception, from the artillery or the infantry: von Brauchitsch, Halder, and Marcks were gunners; von Greiffenburg and Kinzel were infantrymen. Hitler, too, was a conservative in military thought. Only von Paulus was a panzer general with direct experience in the operational and administrative problems, and the potential, of mechanised forces; but he was not the type of man to question or reject what had been decided by his superiors. The invasion plan that evolved, ambitious and daring though it proved to be, was hardly revolutionary in its concept; from the outset, the traditional strategy of *Vernichtungsgedanke* dominated all thought. Foremost in the minds of the military leaders, including Hitler, appears to have been the fear that the Russians, as in 1812, would simply retreat before the invaders into their vast interior, with their forces intact, ready to counter-attack when their enemy's lines of communication had become over-extended, their troops weary, and their equipment worn out. Hence the emphasis placed on the need to destroy the Soviet army west of the Dnepr-Dvina line. Hitler, in his Directive No. 21, laid down that 'The bulk of the Russian Army stationed in western Russia will be destroyed by daring operations led by deeply penetrating armoured spearheads. Russian forces still capable of giving battle will be prevented from withdrawing into the depths of Russia.'[22] This was echoed by the Army Command in its deployment directive of 31 January 1941: 'The first intention of the OKH within the task allocated is, by means of swift and deep thrusts by strong mobile formations north and south of the Pripyat Marsh, to tear open the front of the mass of the Russian Army which it is anticipated will be in western Russia. The enemy groups separated by these penetrations will then be destroyed.'[23]

The Army's directive continued to state categorically: 'The conduct of operations will be based on the principles proved in the Polish campaign.' Foremost amongst these was the idea of the *Kesslschlacht,* the 'cauldron battle,' the decisive manoeuvre of double envelopment ending with the annihilation of the enemy. A closer look at the OKH deployment directive reveals this: 'Army Group Centre will break up the enemy in White Russia by driving forward the strong forces on its wings. It will quickly win the area around Smolensk by uniting the mobile forces advancing north and south of Minsk and so achieve the prerequisites for cooperation between strong elements of its mobile troops and Army Group North in the destruction of the enemy forces fighting in the Baltic States and the Leningrad area.' These two encirclement operations, between them, were designed to destroy the mass of the Red Army in the west. To the south, the original intention for Army Group South was to carry out a bold encirclement of the enemy west of the Dnepr by two concentric attacks, one from southern Poland, the other from Romania. This, however, was amended by Hitler in mid-March, so that the destruction of Soviet troops in Galizia and in the western Ukraine would be achieved by means of a single major flanking movement emanating from southern Poland, moving to the Dnepr at, or below, Kiev and thence south-east 'along the Dnepr in order to prevent a withdrawal of the enemy . . . across the Dnepr and to destroy him by attack from the rear.'[24] In such a manner was Hitler's specification, which he so constantly reiterated, undertaken. On 3 February 1941 he had told his Army leaders that 'It is important to destroy the greater part of the enemy, not just to make them run. This will be achieved only by occupying the areas on the flanks with the strongest forces, while standing fast in the centre, and then outmanoeuvring the enemy in the centre from the flanks.'[25] This was pure 'Schlieffen.'

Understandably, the panzer enthusiasts were unhappy. They, together with one or two generals in OKW, proposed that the panzer arm should be used independently of the rest of the army, in long-range operations aimed at paralysis rather than physical destruction. The General Staff rejected this as an 'extreme solution.'[26] Guderian, especially, 'made no attempt to conceal [his] disappointment and disgust.' He was worried that 'no single clear operational objective seemed to be envisaged.'[27] He and Hoth both wished to exploit the velocity of their armoured formations to the fullest extent, and, at the very least, to reach the Dnepr before closing the first encirclement, which OKH had decided would be nearer the frontier, at Minsk. The encirclement and destruction of the Soviet forces should be left to the infantry; the mechanised forces, stripped to their barest essentials and supplied from the air, should push on with all speed to complete the dislocation of the enemy. Moscow, the political, military, communications, and economic centre of the Soviet Union, should be the geographical objective; paralysis the strategic aim.

Von Blumentritt, Chief of Staff to 4th Army under whose control came Guderian's Panzer Group 2, recognised the essence of the disagreement when he recorded:

> 'Guderian had a different idea—to drive deep, as fast as possible, and leave the encircling of the enemy to be completed by the infantry forces that were following up. Guderian urged the importance of keeping the Russians on the run, and allowing them no time to rally. He wanted to drive straight to to Moscow, and was convinced that he could get there if no time was wasted. Russia's resistance might be paralysed by the thrust at the centre of Stalin's power. Guderian's plan was a very bold one—and meant big risks in maintaining reinforcements and supplies. But it might have been the lesser of two risks. By making the armoured forces turn in each time, and forge a ring around the enemy forces they had by-passed, a lot of time was lost.'[28]

This was similar to the view held by General von Sodenstern, the previously cautious Chief of Staff to Army Group A, who, although considering the whole idea of an invasion to be hopeless, nevertheless produced a plan which aimed not at the physical destruction of the Red Army, but at the crippling of the Soviet leadership by the capture of the three great cities of Leningrad, Kharkov, and, above all, Moscow.

The panzer generals were also unhappy at the restrictions placed on their freedom of action. Caution, rather than daring, was the keynote in the handling of the panzer groups. The OKH deployment directive, while placing emphasis on the role of the panzer groups, was careful not to give them anything approaching full independence. Thus, throughout, there are the following caveats which boded ill for those who valued freedom of operation: 'Army Group South will drive its strong left wing—with mobile forces in the lead—towards Kiev . . . The first task of Panzer Group I will be in cooperation with 17th and 6th Armies. . . . The 6th Army . . . will follow Panzer Group I . . . with all possible speed and strength. It must be ready . . . to cooperate with Panzer Group I. . . .' For Army Group Centre, OKH stipulated: 'Panzer Group 2, in cooperation with 4th Army . . . [and] Panzer Group 3, in cooperation with 9th Army, will break through the enemy forces on the frontier. . . . 4th Army [will] . . . follow advance of Panzer Group 2 . . . 9th Army will . . . follow Panzer Group 3.' In the north: 'Panzer Group 4, in cooperation with 16th and 18th Armies, will break through the enemy front . . . 16th Army will . . . follow Panzer Group 4 . . . 18th Army . . . possibly in cooperation with mobile troops north of Lake Peipus will mop up the enemy in Estonia.'[29]

Cooperation with the infantry, therefore, was to be fundamental to the operation of the panzer groups. Any attempt by the panzer leaders to push ahead and lose contact with the infantry was to be guarded against. The OKH and infantry generals urged that the armoured spearheads be held back during the initial breakthrough, which would be left to the infantry divisions, in order to conserve the strength of the panzers for the exploitation phase. The OKH deployment directive had stipulated: '4th Army will achieve the crossing of the Bug and thereby will open the way to Minsk for Panzer Group 2.'[30] They also wanted the panzer groups to be subordinate to the infantry armies. The panzer generals, however, would not agree. Guderian recorded that they 'knew from experience in France what happens. . . . at the critical moment of success the roads are covered with the endless, slow-moving, horsedrawn columns of the infantry divisions, and the panzers as a result are blocked and slowed up.'[31] Finally, a compromise was agreed on: one or two infantry corps would be placed within each panzer group for the initial attack, and the panzer groups in their turn would be subordinated to an infantry army commander for that period. In the exploitation phase, it was proposed that neither of these conditions would apply. The panzer groups would, however, have to maintain contact with the rest of the army, as laid down in the OKH directive. But this compromise solution did little to allay the tension between the panzer and the infantry generals. In his diary, on 14 March, Halder wrote: 'Panzer Group 3 and [9th] Army not yet perfect. Feel for operational requirements lacking here. Army headquarters evidently cannot assert itself over commanding-general of panzer group [Hoth] and is reluctant to place any infantry units under the command of the panzer group.'[32] And on 19 March: 'Points brought out at conference between Army Commander-in-Chief and panzer division commanders: close control of divisions by corps . . . protection of rear communications . . . close teamwork with infantry.'[33] And, lastly, on 27 March: '. . . 9th Army and Hoth will need direct orders to get them to team up infantry divisions with panzer divisions in the jump-off.'[34] Until the end of the campaign, the panzer commanders were to complain that they were tied too closely to the slower infantry armies; independence of action was not to be theirs.

The so-called 'panzer groups,' therefore, began the invasion emasculated. Only one, Panzer Group 4 in the north, was independent of control by an infantry army, even though a panzer group with its additional infantry divisions was comparable in its size to an army. Of the forty-eight divisions that composed the four groups, eighteen, over one-third, were ordinary infantry formations, one more than the total number of panzer divisions. Thus, the panzer group of 1941 was less an expression of the armoured idea than had been von Kleist's group more than a year previously.

But matters for the rest of the Army were little better. As for the invasion of the west in 1940, so for the invasion of the east in 1941: the state of the German Army was far from that required by the rigours of mobile warfare. That is not to say, however, that in the previous year there had not been a number of changes. Hitler's first idea, expressed in May 1940, even before Dunkirk was taken, was for a peacetime army in which half the 'active' divisions were to be either armoured or motorised infantry. The fall of France did not bring peace, and the Führer's intention became divided between the need to defeat Great Britian, primarily by sea and air, and his desire to attack Soviet Russia, mainly by land. Consequently, on 13 July 1940, even before he had reached his final decision to invade the east, Hitler initiated a new programme of armaments, designed to take account of the conflicting requirements of the two objectives. Production was diverted from the Army to the Luftwaffe and the Navy, so as to take care of the short-term offensive against Britain; the Army was to be reduced to 120 divisions, but at the same time its relative composition was to be altered in preparation for a mobile war. In May 1940, of the 153 divisions in the Field Army, sixteen, one-ninth, were motorised; the new plan called for thirty out of 120, one-quarter, to be motorised. This was to be achieved by increasing the number of panzer divisions from ten to twenty, and the motorised infantry divisions from six to ten. Furthermore, all infantry divisions were to be given organisation and equipment levels similar to those in the First Wave. This was confirmed on 18 July, at a meeting of the Reich Defence Council, which placed the expansion of the mechanised forces and the programmes for synthetic rubber and tyres on 'Priority level No. 1,' together with production of bombers and U-boats.

Yet almost as soon as he had decided on this programme, Hitler began to repent it. Even the same day he initiated it, 13 July, he told Halder that twenty of the thirty-five divisions earmarked for disbandment should be merely sent on prolonged leave. In the event, only seventeen divisions were disbanded by the end of August, three from the Third Wave, the nine of the Ninth Wave, and the four fortification divisions. The nine infantry divisions of the Tenth Wave had never been formed, and all intention to do so was abandoned. On 31 July Hitler reversed his decision of the 13th; to the 120 divisions needed for the invasion of the Soviet Union, no less than a further sixty would be required to garrison the west and Scandinavia so as to secure Hitler's Europe from Great Britain. The new target was 180 divisions. Once again, because of Hitler's impatience and military naïvety, numbers were regarded to be of greater importance than quality. Spring 1941, the date set for 'Barbarossa,' dictated both the pace of events and the nature of the invasion force. No fewer than eleven panzer divisions and four motorised infantry divisions were formed; one infantry division was added to the Seventh Wave; three mountain divisions and five more Waves were established: ten divisions were formed for the Eleventh Wave; six for the Twelfth; nine for the Thirteenth; eight for the Fourteenth; and fifteen for the Fifteenth. In addition, four light divisions (not with tanks, as before, but designed to be as independent as possible of motor transport) and nine security divisions were instituted. In the course of this expansion, nine divisions of the First Wave, together with one of the Second and one of the Third, were transformed either into panzer or motorised infantry divisions, one division of the Second Wave became classified as a formation of the First, and three divisions of the Third Wave (one of which was reactivated after its disbandment in summer 1940) became security divisions. The result of all this was that, by June 1941, the German Army consisted of 162 infantry and mountain divisions, one cavalry division, ten motorised infantry divisions, twenty-one armoured divisions, and nine security divisions—a total of 203. No fewer than eighty-four divisions had been added to the Field Army, which, with headquarters and 'army troops,' brought its strength to 3,800,000 men. To this must be added the 150,000 men of the Waffen SS, disposed among five divisions—one infantry and four motorised infantry, two of which had been raised since May 1940—and other units, including Hitler's guard formation, the *Leibstandarte*. Thus, there had been an increase of 650,000 in the ranks of the Field Army and Waffen SS since the invasion of the west, roughly an eighteen per cent expansion. The Replacement Army numbered 1,200,000 men, the Air Force 1,680,000, and the Navy 404,000. The command organisation of the Field Army was as follows: four army groups (North, Centre, South, and 'D' (in the west)), thirteen armies, four panzer groups, and fifty-eight corps commands.

This rapid and significant expansion of the Army was not accompanied by any corresponding improvement in quality, however. Indeed, it positively precluded such an improvement. The most serious deficiencies came within the panzer arm. Hitler did fulfil his aim of doubling the number of panzer divisions from ten to twenty-one (one of which was called a light division until August 1941), but the method by which he chose to do it was disastrous. When first he made his decision to raise further armoured divisions, he ordered that tank production should simultaneously be increased to 800-1,000 units per month. The Army Ordnance Office was horrified at the prospect, and informed the Führer that such an output would cost two billion marks and involve the employment of 100,000 skilled workers and specialists, already scarce, and would be detrimental to all other armament programmes. Hitler reluctantly agreed to abandon the proposal, with the result that the average monthly production of tanks rose from 182 in the last six months of 1940 to only 212 in the first six months of 1941. The total stock of tanks rose from 3,420 on 1 September 1940 to 5,262 on 1 June 1941, and, of this latter figure, the Germans considered only 4,198 fit for operational service. Thus, the number of front-line machines had risen by less than one-quarter while the divisions to which they were distributed had doubled; the result was a considerable weakening in the armoured strength of the individual panzer divisions. In May 1940 the strongest panzer division possessed 300 tanks; in June 1941 it had only 199, and the average was even lower. Most armoured divisions in 1941 had around 160, organised in one tank regiment of only two battalions (seven had three), thereby completely reversing the original ratio of tank to infantry within the panzer formations.

Such a meddling with the organisation of the armoured arm was looked on unfavourably by Guderian and the other panzer leaders, who saw the dangers that would result from this artificial inflation of the numbers of divisions. Individual formations were now far weaker than before, and the striking-power of the panzer division was severely reduced. Not only had it insufficient tanks to cover the ground, but, and more important, losses from enemy action and mechanical failure would quickly diminish an already limited armoured strength to an unacceptable low level, and disproportionately so in relation to the non-armoured troops in the rest of the division. Furthermore, an unfortunate inflation in military economics had developed; although the panzer brigade staff had been disbanded, the divisional and regimental staff had been expanded, even though the effective tank strength they administered had been reduced by half. In December 1940, Jodl commented: 'If this great campaign has to be fought soon, then it can be done just as well with twelve panzer divisions as twenty-four panzer brigades, because there won't be any more by the spring [of 1941]. We could thus save a mass of the supporting arms and rear services.'[35]

These effects were not offset by any significant improvement in the quality of the tanks, although there were some gains: by June 1941 the PzKw 35(t) had been phased out of front-line service altogether, PzKw Is and IIs figured less prominently, and there was a higher proportion of PzKw IIIs and IVs. Nevertheless, the fact remains that of the invasion force of 3,332 tanks, 1,156 were the long-obsolete PzKw Is (410) and IIs (746) while 772 were Czech PzKw 38(t)s, which equipped five divisions. In other words, 1,928, four-sevenths of the total, were machines that had never been designed to fight in the panzer divisions and, if the Germans had had their way, would never have been included within their wartime organisation. Only 1,404, three-sevenths, were the PzKw IIIs (965) and IVs (439) that had been designed as early as 1936 to completely equip the Reich's armoured force. Although this was an improvement, however slight, on the situation in May 1940, when just under two-sevenths of the invading tanks had been PzKw IIIs and IVs, it was small compensation for the numerical dilution of the divisions. Furthermore, there had been no significant improvements in the machines themselves, with the result that they went into the field against the Soviet Union armed with the 3.7cm, the short-barrelled 5cm, and the short-barralled 7.5cm guns, which were soon to prove woefully inadequate when compared with the best possessed by the Soviets. No action had been taken on Hitler's order that the 3.7cm gun of the PzKw III should be replaced by the long-barrelled 5cm gun, the short-barrelled variant having been preferred by the Army Ordnance Office.

In the other components of the Panzer division, few, if any, improvements had been made since the campaign in the west. A high percentage of transport continued to be wheeled, and tracks were still a rarity. This was to prove a considerable handicap in a country where only three per cent of the roads were hard-surfaced, and much of the terrain was marshy or liable to be turned into a river after a few hours of rainfall. The armoured personnel carriers, the SdKfz 250 and 251, had made but little impact, and relatively few panzer infantry companies were equipped with them (often no more than three per division). Captured foreign transport entirely equipped one panzer division. Guderian was annoyed that the four new motorised infantry divisions, none of which possessed any tracked transport, took large numbers of the scarce trucks that would have been better used in improving the standard of motorisation of the panzer formations. But even then, three of the ten motorised infantry formations had to be equipped with foreign vehicles, most of them French machines that were somewhat delicate compared with those of German make. The motorisation of the new units, too, took a long time to complete. One month before the invasion of the east, Halder noted: 'We shall be lucky if they [panzer and motorised infantry] get all the equipment through in time; training of the divisions equipped last will be incomplete in any event.'[36] Even more disturbing for the

185

Army as a whole and for the mechanised forces in particular, was the severe shortage of tyres—up to fifty per cent of requirements—and of motor fuel, the stocks of which would permit only the concentration of the invasion force for the attack and its movement in battle for two months. On 13 June, just nine days before the start of 'Barbarossa,' General Thomas reported to Halder: 'Fuel reserves will be exhausted in autumn. Aviation fuel will be down to one-half, regular fuel to one-quarter, and fuel oil to one-half requirements.'[37]

Another indication of the neglect of the mechanised force that was apparent despite the doubling of the numbers of its divisions, lay in the increased use made of the *Sturmgeschütz* (assault-gun). This machine was the brainchild of von Manstein, who envisaged it as a self-propelled, close-support gun for the infantry divisions. It was designed around the same chassis as used for the PzKw III, and mounted a short-barrelled 7.5cm gun within a well-armoured superstructure. The major difference between this machine and a tank lay in its lack of a turret with an all-round traverse, which prevented it from dealing with the unexpected situations that continually occur during attack. Design work was initiated in 1936, and production begun in 1940. For the attack on France and Flanders, three batteries, each of six assault-guns, had been formed, although only one battery was ready for action by 5 May 1940. At the time of the invasion of the Soviet Union, however, there were eleven battalions (each of three batteries) and five independent batteries of assault guns; a total of 250 assault guns, out of a stock of some 390, took part in the initial offensive.

To the panzer leaders, the assault guns were unwelcome. Nor was it simply that these new machines did not behave exactly like tanks; there were more important reasons. First, they objected to the whole principle behind the assault-gun development: that of infantry-support. In effect, the establishment of assault-gun battalions was simply a reversion to the principle of panzer brigades designed to cooperate with the infantry divisions, against which Guderian and his supporters had fought so hard before the war. Second, the assault-guns came under the control not of the panzer arm but of the artillery, which meant that there was now an expanding armoured force that was not subordinate to the panzer command, but was, instead, the protégé of a rival, and a conservative, arm of service—one, moreover, that was ambitious for recognition in the field. Finally, by mid-1941, the output of assault-guns amounted to as much as one-fifth (some fifty per month) of the output of tanks. This meant that scarce production facilities and raw materials were being expended on what they considered to be harmful diversion, instead of being concentrated on building up stocks for the badly equipped panzer force.

In the infantry formations there was some improvement in quality. The experience gained during the campaign in the west, and in subsequent training, had improved the already high standard of individual soldier generally found in the German Army. However, the same old problems still dogged the infantry. Of the grand total of 162 infantry and mountain divisions, thirty-six, well over one-fifth, were not regarded as fit for front-line service. (These were all those from the Thirteenth, Fourteenth, and Fifteenth Waves.) Furthermore, eleven of the best divisions had already gone to form the nuclei of the new mechanised formations. Transport continued to be a major problem; on 1 July 1940 Fromm told Halder that 'the activation of new panzer units required so many vehicles that motor transport columns of infantry divisions will have to cut down further.'[38] Expedients were sought; there was even a scheme to mount whole infantry divisions on bicycles, but this was rejected. On

29 September Halder noted that there were 'not enough motor vehicles on hand even to meet the most urgent minimum requirements of General Headquarter troops. We shall have to economise by curtailing the mobility of divisions of the 13th and 14th Waves.'[39] And on 21 January 1941 his diary recorded that the signal corps alone was under-strength by no fewer than 6,000 vehicles. However, further de-motorisation and strict economies enabled the Chief of the General Staff to state on 5 May: 'Motor transport situation still tight, but better than a year ago (before campaign in the west),'[40] and three days later he noted that units assigned to 'Barbarossa' were only 1,430 trucks and 1,256 cars short on establishment and that they might receive a further 300 and 400 respectively before the onset of the campaign. Of the seventy-nine infantry divisions, almost half were equipped with foreign vehicles. The horse was more prominent than before, so for the invasion of the Soviet Union—although the Army amassed 600,000 motor vehicles (including armoured cars)—it was necessary to rely on no fewer than 625,000 of the animals.

The nature of the infantryman's equipment differed little from what it had been in September 1939. After twenty months of war, the main material difference was slight; it lay in the type of the anti-tank guns. Out of the average of seventy-two in each division, up to and including those of the Tenth Wave, six were now the new 5cm type (not in the Third Wave divisions, which had only 3.7cm guns, or in the Fourth and Eleventh Waves, which had six and nine respectively of the captured Czech 4.7cm versions). Thus, the German infantry still went into the field equipped predominantly with the effective 3.7cm 'doorknocker.' Moreover, although equipment levels for all divisions were now supposed to be based on those for the First Wave, there were a number of discrepancies arising from deficiencies, some of them important. Armoured cars, for example, were found only in the divisions of the First, Second, and Twelfth Waves. Instead of the seventy-five anti-tank guns, the twenty light and six heavy infantry guns, the ninety-three light and fifty-four medium mortars, the thirty-six light and twelve heavy field guns, the infantry divisions of the Thirteenth and Fourteenth Waves possessed only twenty-one anti-tank guns, a few light mortars, and twenty-four light field guns of Czech origin. The Fifteenth Wave had even fewer, their two weak infantry regiments and an artillery battalion between them possessing only thirty-six light mortars and twelve light field guns. The light divisions, also with only two infantry regiments, had forty-seven anti-tank guns, twelve light infantry guns, twenty-one light and twelve medium mortars, and twenty-eight light and eight heavy field guns. Among the other formations up to, and including, the Twelfth Wave, the discrepancies were less well-marked, and a reasonable level of equipment was maintained. Some had fewer anti-tank guns or light infantry guns, others a few more light mortars; all had the same number of field guns, medium mortars, and heavy infantry guns. The only significant difference was in the Sixth Wave, which lacked completely an infantry gun component, and in the Third Wave, whose divisions each had but forty-eight anti-tank guns.

The Army's dependence on the support of the Luftwaffe, and the relative weakness of that support, also needs mention. In Poland, in the west, and in the Balkans, the German Air Force had rendered valuable assistance to the ground forces, first by gaining control of the air, thereby allowing the armies to proceed unhindered by attack from that quarter; secondly, by destroying important parts of the enemy's communications system, thereby inducing a kind of paralysis that Guderian might well have wished had been the result of his own actions; and thirdly, by attacking enemy troop concentrations and fortifications, thereby directly assisting the progress of the field forces. Well though the Luftwaffe had performed these tasks, the Army leaders doubted whether they would continue to do so during 'Barbarossa.' But when, for the first and last time, such misgivings were openly voiced, at the Führer conference of 5 December 1940, Hitler refused to entertain any such doubts. Nevertheless, they remained valid until the end of the campaign. More than any other service at this time, the Luftwaffe had suffered from having to wage a two-front, even a three-front, war. Its responsibilities in the Mediterranean and, far more important, in the west and in the defence of the Fatherland, prevented any concentration of its resources for the campaign in the east. Against the west in 1940 it had been able to marshal 2,750 aircraft; against the Soviet Union in 1941, over a considerably larger geographical area, only 2,770 of a total front-line strength of 4,300 aircraft were available, and of these almost one-third were in need of service and repair.

Then, too, there were the Balkans. Early in the morning of 6 April the German Army moved into south-east Europe. By 2 May, Yugoslavia and Greece had been added to the growing list of Hitler's conquests, and the British had again been humbled. Most important of all, the south-eastern flank had been secured for the invasion of the Soviet Union, and the immediate danger of any air attack on the vital Romanian oilfields from bases in Greece had been removed. The plan that OKH had drawn up so hurriedly, but so well, on 27 March had succeeded totally. As in Poland, the Balkan campaign was one the German Army should have won; it was a direct result of striking with the benefit of surprise and of overwhelming material superiority. The Yugoslav Army, never fully mobilised, was crushed before effective resistance could be mounted; the Greek Army, although prepared, lacked modern armaments, especially anti-tank guns and aeroplanes. Only the British Expeditionary Force in Greece had weapons that were effective against German equipment, but its small size, and the failure of the Greeks to support it, undermined its chances of making a successful stand. The defenders failed to exploit the advantages that the mountainous country and poor roads gave them; instead, two German armies, the 2nd under von Weichs and, more important, the 12th under List, won an easy victory over a weak enemy.

The Balkan operation, quick and efficient though it was, had wider, and detrimental, effects on the forthcoming invasion of Soviet Russia. On 27 March, when the decision was taken to invade Yugoslavia and Greece, the date of 'Barbarossa' was postponed from mid-May; on 7 April an OKH order specified that the opening of the attack would be delayed by four weeks, until mid-June. Not until 17 June did Hitler approve the final date for the invasion; it was to be the 22nd. This, many have argued, imposed a delay on 'Barbarossa' that was to prove fatal and cause the Germans to run out of time during their offensive, bringing them to a halt in a premature, and especially severe, Russian winter; but for this, Moscow would have been taken. However, it seems clear that a postponement would have been necessary, Balkans or no, entirely because of the weather. The spring in east Europe had been especially wet, and the ground had suffered as a result. Von Greiffenberg, then Chief of Staff to 12th Army, remembered:

'East of the Bug-San line in Poland, ground operations are [always] very restricted until May, because most roads are muddy and the country generally is a morass. The many unregulated rivers cause widespread flooding. The farther one goes east the more prounouned do these disadvantages become, particularly in the boggy, forest regions of the Rokitro (Pripyat) and Berezina. Thus even in normal times movement is very restricted before mid-May. But 1941 was an exceptional year. The winter had lasted longer. As late as the beginning of June, the Bug in front of our army was over its banks for miles.'[41]

To the north, conditions were just as bad, heavy rain still continuing to fall there during early June. Therefore an attack before the middle of that month would probably have been out of the question in any case; the weather, which in 1940 had been so favourable to the Germans, was in 1941 to become their worst enemy.

The real disadvantage resulting from the Balkan campaign arose out of the diversion of formations from the build up in the east to the south-east. The problem lay not with 2nd Army in Yugoslavia, because six of the nine divisions were replaced in the east by OKH reserves, so that the infantry employed there became in effect the new reserve for 'Barbarossa.' Moreover, all the fighting divisions had been withdrawn from Yugoslavia to the east by the end of May. The situation, though, was very different for 12th Army in Greece, which had disposed of fourteen divisions, nine of them earmarked for the east—five panzer, two motorised infantry (one of them Waffen SS), and two infantry divisions. Although losses in men and equipment had been extremely small, the wear and tear on engines, especially those of the tanks, was significant and no doubt contributed to the high rate of mechanical failure experienced during 'Barbarossa.' Furthermore, the long return journey from Greece to the assembly areas in Poland imposed such delays that two panzer divisions and Hitler's motorised guard formation failed to join Army Group South by the time of the invasion. As a result, von Rundstedt's force lacked about a third of its armoured strength—two of the intended seven divisions—for its initial attack and their loss was sorely felt. Von Kleist later remembered: 'It is true that the forces employed in the Balkans were not large compared with our total strength, but the proportion of tanks employed there was high. The bulk of the tanks that came under me for the offensive . . . had taken part in the Balkan offensive, and needed overhaul, while their crews needed a rest. A large number of them had driven as far south as the Peloponnese, and had to be brought back all that way.'[42]

Two other effects, both long-term, resulted from the Balkan campaign. First, the airborne-led invasion of Crete towards the end of May, although a success, proved very costly in terms of the lives of the attackers and the destruction of their transport aircraft. It also had the effect of discouraging Hitler from attempting any further large-scale airborne operations, although there were many occasions in the forthcoming months when their use on the Eastern Front might have proved invaluable. Secondly, after the occupation of the Balkans, the necessity to guard its coasts and fight the partisans, especially in Yugoslavia, caused the Wehrmacht to expend a not inconsiderable part of its scarce resources in that area. The struggle against the guerilla fighters remained a constant drain on the Germans until the end of the war. By mid-1943 no fewer than fifteen divisions were stationed in the Balkans, and by mid-1944 this number had risen to twenty-five—one-sixth of the total committed to the invasion of the Soviet Union three years previously.

Nor were the Balkans the only area of Europe in which German formations found themselves. In the preceding months Hitler had been anxiously pressing for greater security along the coast of 'Fortress Europe'; when the invading armies crossed the Soviet frontier on 22 June, in addition to the seven divisions in the Balkans, there were eight in Norway, thirty-eight in the west, two in the Fatherland, one in Denmark, and two, both armoured, in North Africa. Thus, of the 208 divisions of the German Field Army and Waffen SS, fifty-eight, one-quarter, were committed elsewhere than in the east. Although just over half of these formations, thirty in all, were infantry divisions of the Thirteenth, Fourteenth, and Fifteenth Waves, not regarded as fit for front-line service, their very existence caused scarce-trained manpower, munitions, equipment, transport, and fuel to be used in areas other than Soviet Russia. The Army was short enough of these resources to resent every corporal and petrol-can that was not allocated to the invasion force.

Much has been made by historians of the Germans having underestimated the Soviet strength when planning 'Barbarossa.' Some have even gone so far as to call it 'the basic error.' Certainly, the initial estimate of the Red Army formations available in European Russia made by the Abwehr in late July 1940 was low—ninety infantry and twenty-three cavalry divisions, together with twenty-eight mechanised brigades. In August, the estimate was increased by six infantry divisions, and it was on this revised figure that operational planning began. It was known that the rest of the Soviet army, some fifty-five infantry divisions, eleven cavalry divisions, and ten mechanised brigades, was in the Far East, protecting Siberia from Japanese incursion, and even if they were sent to the west on the German invasion they would arrive too late to affect the outcome. The German victory, after all, was expected to take little more than two months, and the destruction of the Soviet western forces would be achieved within the first few weeks. Further intelligence reports provided for increases in the German estimates, so that by 30 January 1941, the day before the OKH deployment directive was issued, the Germans believed that the Soviets disposed of 121 infantry and twenty-five cavalry divisions and thirty-one mechanised brigades in western Russia, a total as accurate as it was then possible to obtain.

The quality of this force was an unknown factor, but the Germans thought it to be low. Hitler referred to the Soviet forces as a 'clay colossus without a head,' but added that 'the Russians should not be underestimated, even now.'[43] Stalin's recent purge of his officer corps, which had meant the execution of thirteen of fifteen army commanders, had left the Red Army with a dearth of experienced leadership, and the Germans believed that this had been openly displayed during its disastrous Winter War against Finland in 1939. Equipment, too, was thought to be numerous but obsolete, as, indeed, was true. Of 24,000 tanks (the Germans estimated 10,000), only twenty-seven per cent were in running order, and only 1,475 were superior to the German machines. (These were the T34s and KVIs, of which the Germans had no knowledge.) Many of the divisions were under-strength—the mechanised formations, for example, had just half their complement of tanks—and the whole Red Army was in the process of reorganisation. The disposition of the units in the west was bad, most of them being fairly close to the frontier behind an only partially completed defence line; not one of them was in its tactical position on 22 June. The strategic doctrine of the Soviet Army was fairly crude, based on the concept of vigorous attack or counterattack whenever possible. The plans for the use of armour were confused, some of the tanks being grouped into organisations similar to panzer divisions, while others were distributed in 'penny packets' in support of the infantry.

In mid-June 1941, immediately before the invasion, there was a significant reappraisal of Soviet numerical strength. German intelligence now believed that Russian forces in the west were composed of 154 infantry and twenty-five and a half cavalry divisions, and thirty-seven mechanised brigades, an increase of almost one-quarter over the previous assumption. These figures were probably near the truth, and it dismayed the German military leaders but little. They believed that their 136 divisions, together with those of their allies, could still defeat the enemy. The reasons for this belief were several: the superior quality of the attacking force, both in terms of equipment, training, and tactical and strategic background; the considerable advantage of achieving initial surprise; and the soundness of their invasion plan that would create the conditions by which victory would be gained before the onset of winter. However, there was one aspect of Soviet military organisation of which the Germans took no account—the highly efficient, and ruthless, Soviet mobilisation machinery. This was to succeed in putting more than a million men in the field before July was out. In this, the Osoaviakhim, a national military organisation which had thirty-six million members, thirty per cent of whom were women, played a great part. Thus, although the Germans would kill and capture some seven and a half million Red Army soldiers before the onset of winter—losses that would cripple a European country—the Soviet machine could still produce more.

Nevertheless, it would be wrong to ascribe the German failure to recognise this as the, or even a, major mistake when planning 'Barbarossa.' The magnitude of the Soviet Union's reserves of manpower, and its ability to put them under arms speedily, was not in itself sufficient to defeat the Wehrmacht. Had the German plan succeeded, and had there been a quick occupation of the Soviet Union's key industrial and armament-producing areas in European Russia following on the destruction of her original western armies, it would matter little how many men could emerge from Asiatic Russia. Without sufficient modern armaments, with the industrial area of the Urals bombing range, and denied the communications centre of Moscow, they would have posed little threat to their enemy. Time, not the underestimation of Soviet strength, was the vital factor for Germany. If the advancing armies could achieve, at least, the line Leningrad-Moscow-Rostov before the winter made further movement impossible, before the divisions from the Far East could move west, and before the Soviet mobilisation machinery could produce too many field formations, victory would indeed be possible. But should they fail to reach these objectives, then the divisions from the Far East would arrive, the new formations from the depots would move into the field in ever-increasing numbers, and the Soviet factories would continue to churn out equipment and munitions. Then the Germans, far from home, would face defeat as they stood fighting during a savage winter for every inch of Russian soil, exhausted after several months of campaigning, their supply-lines overstretched, and their losses mounting. Time was of the essence of success, and victory would be won or lost by the soundness, or otherwise, of the German operations.

7

'Barbarossa'—The Campaign

On 22 June, a door opened before us, and we didn't know what was behind it. . . . the heavy uncertainty took me by the throat.

ADOLF HITLER

The greatest land war in recorded history began at 3.30 a.m. on 22 June 1941, the day after the 129th anniversary of Napoleon's attack on Russia in 1812. Halder began his diary entry for the day with the words: 'The morning reports indicate that all armies (except the 11th) have started the offensive according to plan. Tactical surprise of the enemy has apparently been achieved along the entire line.'[1] But beneath this calm, confident attitude lay disquiet. The generals were clearly awed by the magnitude of the task that lay ahead. Fourteen days earlier, with a trace of foreboding, the Chief of the General Staff had written: 'The imposing vastness of the spaces in which our troops are now assembling cannot fail but to strike a deep impression.'[2]

The initial German front was 995 miles long, and there was another 620 miles along the Finnish border. The main front would soon expand to 1,490 miles, and extend to a depth of over 600 miles. Into this great space of steppe, forest, and swamp marched the best of the German Army, amounting to threequarters of its field strength; by the end of the year, 3,500,000 Red Army soldiers were in captivity, and 4,000,000 had died in battle. At one time the Germans occupied some 900,000 square miles of Soviet territory. It had been an historic campaign, a remarkable achievement. But at the same time 'Barbarossa' was a significant failure for German arms. Only one of the objectives, the occupation of the Ukraine, had been achieved, and that only partly; for the rest, the Red Army had not been destroyed, Leningrad had not been reduced, and Moscow had remained Soviet. The plan of operations had proved incapable of meeting with reality. Who was responsible for this failure?

Certainly it was not the staff of the OKW. Warlimont remembered that: 'The Operations Staff of Supreme Headquarters was entirely on the touchline. General Jodl was never once invited either as a visitor or as an observer to the large-scale war-games that the Army Staff held in the autumn of 1940, nor, as far as one knows, did he make any attempt to play any important part in the planning. . . .'[3] Instead, OKW contended itself merely with collating reports for the daily briefings of Hitler, communicating the Führer's desires to the three service commands, establishing contact with Germany's allies, drawing up the time-table for the invasion build-up, and undertaking detailed studies and plans for the economic exploitation of occupied areas of the Soviet Union. The OKW was clearly the Führer's creature, and if he gave it no task to perform, it did nothing. Moreover, it was not the body to question Hitler's decisions. In August 1940 Keitel had presented a memorandum opposing a two-front war, the arguments of which the Führer bluntly refuted; Keitel then tendered his resignation, but it was not accepted . He later recalled:

'Hitler harshly rejected this: did he then have no right to inform me if in his view my judgement were wrong? He really would have to forbid his generals to go into a huff and ask to resign every time somebody lectured them, and in any case *he* had no chance of resigning his office either. He wanted it understood once and for all that it was nobody's right but his to relieve a person of his office if he saw fit, and until then that person would just have to put up with the job; during the previous autumn, he said, he had had to tell Brauchitsch the same as well.'[4]

From that time on, Keitel unhesitatingly and unquestioningly carried out his Führer's wishes. When, a few months later, General Thomas submitted a gloomy report on the dire logistic and economic position of the forthcoming invasion, the Chief of OKW, although no doubt sympathising with its contents, told him that 'the Führer would not allow himself to be influenced in his planning by such economic difficulties,'[5] and there exists no evidence as to whether he passed the report on to Hitler. Jodl, although preferring to deal with Great Britain before embarking on the Soviet Union, and despite his doubts about the economic basis for a war in the east, made no effort to influence his Führer once the decision to invade had been taken. Certainly there is no reason to believe, as is often asserted, that he made any attempt to suggest to the Führer the idea that Leningrad should be the primary objective of the operation. He, like Keitel, existed during the planning and invasion merely as a functionary.

Nor was the responsibility of either Luftwaffe or the Navy Commands any greater than that of OKW. The Luftwaffe was primarily a tactical instrument of war designed to support the Army in the field, and its leaders appeared content to remain passive, ordering their deployment to the requirements of the ground forces. Göring, despite his subsequent protestations to the contrary, does not seem to have questioned either the necessity for, or the possibility of, conquering the Soviet Union; Raeder, on the other hand, until December 1940 openly maintained a critical attitude to Hitler's ideas, and consistently advocated a grand strategy for the Mediterranean and Middle East. However, as the Navy was to play only a minor role in the eastern campaign, the naval staff took but little part in the operational planning. The Army reigned supreme among the services, and it made no attempt to foster any cooperation except for the barest essentials. Commensurate with their traditional predominance in the field of operations, the generals drew up lines of march, allocated units to armies, armies to sectors, organised logistical support, and generally ensured the thorough preparation of every military aspect of the invasion. But important though that work was, the Army leaders were unable to determine the two fundamental elements upon which strategy is based: time and space. It was the Supreme Commander, Adolf Hitler, who alone decided to which objectives the armies would advance, and how long they would take to achieve them, both before and during the campaign. It was here that the fatal error lay.

This is not to absolve the generals of all responsibility for the failings of 'Barbarossa.' Both OKH and Hitler were over-confident from the beginning; both failed to realise that Germany might not emerge victorious before the onset of winter, and thus overlooked the adequate provision of special equipment and clothing; both underestimated the strain that the long distances, the rough communications, and the difficult terrain would have on the poorly mechanised, inadequately supplied German Army; both ignored the strengths of the Soviet military system and overestimated the capabilities of their own; and both rejected any use of the principles of the armoured idea, at the same time reaffirming the dominance of traditional German strategy. Independence of action, speed, and the defeat of the opposing forces by means of command paralysis were disregarded in favour of their opposites—cooperation between infantry and mechanised divisions, secure flanks and the annihilation of the enemy by means of double envelopment, and a battle on an inverted front. If at any time the Army leaders consciously recognised these failings, they omitted to make their objections known to their Supreme Commander.

For the fundamentals of the plan, however, for its allocation of time and space, Hitler must bear full responsibility. On only one aspect was he in agreement with his generals: that the Soviet forces should be destroyed west of the Dvina-Dnepr rivers. For the rest, there was intense conflict, although it was not to come into the open until the middle of the campaign. The Army planned a grand encirclement operation in the south; Hitler abandoned it in favour of a single enveloping thrust. The Army pronounced the Pripyat Marsh to be impassable; Hitler declared that it proved no obstacle. Most important of all, the Army wanted the main effort to be concentrated in the centre, on Moscow; Hitler did not. In praise of the choice of the Army Command, von Manstein wrote:

'OKH . . . rightly contended that the conquest and retention of these undoubtedly important strategic areas [the Baltic, the Ukraine, and the Caucasus] depended first on defeating the Red Army. The main body of the latter, they argued, would be met on the road to Moscow, since that city, as the focal point of Soviet power, was one whose loss the régime dare not risk. There were three reasons for this. One was that—in contrast to 1812—Moscow really did form the political centre of Russia; another was that the loss of the armaments areas around, and east of, Moscow would at least inflict extensive damage on the Soviet war economy. The third, and possibly the most important reason from the strategic point of view, was Moscow's position as the focal point in European Russia's traffic network. Its loss would split the Russian defences in two, and prevent the Soviet command from ever mounting a single, coordinated operation.'[6]

But Hitler had rejected this choice; he had ordered that the primary objectives should lie on the flanks of the invasion, especially on the north. The capital was to him an irrelevance when compared with Leningrad and the Baltic, and with the Ukraine and the Donets Basin. This difference of opinion was to become particularly apparent during the conduct of the campaign. Hitler's choice of objectives took no account of the main advantages possessed by the enemy: the vastness of their country, the lamentable condition of their roads, and the resilience of their mobilisation system. These, the German Army, with its poor state of mechanisation and its rejection of the strategy of the armoured idea, was in any case ill-equipped to overcome. But the dissipation of its efforts to the north and south of the front, and its inability to concentrate from the outset on the single most decisive military objective, the defeat of the Soviet Army in front of Moscow and the occupation of that city, made failure certain. The responsibility for that was solely Hitler's.

The exploits of the panzer arm during 'Barbarossa' were quite remarkable; wherever the German armies advanced, the armoured divisions led the way. There can be no doubt that their fighting qualities contributed significantly to the speed of the German advance. Two examples will serve as illustration: von Manstein's LVI Panzer Corps in Army Group North covered no less than 185 miles in the first four days, and Guderian's Panzer Group 2 advanced 270 miles from Brest-Litovsk to Bobruysk in the first seven, achieving seventy-two miles on the last day. But such thrusts were not the decisive factors of the campaign; the great battles of encirclement and annihilation, in which the armoured groups were but the spearheads of the mass of the army, dominated the progress of the German ground forces. Indeed, it was a strategy that yielded spectacular results. In the seven great *Vernichtungsschlachten* of Bialystok-Minsk, Smolensk, Uman, Gomel, Kiev, on the sea of Azov, and Bryansk-Vyazma, the Red Army lost around 150 divisions and a large portion of its armoured strength. These seven encirclements resulted in the capture of more than two and a quarter million soldiers and ended with the destruction or capture of 9,327 tanks and 16,179 guns. In a further thirteen minor battles of encirclement, another 736,000 Soviet soldiers were made prisoner and 4,960 tanks and 9,033 guns were captured or destroyed. Thus, in twenty encirclement operations, almost three million men, 14,287 tanks and 25,212 guns fell into German hands; and these figures take no account of the large numbers of Red Army soldiers killed at the same time.

In the first stage of the campaign, the most decisive battles were undertaken in Belorussiya by Army Group Centre. Two closely-linked encirclement operations were planned: one, by the 4th and 9th infantry armies, was to destroy the enemy divisions in the 150-mile long Bialystok salient, the weakest point in the Soviet line which gave the Germans an ideal chance to mount a pincer operation similar to that used against the Polish forces in western Poland in 1939; the second, spearheaded by Panzer Groups 2 and 3 in conjunction with 4th and 9th Armies, was to close its jaws 100 miles further east, outside Minsk, thereby catching any enemy formations escaping into the interior of Russia. By such manoeuvres, it was expected to destroy thirty-six Soviet divisions, including ten armoured formations. At first there were delays. Hoth's Panzer Group 3 experienced difficulties in crossing the heavily wooded and virtually trackless terrain, and found initial enemy resistance to be tough. Armour and infantry were concentrated on the few routes available, and close contact with the mass of the army resulted in delays to the panzer spearheads. (On one occasion, one of the panzer divisions was halted for several hours by a column of several thousand lorries belonging to the Luftwaffe.) Hoth's group did not reach the River Nieman, only forty miles beyond the German border, until midday on the 23rd, some thirty-two hours after the advance had begun. To the south, Guderian's Panzer Group 2 experienced difficulty arising from the continued resistance of the border fortress of Brest-Litovsk, which did not fall to units of 4th Army until the fourth day of the attack; congestion resulted from this blocking of a main crossing of the river Bug, and the deployment of the panzer group was adversely affected. By midday on the 26th Hoth had managed to reach a point eighteen miles to the north of Minsk, and that afternoon von Bock ordered Guderian to make contact with his fellow panzer leader and thereby close the jaws of the pincer, which he did the next day. However, it was not until 3 July that resistance inside the cauldron was effectively over. Then, the final count revealed that thirty-two infantry and eight tank divisions had been caught within the Bialystok-Minsk pocket. Some 324,000 soldiers were captured, and 3,332 tanks and 1,809 artillery pieces taken or destroyed.

Success though this may have been, it gave rise to much tension between the commanders involved. As in 1940, the old question arose: how far were the armoured spearheads to advance before halting to consolidate their front and flanks, and were they to wait to be relieved by the fast-marching infantry divisions? In the first days of the campaign, the same fears and hesitations that had been so fatal the previous year were exhibited. On 24 June Hitler, fearing that Soviet troops might break out of the Bialystok pocket to the east, had told von Brauchitsch that the armoured encirclement was not tight enough; Halder noted: 'The same old song! This won't change our conduct of operations.'[7] The next day the Führer repeated his concern in written form; again the Army leaders took no notice. Guderian later wrote: 'He [Hitler] wanted to halt the panzer groups and turn them against the Russians in and about Bialystok. On this occasion, however, the OKH proved strong enough to insist on adherence to the original plan. . . .'[8] On the same day, the 25th, Hitler's Wehrmacht Adjutant, Schmundt, arrived at the headquarters of Army Group Centre to attempt to persuade von Bock to close the pincers at Novogrudok, some seventy-five miles nearer the German border than Minsk. This suggestion was stubbornly resisted.

At the same time as Hitler was pressing for a limitation on the advance of the panzer spearheads, von Bock and Hoth were advocating an extension. On the 23rd, air reconnaissance had reported that Soviet columns were retreating east from the Bialystok salient, and von Bock had become fearful that strong forces might escape the double encirclement. He therefore revived his old idea, abandoned only in May 1941, that Panzer Group 3 should not attempt to close the pincers at Minsk but instead move on 100 miles further east to the Dvina between Vitebsk and Polotsk; meanwhile the infantry of 9th Army could close the northern pincer at Minsk. Thereby, von Bock argued, the Soviet forces would be totally destroyed and the enemy prevented from building a new front on the Dvina river. Hoth, reluctant to lose time by turning in to meet Guderian and begin the inevitable wait for the infantry, agreed entirely with his chief's proposal. But OKH, as firm with von Bock as it had been with Hitler, rejected his request. Halder noted in his diary for the evening of the 23rd:

'In Army Group Centre everything goes according to plan. Hoth has made the farthest advance, whereas Guderian is being checked again and again. This occasions a discussion with the army group as to whether Hoth should continue his drive on Minsk, or had better strike further north for Polotsk. As a matter of fact, von Bock had from the start objected to a joint operation by the two panzer groups in the direction of Smolensk, and wanted Hoth to strike further north. That, however, would have put an almost impassable strip of water and marshland between Hoth and Guderian, enabling the enemy to beat the groups separately.'9

Halder was determined not to allow independent operations; cooperation in encirclement was not to be challenged.

At the same time, tension grew over the continued advance of the panzer spearhead after the closure of the pincers at Minsk. How long should the armoured divisions wait before the marching infantry had caught up with them and consolidated the ground won? Both Guderian and Hoth had pushed on to Minsk with scant regard for maintaining contact with the 4th and 9th infantry armies, under whose command they still came. Von Kluge, commander of 4th Army, uged that the further advance be halted until the cauldron battle was completed and the infantry could release the panzers from their role of securing the encirclement. This, too, accorded with the view of Hitler, who announced that he would agree to the continuation of the offensive to the Dvina and the Dnepr only after the encircled Soviet formations had been rendered sufficiently harmless. The panzer leaders, however, wished to push on with all possible speed towards Smolensk, 200 miles away. Guderian recorded: 'My views concerning the next stage of the operations were as follows: to detach the minimum amount of the panzer group for the destruction of the Russians in the Bialystok-Minsk pocket, while leaving the major part of this operation to the following infantry armies; thus our rapid, mobile, motorised forces would be able to push forward and seize the first operational objective of the campaign, the area Smolensk-Yelnya-Roslavl.'[10] This, too, was the view of von Bock, who, on the 26th, when he had ordered Panzer Group 2 to turn in towards Minsk, also specified that one of its three panzer corps should continue the advance eastwards to Bobruysk, over the Berezina river, a further eighty miles from the panzer spearhead at that time, and ninety miles south-east of Minsk. Guderian had replied that he had already given orders to that effect. On 28 June the corps reached the outskirts of Bobruysk.

Halder, too, was at first in agreement with this course of action. He had committed his view to paper as early as the 24th:

'The time necessary to complete this [the bringing-up of infantry to consolidate the encirclement round Bialystok] will be utilised to allow the units of Guderian's and Hoth's panzer groups to close up on the high ground around Minsk. Meanwhile, strong advanced combat teams can secure the crossings on the Upper Dnepr at Mogilev and Orsha, and on the Upper Dvina at Vitebsk and Polotsk. Continuation of the offensive [thereafter] by the combined panzer groups towards the high ground north-east of Smolensk will be allowed only after consultation with OKH.'[11]

And on 29 June, the eighth day of the offensive, in reference to Hitler's continual concern about the panzer operations, the Chief of the General Staff wrote:

'The Führer's worry that the panzer forces would overreach themselves in the advance has unfortunately prompted the Army Commander at a conference with Army Group Centre to refer to Bobruysk as nothing more important than the objective in a flank cover of the encirclement at Minsk. Guderian, however, quite soundly from an operational point of view, is advancing on Bobruysk with two panzer divisions and is reconnoitring in the direction of the Dnepr; he certainly does that not just to guard his flank but in order to cross the Dnepr as soon as there is an opportunity to do so. Were he not to do that, he would be making a grave mistake. . . . Let us hope that commanders of corps and armies will do the right thing even without express orders, which we are not allowed to issue because of the Führer's instructions to the Army Commander [prohibiting the over-extension of the panzer groups' advance].'[12]

However, it must not be thought that Halder was becoming a convert to the armoured idea. He was careful to stick to the traditional method of strategy; the consolidation of the Minsk pocket remained for him the priority. On the 29th he also wrote: '. . . the outer ring formed by the panzer division is closed, but is still fairly thin, of course. It will take several days before the disposition of our forces . . . can be sufficiently re-organised to allow us to continue the [main] attack towards Smolensk on the dry route Orsha-Vitebsk (not before 4 July).'[13] The next day Halder reaffirmed his allegiance to *Vernichtungsgedanke* by writing: 'Army Group [Centre] must in particular see to it that the infantry forces are brought behind Guderian's and Hoth's panzer groups around the pocket.' To emphasise the dangers of ignoring the principles of this strategy, Halder added: 'In disregard of its orders [Guderian's panzer group] has neglected to attend to the mopping-up of the territory traversed by it, and now has its hands full with local enemy breakthroughs.' On 2 July he noted: 'Guderian is under orders not to withdraw any units from the encircled ring without orders.'[14]

As has already been mentioned, von Kluge was most unhappy at Guderian's further moves eastwards; his priority was the destruction of the pocket to the exclusion of all else. On the 26th he had ordered the panzer group to 'occupy the line Zadvorze (five miles north of Slomin)-Holynka-Zelva-the River Zelvianka, and to hold that line against the enemy advancing from Bialystok [attempting to break out of the pocket].' By the 30th his fears about Russian breakout of the Minsk pocket had still not been allayed. Indeed, as Guderian pointed out, the fierce fighting that continued in the cauldron had:

'. . . made such a deep impression on 4th Army that

they insisted, henceforth, on the pocket being surrounded by strongly occupied and continuous lines. [On 1 July] Field-Marshal Kluge consequently forbade the departure of the 17th Panzer Division [holding the line around the pocket] in the direction of Borisov [over fifty miles on the road to Smolensk] which I had already ordered; he did this despite the fact that the 18th Panzer Division had already reached that town and had secured a bridgehead over the Berezina and that the consolidation of this bridgehead depended to a large extent on the further advance of XLVII Panzer Corps to the Dnepr.'[15]

Nevertheless, orders were orders, and Guderian transmitted von Kluge's command to his troops. But as chance would have it, part of 17th Panzer did not receive the order, and moved on towards Borisov as previously requested. On 2 July Guderian learnt of the error and immediately informed von Kluge's headquarters of the situation. However, such was von Kluge's mistrust of the panzer leaders that he threatened to have Guderian, together with Hoth, the victim of a similar incident, court-marshalled. Von Kluge believed the panzer leaders were conspiring to impose their own conditions on the battlefield, regardless of superior orders. He greatly resented the 'syphoning off' of units eastwards from the Minsk pocket, and only with difficulty did Guderian succeed in persuading him that there was no conspiracy.

On 3 July there came a further blow to the panzer leaders: both the panzer groups of Army Group Centre were placed under von Kluge, and headquarters 4th Army became known as headquarters 4th Panzer Army. The infantry formations of the former 4th Army now came under the command of von Weichs, whose 2nd Army headquarters had previously controlled no troops. The question as to the most efficient way of coordinating the operations of the two panzer groups had been deliberated for some days; Halder noted on 24 June: 'I object to putting Guderian in command of the combined panzer groups.'[16] No doubt OKH was glad to be able to put a strong, conservative general such as von Kluge in a position to control the panzer leaders, whose continual agitation to move east at all possible speed at the expense of consolidating the encirclements was not looked on at all favourably.

A further advance eastwards in the direction of Moscow had been decided on by OKH on 30 June, and Army Group Centre headquarters was told that 'a development of the operations towards Smolensk would be of decisive importance.'[17] The time was ripe for such a move; air reconnaissance had revealed that the Soviets were assembling fresh forces along the Dnepr from Mogilev to Smolensk, and, as Guderian later remarked, 'If the line of the Dnepr was to be captured without waiting for the arrival of the infantry, which would mean the loss of weeks, we would have to hurry.'[18] The next day, 1 July, OKH issued the orders for a further advance to begin on the 3rd. The new objectives were Yelnya on the Desna river for Panzer Group 2, and the region north of Smolensk for Panzer Group 3. The 2nd and 9th armies were to follow the armoured spearheads with all possible speed. The aim was the destruction of the growing Soviet forces on the Dnepr, and the acquisition of the Orsha-Vitebsk-Smolensk triangle, so vital to any continued advance on to the capital.

Accordingly, on the 3rd the general advance eastwards was resumed. Already, thanks to the impatience of Hoth and Guderian and the earlier acquiescence of Halder, a number of armoured units had moved beyond the Minsk pocket; on the right wing, the panzer corps that had crossed the Berezina at Bobruysk on 28 June was already on the way to the Dnepr at Rogachev, which it was to reach on the 4th. Another of Guderian's three corps had secured a bridgehead over the Berezina at Borisov. Units of Hoth's group were also on the way towards the Dvina around the area of Polotsk. Nonetheless, although 4th Panzer Army was well-placed to continue the attack, the fact remained that, by the 3rd, more than six days had elapsed since the armoured pincers had closed at Minsk, and only a further ninety miles had been covered in that time—and then not as part of a general advance but only as the action of individual corps. Such was the delay necessitated by *Vernichtungsgedanke*.

This pause at Minsk was unfortunate for the panzer force. The six days had allowed the Soviets to bring up troops and form some kind of defense against the attackers. On 2 July the formations that had been digging-in along the upper Dvina and upper Dnepr came under the command of Marshal Timoshenko, a martinet who was determined to stiffen Soviet resistance. Furthermore, the day the German advance to Smolensk began, the weather broke, turning the sandy tracks into rivers of mud, and the soft earth into swamp. Von Blumentritt recorded the conditions under which the advance was undertaken:

'It was appallingly difficult country for tank movement—great virgin forests, widespread swamps, terrible roads, and bridges not strong enough to bear the weight of tanks. The resistance also became stiffer, and the Russians began to cover their front with minefields. It was easier for them to block the way because there were so few roads. The great motor highway leading from the frontier to Moscow was unfinished—the one road a westerner would call a "road." . . . Such a country was bad enough for the tanks, but worse still for the transport accompanying them—carrying their fuel,

213

their supplies and all the auxiliary troops they needed. Nearly all this transport consisted of wheeled vehicles, which could not move off the roads, nor move on it if the sand turned into mud. An hour or two of rain reduced the panzer forces to stagnation. It was an extraordinary sight, with groups of them strung out over a hundred-mile stretch, all stuck—until the sun came out and the ground dried. Hoth . . . was delayed by swamps as well as bursts of rain.'[19]

Guderian's and Hoth's five corps attacked over a front of 200 miles, which the latter likened to the fingers of an open hand rather than the clenched fist it should have resembled. The reason for this sprang directly from the requirements of *Vernichtungsgedanke*; Guderian and Hoth were both obliged to advance in the same direction with their individual main objectives less than fifty miles distant from each other (Yelnya and north of Smolensk). The spread in the individual panzer groups themselves was due to the need to protect the flanks of the attacking force which, even before it had reached its objective, would, in part, halt to secure the pocket and become vulnerable to enemy counter-attacks made possible by the delay at Minsk. Hitler's interference also had its effect; the very day the advance resumed Halder privately committed his answer to the Führer's worrying to his diary: '. . . from the tactical point of view there is of course some sense in this worry about the flanks. But that is what the army and corps commanders are there for. Our commanders and staff are our strong point, but at the top they have no confidence in them because they have no conception of the strength represented by a body of commanders all of whom have been trained and educated on the same principles.'[20] Fearing the build-up of enemy forces on the weak line between Army Groups North and South. Hitler directed that Hoth keep one of his panzer corps out along the boundary. Thus, momentum was sadly dissipated and, as Hoth later argued, the broad-front advance on Smolensk became a prime example of how armoured warfare should not be conducted.

Von Kluge remained true to form and held the advance in check when it appeared to him that his panzer leaders were straining at the leash unduly. Guderian later remembered that 'What delayed us most during that time was the hindrance resulting from the doubts of Field-Marshal von Kluge. He was inclined to stop the advance of the panzers at every difficulty arising in the rear.'[21] On 9 July Halder wrote: 'Appearance of a strong and still-growing enemy group between Orsha and Vitebsk has prompted an order from 4th Army headquarters to Panzer Group 2 to put off planned attacks temporarily and instead take over cover of the left wing against enemy attacks and assure contact with Panzer Group 3.'[22] Von Kluge only reluctantly agreed to Guderian's proposal to cross the Dnepr with the panzers before waiting for the infantry divisions, which were then just arriving at the Berezina, to come up. Again von Kluge insisted that the panzer groups hold the ring around the enemy until relieved in force by the infantry, and he appears to have been not over-zealous in forcing the pace of the marching formations, which were, admittedly, tired after covering so many miles from the border, fighting for much of the way. It was not until the 16th that weak advanced-infantry units reached the Dnepr, seven days after they had arrived at the Berezina, a distance of seventy miles to the west. Not until the 20th did the infantry begin to relieve the panzer units east of the Dnepr from their task of holding the Soviet units within their bridgeheads. Guderian, who had reached the objective of Yelnya, was then keen to push on further to the east, but von Bock reminded him of his first duty: to secure the Smolensk pocket. On the 21st, when Guderian had ordered one of his panzer divisions, then on flank protection, to spearhead an attack to close the encirclement and to link up with Hoth, von Kluge intervened and without informing the panzer leader told the division to stay where it was so as not to weaken the almost-formed ring around the enemy. As a result the pocket was not closed until several days later, when Hoth succeeded in doing so from the north.

Consequently, the advance from Minsk to Smolensk had not been a spectacular affair. It took fourteen days, from 3 to 16 July, for Smolensk to be reached, a distance of 150 miles from the position of the foremost panzers on the first day of the attack, and another nineteen, until 5 August, for all resistance within the pocket to be finally subdued. Panzer Group 2 did not cross the Dnepr, some seventy miles from the Berezina, until the 10th and 11th, and was not able to close the jaws of the pincer east of Smolensk until the 26th, by which time large numbers of the enemy had escaped eastwards. Guderian did not occupy Yelnya and the surrounding area, his objective, until 20 July, which meant that his average rate of advance was less than twelve miles a day; in comparison, Minsk had been reached after an average of forty miles a day. However, the Smolensk pocket yielded a rich haul: 310,000 enemy soldiers were taken prisoner, and 3,205 tanks, together with 3,120 guns, were destroyed or captured.

Again, as at Minsk, there had been a considerable delay at Smolensk between the time the panzer divisions reached their objective and the time they were free to continue their advance. The only difference was that at Smolensk the enemy opposition was so fierce, and the control of higher command so great, that no syphoning-off of the mechanised forces eastwards was possible; all their energies were needed to guard the pocket, to attempt to close the pincer, and to ward off strong counter-attacks from the Soviet forces attempting to relieve their encircled comrades. Such was the strength of the resistance that on 30 July the enemy mounted no fewer than thirteen attacks on the Yelnya bridgehead over the Desna. Not until 27 July were there enough infantry divisions of 2nd Army east of the Dnepr to make the German positions there secure, and even then they had come not to relieve Guderian's force, but to reinforce it. Von Kluge, fearing a Soviet breakout to the south, appeared obsessed by the need to retain the enemy troops within the pocket to the exclusion of all else, even to the extent of ignoring the severe enemy pressure on the flanks to the east and south-east, especially at Roslavl. Thus from 20 July until 1 August, Army Group Centre was effectively on the defensive. No further advance was possible.

Once again, then, the requirements of *Vernichtungsgedanke* imposed a delay on the motorised forces. But as the time approached when the panzer troops would be ready to resume the advance eastwards, fresh orders came making such a course of action impossible. On 27 July Guderian had flown to Army Group Centre headquarters, expecting to be told to begin preparations for the push towards Moscow, or at least to Bryansk (some 100 miles south-east on the Desna, a possible objective during a further encirclement operation in the direction of the capital). However, he was mistaken and, to his surprise, 'learned that Hitler had ordered 2nd Panzer Group . . . to go for Gomel in collaboration with 2nd Army.' This meant that, instead of continuing east or south-east, the panzer spearhead would be swung round some 130 degrees to move in a south-westerly direction 150 miles from Smolensk towards Germany. Guderian wrote:

'. . . Hitler was anxious to encircle the eight to ten Russian divisions in the Gomel area. We were informed that Hitler was convinced that large-scale envelopments were not justified: the theory on which they were based was a false one put out by the General Staff corps, and he believed that events in France had proved his point. He preferred an alternative plan by which small enemy forces were to be encircled and destroyed piecemeal and the enemy thus bled to death. All the officers who took part in this conference were of the opinion that this was incorrect: that these manoeuvres on our part simply gave the Russians time to set up new formations and to use their inexhaustible manpower for the creation of fresh defensive lines in the rear area: even more important, we were sure that this strategy would not result in the urgently necessary, rapid conclusion of the campaign.'[23]

Halder, too, was horrified by Hitler's proposal. He wrote on 26 July:

'Such a plan implies a shift of our strategy from the operational to the tactical level. If striking at small local enemy concentrations becomes our sole objective, the campaign will resolve itself into a series of minor successes which will advance our front only by inches. Pursuing such a policy eliminates all tactical risks and enables us gradually to close the gaps between the fronts of the army groups, but the result will be that we feed all our strength into a front expanding in width at the sacrifice of depth, and end up in position warfare.'

His words were prophetic. He continued:

'The Führer's analysis, which at many points is unjustly critical of the field commanders, indicates a complete break with the strategy of large operational conceptions. You cannot beat the Russians with operational successes, he argued, because they simply do not know when they are defeated. . . . it will be necessary to destroy them bit by bit, in small encircling actions of a purely tactical nature. . . . following such a course implies letting the enemy dictate our policy and reduces our operations to a tempo which will not permit us to reach our goal, the Volga. . . . To me, these arguments mark the beginning in the decline of our initial strategy . . . and a willingness to throw away the opportunities afforded us by the impetus of our infantry and armour.'[24]

The campaign was barely a month old when Halder wrote these words. He was correct; under Hitler, even the traditional strategy of decisive manoeuvre was being bastardised and emasculated.

Guderian immediately proposed, 'regardless of what decisions Hitler now may take,' to ignore the Gomel operation and instead to attack Roslavl, thereby 'to dispose of the most dangerous enemy threat to [the] right flank,' and capture 'this important road centre [that] would give . . . mastery of the communications to the east, the south, and the south-west.'[25] Von Bock agreed, provided the six extra infantry divisions asked for, and made Guderian independent of von Kluge by taking his command away from 4th Panzer Army and retitling it *Armeegruppe Guderian*. At the same time a number of panzer divisions were to be withdrawn from the front line and given a few days for rest and maintenance. Furthermore, the Yelnya salient, although it was proving costly to maintain because of the fierce Soviet attacks and the supply problems resulting from its considerable distance (450 miles) from the nearest major railhead, was to be retained. By these measures a situation would be brought about whereby the advance to Moscow could be resumed. The generals' hope was that Hitler would change his mind.

On 1 August the panzers and infantry began the attack on Roslavl; by the 3rd the town was taken, and by the 8th all resistance was eliminated. Some 38,000 prisoners had been taken, and 250 tanks and 359 guns destroyed or captured in what was one of the swiftest and most complete German victories in the east. With the right flank secure, and the road to Moscow before them, the panzer spearhead of Army Group Centre was prepared to resume the advance east by mid-August. Von Bock, Hoth, and Guderian were in complete agreement on this point. Hitler, however, told these officers on 4 August that he had not yet deceided on whether the next objective would be Moscow or the Ukraine. Guderian nevertheless 'decided in any case to make the necessary preparations for an attack on Moscow.'[26] In the event, it was more than seven weeks before his panzers moved again in that direction.

To the north, the advance until early August had been spectacular in terms of distance covered, though not in numbers of prisoners taken. In the first four days von Manstein's panzer corps alone had covered 185 miles on the route to Leningrad, which then lay only 340 miles distant. By 14 July, the twenty-third day of the campaign, the 'Cradle of Bolshevism' was only sixty miles from the foremost panzer spearhead of Panzer Group 4, while the 16th and 18th Armies had cleared most of the Baltic States. An average daily advance of eighteen miles had been achieved. No great battles of encirclement had taken place and, to all intents, it appeared as if Army

Group North's sector was witnessing the type of warfare so urgently desired by Hoth and Guderian in the centre. Indeed, the later comments of General Charles de Beaulieu, the Chief of Staff to Panzer Group 4, appear to support this:

> 'The Commander-in-Chief of Army Group North . . . was confronted with a very different enemy employment than that facing Army Groups Centre and South [which] . . . were faced by Russian forces deployed on a wide shallow front line, with a strong concentration in the great Bialystok salient which positively invited a large-scale encircling movement. . . . But in the north the Russian deployment in the recently occupied Baltic countries, though much looser, was in much greater depth. Their reserves stretched right back into the territory of the old Russian Empire, and a large reserve of Soviet tanks was even located to the east of Pskov [more than 300 miles from the border]. At no point, therefore, did a strategy of encirclement appear feasible. Nevertheless, such a grouping on the part of an enemy still unprepared at the time should have enabled the Germans to surprise the opposition in depth and destroy it piecemeal—but for this an essential condition was superiority of speed and mobility, so that after every partial engagement a deeper and quicker thrust could be made by the attackers.'[27]

This was borne out in von Leeb's army group order of 5 May 1941, which concluded: 'Forward! Don't stop for anything. Never let the enemy consolidate once he has been thrown back.'[28]

But however clearly expressed was the intention for the deep armoured thrusts, practice, tempered as it was by inexperience in handling the panzer formations and by cautious military doctrine, was somewhat different. The first realisation of what was to happen came when a bridgehead over the Dvina at Dvinsk was gained by von Manstein's LVI Corps on 26 June. His corps was isolated 185 miles from the border, the rest of the general advance being some sixty miles distant to the west. But, as von Manstein recalled, he and his officers:

'. . . were less exercised by our present rather isolated position, which would not continue indefinitely, than by the problem of what the next move should be. . . . Instead, our enthusiasm was dampened by an order to widen the bridgehead around Dvinsk and keep the crossings open. We were to wait for XXXXI Panzer Corps and the left wing of 16th Army to move up. . . . While this was certainly the "safe," staff-college solution, we had had other ideas. As we saw it, our sudden appearance so far behind the front must have caused considerable confusion among the enemy. He would obviously make every attempt to throw us back across the river, fetching in troops from any quarter to do so. The sooner we pushed on, therefore, the less chance he would have of offering us any systematic opposition with superior forces. If we pushed on towards Pskov—while, of course, continuing to safeguard the Dvina crossings—and if, at the same time, Panzer Group headquarters pushed the other panzer corps through Dvinsk behind us [instead of fifty miles north up the river, as had already been ordered] it seemed likely that the enemy would have to keep on opposing us with whatever forces he happened to have on hand at the moment, and be incapable for the time being of fighting a set battle. As for the beaten enemy forces south of the Dvina, these could be left to the infantry armies coming up behind. It goes without saying that the further a single panzer corps—or indeed the entire panzer group—ventured into the depths of the Russian hinterland, the greater the hazards became. Against this, it may be said that the safety of a tank formation operating in the enemy's rear largely depends on its ability to keep moving. Once it comes to a halt it will immediately be assailed from all sides by the enemy's reserves.'[29]

Von Manstein was right; as his panzers remained stationary around their bridgehead, the Soviet counter-attacks increased in intensity and frequency, and when, after the sixth day of the halt, the advance began again, enemy resistance had hardened. Von Manstein made the following comment:

'A tank drive such as LVI Panzer Corps made to Dvinsk inevitably generates confusion and panic in the enemy communications zone; it ruptures the enemy's chain of command and makes it virtually impossible for him to coordinate his counter-measures. These advantages had now been waived as a result of [the] . . . decision . . . to consolidate on the Dvina. Whether we should now be fortunate enough fully to regain that lead over the enemy was doubtful, to say the least. Certainly the only chance of doing so lay in the panzer group being able to bring its forces into action as an integrated whole. As will be seen, however, this is precisely what it failed to do. . . .'[30]

From the beginning of the campaign the tactical grouping of Army Group North's forces was far from ideal. Panzer Group 4 possessed only two panzer corps, XXXXI and LVI, and both were sent forward on parallel lines of advance without even a division in reserve. A dissipation of limited armoured strength was thus brought about, further worsened by von Leeb's concept of future operations. He believed that his first task was to destroy the enemy in the Baltic region, and only then to occupy Leningrad. Therefore he proposed that Panzer Group 4 should advance as the apex of a wedge aimed at Lake Ilmen, 125 miles south-south-west of Leningrad, while 18th Army cleared the Baltic States, and 16th Army the area between the panzer group and the army group's boundary. Hoepner, however, disagreed with this. Von Leeb's proposed advance meant that the motorised formations would have to move through an area devoid of roads and covered by forest and swamp. Moreover, the panzer leader contended that Leningrad must be the first objective, and that the armoured thrust should therefore be between the Peipus and Ilmen lakes on the direct route to the city. A compromise was then arrived at, one that satisfied Hoepner not at all. Von Manstein's LVI Panzer Corps was to advance through Novorzhev towards Lake Ilmen, while XXXXI Panzer Corps would move via Ostrov to Leningrad. Hoepner appealed to OKH, but no help came from that quarter. Halder noted in his diary for 28 June that 'the objectives were of course dependent on the directives which we had not yet issued, but which were certainly overdue.'[31] Not until 9 July would firm orders come from the Army Command; meanwhile, the advance was resumed on 2 July along the lines of von Leeb's compromise.

At first all went well with the renewed attack, due in no small measure to the surprise inflicted on the Soviets by the double thrust of Panzer Group 4. Halder noted on 8 July: 'The infantry armies are pressing on in rapid marches on a wide front and with great depth, with their advanced combat teams following closely behind the armour.'[32] Von Manstein, however, remained sceptical, for he feared the marshy and impenetrable terrain beyond the old Soviet frontier, seventy-five miles east of the Dvina. His misgivings proved correct, and after a week of inconclusive fighting any idea of a further advance through the wooded swamps towards Novorzhev had to be abandoned. On 9 July LVI Panzer Corps was accordingly diverted to Ostrov, through which XXXXI Panzer Corps had already passed five days earlier on its way to Pskov, seventy miles north, which it reached on the 8th. There XXXXI Panzer Corps rested. Now that the two parts of the panzer group were more or less reunited on the same line of attack, von Manstein 'hoped for a rapid, direct, and uniform advance on Leningrad. . . . this offered the best chance not only of effecting the quick capture of the city but also of cutting off the enemy forces retreating through Livonia into Estonia before 18th Army. The task of safeguarding this operation on its open eastern flank would have had to devolve on 16th Army as it moved up behind Panzer Group 4.'[33] It was not to be. On 7 July von Brauchitsch had approved Hoepner's plan for a bold armoured stroke on Leningrad, with XXXXI Panzer Corps proceeding directly through Luga, on the river of that name and more than 100 miles from Pskov, and LVI Panzer Corps executing a flanking movement to approach the city from the east via Lake Ilmen in order to break the line of communications between Moscow and Leningrad. Von Manstein commented: 'Important though this latter task was, these orders must once again have led to the two corps becoming widely dispersed, as a result of which each was liable to be deprived of the necessary striking power. The danger was increased by the fact that much of the country to be crossed this side of Leningrad was marshy or wooded and hardly suited for large armoured formations.'[34]

The advance began on 10 July. The XXXXI Panzer

Corps immediately ran into trouble with the terrain which, on the route to Luga, was dense forest and marsh. Progress was less than seven miles a day, and on the 12th it was decided to switch the line of advance from Luga to the area of Sabsk, 100 miles north up the Luga river, where the ground was more suited to mechanised forces. Any idea of waiting for the arrival of the infantry—the only type of soldier that was of any use in the forests and swamps—was rejected by the panzer leaders and von Leeb; the idea of a fast, armoured thrust on Leningrad, decided upon on 7 July, still held good. By 14 July, XXXXI Panzer Corps had established two bridgeheads over the Luga near Sabsk; Leningrad was only sixty miles distant, across relatively easy terrain, and few enemy troops were in a position to put up any stiff resistance. Hoepner prepared for his final drive, which he reckoned could begin on 20 July. He was confident that the city could be occupied.

Again, von Manstein was unhappy about the new line of advance for XXXXI Panzer Corps. It meant that the two panzer corps were separated by more than 100 miles of nearly impenetrable wooded swamp, and there was no opportunity for mutual support. The infantry were still miles behind. The LVI Panzer Corps, moving slowly, found itself even more isolated and coming under increasing enemy pressure. Hitler, too, was growing more and more concerned. He had taken considerable interest in the tactical moves on the northern front, and Keitel had acquired the habit of telephoning or telegraphing a daily list of 'Führer worries' to army group headquarters. On 11 July the Chief of OKW had informed Halder that Hitler was worried lest Panzer Group 4 in its race to Leningrad should lose contact with the infantry, although on the same day the Chief of the General Staff noted: 'Hoepner has made some frontal advances; and now, with the infantry divisions arriving from the rear having replaced the armour on his flank, he is concentrating his forces northwards.'[35] Hitler later expressed great concern at the large gap between the two panzer corps (as also, on 14 July, did Halder). Thus, Army Group North was told to halt Hoepner's advance on the Luga; Halder complained at the time that Hitler's uninformed interference in such matters was becoming intolerable. On 19 July Hitler issued Directive No. 33, which contained the following: 'The advance on Leningrad will be resumed only when 18th Army has made contact with Panzer Group 4, and the extensive flank in the east is adequately protected by 16th Army. At the same time Army Group North must endeavour to prevent Russian forces still in action in Estonia from withdrawing to Leningrad.'[36]

Furthermore, such was the Führer's failure to allot priorities and his desire to do everything all at once, even with insufficient resources, that he denied the panzer group the infantry support it so urgently required in the marshy, forested terrain where mobility was limited, and where wheels that sank in mud became a liability. Because of the shape of the Baltic region allocated to Army Group North, the further east the invaders moved, the longer became their front. Moveover, whereas the army group was advancing north-east towards Leningrad, its neighbour, Army Group South, was moving due east in the direction of Moscow, with the result that it was becoming increasingly difficult for the two forces to keep in contact. Hitler, wishing to dominate the Baltic States as soon as possible, kept requiring that more and more infantry divisions of 18th Army should cease supporting Panzer Group 4 and move westwards to clear the region and secure the ports. He expressed the opinion that Leningrad should not be captured until the Baltic States had been cleared of all enemy troops. At the same time he insisted that, come what may, the right flank of Army

Group North should be kept in close contact with Army Group Centre, and even give support to it if necessary. Thus, nearly sixty per cent of 16th Army's strength was committed to the south flank, with the result that LVI Panzer Corps was left virtually unsupported. The terrain and the opposition combined to slow down the advance and severely deplete the material resources of panzer corps. Not until the 22nd July, when the LVI Panzer Corps had the support of an infantry corps from 18th Army, did Soltsy fall. It had taken von Manstein twelve days to cover the ninety miles from Ostrov; any further advance was then checked twelve miles west of Lake Ilmen. Von Manstein told von Paulus on 26 July that he was of the opinion that the corps should be taken out of the area where rapid movement was impossible, and instead used against Moscow. The Deputy Chief of the General Staff agreed with him. If not, von Manstein continued, it was vital to have the support of the infantry divisions until the wooded zone was cleared, otherwise the panzer corps would have no strength left for the final attack on Leningrad; he thought the best use of his corps in the north would be to combine it with XXXXI Panzer Corps on the Luga. Von Paulus again concurred wholeheartedly.

The advance of Panzer Group 4 from the Dvina to the Luga had been bedevilled by three factors: the splitting of its force; the bad, at times impassable, terrain on the approaches to Leningrad; and the lack of infantry support. Although Hoepner, supported by von Leeb, had, at least since the crossing of the Dvina, wished for a speedy armoured thrust on Leningrad, and although the Soviet forces were relatively weak, the isolation of the two corps and the forested marshes, through which they were directed, had meant that panzer divisions alone were not enough. The support of the infantry was vital: only they could master the dense, tree-covered marshes through which the bulky tanks could not pass and into which the wheeled transport just sank. But, thanks to Hitler's interference, it was not until the second half of July that this support was given, and then only by two infantry corps—one to XXXI Panzer Corps, the other to the LVI. Army Group North then determined to resume the advance on Leningrad. On Hitler's orders, the XXXI Panzer Corps had been standing only sixty miles from the city since 14 July, and was being subjected to increased enemy pressure. A date for the final attack was set provisionally for the 22nd, exactly one month after the invasion had begun. Hoepner hoped for success; large-scale Soviet counter-attacks were not expected, and the leaders of Leningrad were unprepared for defence. Even had the city not been occupied (Hitler had decided as early as 8 July that it should be only encircled, and then razed to the ground by the Luftwaffe, as this would save supporting the population during the winter), certainly a close encirclement would have been possible one and a half months earlier than actually happened.

However, Hitler's demands, the slowness of LVI Panzer Corps' advance, and the growing doubts about the advisability of a sudden dash by XXXI Panzer Corps, even though reinforced by infantry, led to the postponement of the attack, first until 26 July and then until the 28th. Infantry of the 16th Army were awaited to reinforce von Manstein's force, and Hitler strongly advocated that the bulk of XXXI Panzer Corps should be transferred to LVI Panzer Corps' area, by then around the town of Luga. This, however, was successfully resisted by von Leeb. On the 23rd Hitler had issued his Directive No. 33a, which specified:

'Panzer Group 3 will come under temporary command of Army Group North to secure its right flank and to surround the enemy in the Leningrad area . . . [this] will enable Army Group North to employ strong forces of infantry for an attack in the direction of Leningrad, and to avoid expending its mobile forces in frontal attacks over difficult terrain. . . . Panzer Group 3 is to be returned to Army Group Centre on the completion of its task. The High Command of the Army will plan further operations so that large parts of Army Group North, including Panzer Group 4 . . . may be moved back to Germany.'[37]

On the 30th, this was followed by Directive No. 34:

'In the northern sector of the Eastern Front the main attack will continue between Lake Ilmen and Narva towards Leningrad, with the aim of encircling Leningrad and making contact with the Finnish Army. . . . The intended thrust by Panzer Group 3 against the high ground around Valdi will be postponed until armoured formations are fully ready for action. . . . Estonia must first of all be mopped up by all the forces of 18th Army. Only then may divisions advance towards Leningrad.'[38]

A delay was now inevitable. The attack had already been stayed too long, as von Leeb knew, but there was now only one course left open: to wait for the formations of 16th and 18th Armies to break through the swamp, forest, and ever-growing enemy troop concentrations. The date for the attack was set at 8 August, twenty-five days after the Luga river had been reached. The plan was for two thrusts by Panzer Group 4, one from Luga, the other from the Sabsk area, to converge on Krasnogvardeisk, twenty-five miles from Leningrad, while two army corps would attack from the west of Lake Ilmen towards Novgorod. The main emphasis of the advance would thus be on the right flank, as Hitler wished, in the most difficult of terrain, whereas before it was to have been on the left, where suitable tank country faced the XXXXI Panzer Corps. In the early morning of 8 August, just as the enemy resistance in Guderian's pocket of Roslavl to the south was collapsing, the tanks and infantry of Army Group North moved towards Leningrad. Success was not to greet their endeavours.

Events on the southern sector of the German front were less momentous than those in the north. Von Rundstedt's Army Group Centre faced the strongest concentrations of Soviet troops, for it was at this point, the Ukraine, that Stalin believed any German attack would be mounted. The invaders had disposed of only forty divisions, plus a number of Romanian and Hungarian formations, to face fifty-six, commanded by some of the most able of the Red Army generals. The offensive capacity of von Rundstedt's force had been weakened by the allocation of units to the Balkan campaign, and further limited by Hitler's decision not to agree to OKH's proposal to mount a strong offensive movement from Romania, through ideal tank country. This, when allied with an attack from southern Poland, would have allowed a deep, double encirclement of the Soviet formations in the Borislav-Przemyśl salient similar to the advances around the Bialystok salient and beyond, to Minsk. Instead, the weak German and Romanian forces in Romania, devoid of armoured formations, did not even attack for the first seven days of the campaign but remained passive, safeguarding the vital Ploiesti oilfields and taking care not to provoke a Soviet counteroffensive. After the week had elapsed, an advance into the Ukraine and down to the Black Sea to Odessa was undertaken. The German weight in the south, therefore, fell entirely on the northern flank of the Borislav-

Przemyśl salient, where von Kleist's Panzer Group 1, aided and guarded on its left flank by von Reichenau's 6th Army, under whose control it came, moved to Kiev on the Dnepr, some 270 miles from the border, and then turned south-east, following the river so as to secure bridgeheads and encircle the main Soviet forces west of its line of advance. At the same time, von Stülpnagel's 17th Army, on the right flank of the panzer group, moved through Vinnitsa, 130 miles south-west of Kiev, towards the Dnepr. By such means a double encirclement could be achieved, although not, of course, on the same grand scale as might have been possible. Furthermore, unlike the country to the south of the Ukraine, the terrain traversed by Panzer Group 1 and 6th Army was far from ideal for panzer operations; the troops were forced to advance through the woodlands of Galizia and the west Ukraine and the broken swampland south of the Pripyat.

The portents for a quick, decisive encirclement were not good, and the rate of advance of von Rundstedt's force was accordingly slow. On 23 June Halder noted in his diary: 'The situation looks more difficult on Army Group South's sector, because, in abandoning the original plan of operations based on Romania, we have thrown away our best strategic opportunity. We shall have to confine ourselves to probing for the soft spot and then drive an armoured wedge through it as hard as we can.'[39] But the soft spot was difficult to find. Panzer Group 1 and 6th Army experienced great difficulties; Halder wrote on the 25th that they were 'advancing slowly, unfortunately with considerable losses. The enemy on this front has energetic leadership.'[40] By comparison with Hoepner's achievement, the armoured spearhead of Army Group South's advance was poor. Continual Soviet attacks, designed to separate the panzer divisions from the supporting infantry formations, unsuitable ground, and the not-too-dashing leadership of von Kleist combined to produce an average advance of just under ten miles a day until 10 July, by which time Kiev had not even been reached. It took a further twenty-three days, to 2 August, to advance the 130 miles to Pervomaysk in order to meet 17th Army and seal the first encirclement around the Soviets. The *Kesselschlacht*, known as Uman, which ended on 8 August, was, by the standards of Army Group Centre, small. Only 103,000 Red Army soldiers were captured, and 317 tanks and 1,100 guns taken or destroyed. Large Soviet forces still remained to be trapped, especially those south of the Pripyat Marshes with whom 6th Army was having difficulties. Indeed, the diversion of 6th Army in this direction was the only cause for any separation between its infantry divisions and the motorised formations of Panzer Group 1; von Kleist, von Reichenau, and von Rundstedt all took care to maintain contact between the two, a fact which also contributed to the slow rate of advance which averaged only seven miles a day from 22 June until 2 August. So much for the deep, fast thrusts of armoured warfare. In the extreme south, 11th Army and the Hungarians, who began their advance on 1 July, achieved a rate of advance of only eight miles a day through the lonely, hot, wide expanses. It took two months to cross the 400 miles to the Dnepr, a distance that Panzer Group 4 in the Baltic had traversed, through more difficult terrain, in two weeks. The movement, particularly slow even for infantry, was brought about partly by daily cloudbursts, which turned the rich black soil into liquid glue, and partly by enemy action, especially by tank troops.

As in the north and the centre, there was in the south a conflict of attitudes over the handling of the advance. The question as to exactly where the main advance was to reach before turning in to encircle the enemy was considered as early as the eighth day. In his diary,

Halder wrote:

> 'In the next moves, the main objective . . . must
> be to break through the Russian rear positions on
> the line Belokorivchi-Navogorod Volynskij-Mogilev
> Pod-mouth of the Dnestr, without engaging in
> major frontal attacks, and then swing south still
> west of the Dnepr. . . . For this breakthrough
> Panzer Group 1 must be furnished with infantry
> (which apparently were deliberately excluded when
> Panzer Group 1 and 6th Army were separated from
> each other [after the initial advance]).'[41]

On 5 July the Chief of the General Staff noted: 'Chief of
Staff Army Group South sends an interesting situation
estimate. It shows how widely Army Group South, which
has decided to direct its main effort against Berdichev
(non-existent gap in the fortified line), diverges from our
plan (main concentration on the north wing).'[42] In other
words, von Rundstedt proposed a wider, more ambitious
encirclement than OKH were prepared to accept. On the
7th Halder wrote:

> '. . . breakthrough in the central sector of Army
> Group South is under way. . . . Telephone conver-
> sation with General von Sodenstern [Chief of Staff]
> on next moves. The thing tomorrow is to move
> Kleist's panzer group in such a direction that we
> can turn to form an "inner ring" [i.e. a tight
> encirclement] forthwith, resorting to an "outer
> ring" [i.e. a wide encirclement] only if we are
> compelled to do so [i.e. by escape of the enemy east-
> wards]. The trouble is that the further the armour
> penetrates into enemy territory in such a case, the
> quicker our infantry loses contact with them and
> the enemy forces marked for destruction escape in

masses through the resulting gaps.'[34]

Halder was not going to let what had happened at Minsk
be repeated; the field commanders were so ambitious, so
greedy for gains that they forgot such realities, or so he
thought. On the 9th he noted: 'The burning question
now is the further employment of Panzer Group 1. Army
Group [South] states its intention to strike with its north
group (III Corps) to Kiev and with the bulk of the panzer
group to Belaya Tserkov, and then to push in south or
south-east direction.' Now the Führer intervened; all his
fears concerning wide encirclement came again to the
fore. Halder continued:

'In the meantime, the Führer has called up von
Brauchitsch and told him that he wants the
panzer group to swing the elements that have
penetrated to Berdichev [90 miles from Kiev] to the
south in the direction of Vinnitsa, [75 miles to the
south], in order to effect an early junction with
11th Army. At the evening situation conference
this leads to an agitated exchange about the
direction in which Panzer Group 1 ought to be
moved. My standpoint is as follows: We must on no
account ignore Kiev. There is so much evidence of
enemy confusion that chances of taking Kiev by
some sort of surprise thrust look good. [He added
that the armour must not be risked if it was
impossible to achieve surprise.] . . . Thus the ring
to be formed will run from Berdichev through
Belaya Tserkov and to the sector of 11th Army.
Sealing the ring is the primary objective. Kiev and
Dnepr crossings south of Kiev are secondary
objectives. The Army Commander outlines this
scheme to the Führer. He does not object, but
apparently is not yet converted and emphasises that

he expects nothing from the Kiev operation.'[44]

Thus, OKH and Army Group South were now in agreement about the future moves, but the Führer was unconvinced. At 1.30 a.m. the following morning, 10 July, Hitler phoned von Brauchitsch, the content of his conversation being summed up by Halder:

'He cannot put his mind to rest for fear that tanks might be committed against Kiev and so needlessly sacrificed [it must be remembered that two days previously he had specified that the panzer groups should not advance into Moscow or Leningrad, but instead close round outside them and let the Air Force reduce the cities]. . . . The encircling ring is to run from Berdichev through Vinnitsa to 11th Army. Accordingly the following order goes out to Army Group South: the Führer does not want tanks to be brought to bear against Keiv, beyond what is necessary for reconnaissance and security . . . [only those forces of Panzer Group 1 not needed for Berdichev-Vinnitsa] will strike for Belaya Tserkov and then south [the wider encirclement].'

This was the beginning of a day of frantic activity. At 11.00 a.m. von Brauchitsch recalled his Chief of General Staff from the headquarters of Army Group South to tell him he had heard again from Hitler. This time the Führer, while reaffirming his intention to move south once Zhitomir-Berdichev had been reached, nevertheless granted that, if there were no large bodies of enemy troops to encircle (as von Rundstedt argued), then Panzer Group 1 could attack Kiev. Von Rundstedt believed that the ring through Vinnitsa would be too close and would miss many enemy units; it should therefore go through Belaya Tserkov astride the retreat route to Kiev, then move south-west to link up with 11th Army. If this should prove inadvisable, there were two courses of action left: to advance south-east and south-west of Dnepr, or across Dnepr at Kiev south-east and then east. The Army Commander agreed with this view, which was in effect a compromise between the Führer's two alternatives. Halder wrote: 'The Army Commander will make no decision that would not have the Führer's approval. It is now up to me to get the Führer to agree.' At 11.30 a.m. his diary entry read: '. . . can't get the Führer (sleeping) to the telephone. Tell Keitel need to get as many enemy as possible and that no plan should rely on 11th Army as its capabilities are low.' At 12.30 p.m. '. . . telephone call from OKW. Führer approves proposed plan, but wants to make sure nothing untoward happens on the northern flank of the panzer group [towards Kiev].'[45] At 1.00 p.m. Halder informed von Brauchitsch of the Supreme Commander's views. The argument was over; Hitler's fears were to prove baseless and von Rundstedt's views were to be vindicated. The *Kesselschlacht* of Uman was the result.

8

'Barbarossa'—The Failure

A tactical success is only really decisive if it is gained at the strategically correct spot.
VON MOLTKE THE ELDER
Chief of the General Staff, 1857–1871

When the first phase of 'Barbarossa' ended on 8 August, just over six weeks after the opening of the campaign, the situation on the Eastern Front was as follows: in the north, the Germans were within sixty miles of Leningrad and poised for the attack that might well end with the encirclement of the city; in the centre, two large, and one small, battles of annihilation had been won, and Moscow lay only 200 miles away, under two weeks' advance, with few Soviet forces to oppose the passage; and in the south, the first encirclement battle had just been concluded and the Dnepr was only fifty miles from the main force. The one immediate tactical worry lay in the large concentration of Soviet forces south of the Pripyat Marsh, between Army Groups Centre and South. Everywhere else the

238

enemy was disorganised; roughly one and a quarter million of his troops had been captured.

In the east, the state of the German Army at this time was far from good. By 31 July the Germans had suffered 213,301 casualties, around fifteen per cent of their total invasion force, and had lost 863 tanks through enemy action or breakdown beyond repair, nearly one-quarter of the original number. Replacements could not keep pace with losses. The average strength of the infantry divisions was reduced by twenty per cent, the combat strength of the panzer divisions in Army Group Centre was down by forty per cent, while those in Army Group South were reduced by no less than sixty per cent. The logistical situation was more critical. The shortage of motor fuel was made worse by the fact that the appalling roads and difficult terrain caused the vehicles to consume almost twice the normal quantity. (This was, however, partially offset by petrol captured from the Soviets.) Moreover, the poor quality of much of the transport was becoming evident on the unsurfaced roads; many of the large trucks had proved too heavy, and by late July the high rate of mechanical breakdown and loss through enemy action had reduced motor transport units in Army Group Centre to almost half strength, while in the north some had as many as fifty-six per cent of their vehicles out of action. In the south, von Rundstedt's situation was as bad, if not worse. The reliance on horses, especially on the light, agile Russian breeds, and the small *panje* wagons, became daily greater.

Even more serious was the breakdown in the railway supply system. For Army Group North there was no problem; its relatively small size and the comparatively good rail facilities in the Baltic States ensured that it received the daily average of eighteen trains a day it needed. But for Army Groups Centre and South, the position was critical. It had proved impossible to convert sufficient of the Russian rail-track to the German gauge; Yelnya, the furthest eastern point of Army Group Centre, was no less than 450 miles from the nearest adequate railhead, and 120 miles from a very inadequate one. There was also a shortage of locomotives. Thus, in late July and early August, of the twenty-five goods trains required each day, Army Group Centre received between eight and fifteen, and Army Group South's daily average was only ten. It was thus impossible to replenish losses, let alone build up stocks. The Quartermaster-General's task was made even more difficult by his uncertainty as to where the weight of the attack in the second phase would fall: in the north, as Hitler had originally intended; in the centre, the choice of OKH; or in the south, which was now attracting the Führer's attention? Certainly, Wagner knew that a simultaneous advance on all three sectors would be an impossibility, and that a pause in the attack east, however short, was necessary.

Against this background must be viewed the crucial decision of 1941. Where was the main weight of the second phase of the invasion to lie—north, centre, or south? The view of OKH was that Moscow should still remain the first objective. This had not always been so; for a short period, the early successes had served to turn attention away from the capital. As early as 3 July, when the panzer divisions were beginning their advance from Minsk to Smolensk, the opinion of the Army Command was that victory already belonged to them. Halder wrote in his diary for that day:

'On the whole, then, it may already be said that the aim of shattering the bulk of the Russian Army this side of the Dvina and Dnepr has been accomplished. I do not doubt the statement of the captured Russian corps general that, east of Dvina and the Dnepr, we would encounter nothing more than partial forces, not strong enough to hinder the realisation of German operational plans. It is thus probably no overstatement to say that the Russian campaign has been won in the space of two weeks. Of course, this does not yet mean that it is closed. The sheer geographical vastness of the country and the stubbornness of the resistance, which is carried on with every means, will claim our efforts for many more weeks to come.'[1]

Although the Chief of the General Staff realised that hard fighting still remained ahead, he clearly believed that the pursuit phase of the operation was near at hand: 'Once we are across the Dvina and Dnepr it will be less a question of smashing enemy armies than denying the enemy the possession of his production centres.'[2] Because of the size of the success so far, and because the future appeared not to be in doubt, Halder felt there was less need to capture Moscow immediately than he had previously believed. Other priorities loomed up. As early as 30 June Halder had even suggested to Hitler that armoured formations from the central front could be diverted to the north in order to clear up the situation there before the infantry divisions had completed their concentration in the Smolensk area prior to the attack on Moscow. On 11 July, as Guderian crossed the Dnepr, Halder wrote:

'. . . there is one question which . . . this battle of Smolensk will not settle for us, and that is the question of the enemy's armour. In every instance, large bodies, if not all, manage to escape encircle-ment, and, in the end, their armour may well be the only fighting force left to the Russians for carrying on the war. The [Soviet] strategy . . . would have to be visualized on the basis of operations by two or

241

three major ... groups of armour, supported by industrial centres and peacetime garrisons, and by the remnants of the Russian Air Force.'[3]

Thus a wide-ranging advance might be necessary. The next day he recorded: 'I am not all that wedded to the idea of hurrying the panzer groups eastwards. I can well visualise the necessity for turning considerable portions of Hoth's forces to the north. ... Guderian must turn southwards to encircle the new enemy appearing on his southern wing. ...' Then he added prophetically: '... perhaps to drive down even as far as the Kiev area. ...'[4] Later that day, Heusinger reported to the Chief of the General Staff, who wrote: 'Planning on continuance of operations with the object of preventing a frontal retreat of the enemy and ensuring the destruction of the largest possible enemy force [no mention of Moscow]. The operations are evolved from ideas outlined to me by the Army Commander, and crystallise first of all in plans for a new drive by Panzer Group 3 aimed at liquidating the concentration of twelve to fourteen divisions now opposite von Leeb's right wing.' That evening Halder noted: 'Hoth is getting on well and is expanding his front to the north. In doing so he is anticipating our wishes.'[5] The following day, the 13th, revealed how much the views of Hitler and of OKH were now in accord. Halder's dairy noted the Army's proposal: 'Next objectives. We shall temporarily halt the dash towards Moscow by Panzer Groups 2 and 3, with the object of destroying as much of the enemy strength as possible on the present front.' To this, Hitler replied: 'A quick advance east is less important than smashing the enemy's military strength. The enemy army opposite von Leeb's right wing ... must be attacked from the rear by the motorised forces of Panzer Group 3.'[6]

But OKH's new preoccupation with the north began

before the battle for the Smolensk pocket had really started. Even then, Halder had made the point that 'the prerequisite for either move is that Hoth and Guderian should break into the open to the east and so gain freedom of movement.'[7] Yet as the Smolensk *Kessel-schlacht* grew in intensity, and as it became clear that a breakthrough to the east was becoming increasingly difficult, a note of alarm crept into the deliberations at the Army High Command. On 15 July Halder noted with concern: 'The Russian troops are fighting as ever with wild ferocity and enormous human sacrifice.'[8] Clearly, the Red Army was still not finished; the Germans, on the other hand, were showing signs of weariness. The 'diluted' armoured divisions, especially, were tired. On the 16th Halder wrote:

'The striking power of the panzer divisions is slowly declining. When the current objectives (Smolensk, Leningrad, and Uman) have been reached, a break will be necessary in order to give the units a rest, and, if advisable, to merge and refit several units. Guderian thinks he can do that in three to four days. I believe much more time will be required. The supply system of Army Group Centre will not be functioning at full capacity before 25 July. By that time the panzer groups will again be ready for new operations.'[9]

To Soviet resistance and German tiredness were added the arguments of Army Group Centre, anxious to get to Moscow. On 13 July Halder was told that von Bock 'holds that the chances are very good for our tank spearheads to smash through to Moscow. . . . He objects strongly to detaching forces in a north-easterly direction. . . . All forces must be kept together to strengthen the thrust to the east.'[10]

243

By the middle of July, the elation of earlier days at OKH had turned into gloom. The generals were concerned at the obvious resilience of their enemy and the ever-growing weaknesses of their own troops. The vast distances still to be covered were highlighted by the problems of closing and holding the Smolensk pocket, and by the slowness of von Rundstedt's advance in the south. On 20 July Halder wrote: 'The most visible expression is the severe depression into which [von Brauchitsch] has been plunged.'[11] Then, on the 23 July, OKH issued a memorandum drawn up several days before, which said:

> 'Decisions concerning future operations are based on the belief that once the first operational objectives [Dvina-Dnepr line] . . . have been reached, the bulk of the Russian Army capable of operational employment will have been beaten. [Then it added a note of caution.] On the other hand it must be reckoned that, by reason of his strong reserves of manpower and by further ruthless expenditure of his forces, the enemy will be able to continue to offer stubborn resistance to the German advance. In this connexion, the point of main effort of the enemy's defence may be expected to be in the Ukraine, in front of Moscow, and in front of Leningrad. The intention of the OKH is to defeat the existing or newly created enemy forces, and by a speedy capture of the most important industrial areas in the Ukraine west of the Volga, in the area Tula-Gorkiy-Rybinsk-Moscow, and around Leningrad to deprive the enemy of the possibility of material rearmament.'[12]

The need for further destruction of enemy troops beyond the Dvina-Dnepr line was now recognised, and the area around Moscow was restored at least to parity with Leningrad and the Ukraine. However, in a very few days, new strategic proposals from Hitler, evidence of strengthening Soviet resistance to Army Group Centre's fight for the Smolensk pocket, and further signs of increases in enemy forces, were to lead OKH back to its former position. Moscow was again to become the prime objective; by the 28th Halder was describing its attainment as 'crucial.'[13] This was justified by the old arguments: Moscow was the capital of the Soviet Union, the centre of government and communications, as well as a significant industrial base; and, most important of all, it was before Moscow that the Soviets were expected to commit the major portion of their remaining forces. It was here that the Red Army would be defeated. The brief flirtation by OKH with Hitler's operational objectives was soon over.

Hitler's view on the next objective to be pursued is less easy to comprehend. He was aware of the vital importance of the decision to be taken, and that is perhaps why he took so long in taking it, fearful as ever of committing himself irrevocably. As early as 4 July, when only success was greeting German endeavours, he recognised there were three choices confronting him: to adhere to the 'Barbarossa' plan and ensure the capture of Leningrad; to continue Army Group Centre's successful advance towards Moscow on the basis that Soviet resistance had collapsed speedily, and that Leningrad could be taken by Army Group North alone; or to switch the weight of the attack to the south for an advance deep into the Caucasus, with its oilfields as the strategic objective. In common with OKH at that time, the Führer saw no need to worry further about the Red Army's continued capacity for resistance. As Warlimont wrote: 'Hitler himself stated to his immediate entourage on 4 July: "to all intents and purposes the Russians have lost the war," and congratulated himself on what a good thing it was "that we smashed the Russian armour and air forces right at the beginning." '[14]

Hitler, like OKH, had his head turned by success. On 8 July, the seventeenth day of the campaign, Halder wrote:

'The Führer has in mind the following "perfect solution". . . . Army Group North accomplishes with its own forces the mission assigned to it in the original operational plan. Army Group Centre . . . will . . . open the way to Moscow. Once the two panzer groups have reached the areas assigned to them by the operational plan [of 31 January 1941] (a) Hoth can he halted (to assist von Leeb *if necessary* [author's italics]) or else continue operating in an easterly direction . . . with a view to investing Moscow. . . . (b) Guderian can strike in a south or south-easterly direction east of the Dnepr cooperating with Army Group South.'[15]

This represented a considerable departure from Hitler's previous idea, which placed Leningrad above all else; now he believed that all three objectives in the north, centre, and south could be pursued concurrently.

The views of Hitler and OKH were, for a short time, not dissimilar. Contrary to what had become normal practice, Jodl was concerned to foster this, and attempted to bring OKH into the discussions on the subject. On 5 July he commented: 'Since this decision might be decisive for the whole war . . . it [is] essential that the Army Commander-in-Chief should discuss his views and intentions with the Führer. . . .'[16] The consensus of opinion resulted in Hitler's Directive No. 33, dated 19 July, which read: 'The aim of the next operations must be to prevent any further sizeable enemy forces from withdrawing into the depths of Russia, and to wipe them out.' This was to be achieved thus: in the south, one enemy troop concentration was to be 'quickly and decisively defeated and annihilated by cooperation between forces on the south flank of Army Group Centre and the northern flank of Army Group South. While infantry divisions of Army Group Centre move south-ward, other forces, chiefly motorised . . . will advance south-eastwards' in order to destroy Soviet forces on the east bank of the Dnepr. In the centre, von Bock's army group would continue the 'advance to Moscow with infantry formations and will use those motorised units which are not employed in the rear of the Dnepr line to cut communications between Moscow and Leningrad, and so to cover the right flank of the advance on Leningrad by Army Group North.'[17] A virtual standstill on the central front would be accompanied by reinforced manoeuvres to the north and south.

It might be thought that at this moment OKH had given Hitler, voluntarily, all he wanted concerning the implementation of his 'Barbarossa' plan. Moscow, in direct contradiction of all that the Army leaders had said previously, was now very much a secondary objective. But the Führer was not satisfied. His eyes ranged further afield, and his desire to do everything at once caused him to decide on the inclusion of the Caucasian oilfields as a new objective to be reached before winter. Thus was a further 350 miles added to Army Group South's task. On 23 July, by which time the Army leaders were reverting to their original idea, Hitler issued his Supplement to Directive No. 33 without consultation with OKH. Consensus was at an end. He now proposed to concentrate Panzer Groups 1 and 2 under the command of 4th Panzer Army which, 'with the support of infantry and mountain divisions, will occupy the Kharkov industrial area and thrust forward across the Don to Caucasia.'[18] In the centre, Hitler gave the task of the

247

capture of Moscow to the infantry divisions of Army Group Centre, which would be devoid of armour. Panzer Group 3 would come under the command of Army Group North as already indicated. Once both Moscow and Leningrad had been captured, Panzer Group 3, again under Army Group Centre, might be used for thrusting still further east to the Volga. Once Leningrad had fallen, however, Panzer Group 4 and large parts of Army Group North were to be moved back to Germany.

The Army leaders were aghast at this radical revision of the 'Barbarossa' plan, especially in view of the stiffening Soviet opposition. At once they reverted fully to the advocacy of their first objective: Moscow. Even Jodl had attempted to prevent the adoption of the aim expressed in the Supplement. On the day it was issued, Halder saw the Führer and outlined the views of OKH. But his strong representations had no effect. He wrote in his diary for the 23rd:

'He has decided on his objectives and sticks to them without considering what the enemy may do, or taking account of any other points of view. This means that von Bock will have to give up his armoured groups and move on Moscow with infantry alone. In any case, the Führer right now is not interested in Moscow; all he cares about is Leningrad. This sets off a long-winded tirade on how von Leeb's operation ought to have been conducted and why Panzer Group 3 now has to be thrown into the battle to destroy the enemy at Leningrad. The chief object of the operations is viewed by him in the smashing of the enemy, a task which he believes would probably be accomplished by the time we are abreast of Moscow [at Leningrad and in the Donets Basin]. Subsequently (and into the rainy autumn season) he imagines one could drive to the Volga and into the Caucasus with panzer divisions alone. . . . I hope he is right, but all one can say is that time spent in such a conference is a sad waste.'[19]

Three days later, on the 26th, Halder again tried to convince the Führer of the errors in his views. Hitler, now advocating the Gomel operation, was prepared to hold 'long-winded and sometimes violent arguments with the Army leaders over missed opportunities for encirclement.'[20] Halder's view was that Hitler's plan would not only leave von Bock so weak as to be unable to move on to Moscow, but that it would lead to a front expanding in width but not in depth, and end in static warfare. Hitler, however, simply rejected Halder's arguments regarding the importance of Moscow without producing any real reasons against them. He merely advanced the economic argument—that it was essential for the German war effort to seize the industrial area and coalfields of the Donets Basin, and the oil of the Caucasus.

Whether because of the arguments put forward so strongly by Halder, or the unfavourable reports that were then coming in from Army Groups Centre and North, or a combination of both, Hitler changed his mind once more. On 30 July, Jodl announced to a wary Halder: 'The Führer has arrived at a new conception of the next phase of the campaign.'[21] Later that day, Hitler issued Directive No. 34, which opened: 'The development of the situation in the last few days, the appearance of strong enemy forces on the front and to the flanks of Army Group Centre, the supply position, and the need to give Panzer Groups 2 and 3 about ten days to rehabilitate their units make it necessary to postpone for the moment the further tasks and objectives laid down in Directive No. 33 of 19 July and in the supplement of 23 July.'[22] Now the attack on Leningrad was to take place without the aid of

Panzer Group 3, and operations in the southern sector were to be undertaken only by formations of Army Group South. The operation into the Caucasus was abandoned, and activities were to be limited to the west of the Dnepr. On the central sector of the front, von Bock's army group was to go over to the defensive, the Panzer Groups 2 and 3 were to be withdrawn from the front line and rehabilitated. All at OKH, as at OKW, were relieved. Halder wrote: 'This solution means that all thinking soldiers are now freed from the frightful spectre of the last few days, during which time it looked as if the entire eastern operation would be bogged down as a result of the Führer's stubbornness. At last a little light on the horizon once more.'[23] However, the plan did not go far enough. No mention was made of Moscow, apart from ordering air attacks on the city, and only the vaguest of references was made to further operations on the central front. Apart from advancing north-eastwards sufficiently far to protect the right flank of Army Group North, Army Group Centre was to mount only 'attacks with limited objectives' so as 'to secure favourable springboards for our offensive against the Soviet 21st Army [to the east].' The main emphasis remained on the flanks to the north and south. Halder noted irritably on the 31st: 'OKH issues its implementation order to the last Führer directive. Unfortunately I cannot induce the Army Commander to inject the slightest overtone expressive of a will of his own in this order. Its wording is dictated by an anxiety to avoid anything that could be suspected as opposition to his superior.'[24] As Major von Bredow, the OKH liaison officer, put it to Guderian the next day: 'The OKH and the Chief of the General Staff are engaged in a thankless undertaking, since the conduct of all operations is being controlled from the very highest level. Final decisions have not yet been taken. . . .'[25]

Hitler's mind was clearly not yet at rest. Over the next

few days, the generals' fears grew unchecked. Between 4 and 6 August the Führer visited the headquarters of both Army Groups Centre and South, only to hear a unanimous plea for a resumption of the offensive towards Moscow. But in his comments to the generals, he gave them little hope. Guderian remembered:

'Hitler designated the industrial area about Leningrad as his primary objective. He had not decided whether Moscow or the Ukraine would come next. He seemed to incline towards the latter target for a number of reasons: first, Army Group South seemed to be laying the groundwork for a victory in that area; secondly, he believed that the raw materials and agricultural produce of the Ukraine were necessary to Germany for the further prosecution of the war; and finally he thought it essential that the Crimea, "that Soviet aircraft-carrier operating against the Romanian oilfields," be neutralised. He hoped to be in possession of Moscow and Kharkov by the time winter began.'[26]

Of this conference at Army Group Centre's headquarters, Keitel recorded that Hitler:

'. . . came up against a blank wall of refusal, the two tank generals even going so far as to announce that their units were so battle-weary that they would need two or three weeks to regroup and to overhaul their tanks before they would be fully operational again. Obviously we had no means of checking these claims; the two generals remained uncooperative—despite the award to them of the Oak Leaves to their Knight's Crosses—and refused to admit any possibility of alternative employment for their units, at any rate on such remote sections of the front. Von Bock naturally had no desire to lose them and trumped the same story. All three of them were aware of the [OKH's] ... plan of attack, and saw it as their panacea. ... [it] had electrified them all.'[27]

At this point Jodl, who had long been in sympathy with the Army's desire to advance on Moscow, entered the fray. On 7 August he and Halder had joint talks, 'something which had not happened for as long as anybody could remember,'[28] and on the 10th he presented to Hitler an OKW appreciation of the situation that was in full agreement with OKH. Warlimont recorded that:

'This began by proving ... that the enemy was strongest opposite the centre of the front, and that therefore the most important objective was the annihilation of this enemy grouping, followed by the capture of Moscow. Operations from the centre into the areas of Army Groups North and South were attractive, but must be subordinated to the Moscow decision or postponed to a later date. The attack on Moscow would begin at the end of August, with the infantry divisions in the centre and the armoured groups on the flanks.'[29]

The early capture of Moscow became all the more urgent with the appearance of reports showing large-scale Soviet reorganisation along the central front, which indicated that field fortifications were being built in great depth, behind which mobile reserves were being formed. Halder had commented on 8 August that this enemy policy was a clear break with the past and was 'similar to that pursued by the French in the second phase of the western campaign, that is to form strong islands of resistance ...

which would serve as the backbone of . . . the new defence line.' Time was running out; the only solution was for Army Group Centre to 'concentrate its forces to the last man to destroy the main body of the enemy's strength.'[30] This was reinforced by further estimates of German weakness and Soviet strength. A day earlier, the Chief of the General Staff had been told by Wagner that after 1 October fuel oil and petrol would be in such short supply that a further major offensive would be impossible. On 11 August Halder noted alarmingly:

'The whole situation makes it increasingly plain that we have underestimated the Russian colossus, which consistently prepared for war with that utterly ruthless determination so characteristic of totalitarian states. This applies to organisational and economic resources, as well as to the communications system and, most of all, to the strict military potential. At the outset of the war we reckoned with about 200 enemy divisions. Now we have already counted 360. These divisions indeed are not armed and equipped according to our standards, and their tactical leadership is often poor. But there they are, and if we smash a dozen of them, the Russians simply put up another dozen. The time factor favours them, as they are near their own resources, whereas we are moving farther and farther away from ours. And so our troops, sprawled over an immense front line, without any depth, are subjected to the enemy's incessant attacks. Sometimes these are successful, because in these enormous spaces too many gaps have to be left open.'[31]

Hitler, when he finally made his choice, decided on a compromise. On 12 August, a Supplement to Directive

No. 34 was issued; this was intended to contain the final operational plan. In the north there was to be no change, as it was expected that the attack in progress would result in the encirclement of Leningrad and a junction with the Finns. In the south von Rundstedt's army group was to consolidate its position west of the Dnepr and then cross the river, destroy the Soviet forces on the east side, and occupy the Crimean peninsula, the Donets Basin, and the industrial region of Kharkov. In the centre 'the most important task' became the elimination of 'the enemy flanking positions, projecting deeply to the west, with which he is holding down large forces of infantry on both flanks of Army Group Centre. For this purpose close cooperation . . . between the adjoining flanks of Army Group South and . . . Centre is particularly important.' On the northern flank of von Bock's force the enemy was also to be defeated, and the security of Army Group North's right flank was to be achieved. Hitler continued:

'Only after these threats to our flanks have been entirely overcome and armoured formations have been rehabilitated, will it be possible to continue the offensive, on a wide front and with echeloning of both flanks, against the strong enemy forces which have been concentrated for the defence of the enemy. The object of operations must then be to deprive the enemy, before the coming of winter, of his government, armament, and traffic centre around Moscow, and thus prevent the rebuilding of his defeated forces and the orderly working of government control.'[32]

On the 15th the order was issued for Army Group Centre to go on the defensive; the attack on Moscow was finally abandoned for the time being, to be reopened only after movements to the north and, most important, to the south.

The Army leaders, aware of the far-reaching consequences of this decision, were far from happy at the compromise. On 13 August Halder had written: 'Attack on Moscow by Army Group Centre is approved, but approval is made conditional on so many factors . . . that the freedom of action which we need for the execution of the plan is severely restricted.'[33] Two days later, when Hitler demanded that units from Hoth's panzer group be sent to assist Army Group North which was then coming under enemy pressure at Luga, the Chief of the General Staff noted crossly: 'Once again they [OKW] are making that old mistake that has the result that an audacious thrust by a single Russian division ties up three to four German divisions—such methods are not conducive to success.' Nevertheless, he reluctantly admitted: 'So then, there will be no way of getting round issuing that order for the transfer of a motorised corps to Army Group North. To my mind it is a grave mistake for which we shall pay heavily.'[34]

Feelings among the Army leaders ran so high that they determined to put up a strong resistance such as they had not done since October and November 1939. On 18 August, while the motorised corps was on its way to the north, von Brauchitsch submitted the views of OKH to Hitler in the form of a closely argued memorandum drawn up by the Operations Section of the General Staff under Heusinger. Once again, the Army advocated a decisive thrust to Moscow:

'The distribution of the enemy forces indicates that at the present time, after the annihilation of the enemy forces facing Army Group South [in the battle of Uman], and with the impending successes of Army Group North, the bulk of the intact military forces of the enemy is in front of Army

255

Group Centre. The enemy therefore appear to regard an attack by Army Group Centre in the direction of Moscow as the main threat. . . . The future objectives of Army Groups South and North are, apart from the defeat of the enemy forces confronting them, in the first instance to capture essential industrial areas and to eliminate the Russian fleet. The immediate objective of Army Group Centre, on the other hand, is, above all, the destruction of the strong enemy forces confronting it, thereby breaking down the enemy's defences. If we succeed in smashing these enemy forces, the Russians will no longer be capable of establishing a defensive position. This will create the necessary conditions for the occupation of the industrial area of Moscow. Only the elimination of this industrial area, together with the successes of Army Groups South and North, will remove the possibility of the enemy rebuilding their defeated armed forces and re-establishing them on an operationally effective basis. The decision about the operational objective for Army Group Centre must take into account the following basic points:

(a) The time factor. The offensive by Army Group Centre cannot continue after October on account of the weather conditions . . . we will not be able to push forward with the motorised units on their own without support from the infantry.

(b) Even after refuelling, the motorised units can be effective only over short distances and with diminishing combat strength. As a result, they must be used only for the essential tasks involved in the decisive operation.

(c) The suggested operation can be successful only if the forces of Army Group Centre are systematically concentrated on this single goal to the exclusion of other tactical actions which are not essential for the success of the operation. Otherwise, time and energy will not suffice to deal a decisive blow . . . during the course of this year.'[35]

On 21 August came Hitler's written reply rejecting the Army's proposal, although not answering specifically the points it raised. He argued:

'The objective of this campaign is finally to eliminate Russia as a Continental ally of Great Britain. . . . This objective can only be achieved: (a) through the annihilation of the Russian combat forces; (b) through the occupation, or at least destruction, of the economic bases which are essential for a reorganisation of the Russian forces. . . . In accordance with the initial decision on the relative importance of the individual combat zones in the east, the following are and remain the most essential points: 1) the destruction of the Russian position in the Baltic; and 2) the occupation of the Ukrainian areas and those round the Black Sea which are essential in terms of raw materials for the planned reconstruction of the Russian armed forces. 3) . . . in addition, there is concern for our own oil in Romania and the necessity of pressing on as fast as possible to a position which offers Iran at least the prospect of assistance in the foreseeable future.

As a result of the circumstances which have developed, partly because an order of mine, or rather of the OKW, was ignored, Army Group North is clearly not in a position, within a short space of time and with the forces at its disposal, to advance on Leningrad with a right-flanking movement and thereby to be certain of surrounding and destroying this base and the Russian forces defending it. The situation now demands that Army Group North should be rapidly supplied with the forces which were intended for it at the beginning of the campaign. . . . I hope that the three divisions which are being sent will suffice to enable Army Group North to achieve its objective and to deal with any crises. The cleaning-up and securing of its south-eastern flank can, however, be carried out only by forces of Army Group Centre.'

Only when its objectives had been attained would Army Group North:

'. . . help the advance of Army Group Centre on Moscow. . . . even more important is the clearing up of the situation between Army Group Centre and Army Group South. This is a strategic opportunity such as fate only very rarely provides in war. The enemy is in a salient nearly 300 kilometres long, triangular in shape and surrounded by two army groups. It can be destroyed only if at this time army group considerations are not allowed to predominate but are subordinated to the interests of the over-all conduct of the campaign. The objection that time would then be lost and that the units would no longer be technically equipped for their advance on Moscow is not decisive in view of this opportunity. . . . after the destruction of the Russian forces, which are still threatening the flank of Army Group Centre, the task of advancing on Moscow will not be more difficult, but considerably easier. For either the Russians will withdraw part of their forces from the central front to cover the gap opening up in the south, or they will immediately bring up the forces which are being created in the rear. In either event, the situation will be better than if Army Group Centre tried to advance with the undefeated Russian 5th Army as well as the Russian forces east and west of Kiev acting as a continual threat to its flanks and with the Russians able, in addition, to bring new formations from the rear as reinforcements.'[36]

The next day, the 22nd, Hitler sent a personal memorandum to von Brauchitsch, in which he criticised the Army's conduct of operations and blamed its leaders for the failure of the original 'Barbarossa' plan. The control exercised by OKH had been too loose, he argued, and the Army Commander-in-Chief had allowed his subordinates to have more influence over strategy than was desirable. The result was that the armoured forces in the centre had acted with too great a degree of independence, pushing too far ahead of the infantry, failing to surround the enemy strongly enough, and extending the advance so far eastwards as to threaten the very concept of the operation. Instead of attacking to Yelnya, beyond Smolensk, the panzer groups should have been halted after crossing the Dnepr and have been freed for flanking operations to assist Army Groups North and South, as he had always intended. Instead, the panzers had pushed on, contact with the following infantry had been lost, and many Soviet troops had managed to break out of the weakly held envelopment. After the battle for the Smolensk pocket, neither the time nor the terrain for the vital move north to Leningrad by Hoth's group was favourable. Hitler ended by comparing the Army Commander unfavourably with Göring, and accusing von Brauchitsch of lack of leadership and of not having the necessary grip on operations.

Hitler's criticisms were manifestly unfair. The OKH deployment directive of January 1941, which he had himself approved, had mentioned specifically that 'Army Group Centre . . . will quickly win the area around Smolensk' so as to 'achieve the prerequisites for cooperation between strong elements of its mobile troops and Army Group North.'[37] This is exactly what the Army leaders had done, and no more. At no point during the advance had Hitler dissented from this objective. On 8 July, for example, he had told von Brauchitsch and Halder that the ideal solution would be to leave Army Group North to gain its objective 'with its own forces.'[38] Indeed, in the first weeks of the campaign, Hitler and the Army Command were in unusual accord. Warlimont remembered that Hitler's 'appreciation of the situation . . . agreed generally with that of the Army. Accordingly during these early weeks he did not meddle with the conduct of operations in the east, apart from certain pressure and nagging at OKH to get them to close the great "pocket" [Minsk] more rapidly and securely, and later, just as in the west, being beset by "fear" for the flanks of the armoured thrusts which had driven so far ahead.'[39]

Halder's reaction to Hitler's criticisms of 22 August was immediate and strong. He wrote in his diary for the day:

'In my view the situation resulting from the Führer's interference is intolerable for the Army. These individual instructions from the Führer produce a situation of order, counter-order, and disorder and no one can be held responsible but he himself personally; OKH as now constituted is engaged on its fourth victorious campaign and its reputation should not be sullied by the instructions now received. In addition, the way the Commander-in-Chief has been treated is a scandal. I have accordingly suggested to [him] . . . that he should ask to be relieved of his office and propose that I should also be relieved at the same time.'[40]

At last, Halder had understood that the Führer's usurpation of the Army's operational autonomy had gone too far to bear any longer. His only fault was that he should have resolved upon such drastic action two years earlier, when Hitler had decided how and when the invasion of the west was to take place; it was now rather like shutting the stable door after the horse had bolted. Von Brauchitsch, little more than a man of straw in his master's hands, refused Halder's suggestion, giving the reason, which was probably quite correct, that 'in practice he would not be relieved and that therefore nothing would be changed.'[41] Eight days later, on the 30th, a private meeting between the Army Commander and the dictator took place, when there was a reconciliation which von Brauchitsch maintained cancelled Hitler's insulting memorandum. Warlimont, however, thought otherwise: 'For those who knew the background . . . there can be little doubt that, although for the moment he pretended to imitate it, Hitler took Brauchitsch's chivalrous attitude merely as a sign of weakness and lack of character, and considered the outcome of this encounter simply as another victory over his opponents in the Army.'[42] Halder wrote sarcastically that same day: '. . . the result is bliss and harmony! Everything is just lovely again! Of course, nothing has changed, except that we are now supposed to wait upon not only the Führer but also the Reichsmarschall with separate reports on the railways situation, supply, signal communications, and ground forces replacements.'[43]

While, on 22 August, von Brauchitsch was prepared to submit to the Führer's will, and subsequently confirmed this on the 30th, Halder was determined to make one last attempt to convince his Supreme Commander of the error of his ways. On the 23rd he informed the generals of Army Group Centre of Hitler's decision. Guderian remarked that the Chief of the General Staff 'seemed deeply upset at this shattering of his hopes.' The panzer leaders put forward their reasons why an immediate advance on Moscow was desirable, and Halder, on von Bock's suggestion, decided that Guderian should accompany him to Führer headquarters to put the arguments personally to Hitler. Guderian wrote of the meeting, which took place on the same day: 'I reported at once to . . . von Brauchitsch, who greeted me with the following words: "I forbid you to mention the question of Moscow to the Führer. The operation to the south has been ordered. The problem now is simply how it is to be carried out. Discussion is pointless."' However, during the meeting, at which neither von Brauchitsch nor Halder was present, Hitler himself brought up the subject, and Guderian was able to put forward his reasons, which were listened to without interruption. In reply, the Führer again reiterated the economic importance of the Ukraine, declaring 'My generals know nothing about the economic aspects of war.' Guderian noted that he 'saw for the first time that . . . all those present nodded in agreement with every sentence that Hitler uttered.'[44] Guderian, having failed in his impossible mission, then returned to his command. That night, OKH sent an order to Army Group Centre concerning future operations, the object of which was 'to destroy as much of the strength of the Russian 5th Army as possible, and to open the Dnepr crossings for Army Group South with maximum speed.'[45] The final aim was a grand double encirclement operation, in which the inner jaws would be closed by 2nd, 6th, and 17th armies, and the outer by Panzer Groups 1 and 2. The cauldron was to be 130 miles in width and depth. Once again, the German Army would perform in the classic tradition of *Ver-*

nichtungsgedanke; it was to be the greatest battle of annihilation in history. Four enemy armies were largely destroyed, together with parts of two others. By the time the battle of Kiev was over on 26 September, the Germans had captured 665,000 prisoners and destroyed or taken 884 tanks and 3,178 guns.

The drive south had already been begun by Guderian's group before the decision of 23 August. After the encirclement at Roslavl, one of his panzer corps had continued to Krichev, a few miles to the south, where a further 16,000 prisoners were taken by 14 August. Against his better judgement, Guderian had been ordered by OKH to exploit this success by pushing on to Gomel to destroy the enemy there in cooperation with 2nd Army, in pursuance of Hitler's order of 26 July. The panzer leader commented: 'As I saw it, such a march to the south-west would constitute a step backwards.'[46] However, by 24 August the panzer corps had captured Novozybkov, more than 100 miles south-west of Roslavl, and was well positioned to embark on the advance ordered by Hitler the day before.

From the beginning of the Kiev encirclement, Guderian was bedevilled with interference from higher command. He wished to pursue his advance southwards with all his forces as he alone thought best; he was particularly keen to attack strongly on his eastern, left flank, where the enemy threatened his movements. But Halder, feeling that the panzer leader had given way to Hitler during the meeting on the 23 August, and had therefore betrayed the Army's intention, was in no mood to allow the headstrong Guderian any latitude; OKH would control operations firmly, and contact would not be lost between the panzers and the infantry. As early as the 25th, the Chief of the General Staff wrote in his diary: 'The intention of the panzer group to strike out . . . with its left wing . . . leads too far eastwards. Everything depends on its assisting 2nd Army [to the west] across the Desna and then the 6th Army across the Dnepr.'[47] On the 27th Halder asked Army Group Centre 'not to allow Guderian to run east, but keep him in readiness for the 2nd Army's crossing of the Desna.' Moreover, despite his strong protests, one third of Guderian's force was kept back in reserve for the central sector, then under enemy attack. Again, on the 27th, Halder recorded a message from von Bock: 'Guderian rages, since he fails to make progress because of being attacked from the right and left flanks, and demands reinforcement in the form of the rest of the fast units of his group. Von Bock feels unable to do this. . . . I am of the same opinion and request him not to give way to Guderian. . . . In addition, I ask him to keep a tight rein on Guderian.'[48] The next day, after von Paulus had pleaded the panzer leader's case for the release of the panzer corps, Halder commented: 'I realise the difficulty of the situation. But in the final analysis all war consists of difficulties. Guderian will not tolerate any army commander and demands that everybody up to the highest position should bow to the ideas he produces from a restricted point of view. Regrettably, von Paulus has allowed himself to be caught. I will not give way to Guderian. He has got himself into this fix. Now he can get himself out of it.'[49]

Seldom had Guderian come under such vitriolic attack; OKH had never been firmer in holding out against the pressures of this 'firebrand.' The advance was to be properly conducted according to well-established military principles. The panzer group would not be allowed to overreach itself; it would maintain contact with the infantry; it would adhere to its task of assisting 2nd and 6th Armies instead of pushing the encirclement too far to the east so as to secure its flank; and a mobile reserve would be kept back at the disposal of the army group, to be committed whenever necessary (there might well have been an idea that this panzer corps should be preserved for the advance on Moscow). If, as had happened, Guderian should want to advance in a direction that OKH believed would threaten the coordination of the general advance, no help would be given him to continue to do so. Between 24 and 26 August, when a bridgehead across the Desna was effected, Guderian's foremost panzer corps covered more than eighty miles; in the view of the Chief of the General Staff, he had needlessly overreached himself and exposed his flank. Halder's diary provides a full record of the controversy. For 29 August it contains the following entry:

'Guderian's situation is none too pretty. He is being very hard pressed from the west by enemy elements evading the thrust of 2nd Army, from the east by the newly armed enemy forces, and on top of that has to cope with frontal opposition. And this front consists of only 3rd Panzer and 10th Motorised Infantry Divisions, which are rather far apart at that. It's all Guderian's fault. He devised this plan of attack [a reference to Guderian's meeting with Hitler on the 23rd] and even the most naïve enemy could not be expected to stand passively by while an enemy flank is parading past his front. So the attacks from the east are only what he might have expected. Moreover, with Guderian straining away from 2nd Army instead of keeping close to it, a gap has developed through which the enemy is escaping to the east, that in turn accounts for the attacks against Guderian from the west.'[50]

And on the 31st: '. . . his movements are paralysed. Now

he is blaming everyone in sight for his predicament and hurls accusations and recriminations in all directions. . . . Personal relationships between von Bock and Guderian are increasingly deteriorating. Guderian is striking a tone which von Bock cannot tolerate on any account. He even appeals to the Führer for a decision, so as to get his head. This is unparalleled cheek.'[51]

For his part, Guderian felt that the advance on his left flank should be pursued at all costs, for there, he was convinced, he had found a weak spot, if not a gap, in the enemy's defences; he was not to be tied to an infantry army and thereby forced to give up any idea of exploiting this opportunity. But for success he needed his divisions held back in reserve. His continual pleading for reinforcement began to bear fruit only as late as 2 September, and even then the trickle that was allowed satisfied him not at all. On 1 September he demanded from the Führer that he be sent the whole of his panzer corps kept in reserve, but OKH intercepted his radio call and listened to what he said. This resulted, in Guderian's words, 'in a positive uproar.'[52] On 4 September, Lieutenant-Colonel Nagel, an OKH liaison officer, was even dismissed for daring to advocate Guderian's argument, being described as a 'loudspeaker and propagandist,'[53] and von Bock asked OKH to relieve Guderian of his command. By this time, Hitler, too, was 'very exasperated'[54] with the panzer leader. The consequence was, in Guderian's words:

'A telephone message from army group had informed us that OKW was dissatisfied with the operations of the panzer group and particularly with the employment of XLVII Panzer Corps on the eastern bank of the Desna. A report . . . was demanded. That night an order came from OKH in which it was stated that the attack by XLVII Panzer

266

Corps was to be discontinued, and the corps transferred back to the west bank of the Desna. These orders were cast in an uncouth language which offended me. The effect of the order on XLVII Panzer Corps was crushing . . . [it believed itself] to be on the brink of victory. The withdrawal of the corps and its redeployment on the west bank would require more time than was needed for the completion of the attack.'[55]

As a result of the interference from OKH, von Bock, and the Führer, Guderian found himself forced to conduct the attack south against strong opposition to meet von Kleist with just one panzer corps, the XXIV, spearheaded by a single armoured division, 3rd Panzer. The requirements of the higher commands to maintain contact with 2nd Army on the right, to keep back a corps in reserve, and to refrain from advancing too far on the left, had brought about this absurd situation. On 16 September, when Guderian's group finally met with von Kleist's, the 3rd Panzer Division had but ten tanks left fit for action, of which six were PzKw IIs.

On 23 August Hitler had taken a firm decision to turn his main effort away from Moscow and disperse it to the two ends of the 1,000-mile eastern front, to the Baltic and to the Ukraine. The weary armoured formations of Army Group Centre, just 200 miles from the Soviet capital, were ordered to advance more than 400 miles to the north and to the south, while the equally tired infantry consolidated the front and fought off ever more violent enemy counter-attacks. On 5 September, only thirteen days later, Hitler decided that the emphasis of the German advance should be changed again. In his Directive No. 35 of the following day, he stated:

'Combined with the progressive encirclement of the Leningrad area, the initial successes against the enemy forces in the area between the flanks of Army Groups South and Centre have provided favourable conditions for a decisive operation against the Timoshenko army group which is attacking on the central front. This army group must be defeated and annihilated in the limited time which remains before the onset of winter weather. For this purpose it is necessary to concentrate all the forces of the Army and Air Force which can be spared on the flanks and which can be brought up in time.'[56]

On 19 September the OKH deployment order gave the code-name *Taifun* (Typhoon) to the forthcoming operation towards Moscow.

The planning for Operation Typhoon was undertaken by OKH, in conjunction with Army Group Centre, and was subject to Hitler's approval. The offensive was to be carried out by seventy divisions, of which just under one-third were mechanised (14 panzer and 8 motorised infantry). This was the highest proportion of mechanised units to infantry units ever to be achieved by an attacking force of the German Army in the years of victory. Moreover, efforts had been made to re-establish the panzer groups to full strength, at least in tanks—Panzer Groups 2, 3 and 4 now possessed 50, 75, and 100 per cent respectively of their established tank complements. As a result, 1,500 tanks would spearhead the offensive. However, this did not betoken any conversion to the principles of the armoured idea. Yet again, the panzer groups were to be subordinated to infantry armies; and again double encirclement was seen to be the method by which victory would be achieved. There exists no evidence that a direct thrust to Moscow by the mechanised forces was ever even contemplated. The plan that evolved was pure *Vernichtungsgedanke*. The main operation would take place opposite the capital; there the northern pincer, consisting of 9th Army and Panzer Group 3, would meet the southern pincer, made up of 4th Army and Panzer Group 4, at Vyazma, eighty miles in the Soviet rear and more than 100 miles west of Moscow. Once this was achieved, a second similar operation would invest the enemy capital. To the south, 2nd Army and a part of Panzer Group 2 (or 2nd Panzer Army as it was to be designated after 6 October) would undertake a subsidiary encirclement operation, the pincers meeting at Bryansk, some thirty-seven miles behind the Soviet front, while the rest of Guderian's force would proceed to Tula, 105 miles to the south of Moscow, an advance which not only protected the flank of the main operation, but also put the panzer group in a good position for the subsequent envelopment of the capital. Thus, the attack on Moscow would be undertaken over an initial front of 400 miles, the unusual length being made necessary by the inability of Panzer Group 2 to return any further north by the time the offensive was to begin. The role of Army Groups North and South in 'Typhoon' would be restricted to operations that would secure the flanks of the central advance.

Time was crucial to the whole operation. On the central sector of the front, two relatively dry summer months had passed without any advance at all; indeed, there had actually been a small withdrawal, when on 5 September, in order to save casualties, the Germans had yielded up the Yelnya salient. Now, in the middle of autumn, Hitler proposed to cross the 200 miles to Moscow, in face of stronger enemy opposition, and at a time when the weather did not favour mobile operations. In this part of the Soviet Union, heavy rains usually come in late September or early October, turning the earth and tracks into a sea of mud; at the end of October and in November, frost hardens the ground, and in December snow begins to settle. To an Army equipped to meet these vicissitudes, a wet autumn and a hard winter need not have rendered operations impossible. Only in the most extreme conditions would tracked vehicles be unable to move in mud or in snow; only if denied adequate food and clothing would soldiers be incapable of action in the extreme cold; and only if special preparations, such as antifreeze for vehicle radiators, were not available would transport and guns cease to function in deep winter. But the German Army was not so equipped; tracked vehicles were a rarity; winter clothing was scarce; winter precautions were minimal. All this was made infinitely worse by the lack of any comprehensive system of surfaced roads in the Soviet Union. The effects of rainfall had already been experienced by the Germans from almost the very beginning of 'Barbarossa,' but it was not until early September that the heavy rains began, although intermittently. For example, Guderian recorded of the Kiev encirclement:

'During the whole night it poured with rain. My drive ... on the 11th [September], therefore, proved very difficult. I had covered 100 miles in ten hours, on the 11th eighty miles in ten and a quarter hours. The boggy roads made any faster progress impossible. These time-wasting drives gave me sufficient insight into the difficulties that lay ahead of us. Only a man who has personally experienced what life on those canals of mud we called roads was like can form any picture of what the troops and their equipment had to put up with, and can truly judge the situation at the front and the consequent effect on our operations.'[57]

And yet Hitler and OKH were pinning their hopes of success on good weather in a season not noted for it. Guderian summed it up: 'It all depended on this: would the German Army, before the onset of winter and, indeed, before the autumn mud set in, still be capable of achieving decisive results? . . . Was there still sufficient time . . . to succeed?'[58]

At first all went extraordinarily well. On 30 September, in bright sunshine, 2nd Army and Panzer Group 2 began their advance; by 3 October Guderian had taken Orël, 130 miles in the Soviet rear, and by the 9th he had linked up with 2nd Army to complete the Bryansk pocket. All resistance in the 'cauldron' was eliminated by the 20th. To the north, the main offensive began on 2 October, also in good weather; by 7 October the pincers had met at Vyazma, and the fighting around the pocket ended on the 14th. These two encirclements gave the Germans no less than 673,000 Soviet prisoners, and ensured the capture or destruction of 1,242 tanks and 5,412 guns. Orders for the exploitation of this success were not slow in coming, and on 7 October von Bock had set the next objectives, which included the encirclement, but not the capture, of Moscow. Speed was urged on the soldiers, although, as usual, the mechanised forces were not allowed to push ahead from the pockets until relieved by the infantry divisions. Confidence was high. On the 8th Halder found it possible to write: 'To save Moscow the enemy will try to bring up reinforcements, especially from the north. But any such miscellaneous force, scraped together in an emergency, will not suffice against our superior strength, and, provided our strategy is any good at all (and provided the weather is not too bad), we shall succeed in investing Moscow.'[59]

It was not to be. Even before Halder had written these words, the weather broke. Guderian was the first to experience the consequences, when, on the night of 6-7

October, snow fell on his part of the front. At first it did not settle, but was followed by incessant rain. Guderian wrote: '. . . the roads rapidly became nothing but canals of bottomless mud, along which our vehicles could advance only at snail's pace and with great wear to the engines. . . . The next few weeks were dominated by the mud. Wheeled vehicles could advance only with the help of tracked vehicles. These latter, having to perform tasks for which they were not intended, rapidly wore out.'[60] The supply of the armoured spearheads now became a considerable problem, with which the Luftwaffe, for all its effort, was simply not equipped to deal. Those tracked vehicles that survived the mud were in great danger of coming to a standstill through lack of petrol. By the 28th, Guderian remembered, 'We could advance only as fast as our supply situation would allow. Travelling along the now completely disintegrated Orël-Tula road our vehicles could occasionally achieve a maximum speed of twelve miles per hour.' In response to Hitler's instructions concerning 'fast-moving units,' Guderian noted: 'There were no "fast-moving units" any more. Hitler was living in a world of fantasy.'[61] On average, Guderian's foremost units were now advancing only five miles a day. It was not until mid-October that the weather broke on the rest of Army Group Centre's front, with the same results. Whole divisions came to a halt; thousands of horses died of overexertion; guns and vehicles sank in the mud; troops went without proper rations for days; infantrymen's boots fell to pieces, or were lost in the mire. The attack quickly foundered, and made hardly any progress in the latter half of the month. Moscow lay only fifty miles away, but until the ground hardened it was impassible in the face of ever-increasing enemy opposition. On the 30 October OKH ordered a halt.

The situation in which the German Army found itself was

by far the most critical of the war up to that date. Losses had been high; an OKH assessment of 6 November estimated that the 101 infantry divisions in the east possessed a fighting strength equivalent to sixty-five divisions at full strength, while the seventeen panzer divisions had been reduced to the effectiveness of only six. In all, the combat power of the invasion force of the 136 battered German divisions was now equal to only eighty-three. Only thirty per cent of the trucks were still in working order. Moreover, of the thirty-one supply trains required daily by Army Group Centre, only sixteen were being provided. Fuel was low; reliance on horses was high, and increasing. Winter clothing for the troops was almost completely lacking. Furthermore, because there were only three major approach routes to the capital in von Bock's area of operations, there was considerable confusion in the supply lines of the advancing forces—4th and 9th Armies and Panzer Group 3 all competed for space on two roads, while 2nd Army and Panzer Group 4 shared the other. Against this background, a decision had to be made whether to continue the advance or to retreat. General Fromm even believed it was time to make peace proposals. Others did not go so far as this, advocating rather a move back to the positions the army group had held during the summer months, where some form of a defensive line had been constructed and where the supply of the troops would be considerably easier. There the troops could take up winter quarters, beat off Soviet counter-attacks, re-form, and plan a spring offensive.

The Army leaders, however, took a different view. Von Brauchitsch and Halder were convinced that the Red Army must be at the end of its tether; that one further advance was all that was needed to gain the capital. They argued that the acquisition of the Moscow-Vologda-Saratov line would be decisive. Not only would it mean the loss to the Soviets of any rail communication between the main theatres of operation, the Caucasus, the Urals, and the incoming Allied seaborne aid from the Baltic, it would also deprive the enemy of a main industrial and armament area and so prevent any full re-equipping of his armed forces. Furthermore, because of the area's importance, it was here that the last stand of the Red Army was expected; it was here, therefore, that it would be finally encircled and destroyed. Von Bock, who, like the OKH generals, had always attached the greatest importance to the capture of Moscow, also advocated continued advance. On 13 November a conference was held at Orsha between the commanders and the chiefs of staff of the army groups and the armies subordinate to them. After a discussion, and despite opposition, the order for the resumption of the attack was issued. The objectives were far-reaching: 2nd Panzer Army, for example, was assigned the city of Gorkiy, 250 miles east of Moscow, which led von Liebenstein, the chief of staff, to protest that 'This was not the month of May and [they] were not fighting in France!' Guderian immediately informed von Bock that his panzer army 'was no longer capable of carrying out the orders that had been issued it.'[62] One of his panzer corps, which had an establishment of 600 tanks, had only fifty left. On further protests from von Kluge, who believed that such an advance was a fantasy at that time of the year, von Bock came to share his opinion, saying he believed that it was almost impossible to reach the capital 'in view of the condition of his troops,'[63] let alone to carry the offensive beyond. Because of the importance of attacking before the deep snow fell, a more limited attack aimed directly at Moscow was ordered, even before the Germans had built up their strength.

The Army leaders had taken a bold decision, a gamble that was fully justified by the facts as they knew them.

The Red Army had already suffered catastrophic losses in front of Moscow; the capital lay only fifty miles distant; and the importance of the objective had diminished not at all. Furthermore, the abandonment of the advance after the greatest victory of the campaign—the Vyazma-Bryansk encirclements—and when Moscow was so near, would never have been accepted by the Führer. Success was now a question of one final effort—in von Bock's words, 'the last battalion will decide the issue.'[64]

On 15 November the new offensive opened on the left wing, followed on the 17th by the right wing. The ground had indeed become hard, but the furthest advance was but fifty miles, and that not in the direction of Moscow. This time it was not rain that paralysed the attack; it was the tremendous drop in temperature. Even before the 15th the cold was becoming crippling; on the night of 3–4 November the first frost set in; on the 12th the temperature dropped to –5°F, and the next day to –8°F. Guderian remembered some of its effects: 'Ice was causing a lot of trouble, since the calks for the tanks had not yet arrived. The cold made the telescopic sights useless; the salve which was supposed to prevent this also had not arrived. In order to start the engines of the tanks, fires had to be lit beneath them. Fuel was freezing on occasions, and the oil became viscous.'[65] Vehicles were frozen into the snow up to their axles; when halted, their engines had to be started up every four hours, and their transmissions operated, so that the strain on the metal, made brittle by the cold, was eased. Owing to the lack of antifreeze, some would even freeze while running. Oil became like tar; the plates of vehicle batteries buckled; guns of all types became inoperable as the oil in their recoil systems solidified—only one in five of the tank guns could fire; and the narrow tracks of the German tanks sank deep into the soft snow, giving them a poor performance compared with their Soviet counterparts.

Small arms, too, froze solid; the grenade was the only weapon that retained its efficiency. On 21 November Guderian wrote to his wife: 'The icy cold, the lack of shelter, the shortage of clothing, the heavy losses of men and equipment, the wretched state of our fuel supplies, all this makes the duties of a commander a misery, and the longer it goes on the more I am crushed by the responsibility which I have to bear. . . .'[66] After the war, he remembered: 'Only he who saw the endless expanse of Russian snow during this winter of our misery, and felt the icy wind that blew across it, burying in snow every object in its path; who drove for hour after hour through no-man's land only at last to find too thin shelter with insufficiently clothed, half-starved men; and who also saw by contrast the well-fed, warmly clad, and fresh Siberians [the Soviet reinforcements recently arrived], fully equipped for winter fighting—only a man who knew all that can truly judge the events which now occurred.'[67]

Yet the offensive continued; the endurance of the German soldiers, most of whom were without winter clothing, was magnificent. By 27 November the advanced units of Panzer Group 3 were only nineteen miles from the capital; but the field commanders, quite rightly, were convinced that further advance was impossible. On 29 November von Bock reported to Halder that 'if within a few days they do not force the front north-west of Moscow to collapse, the offensive must be abandoned. It would merely lead to a soulless frontal struggle with an enemy who apparently still had large reserves of men and material.'[65] Two days later he wrote:

'After further bloody struggles the offensive will bring a restricted gain of ground and it will destroy part of the enemy's forces, but it is most unlikely to bring about strategic success. The idea that the enemy facing the army group was on the point of collapse was, as the fighting of the last fortnight shows, a pipe-dream. To remain outside the gates of Moscow, where the rail and road systems connect with almost the whole of eastern Russia, means heavy defensive fighting for us against an enemy vastly superior in numbers. Further offensive action therefore seems to be senseless and aimless, especially as the time is coming very near when the physical strength of the troops will be completely exhausted.'[69]

The Army High Command, however, was reluctant to concede failure. When Guderian spoke to von Brauchitsch by telephone on 23 November, he noted that 'The Commander-in-Chief of the Army was, plainly, not allowed to make a decision. In his answer he ignored the actual difficulties, refused to agree to my proposals [to go over to the defensive], and ordered the attack to continue.'[70] But OKH could not withstand reality for long; on 27 November Wagner reported to Halder and the senior officers of the General Staff that 'we are at an end of our resources in both personnel and material. We are about to be confronted with the dangers of deep winter. . . . Situation is particularly difficult north of Moscow. . . . Horses—situation very serious; distressing lack of forage. Clothing—very bad, no means of improvement in sight.'[71] Three days later Halder noted 'total losses on the Eastern Front (not counting sick) 743,112 [since 22 June], i.e. 23.12 per cent of the average total strength of 3.2 million. . . . On the Eastern Front the Army is short of 340,000 men, i.e. 50 per cent of the fighting strength of the infantry. Companies have a fighting strength of 50-60 men. At home there are only 33,000 men available. Only at most 50 per cent of load-carrying vehicles are runners. Time needed for the rehabilitation of an armoured division is six months. . . .

We cannot replace even 50 per cent of our motorcycle losses.' Of the 500,000 trucks that had begun the campaign, 150,000 were total losses, and a further 275,000 needed repair. After the obvious failure of the last, desperate push in the first few days of December, OKH was finally convinced of the hopelessness of the situation. On the 4th it allowed the commander of Army Group Centre the discretion whether to carry on with the offensive or not; on the 5th, the 167th day of the campaign, von Bock called off the attack and ordered a withdrawal from over-exposed positions, and the Army leaders approved his move. Halder noted: 'They are at the end of their strength.'[73] Von Brauchitsch, his health broken, determined on resignation.

The next day, at a conference with the Führer, the Army Commander and his Chief of General Staff did all they could to impress on Hitler the dire straits in which Army Group Centre found itself. Halder noted that 'he refuses to take any account of comparative figures of strengths. To him our superiority is proved by the number of prisoners taken.'[74] Although Hitler reluctantly agreed that there should be a pause in the attack, he insisted that the objectives should be maintained and pursued as soon as possible. It was not until 8 December that he was forced to realise that the offensive should be abandoned completely. In Directive No. 39 he conceded defeat: 'The severe winter weather which has come surprisingly early in the east, and the consequent difficulties in bringing up supplies, compel us to abandon immediately all major offensive operations and go over to the defensive.'[75] Only in the extreme north and south was offensive action to continue; the lower Don-Donets line and Sevastopol were to be captured as soon as possible, and Leningrad encircled. Meanwhile, every attempt would be made to bring the eastern armies up to strength for the 1942 campaign, although the resources of the Army in the west were to be only temporarily weakened and would be maintained so that it was still capable of coastal defence and of carrying out the occupation of Vichy France.

The attack on Moscow was over; but the fighting certainly was not. On the night of 5 December, the day Army Group Centre had come to a halt, the Red Army launched the first of a series of counter-attacks which were to last until March. Of this period, Guderian wrote: 'We had suffered a grievous defeat in the failure to reach the capital which was to be seriously aggravated during the next few weeks thanks to the rigidity of our Supreme Command: despite all our reports, these men far away in East Prussia could form no true concept of the real conditions of the winter war in which their soldiers were now engaged. This ignorance led to repeatedly exorbitant demands being made on the fighting troops.'[76]

After 5 December there were two courses of action open to the military leaders: either a withdrawal until the following spring to a suitable defensive line, where positions had already been prepared, or an unyielding defence outside the gates of Moscow, in which any retreat was strictly forbidden. There were arguments for both courses. Von Bock's sixty-seven exhausted divisions were committed to a wide front that curved in a large, extended 600-mile salient, exposed to attack, difficult to defend, and for which there were no reserves to meet the Soviet counter-offensive. This problem could have been solved by a withdrawal to prepared positions nearer the supply bases, which would have had the effect of shortening the front and allowing a higher ratio of force to space. Moreover, the shelter afforded by these prepared positions would have prevented the high casualties brought about by the intense cold—by 8 December the temperature had fallen to -30°C. Had the Germans moved back to either Vyazma or Smolensk, the enemy would be forced to fight a major battle at the end of a 200-mile line of communication in deep snow, which the Soviet Army was ill-equipped to do. Such a withdrawal was favoured by all the front-line generals almost without exception. Initially, too, Hitler appears to have favoured some sort of a rearward move. In his Directive No. 39 of 8 December he specified three factors that should be observed when the Army went over to the defensive; areas 'of great operational or economic importance to the enemy' were to be held; the soldiers were to be allowed 'to rest and recuperate as much as possible'; and 'Conditions suitable for the resumption of large-scale offensive operations in 1942' were to be established. None of these precluded a withdrawal. Hitler continued: 'The main body of the Army . . . will, as soon as possible, go over to the defensive along a lightly tenable front to be fixed by the Commander-in-Chief of the Army. . . . Where the front had been withdrawn without being forced by the enemy, rear areas will be established in advance which offer troops better living conditions and defensive possibilities than the former positions. . . . The front line must be chosen with an eye to easy quartering and defence, and simplification of supply problems. . . .'[77]

Soon the Führer was to contradict himself. On 13 December, in accordance with Hitler's will, von Brauchitsch issued an order to commanders telling them to break off contact with the enemy and withdraw ninety miles; the very next day the Führer countermanded this. On the 15th von Brauchitsch again proposed a withdrawal, which Hitler overrode the next day, ordering: 'A general withdrawal is out of the question. The enemy has made substantial penetration only in a few places. The idea that we should prepare rear positions is just drivelling nonsense. The only trouble at the front is that the enemy outnumbers us in soldiers. He does not have any more artillery. His soldiers are not nearly as good as ours.'[78] A fanatical resistance was to be undertaken, without regard to the enemy on the flanks or the rear. Hitler was concerned that any withdrawal under enemy pressure would soon degenerate into a rout which would end, at the best, in the loss of most heavy equipment and, at the worst, in the destruction of Army Group Centre. Just as important in the Führer's eyes was the impact that any retreat would entail on the morale of the German nation, and the lowering of his status as a warlord in the eyes of the world. Moreover, he was convinced that 'will power' could override the crisis; that rigidity and tenacity would suffice to stem the Soviet tide. Keitel was fully in agreement with his Führer's decision: '. . . he correctly realised that to withdraw even by only a few miles, was synonymous with writing off all our heavy armaments; in which case the troops themselves could be considered lost. . . .'[79] Others, however, disagreed, and a large number of generals were replaced for acting on their convictions. Both Guderian and Hoepner were dismissed in disgrace for having dared pull their troops back without approval from the Führer.

The views of the military amateur were not in accord with those of the professionals. As it was, the front was forced back in a series of piecemeal withdrawals over distances of between 100 and 200 miles in the five weeks from 5 December, and losses in men and equipment were extremely high. By Christmas Eve Guderian had only forty tanks left in action. Between December 1941 and the middle of March 1942 Army Group Centre lost 256,000 men, and suffered a crippling sickness rate of some 350,000 men, a large proportion being the result of frostbite. In the same period it lost around 55,000 motor vehicles, 1,800 tanks, 140 heavy infantry guns, and so on down to 10,000 machine-guns. Material losses were considerably higher than during the summer victories.

For example, during the first six months of 'Barbarossa,' the average monthly loss of trucks was 1,223, and of light and heavy field howitzers, 193; in the following four months of winter, no less that 5,095 and 391 respectively were destroyed or captured. The suffering of the individual soldier, from cold and lack of food, to say nothing of the shortage of weapons and ammunition, was immense. On 2 February an agitated Halder noted: 'The scenes in this battle . . . are absolutely grotesque and testify to the degree to which this war has degenerated into a sort of slogging-bout which has no resemblance whatever to any form of warfare we have known.'[80] Yet in spite of this the German line did not break; by mid-March the Soviet offensive, at the end of its resources, came to a halt. There is no reason to suppose that a well-conducted, staged withdrawal, as was attempted by several first-class commanders at the time, would not have succeeded with, at most, the same loss that was in any case suffered, and probably with far less.

Moreover, the Germans were extremely fortunate not to suffer greater casualties, and to succeed in avoiding the enemy's repeated attempts at envelopment. Von Blumentritt gave a graphic description of what might have happened to 4th Army had it not been for mistakes on part of the enemy:

'Following the final check before Moscow . . . von Kluge advised the Supreme Command that it would be wise to make a general withdrawal to the Ugra, between Kaluga and Vyazma, a line which had already been partially prepared. There was prolonged deliberation at the Führer's headquarters over this proposal before reluctant permission was granted. Meanwhile the Russian counter-offensive developed in a menacing way, especially on the flanks. The withdrawal was just beginning when a fresh order came from the Führer, saying: "The 4th Army is not to retire a single step." . . . 4th Army became isolated in its forward position, and in imminent danger of encirclement. . . . Soon the danger became acute, for a Russian cavalry corps pressed round our right flank well to the rear of it. . . . Such was the grim situation of 4th Army on 24 December—and it had arisen from Hitler's refusal to permit a timely step back. . . . I and my staff spent Christmas Day in a small hut . . . with tommy-guns on the table and sounds of shooting all around us. Just as it seemed that nothing could save us from begin cut off, we found that the Russians were moving on westward, instead of turning up north astride our rear. They certainly missed their opportunity.'[81]

It was the endurance of the German soldier, the skill of his front-line generals, and the mistakes of the enemy that saved Army Group Centre, not Hitler. The utter ineptitude of his military leadership is revealed in the following extracts from the Chief of the General Staff's diary:

'19 December . . . [Hitler] orders to hold present positions. Not worried about any threats to the flanks. . . . 9 January . . . Several phone calls with von Kluge and Jodl. We have reached the point where a decision on taking back the front is absolutely essential, but the Führer cannot make up his mind yet and wants to talk to von Kluge directly. So, to our distress, the decision on this burning question is put off again, while we lose precious time. . . . 10 January . . . owing to adverse weather, von Kluge could not fly to the Führer. The decisive conference on the continuation of the

operations is therefore put off [to the next day]. . . .
11 January . . . The whole day with von Kluge at
Führer headquarters. The Führer upholds his order
to defend every inch of the ground. . . . The
situation is now becoming really critical. . . . 14
January . . . von Kluge reports that he must move
back if he wants to extricate himself. . . . The
Führer appreciates the necessity for taking back the
front, but will make no decision. This kind of
leadership can only lead to the annihilation of the
Army. . . . 20 January . . . The front is being taken
back gradually.'[82]

Halder's comment after the war was most apposite:
'Events proved stronger than Hitler's order. In spite of
the superhuman efforts of the troops, the front was
pressed back step by step and in some places even torn
open. When the force of the Russian attack had finally
been spent, the battered army held a deeply bulging line,
and even had to accept the fact that a substantial body of
its troops was cut off.'[83] By the time the Soviet counter-
offensive drew to a close, the German front had stabilised
along similar to, although more unfavourable than, that
proposed by von Bock four months earlier. Even Hitler
could not contravene reality; his attempt to do so,
however, had been costly in the lives of his soldiers.

9

The New Commander-in-Chief

'*I can take no more*'
FIELD-MARSHAL WALTHER von BRAUCHITSCH
Commander-in-Chief of the German Army, 1938–41

The assault on Moscow had failed; the fears of the generals, expressed so forcibly in the summer, had been realised in the winter. The campaign that had opened with such high hopes in June had come to a bitter end just six months later. Keitel, in an effort to understand the reasons for this, wrote:

'. . . during the summer of 1941 it almost seemed as though the eastern colossus would succumb to the mighty blows inflicted by the German Army, for the first and probably the best Soviet front-line army had, in fact, been all but wiped out by that autumn. . . . One wonders what army in the world could have withstood such annihilating blows, had the vast expanse of Russia, her manpower reserves, had the Russian winter not come to its assistance?'[1]

Perhaps, but von Bock's sober assessment, written on 7 December 1941, shows a clearer grasp of the reasons for failure:

> 'Three things have led to the present crisis: 1) the setting-in of the autumn mud season. . . . 2) the failure of the railways. . . . 3) the underestimation of the enemy's resistance and of his reserves of men and material. The Russians have understood how to increase our transport difficulties by destroying almost all the bridges on the main lines and roads to such an extent that the front lacks the basic necessities of life and of fighting equipment. . . . The Russians have managed in a surprisingly short time to reconstitute divisions which had been smashed, to bring new ones from Siberia, Iran, and the Caucasus up to the threatened front, and to replace the artillery which had been lost by numerous rocket launchers. There are now twenty-four more divisions in the sector of this army group than there were on 15 November. By contrast, the strength of the German divisions has sunk to less than a half as a result of the unbroken fighting and of the winter . . . the fighting strength of the tanks is even less. The losses of officers and NCOs are terribly high, and at the moment replacements for them are even more difficult to get than new troops.'[2]

Where lay the responsibility for these reasons for failure? They lay with Hitler. Had he listened to the advice of his generals in August, he would probably have been in the capital by October. But, as has been seen, he took another course. Time, the most valuable of commodities, had been lost; time in which the autumn mud season had drawn perilously near, in which the effect of the failure of the railways had had time to accumulate, and, most important, in which the enemy could build up his strength. By the middle of July, when von Bock was reporting that his chances were good for capturing Moscow by means of quick armoured thrusts, the Soviets had no tanks defending the Yartsevo-Vyazma-Moscow axis, and their divisions averaged fewer than 6,000 men in strength. No more than 50,000 soldiers could have stood between the Germans and the capital. By October the position had changed radically; no fewer than 800,000 men and 770 tanks, half the entire strength of the Red Army in the west, faced von Bock's offensive, and three defensive lines that had not been there in August had been erected around the capital. Operation Typhoon did indeed succeed in annihilating this force; by mid-November, after suffering losses of up to 700,000 men, the Soviets had but 90,000 men and only a few tanks defending Moscow. But then, at this decisive point, the weather broke. The Germans, exhausted by their efforts over the previous months, and denied adequate supplies, were unable to cross the hundred miles to Moscow, even against such weak opposition. Time was again on the side of the Red Army, and by the middle of November sixty rifle divisions, seventeen tank brigades, and fourteen cavalry divisions faced thirty-eight infantry, thirteen panzer, and seven motorised infantry divisions. Many of the Soviet formations might have been understrength, but all of the Germans were exhausted. When it became clear that the Japanese would not attack in Siberia, divisions from the Far East began to arrive in large numbers, composed of men highly trained and well-equipped for operating in the intense cold of a Russian winter. By early December, on the eve of their counter-attack, the Soviets had 718,000

men, 7,985 guns and mortars, and 721 tanks, mostly
T34s, on their central front. The Germans, outnumbered
and ill-equipped for winter warfare, proved incapable of
reaching their objective. The result was the first major
defeat for German arms in the war.

It is, of course, a purely hypothetical question whether
the German Army could have reached Moscow in the
autumn had Hitler allowed it to attempt to do so. All that
can be said is that the chances seemed good; certainly
this was the consensus of military opinion at the time. It
is only possible to guess at the impact that the loss of
Moscow would have had on the Soviet colossus, but the
argument of Kesselring appears not unreasonable:

> 'If on conclusion of the encirclement battle of
> Smolensk . . . the offensive had been continued
> against Moscow after a reasonable breather, it is my
> belief that Moscow would have fallen into our
> hands before the winter and before the arrival of
> the Siberian divisions. The capture of Moscow
> would have been decisive in that the whole of
> Russia in Europe would have been cut off from its
> Asiatic potential and the seizure of the vital
> economic centres of Leningrad, the Donets Basin,
> and the Maykop oilfields in 1942 would have been
> no insoluble task.'[3]

Such was the potential that Hitler had lost; more
crucially, he had also paved the way for the total defeat of
the German Army in the field.

On the flanks of the German Eastern Front, operations
had continued during the final advance on Moscow. In
the south, von Rundstedt's weakened army group had
been given new tasks by the Führer, despite the fact that
it now possessed only forty German divisions, of which

three were panzer and two motorised infantry, and had suffered severe shortages of supplies, especially petrol. Von Rundstedt recalled:

> 'After accomplishing my first objective, which was the encirclement and destruction of the enemy forces west of the Dnepr, I was given my second objective. It was to advance eastwards and take Maykop and Stalingrad. We laughed aloud when we received these orders, for winter had already come and we were almost 700 kilometres away from these cities. Hitler thought that with the frost making the roads hard we could advance towards Stalingrad very quickly. At the same time I was told to advance towards Maykop because oil was urgently needed, and I was also expected to clean up the Crimea in order to deprive the Russians of their airfields in this area.'[4]

Thus, Army Group South was expected to be capable of achieving three objectives at once. None was achieved in 1941; in the Crimea, Sevastopol continued its stubborn resistance, and 11th Army was forced to waste its energies which would have been spent more properly on the main attack to the Caucasus; in the Ukraine the Germans managed to get no further than Rostov, the 'gateway' to the Caucasus; and on the road to Stalingrad, they only passed Kharkov, still on the west bank of the Donets. Their inability to gain these three objectives simultaneously need not be regarded as a failure, for they were certainly too ambitious for a force with the limited resources of Army Group South.

However, in their main attack the Germans were to experience their first setback of the war, at Rostov-on-the-Don. The advance south-east to the Caucasus was led by von Kleist's Panzer Group 1, renamed 1st Panzer

Army on 5 October, with 17th and 6th Armies in support. Halder was concerned that such an advance would leave a dangerous gap between Army Groups Centre and South, and von Rundstedt was disturbed by the risks of advancing a further 400 miles beyond the Dnepr and exposing and overstretching his left flank. Hitler dismissed these fears with the confident argument that the Soviets were by then incapable of offering any serious opposition. However, as in the central sector of the front, so in the south. On 6 October the weather broke and the ground turned to mire; by the 11th, 6th and 17th Armies were at a standstill. But it was not until the 14th that 1st Panzer Army was similarly affected, with the result that the supporting infantry armies were kept from maintaining close contact with the vulnerable, but still advancing, spearhead. Nevertheless the attack continued. On the 17th Taganrog fell; on the 30th Kharkov was reached, and on 20 November Rostov was entered. Although their achievement was hailed as a great victory by Germany's propaganda machine, von Rundstedt and his officers knew that the reality of their position was other than Geobbels would have it.

With insufficient resources, an over-extended flank, and a rate of advance that was far too slow to keep the enemy off balance, the army group was vulnerable to Soviet counter-attack. At the end of November this came, with, as its object, the severance of 1st Panzer Army from the rest of von Rundstedt's army group. As 6th Army was stuck in the mud, and 17th Army too far back to relieve the armoured spearheads, there was nothing for it but to evacuate Rostov and fall back over the Mius to Taganrog. On 28 November the Germans left the city. But on the 30th Hitler ordered 'no retreat.' Von Rundstedt remembered:

'The Russians attacked at Rostov from the north

and south about the end of November, and, realising that I couldn't hold the city, I ordered it to be evacuated. I had previously asked for permission to withdraw this extended armoured spearhead to the Mius river, about 100 kilometres west of Rostov. I was told that I could do this and we began to withdraw very slowly, fighting all the way. Suddenly an order came to me from the Führer: "Remain where you are, and retreat no further," it said. I immediately wired back: "It is madness to attempt to hold. In the first place the troops cannot do it, and in the second place if they do not retreat they will be destroyed. I repeat that this order be rescinded or that you find someone else." That same night the Führer's reply arrived: "I am acceding to your request," it read, "please give up your command." I then went home.'[5]

Von Rundstedt was replaced by von Reichnau. The attacks continued unabated, and Halder wrote in his diary for 1 December: '1st Panzer Army is convinced intermediate position [between Rostov and Taganrog] cannot be held. . . . It cannot understand why our troops should stand here and have the enemy punch through their line when five miles back there is a much better position.'[6] Nor could von Reichnau. His request to the Führer for a withdrawal met with compliance; in the afternoon of 1 December, less than twenty-four hours after von Rundstedt had been relieved of his command, permission was given to move back across the Mius. Halder noted wryly: 'We have arrived where we were yesterday evening. Meanwhile we have lost energy and time, and von Rundstedt.'[7]

To the north, too, the Germans had suffered a major setback, although this was not at first apparent to them. Leningrad had not fallen; it had not even been fully encircled. As Warlimont said later: 'Hitler gave another fateful halt order just when the vanguards of Army Group North had reached the outskirts of the city [on 10 September]. Apparently he thereby wanted to avoid the loss of human life and material to be expected from fighting in the streets and squares of this Soviet metropolis against an outraged population, and hoped to gain the same ends by cutting off the city from all lines of supply.'[8] But although all road and rail communications to the city had been cut, the Lake of Ladoga, which froze over on 18 November, still remained in Soviet hands as the vital lifeline to Leningrad. On 25 November the Germans went over to the defensive; deprived of Panzer Group 4, then in the central sector of the front, von Leeb was left with only one Spanish and thirty German divisions to withstand the inevitable Soviet counter-offensive. When this broke, the ring around Leningrad remained intact, but Hitler's 'no withdrawal' order ensured that other parts of the front were penetrated, and troops encircled, much to von Leeb's disquiet. The most renowned of these pockets was at Demyansk, where 90,000 men in an area forty by twenty miles were kept supplied for two and a half months by the Luftwaffe until, by 21 April 1942, a corridor was forced through to the defenders. This had been a notable achievement by the Air Force, which succeeded in getting a daily average of 273 tons of supplies to the troops, and it won the Führer's praise. Demyansk, above all other battles during the Soviet counter-offensive, proved to Hitler's own satisfaction that his policy of 'no withdrawal' was correct, and with this as his justification he was to embark on exactly the same course the following winter. It was to result in the débâcle at Stalingrad.

Failure at the gates of Moscow, the first significant setback suffered by Hitler since 1933, inevitably brought with it serious consequences for the Army leadership, innocent though it was of the causes. Relations between the Supreme Commander and OKH, which had blown hot and cold during the campaign, were at their lowest level. On 7 December, Halder noted in his diary: 'The experiences of today have been shattering and humiliating. The Commander-in-Chief is little more than a post-box. The Führer is dealing over his head with commanders-in-chief of army groups.'[9] Already Hitler had dismissed one army group commander, von Rundstedt, without even consulting OKH; now he was personally directing the battle as well. On 6 December von Brauchitsch, weakened considerably from ill-health (he had been suffering heart-attacks since November) and torn between his conceptions of duty and honour, had offered his resignation, only to be told by the Führer that he was too busy with more important matters to be bothered by it. Eleven days later the Army Commander was summoned to Hitler's presence and informed that he was to be relieved. All suggestions of a successor were rejected with the exception of one, when Schmundt proposed what was no doubt already in the dictator's mind—that Hitler himself should be the new Commander-in-Chief. On the 19th von Brauchitsch's retirement was announced, and the Führer informed his soldiers that henceforth he would assume active command of the Army. He told Halder: 'Anyone can do the little job of directing operations in war. The task of the Commander-in-Chief is to educate the Army to be National Socialist. I do not know any Army general who can do this as I want it done. I have therefore decided to take over command of the Army myself.'[10] At the same time, although Halder was to maintain his position as Chief of the General Staff, Keitel was to take over all the other 'administrative functions' of OKH. Thus, in mid-December 1941 Hitler concluded a process which had begun in early 1938.

Then, the political independence of the soldiers had received a significant setback, and was soon to exist no more; now the operational autonomy of the Army, already severely breached on many occasions, was to end abruptly. The corporal of the First World War had, indeed, become the warlord of the Second.

Hitler's disillusion with, and contempt for, his generals reached a high point at the end of 1941. Three months later he could speak of von Brauchitsch 'only in terms of contempt. A vain cowardly wretch who could not appraise the situation, much less master it. By his constant interference and consistent disobedience he completely spoiled the entire plan. . . .'[11] Of the other generals, too, the Führer had a low opinion: 'The senior officers who have risen from the General Staff are incapable of withstanding severe strain and major tests of character.'[12] During the winter crisis his temper grew shorter, and his dislike more marked. Halder's diary for this period is full of the Führer's outbursts. For example, on 30 November, as von Rundstedt was pulling back from Rostov, Halder noted: 'The interview [between Hitler and von Brauchitsch] appears to have been more than disagreeable, with the Führer doing all the talking, pouring out reproaches and abuse, and shouting orders as fast as they came into his head.'[13] On 2 January Halder wrote: 'The withdrawals of 9th Army [under extreme pressure] against the will of the supreme Commander occasion mad outbursts on his part at the morning conference. OKH is charged with having introduced parliamentary procedures into the Army [a high abuse!], and with lacking incisiveness of direction. These ravings, interspersed with utterly baseless accusations, waste our time and undermine any effective cooperation.'[14] And the next day: 'Another dramatic scene with the Führer, who calls into question the generals' courage to make hard decisions.'[15]

Thus, between December 1941 and April 1942 there came about a considerable transformation in the leadership of the German Army. On 1 December von Rundstedt was removed, and von Reichenau put in his place; on 18 December von Bock, suffering from a bad stomach, left Army Group Centre, and was succeeded by von Kluge; on 19 December von Brauchitsch was replaced by Hitler; on 16 January von Leeb, frustrated by his loss of operational freedom, was relieved of his command as requested, to be replaced by von Küchler; on 17 January von Reichenau died of a stroke, and von Bock returned to the front to take up command of Army Group South. In addition, thirty-five army, corps, and divisional generals, including Guderian and Hoepner, were dismissed. Gone with them was the respect that had traditionally been accorded to members of the Army General Staff. From then on, none of its members was to be safe from the Führer's wrath. Warlimont remembered one instance of this:

'In the Reich Chancery . . . Brauchitsch's departure was followed by a busy perusal of the list of generals and their chiefs of staff whom Brauchitsch might have seen on his trip. Then Hitler came across the name of Hossbach, his former aide-de-camp, whom he had dismissed on 4 February 1938, and very brusquely transferred him to field duty. Hitler added, as I learned later, that Hossbach was "one of those defeatist General Staff officers" who should not be allowed to influence an able commander (General Strauss). Under the circumstances this incident made a painful and lasting impression among the older General Staff officers.'[16]

This was but one of the manifestations of the Army's

political and operational impotence; the most damaging were Hitler's inflated regard for himself as a military leader, and the power he had come to possess over the Army, which he was determined to exercise to the full. The impotence of the Army High Command in operational matters was the end of a process that had begun so innocently with the several suggestions made by the Führer during the Polish campaign. The offensives against Norway and the west had further extended this precedent to unacceptable limits, while the invasion of the Soviet Union had seen the matter taken to its logical conclusion with the choice of objectives. By September 1941, it was clear that the General Staff could never hope to prevail against Hitler's direction of the battle; and by the end of the year the Army leaders were even isolated from their generals in the field. Von Brauchitsch was Army Commander-in-Chief only in name; Hitler had already assumed his power. The transfer of his title was but a formality. After December 1941 and the bitter fighting of the winter of early 1942, Hitler placed the weight of the blame for the failure in front of Moscow on the military commanders, both in OKH and in the field; he was convinced that his 'no retreat' order had saved the Army. This was but the last of a number of events stretching back to 1936, in which he believed that his intuition had shown itself to be immeasurably superior to the professional expertise of the generals. This, he was convinced, would continue; he would take no heed to their advice or warnings.

The fact that Hitler had assumed the full authority of the Army Commander, was, in itself, no reason why OKH should continue to lose its importance relative to OKW. There were two other solutions to the problem as to how the division of operational responsibility should be divided between the commands: either the merger of the two staffs, both of whom were now directly answerable to Hitler, or the absorption of OKW into the larger, and better equipped, OKH. However, neither of these courses was to be followed; combination of the two officers would have been against one of Hitler's fundamental political principles—the division of authority. Furthermore, the dominance of the Army Command, after all its supposed opposition to his wishes, would have been highly distasteful to him. Hitler's suspicion of OKH and his dislike of its methods were ingrained. He once remarked: 'General Staff officers do too much thinking for me. They make everything too complicated. That goes even for Halder. It is a good thing that I have done away with the joint responsibility of the General Staff.' As Warlimont noted: 'Hitler did not want unity; he preferred diversity, such unity as there was being concentrated in his person alone.'[17]

Ironically, however, it had been the Army itself that, in the period between July 1940 and June 1941, had first extended the authority of OKW. Von Brauchitsch, still resentful at OKW's role during the Norwegian campaign, and no doubt annoyed by Hitler's interference in the plans for the Army of Norway, had declared on 18 March 1941 that 'he was leaving it to the OKW to issue all orders'[18] for the operations in Finnish Lapland. Halder disagreed, but to no avail. The result was that OKW controlled the operations of the Army units in that theatre, but, because it had not the organisation for the job, it left their supply, replacements, and organisation to OKH. This situation was made even more bizarre by the fact that OKH continued to advise Marshal Mannerheim, the Finnish Commander, on operational matters. Of this peculiar arrangement, Warlimont commented: '. . . a second "OKW theatre of war" was set up in Finland [to add to Norway] . . . now the Commander-in-Chief of the Army of his own accord surrendered to OKW, in other

297

words to Hitler, his responsibility for, and his powers of command over, a considerable number of Army formations in a purely land theatre of war.'[19] Once again the Army had yielded its operational autonomy, but this time without being ordered, or even asked, to do so. It was a poor reflection on the quality of von Brauchitsch's leadership.

During 'Barbarossa,' the influence of OKW, which during the planning of the invasion had been negligible, began to grow. Instead of remaining in Berlin, or surrounding himself with the Operations Staff of OKH, Hitler chose to situate his well-guarded Führer headquarters, code-named the *Wolfschanze* (Wolf's Lair), in East Prussia, a lonely place, remote from the front, far from the capital, and an hour away, by road, from the Army Command. Surrounding the Führer were the officers of OKW, who provided him with his daily briefings, and received and passed on his orders. Von Brauchitsch, Halder, and von Paulus met with Hitler only twenty-two times between 22 June and 19 December, whereas Keitel and Jodl saw and ate with him every day. Such an environment suited Hitler's temperament— especially his suspicion, his determination to exercise his authority as warlord, his inadequacies in military training, and his capacity to subordinate reality to wishful thinking. The OKW staff did nothing except foster this. Warlimont remembered: 'His permanent entourage . . . believing as they did that he had second sight and could not go wrong, egged him on rather than restraining him; moreover he was actually confirmed in his determination to play the part of supreme military leader by the fact that in Norway and northern Finland he was in direct command; the buffer of OKH did not exist there, and he could run affairs as he pleased.'[20] Furthermore, there still remained within the circle around Hitler that distrust and contempt for the Army

Command of old, which so pleased the dictator. For example, Goebbels wrote in his diary that 'Schmundt complained bitterly about the indolence of a number of senior officers who either do not want, or in some cases are unable, to understand the Führer.'[21] At least for the moment, Hitler had no fear of the OKW and OKH combining to thwart his wishes.

The OKW, then, suited Hitler well, despite the fact that it was ill-equipped for its growing responsibilities. From the early summer of 1941 he began to use it in the place of OKH as his command organisation in all theatres of war except in the east. Warlimont wrote: 'He was entirely unmoved by the obvious disadvantages of this peculiar command organisation, and apparently encountered no objection from any quarter.'[22] On 15 October 1941 Hitler instituted the post of Commander-in-Chief of the Armed Forces, South-East, to control the Balkans, the Aegean, and Crete up to Dalmatia; he was to receive his orders from, and report to, OKW. From the autumn the Mediterranean also became an OKW theatre. Although supreme command there nominally belonged to the Italians, the importance of Rommel's activities in North Africa and the problems of communications across the Mediterranean caused Hitler to attempt to exert more influence over that area. Although no order was issued specifically transferring responsibility from OKH to OKW, the Führer made greater use of the latter at the expense of the former. On 1 December the Luftwaffe general, Kesselring, was made Commander-in-Chief, South, directly responsible to OKW. This was similar to the position as it developed in the west; again, no specific order was ever given, but on 20 October command was effectively moved from OKH to OKW by the Führer's direction to the Wehrmacht Command to build up the defence of the occupied English Channel Islands. This was followed in December by Hitler's decision to build a new West Wall to protect the Arctic, North Sea, and Atlantic coasts, the responsibility for which he gave to OKW. The Commander-in-Chief, West, was also made responsible to the Wehrmacht Command. By such means OKW was provided with a role; as a command organisation responsible for the over-all direction of the war it was impotent, but as one concerned with the individual services in individual theatres, it was to have an influence at least as great, or as little, as that of OKH.

By mid-December 1941 the OKW had replaced OKH as the responsible command in Norway, Finland, the west, the south-east, and the Mediterranean, and Hitler had succeeded in taking full control of the conduct of ground operations in the Eastern Front in place of von Brauchitsch and his staff. Thus, because of the division of authority between OKW and OKH, no single organisation possessed command over all the units of the Army in all the theatres of operation; this power was in the hands of just one man: Adolf Hitler. He was in every sense the supreme warlord. It was his tragedy, and the Army's, that he was to pay no heed to von Moltke's dictum: 'Only humility leads to victory; arrogance and self-conceit to defeat.'

A Note on Sources

I have relied upon a wide range of sources, both original
and secondary, and have drawn as much on many of the
well-known works on the period as on the fine collections
of documents found in the archives of the Imperial War
Museum (IWM), the Public Record Office (PRO) and
the Liddell Hart Papers (LHP). Of particular use have
been the collection of captured German documents
found in the IWM, and the interrogation reports and
translations of documents prepared for the War Crimes
Military Tribunal in 1945 and 1946, found in the LHP.

I have made extensive use of quotations, and would
like to place on record my indebtedness to the following
published works which must be regarded as basic texts
for all students of the German Army:

Heinz Guderian, *Panzer Leader*, Michael Joseph, 1952.
Wilhelm Keitel, *Memoirs*, with introduction and
    epilogue by Walter Görlitz, William Kimber, 1965.
Albert Kesselring, *Memoirs*, Kimbler, 1953.
B. H. Liddell Hart, *The Other Side of the Hill* (revised),
    Cassell, 1951.
Erich von Manstein, *Lost Victories*, Methuen, 1958.
Erwin Rommel, edited by B. H. Liddell Hart, *The*

Rommel Papers, Collins, 1953.

Walter Warlimont, *Inside Hitler's Headquarters*, Weidenfeld and Nicolson, 1964.

Siegfried Westphal, *The German Army in the West*, Cassell, 1951.

My quotations from men such as Halder, Jodl and Zeitzler come from translations of captured documents and interrogation reports.

I also owe a great deal to the information contained in books by the following authors: B. H. Liddell Hart, J. F. C. Fuller, R. O'Neill, J. Wheeler-Bennett, K. Demeter, H. Deutsch and H. Rosinski.

I should also like to thank two Americans, John Calder and Otto Kuhn, for making available to me their, as yet, unpublished manuscripts on the German Army 1933 to 1939; although much of their material can be found in published works, their compilations are of considerable value to a researcher.

Notes

1 *Poland*

1. Friedrich Heiss, *Der Sieg im Osten*, Berlin, 1940, p. 19.
2. Ibid., p. 15.
3. IWM, AL 1446.
4. Heiss, p. 119.
5. Ibid., p. 18.
6. Ibid., p. 18.
7. Erich von Manstein, *Lost Victories*, London, 1958, pp. 62–3.
8. LHP, letter from Guderian to Liddell Hart, dated 20 Dec. 1949.
9. B. H. Liddell Hart, *History of the Second World War*, London, 1970, pp. 29–30.
10. IWM, AL 1448.
11. Ibid.

2 *Military Impotence*

1. Walter Warlimont, *Inside Hitler's Headquarters 1939–45*, London 1964, p. 5.

2. Halder, *Kriegstagebuch* (KTB), 24 Aug. 1939.
3. Ibid., undated entry at end of the first volume (ends 10 Sept. 1939).
4. Ibid., 25 Sept. 1939.
5. Ibid., 27 Sept. 1939.
6. IWM, War Directive No. 6.
7. Ibid., No. 1.
8. Adolf Hitler, *My New Order* (Speeches), New York, 1941, p. 102.
9. Halder, KTB, 29 Sept. 1939.
10. Ibid., 8 Oct. 1939.
11. Wilhelm Keitel, *The Memoirs of Field-Marshal Keitel*, London, 1965, p. 99.
12. Warlimont, pp. 36–7.
13. Manstein, p. 72.
14. Ibid., pp. 72–84.
15. Warlimont, p. 57.
16. Manstein, p. 93.
17. Keitel, p. 100.
18. Halder, KTB, 4 Oct. 1939.
19. Harold Deutsch, *The Conspiracy Against Hitler in the Twilight War*, Minneapolis, 1968, p. 72.
20. Halder, KTB, 11 Oct. 1939.
21. Manstein, p. 85.
22. Keitel, p. 102.
23. Manstein, p. 87.
24. Deutsch, p. 229.
25. John Wheeler-Bennett, *Nemesis of Power*, London, 1964, p. 459.
26. Deutsch, *Twilight Conspiracy*, p. 197.
27. Ibid., p. 235.
28. Ibid., p. 240.
29. Ibid., p. 246.
30. Halder, KTB, 7 Jan. 1940.
31. Wheeler-Bennett, p. 492.
32. Deutsch, *Twilight Conspiracy*, p. 259.

33. Heinz Guderian, *Panzer Leader*, New York, 1957, p. 64.
34. Taylor, *The March of Conquest*, New York, 1958, p. 57.
35. Manstein, p. 88.
36. Deutsch, *Twilight Conspiracy*, p. 262.
37. Halder, KTB, 23 Nov. 1939.
38. Guderian, p. 66.
39. Ibid., p. 66.
40. Ibid., p. 66.
41. Jodl, KTB, 18 Oct. 1939.
42. Warlimont, p. 45.
43. Ibid., pp. 56–8.
44. Ibid., p. 62.
45. Ibid., p. 56.
46. Ibid., p. 79.
47. Jodl, KTB, 13 Dec. 1939.
48. Warlimont, p. 71.
49. Ibid., p. 72.
50. Halder, KTB, 21 Feb. 1940.
51. Ibid., 21 Feb. 1940.
52. Warlimont, pp. 75–6.
53. Jodl, KTB, 19 April 1940.
54. LHP, files on German generals.
55. Warlimont, p. 76.
56. Ibid., pp. 79–80.
57. LHP, Wavell.
58. Jodl, KTB, 14 April 1940.
59. Halder, KTB, 14 April 1940.
60. Jodl, KTB, 17 April 1940.
61. Ibid., 19 April 1940.
62. Gordon Craig, *The Politics of the German Army 1640–1945*, London, 1955, p. 502.

3 *The West—The Plans*

1. IWM, War Directive No. 6.
2. Ibid., No. 10.
3. Taylor, *The March of Conquest*, p. 162.
4. Manstein, p. 97.
5. Author's collection, Operation Yellow, second version.
6. Manstein, p. 98.
7. IWM, War Directive, No. 8.
8. Taylor, *The March of Conquest*, p. 165.
9. Jodl, KTB, 30 Oct. 1939.
10. L. F. Ellis, *The War in France and Flanders*, London, 1953, p. 338.
11. IWM, War Directive No. 8.
12. Jodl, KTB, 13 Feb. 1940.
13. IWM, AL 7956.
14. Ibid.
15. Ibid., AL 795C.
16. Manstein, p. 108.
17. Halder, KTB, 21 Jan. 1940.
18. IWM, Al 795.
19. Ibid., AL 795B.
20. Ibid.
21. Ibid.
22. Ibid.
23. Ibid.
24. Ibid., AL 1092.
25. Ibid., AL 7950.
26. Guderian, p. 74.
27. Ibid., p. 72.
28. IWM, AL 795B.
29. Halder, KTB, 6 Mar. 1940.
30. Guderian, p. 69.
31. Ibid., pp. 69–70.
32. Halder, KTB, 14 Feb. 1940.

33. Manstein, p. 100.
34. Guderian, pp. 70–1.
35. Halder, KTB, 17 Mar. 1940.
36. Guderian, p. 70.
37. Halder, KTB, 4 Feb. 1940.
38. Ibid.
39. Ibid., 28 Apr. 1940.
40. Ibid., 2 May 1940.
41. Larry Addington, *The Blitzkrieg Era and the German General Staff*, New Brunswick, 1971, p. 85–6.

4   *The West—The Campaign*

1. J. F. C. Fuller, *Conduct of War*, London, 1961, p. 258–9.
2. Ibid., pp. 257–8.
3. Liddel Hart, *History of the Second World War*, p. 66.
4. LHP, letter from Guderian to Liddell Hart dated 24 Jan. 1949.
5. Halder, KTB, 12 May 1940.
6. B. H. Liddell Hart, *The Other Side of the Hill*, London, 1951, p. 173.
7. Guderian, p. 71.
8. H. A. Jacobsen, *Dokumente zur Vorgeschichte des Westfeldzuges, 1939–40*, Vol. 2, Göttingen, 1956, p. 32.
9. Liddell Hart, *The Other Side of the Hill*, pp. 177–8.
10. Halder, KTB, 16 May 1940.
11. Jacobsen, p. 34.
12. Ibid., p. 38.
13. Liddell Hart, *The Other Side of the Hill*, p. 179.
14. Ibid., pp. 178–9.
15. Jacobsen, p. 40.
16. Ibid., p. 42.

17. Halder, KTB, 17 May 1940.
18. Halder, KTB.
19. Jodl, KTB, 18 May 1940.
20. Ibid.
21. Halder, KTB, 18 May 1940.
22. Ibid.
23. Ibid.
24. LHP, file on invasion of the West.
25. Jacobsen, p. 47.
26. Guderian, p. 89.
27. Jodl, KTB, 20 May 1940.
28. Liddell Hart, *The Other Side of the Hill*, p. 184.
29. Ellis, p. 95.
30. Ibid., p. 96.
31. Jacobsen, p. 61.
32. Guderian, pp. 91-2.
33. Ellis, p. 158.
34. Ibid., p. 158.
35. IWM, 1L 1092B.
36. LHP, file on invasion of the West.
37. Ellis, p. 151.
38. Ibid., p. 138.
39. Ibid., p. 348.
40. Ibid., p. 348.
41. Warlimont, p. 98.
42. Jacobsen, p. 74.
43. Jodl, KTB, 24 May 1940.
44. Ellis, p. 139.
45. IWM, War Directive No. 13.
46. Guderian, p. 94.
47. Halder, KTB, 24 May 1940.
48. Ibid.
49. Jacobsen, p. 74.
50. Ellis, p. 150.
51. Ibid., p. 150.
52. Halder, KTB, 25 May 1940.

53. Jodl, KTB, 25 May 1940.
54. Ellis, p. 150.
55. Ibid., p. 151.
56. Jacobsen, p. 56.
57. Halder, KTB, 26 May 1940.
58. Ibid.
59. Jodl, KTB, 26 May 1940.
60. Halder, KTB, 26 May 1940.
61. Guderian, p. 96.
62. Ellis, p. 192.
63. Ibid., p. 191.
64. Ibid., p. 192.
65. Ibid., p. 208.
66. Jacobsen, pp. 147–51.
67. Halder, KTB, 30 May 1940.
68. Guderian, p. 99.
69. Albert Kesselring, *Memoirs*, London, 1953, p. 60.
70. Guderian, p. 104.
71. F. W. Mellenthin, *Panzer Battles 1939–45*, London, 1955, p. 22.
72. Liddell Hart, *The Other Side of the Hill*, p. 168.
73. Halder, KTB, 6 June 1940.
74. Ibid., 10 June 1940.
75. Ibid., 13 June 1940.
76. Ibid., 19 June 1940.
77. Guderian, p. 105.
78. LHP, file on invasion of the West.
79. Ibid.

5 *Decisions*

1. Manstein, p. 150.
2. Halder, KTB, 3 Sept. 1940.
3. Taylor, *March of Conquest*, p. 346.
4. Halder, KTB, 23 May 1940.

5. Keitel, p. 110.
6. Warlimont, pp. 89–90.
7. Barry Leach, *German Strategy against Russia, 1939–41*, London, 1973, p. 52.
8. Ibid., p. 53.
9. Halder, KTB, 22 June 1940.
10. Ibid., 15 June 1940.
11. IWM, War Directive No. 16.
12. Halder, KTB, 6 Aug. 1940.
13. Siegfried Westphal, *The German Army in the West*, London, 1951, p. 89.
14. LHP, file on Operation 'Sealion.'
15. Manstein, p. 167.
16. IWM, War Directive No. 19.
17. Halder, KTB, 27 Mar. 1941.
18. IWM, War Directive No. 26.
19. Halder, KTB, 22 July 1940.
20. Leach, p. 54.
21. Halder, KTB, 4 July 1940.
22. Ibid., 3 July 1940.
23. Ibid., 13 July 1940.
24. Ibid., 30 July 1940.
25. Ibid., 5 Dec. 1940.
26. Ibid., 31 July 1940.
27. IWM, War Directive No. 18.
28. Halder, KTB, 5 Dec. 1940.
29. IWM, War Directive No. 21.
30. Halder, KTB, 28 Jan. 1941.
31. Leach, p. 141.
32. Ibid., p. 141.
33. Ibid., p. 142.
34. Ibid., p. 159.

1. Halder, KTB, 3 July 1940.
2. Ibid., 22 July 1940.
3. Ibid., 31 July 1940.
4. Ibid., 26 July 1940.
5. Ibid., 1 Aug. 1940.
6. Author's collection, Marcks Plan.
7. Leach, p. 106.
8. Halder, KTB, 5 Dec. 1940.
9. Author's collection, Lossberg Study.
10. IWM, War Directive No. 21.
11. Halder, KTB, 9 Jan. 1941.
12. Warlimont, p. 138.
13. Ibid., p. 140.
14. Author's collection, OKH Deployment Plan.
15. Ibid.
16. Halder, KTB, 3 Feb. 1941.
17. Ibid., 17 Mar. 1941.
18. Leach, p. 163.
19. Ibid., p. 164.
20. Warlimont, pp. 141–2.
21. Author's collection, OKH Deployment Plan.
22. IWM, War Directive No. 21.
23. Author's collection, OKH Deployment Plan.
24. Ibid.
25. Halder, KTB, 3 Feb. 1941.
26. Leach, p. 106.
27. Guderian, p. 117.
28. Liddell Hart, *The Other Side of the Hill*, p. 272.
29. Author's collection, OKH Deployment Plan.
30. Ibid.
31. Guderian, p. 122.
32. Halder, KTB, 14 Mar. 1941.
33. Ibid., 19 Mar. 1941.
34. Ibid., 27 Mar. 1941.

35. Leach, p. 135.
36. Halder, KTB, 20 May 1941.
37. Ibid., 13 June 1941.
38. Ibid., 1 July 1940.
39. Ibid., 29 Sept. 1940.
40. Ibid., 5 May 1941.
41. Liddell Hart, *The Other Side of the Hill*, pp. 254-5.
42. Ibid., p. 251.
43. Leach, p. 94.

7 *'Barbarossa'—The Campaign*

1. Halder, KTB, 22 June 1941.
2. Ibid., 9 June 1941.
3. Warlimont, p. 135.
4. Keitel, p. 127.
5. Leach, p. 144.
6. Manstein, p. 177.
7. Halder, KTB, 24 June 1941.
8. Guderian, p. 129.
9. Halder, KTB, 23 June 1941.
10. Guderian, p. 131.
11. Halder, KTB, 24 June 1941.
12. Ibid., 29 June 1941.
13. Ibid., 29 June 1941.
14. Ibid., 2 July 1941.
15. Guderian, pp. 131-5.
16. Halder, KTB, 24 June 1941.
17. Guderian, p. 132:
18. Ibid., p. 134.
19. Liddell Hart, *The Other Side of the Hill*, p. 272.
20. Halder, KTB, 3 July 1941.
21. Liddell Hart, *The Other Side of the Hill*, p. 272.
22. Halder, KTB, 9 July 1941.
23. Guderian, p. 149.

24. Halder, KTB, 26 July 1941.
25. Guderian, p. 150.
26. Ibid., p. 154.
27. Purnell's *History of the Second World War*, p. 702.
28. Ibid.
29. Manstein, pp. 184–5.
30. Ibid., p. 186.
31. Halder, KTB, 28 June 1941.
32. Ibid., 8 July 1941.
33. Manstein, p. 193.
34. Ibid., p. 193.
35. Halder, KTB, 11 July 1941.
36. IWM, War Directive No. 33.
37. Ibid., No. 33a.
38. Ibid., No. 40.
39. Halder, KTB, 23 June 1941.
40. Ibid., 25 June 1941.
41. Ibid., 29 June 1941.
42. Ibid., 5 July 1941.
43. Ibid., 7 July 1941.
44. Ibid., 9 July 1941.
45. Ibid., 10 July 1941.

8 *'Barbarossa'—The Failure*

1. Halder, KTB, 3 July 1941.
2. Ibid.
3. Ibid., 11 July 1941.
4. Ibid., 12 July 1941.
5. Ibid.
6. Ibid., 13 July 1941.
7. Ibid., 12 July 1941.
8. Ibid., 15 July 1941.
9. Ibid., 16 July 1941.
10. Ibid., 13 July 1941.

11. Ibid., 20 July 1941.
12. Author's collection, OKH Memorandum.
13. Halder, KTB, 28 July 1941.
14. Warlimont, p.
15. Halder, KTB, 8 July 1941.
16. Jodl, KTB, 5 July 1941.
17. IWM, War Directive No. 33.
18. Ibid.
19. Halder, KTB, 23 July 1941.
20. Ibid., 26 July 1941.
21. Ibid., 30 July 1941.
22. IWM, War Directive No. 34.
23. Halder, KTB, 30 July 1941.
24. Ibid., 31 July 1941.
25. Guderian, p. 151.
26. Ibid., p. 153.
27. Keitel, p. 150.
28. Warlimont, p. 187.
29. Ibid., p. 187.
30. Halder, KTB, 8 Aug. 1941.
31. Halder, KTB, 11 Aug. 1941.
32. IWM War Directive No. 34, Supplement.
33. Halder, KTB, 13 Aug. 1941.
34. Ibid., 15 Aug. 1941.
35. Author's collection, OKH Memorandum.
36. Ibid., Hitler's reply to Memorandum.
37. Ibid., OKH Deployment Directive.
38. Halder, KTB, 8 July 1941.
39. Warlimont, p. 180.
40. Halder, KTB, 22 Aug. 1941.
41. Ibid., 22 Aug. 1941.
42. Warlimont, pp. 191–2.
43. Halder, KTB, 30 Aug. 1941.
44. Guderian, pp. 158–62
45. Ibid., p. 162.
46. Ibid., p. 157.

47. Halder, KTB, 25 Aug. 1941.
48. Ibid., 27 Aug. 1941.
49. Ibid., 28 Aug. 1941.
50. Ibid., 29 Aug. 1941.
51. Ibid., 31 Aug. 1941.
52. Guderian, p. 165.
53. Ibid., p. 166.
54. Halder, KTB, 4 Sept. 1941.
55. Guderian, pp. 167-8.
56. IWM, War Directive No. 35.
57. Guderian, pp. 173-4.
58. Ibid., p. 174.
59. Halder, KTB, 8 Oct. 1941.
60. Guderian, pp. 179-82.
61. Ibid., p. 186.
62. Ibid., p. 188.
63. KTB, 11 Nov. 1941.
64. Liddell Hart, *History of the Second Word War*, p. 168.
65. Guderian, pp. 189-90.
66. Ibid., p. 192.
67. Ibid., p. 194.
68. Halder, KTB, 29 Nov. 1941.
69. Ibid., 1 Dec. 41.
70. Guderian, p. 193.
71. Halder, KTB, 27 Nov. 1941.
72. Ibid., 30 Nov. 1941.
73. Ibid., 5 Dec. 1941.
74. Ibid., 6 Dec. 1941.
75. IWM, War Directive No. 39.
76. Guderian, p. 199.
77. IWM, War Directive No. 39.
78. Halder, KTB, 16 Dec. 1941.
79. Keitel, p. 166.
80. Halder, KTB, 2 Feb. 1942.
81. Liddell Hart, *The Other Side of the Hill*, pp. 289-90.
82. Halder, KTB, 19 Dec. 1941-20 Jan. 1942.

83. Halder, *Hitler as Warlord*, p. 51.

9 *The New Commander-in-Chief*

1. Keitel, p. 145.
2. Author's collection, von Bock memorandum.
3. Kesselring, p. 78.
4. LHP, von Rundstedt file.
5. Ibid.
6. Halder, KTB, 1 Dec. 1941.
7. Ibid.
8. Liddell Hart, *The Other Side of the Hill*, p. 278.
9. Halder, KTB, 7 Dec. 1941.
10. Halder, *Hitler as Warlord*, p. 49.
11. Warlimont, p. 212.
12. Ibid., p. 213.
13. Halder, KTB, 30 Nov. 1941.
14. Ibid., 2 Jan. 1942.
15. Ibid., 3 Jan. 1942.
16. LHP, Warlimont file.
17. Warlimont, pp. 216–7.
18. Ibid., p. 142.
19. Ibid., p. 142.
20. Ibid., p. 179.
21. Ibid., p. 214.
22. Ibid., p. 196.

Select Bibliography

ADDINGTON, LARRY H.: *The Blitzkrieg Era and the German General Staff, 1865–1941.* New Brunswick: Rutgers, 1971.

ALLEN, WILLIAM SHERIDAN: *The Nazi Seizure of Power.* New York: Watts, 1965.

BAUER, EDDY: *Panzer Krieg* (2 Vols.) Bonn: Offene Wörte, 1965.

BECKER, CAJUS: *The Luftwaffe War Diaries.* London: Macdonald and Jane's, 1967.

BELFIELD, E. and ESSAME, A.: *The Battle for Normandy.* London: Batsford, 1965.

BENOIST-MÉCHIN, J.: *Sixty Days that Shook the West.* London: Jonathan Cape, 1963.

BERNHARDT, WALTER: *Die Deutsche Aufrüstung, 1934–39. Frankfurt am Main: Bernard und Graefe, 1969.*

BLAU, GEORGE E.: *The German Campaign in Russia: Planning and Operations, 1940–42.* Washington D.C.: U.S. Department of the Army, 1955.

BLUMENSON, MARTIN: *Breakout and Pursuit.* Washinton D.C.: U.S. Army Military History Department, 1961.

BLUMENTRITT, GÜNTHER: *Von Rundstedt, The Soldier and The Man*. London: Odhams, 1952.

BRACHER, KARL: *The German Dictatorship*. New York: Praeger, 1970

BRACKMANN, ALBERT *et al.*: *Unser Kampf in Polen*. Munich: Bruckmann, 1959.

BROSZAT, MARTIN: *German National Socialism 1919–1945*. Santa Barbara, California: American Bibliographical Center-Clio Press, 1966.

BULLOCK, ALAN: *Hitler, A Study in Tyranny*. New York: Harper & Row, 1964.

CARREL, PAUL: *Hitler's War on Russia*. London: Harrap, 1964.
    Scorched Earth. London: Harrap, 1970.

CECIL, ROBERT: *Hitler's Decision to Invade Russia 1941*. New York: David McKay, 1976.

CHAPMAN, GUY: *Why France Fell*. London: Cassell, 1968.

CHURCHILL, WINSTON S.: *History of The Second World War*. London: Cassell, 1949.

CLARK, ALAN: *Barbarossa*. London: Hutchinson, 1965.

COLE, HUGH M.: *Ardennes and the Battle of the Bulge*. Washington D.C.: U.S. Army Military History Department, 1965.

COOPER, MATTHEW, and LUCAS, JAMES: *Panzer, The Armoured Force of the Third Reich*. London: Macdonald and Jane's, 1976.

CRAIG, GORDON: *The Politics of the Prussian Army 1650–1945*. New York: Oxford University Press, 1964.

CREVELD, MARTIN VAN: *Hitler's Strategy 1940–41*. New York: Cambridge University Press, 1973.

DALLIN, ALEXANDER: *German Rule in Russia, 1941–45*. London: Macmillian, 1951.

DELARUE, JACQUES: *The Gestapo.* New York: William Morrow, 1964.

DEMETER, KARL: *The German Officer Corps in Society and State, 1860–1945.* London: Weidenfeld and Nicolson, 1965.

DEUTSCH, HAROLD: *The Conspiracy against Hitler in the Twilight War.* Minneapolis: University of Minnesota, 1968.

    Hitler and His Generals, The Hidden Crisis. January–June 1938. Minneapolis: University of Minnesota, 1974.

DÖNITZ, Admiral KARL: *Memoirs.* London: Weidenfeld and Nicolson, 1958.

EARLE, EDWARD MEAD: *Makers of Modern Strategy.* Princeton: Princeton University Press, 1943.

EBELING, Dr. H.: *The Political Role of the German General Staff between 1918 and 1938.* London: New Europe, 1945.

ELLIS, L. F.: *The War in France and Flanders.* London: H.M.S.O., 1953.

    Victory in the West (2 Vols.) London: H.M.S.O., 1968.

ERICKSON, JOHN: *The Road to Stalingrad.* New York: Harper & Row, 1975.

ESEBECK, HANNS GERT Von: *Afrikanische Schicksalsjahre.* Wiesbaden: Limes, 1950.

ESSAME, H.: *Battle for Germany.* London: Batsford, 1969.

FEST, JOACHIM: *The Face of the Third Reich.* New York: Pantheon 1970.

    Hitler. New York: Random, 1975.

FRANK, FRIEDRICH, *et al.*: *Unser Kampf in Holland, Belgien und Flandern.* Munich: Bruckmann, 1941.

FRIED, HANS ERNEST: *The Guilt of the German Army.*

New York: Macmillan, 1943.

FULLER, Major-General J. F. C.: *Armoured Warfare.*
London: Eyre and Spottiswoode, 1943.

    Conduct of War. New York: Funk & Wagnalls,
1961.

    The Decisive Battles of the Western World (3 Vols).
London: Eyre and Spottiswoode, 1956.

    Machine Warfare. London: Hutchinson, 1942.

    The Second World War. New York: Hawthorn,
1969.

GAULLE, CHARLES De: *The Army of the Future.*
London: Hutchinson, 1940.

GEYR Von SCHWEPPENBURG, L.: *The Critical Years.*
London: Allen Wingate, 1952.

GILBERT, FELIX: *Hitler Directs His War.* Hauppauge,
N.Y.: Universal Publishing, 1971.

GOEBBELS, JOSEF: *The Goebbels Diaries.* (Ed. Louis P.
Lochner). Wesport, Conn.: Greenwood Press, repr
of 1948 ed.

GÖRLITZ, WALTER: *The German General Staff.* London: Hollis and Carter, 1953.

GREINER, E.: *Die Oberste Wehrmachtführung, 1939–
1943.* Wiesbaden: Limes, 1951.

GRUNBERGER, RICHARD: *A Social History of the Third
Reich.* London: Weidenfeld and Nicolson, 1971;
Penguin, 1974.

GUDERIAN, HEINZ: *Panzer Leader.* New York: Ballan-
tine, 1957. abr ed. 1976.

    Mit dem Panzern in Ost und West. Göttingen:
Volk und Reich, 1942.

HALDER, FRANZ: *Hitler as Warlord.* London: Putnam,
1950.

    Kriegstagebuch, 1939–1942.

HARRISON, G. A.: *Cross Channel Attack.* Washington

D.C.: Army Military History Department, 1951.

HEIDEN, KONRAD: *Der Führer*. New York: Howard Fertig, repr of 1944 ed.

HEISS, FRIEDRICH: *Der Sieg im Osten*. Berlin: Volk und Reich, 1940.

HIGGINS, TRUMBALL: *Hitler and Russia*. London: Macmillan, 1966.

HILLGRUBER, ANDREAS: *Hitlers Strategie*. Frankfurt am Main: Bernard und Graefe, 1965.

HINSLEY, F. H.: *Hitler's Strategy*. Cambridge: Cambridge University Press, 1951.

HITLER, ADOLF: *My New Order* (Speeches). New York: Octagon Books, repr of 1941 ed.
  Table Talk. (Ed. H. Trevor-Roper). London: Weidenfeld and Nicolson, 1953.
  War Directives, 1939–45 (Ed. H. Trevor-Roper). London: Sidgwick and Jackson, 1964; Pan, 1966.

HOFFMANN, PETER: *The History of the German Resistance, 1933–1945*. Cambridge, Mass.: M.I.T. Press, 1976.

HÖHNE, HEINZ: *The Order of the Death's Head*. New York: Coward, McCann & Geoghegan, 1970.

HORN, A.: *To Lose a Battle*. New York: Macmillan, 1969.

HOSSBACH, FRIEDRICH: *Zwischen Wehrmacht und Hitler*. Göttingen: Vardenhoek und Ruprecht, 1965.

HOTH, HERMANN: *Panzer Operationen*. (Die Wehrmacht im Kampf, vol. II) Heidelberg: Vowinkel, 1956.

HOWARD, MICHAEL: *The Mediterranean Strategy in the Second World War*. London: Weidenfeld and Nicolson, 1968.

HUNTINGTON, SAMUEL P.: *The Soldier and the State*. Cambridge, Mass.: Harvard University, 1957.

INTERNATIONAL MILITARY TRIBUNAL: *The Trial of the German Major War Criminals: Proceedings of the International Military Tribunal Sitting at Nuremberg, Germany* (23 Vols.). London: H.M.S.O., 1949–51.

IRVING, DAVID: *Hitler's War*. New York: Viking Press, 1977.

JACOBSEN, H. A.: *Dokumente zur Vorgeschichte des Westfeldzuges, 1939–1940* (2 Vols.). Göttingen: Musterschmidt, 1956.
  Fall Gelb: der Kampf um den deutschen Operationsplan der Westoffensive, 1940. Wiesbaden: Steiner, 1957.

JACOBSEN, H.A. and ROHWER, J.: *Der Zweite Weltkriege in Chronik und Dokumentum*. Darmstadt: Wehr und Wissen, 1961.

JODL, ALFRED: *Kriegstagebuch 1938–1945*—fragments prepared by the International Military Tribunal.

KEILIG, WOLF: *Das Heer* (3 Vols.). Bad Neuheim: Podzun, 1956 and various dates.

KEITEL, WILHELM: *The Memoirs of Field-Marshal Keitel*, with an introduction and epilogue by Walter Görlitz. London: William Kimber, 1965.

KENNEDY, R.M.: *The German Campaign in Poland, 1939*. Washington D.C.: Department of the Army, 1956.

KESSELRING, ALBERT: *Kesselring*. Wesport, Conn.: Greenwood Press, repr of 1954 ed.

KRAUSNICK, HELMUT *et al.*: *Anatomy of the SS State*. London: Collins, 1968.

LAFFIN, JOHN: *Jackboot*. London: Cassell, 1965.

LEACH, BARRY A.: *German Strategy against Russia, 1939–1941*. New York: Oxford University Press, 1973.

LESTER, J. R.: *Tank Warfare*. London: Allen and

Unwin, 1943.

LEWIN, ROLAND: *Rommel as a Military Commander*. London: Batsford, 1968.

LIDDELL HART, B. H.: *The Other Side of the Hill*. London: Cassell (revised and enlarged), 1951.

    A History of the Second World War. New York: Putnam, 1971.

    Strategy. New York: Praeger (revised), 1961.

    The Tanks—The History of the Royal Tank Regiment 1914–45 (2 Vols.). London: Cassell, 1959.

LUDENDORFF, ERICH: *The Nation at War*. London: Hutchinson, 1936.

MACKSEY, KENNETH: *Guderian: Creator of the Blitzkrieg*. New York: Stein and Day, 1976.

MANSTEIN, ERICH Von: *Lost Victories*. London: Methuen, 1958.

MASON, H. M.: *The Rise of the Luftwaffe, 1918–1940*. New York: Dial, 1973.

MELLENTHIN, F. Von; *Panzer Battles*. Norman, Okla.: University of Oklahoma Press, 1972.

MIDDELDORF, E.: *Taktik im Russlandfeldzug*. Berlin: E. S. Mittler und Sohn, 1956.

MIKSCHE, F. O.: *Blitzkrieg*. London: Faber and Faber, 1941.

MILWARD, ALAN S.: *The German Economy at War*. Atlantic Highlands, N. J.: Humanities Press, 1965.

MÜLLER-HILLEBRAND, B.: *Das Heer, 1933–1945* (3 Vols.) Frankfurt am Main: E. S. Mittler und Sohn, 1954, 1956, 1969.

    The Organisational Problems of the Army High Command and their Solutions, 1938–1945. U.S. Army, Europe, Historical Division, 1953.

MUNZEL, O.: *Die Deutschen Gepanzerten Truppen bis 1945*. Hertford: Maximilian, 1965.

    Heinz Guderian—Panzer Marsch. Munich: Schild,

1955.
> *Panzertaktik.* Heidelberg: Vowinkel, 1959.

NEHRING, W.: *Die Geschichte de deutschen Panzerwaffe, 1916 bis 1945.* Berlin: Propyläen, 1969.

OBERKOMMANDO DES HEERES: *Jahrbücher des deutschen Heeres, 1940, 1941, 1942.* Leipzig: Breitkopf und Härtel, 1940, 1941, 1942.
> *Die Truppenführung.* HDV 300.

OBERKOMMANDO DER WEHRMACHT: *Glückhäfte Strategie.* Berlin: 1942.
> *Kriegestagebuch* (5 Vols.) Frankfurt am Main: Bernard und Graefe, 1961-63.
> *Sieg über Frankreich.* Berlin: 1940.
> *Der Sieg in Polen. Berlin: Andermann, 1940.*
> *Sieg im Westen.* Berlin: 1940.
> *Die Wehrmacht, 1940, 1941.* Berlin: Die Wehrmacht, 1940, 1941.

OGORKIEWICZ, RICHARD M.: *Armour.* New York: Arco, 1970.

O'NEILL, ROBERT: *The German Army and the Nazi Party, 1933-39.* New York: Heineman, 1967.

ORLOW, DIETRICH: *The History of the Nazi Party.* Vol. 1—1919-33, Vol. 2—1933-45. Pittsburgh: University of Pittsburgh Press, 1969, 1973.

PHILIPPI, ALFRED, und HEIM, FERDINAND: *Der Feldzug gegen Sowjetrussland, 1941-45.* Stuttgart: Kohlhammer, 1962.

PIELALKIEWICZ, JANUSZ: *Pferd und Reiter im II Weltkrieg.* Munich: Sudwest, 1976.

PLAYFAIR, I. S.: *The Mediterranean and Middle East.* (4 Vols.) London: H.M.S.O., 1954.

RAUSCHNING, HERMANN: *Hitler Speaks,* London:

Butterworth, 1939.

REITLINGER, GERALD: *The Final Solution*. London: Vallentine, Mitchell, 1953.

RICH, NORMAN: *Hitler's War Aims*. (2 Vols.) New York: Norton, 1973, 1974.

ROBERTSON, E. M.: *Hitler's Pre-War Policy and Military Plans, 1933–39*. London: Longmans, 1963.

ROHER, J. *et al.*: *Decisive Battles of World War II: The German View*. London: Deutsch, 1965.

ROMMEL, ERWIN: *Papers*. (Ed. B. H. Liddell Hart) New York: Harcourt Brace Jovanovich, 1953.

ROSINSKI, HERBERT: *The German Army*. New York: Praeger, 1966.

SCHRAMM, PERCY ERNST: *Hitler: The Man and the Military Leader*. New York: Watts, 1971.

SCHRAMM, WILHELM RITTER Von: *Conspiracy among Generals*. New York, Scribner, 1957.

SEATON, ALBERT: *The Russo-German War, 1941–45*. London: Barker, 1971.

SEECKT, HANS Von: *Thoughts of a Soldier*. London: Benn, 1930.

SENFF, H.: *Die Entwicklung der Panzerwaffe im deutschen Heer zwischen der beiden Weltkriegen*. Berlin: E. S. Mittler und Sohn, 1969.

SENGER und ETTERLIN, Dr. F. Von: *Die deutschen Panzer 1926–45*. Munich: Lehmanns, 1959.

　Die Panzergrenadiere. Munich: Lehmanns, 1961.

SHIRER, WILLIAM L.: *Berlin Diary*. New York: Knopf, 1941.

　The Rise and Fall of the Third Reich. New York, Simon and Schuster, 1960; London: Pan, 1964.

SHULMAN, MILTON: *Defeat in the West*. Westport, Conn.: Greenwood Press, repr of 1948 ed.

SIEGLER, F.: *Die höheren Dienstellen der deutschen Wehrmacht, 1933–45*. Stuttgart: Deutsche Verlagsanstalt, 1953.

SPEER, ALBERT: *Inside the Third Reich. New York: Macmillan.* Sphere, 1971.

SPEIDEL, H.: *We Defended Normandy.* London: Jenkins, 1951.

STEIN, GEORGE H.: *The Waffen SS.* Ithaca, N.Y.: Cornell University Press, 1966.

STRAWSON, JOHN: *Hitler as a Military Commander.* London: Batsford, 1971.

TAYLOR, A. J. P.: *The Origins of the Second World War.* New York: Atheneum, 1962.

TAYLOR, TELFORD: *Sword and Swastika.* Magnolia, Mass.: Peter Smith, repr of 1953 ed.

TOLAND, JOHN: *Adolf Hitler.* New York: Doubleday, 1976.

TREVOR-ROPER, H. R.: *The Last Days of Hitler.* New York: Macmillan, 3rd ed 1962.
    Hitler's War Directives. London: Sidgwick and Jackson, 1964; Pan, 1966.

U.S. GOVERNMENT PRINTING OFFICE: *Nazi Conspiracy and Aggression* (10 Vols.). Washington D.C., 1946.

U.S. WAR DEPARTMENT: *Handbook of German Military Forces.* Washington D.C., 1941.

WARLIMONT, WALTER: *Inside Hitler's Headquarters, 1939–45.* London: Weidenfeld and Nicolson, 1964.

WERNER, MAX: *The Military Strength of the Powers.* London: Gollancz, 1939.

WERTH, ALEXANDER: *Russia at War, 1941–1945.* New York: Dutton, 1964.

WESTPHAL, SIEGFRIED: *The German Army in the West.* London: Cassell, 1951.

WHEELER-BENNETT, JOHN: *The Nemesis of Power.*

New York: St. Martin, 1964.

WILLIAMS, JOHN: *The Ides of May. The Defeat of France May–June, 1940*. London: Constable, 1968.

WILMOT, CHESTER: *The Struggle for Europe*. Westport, Conn.: Greenwood Press, repr of 1952 ed.

WINTRINGHAM, TOM: *New Ways of War*. London: Penguin, 1940.

    Peoples' War. London: Penguin, 1942.

YOUNG, Brigadier DESMOND: *Rommel, The Desert Fox*. New York: Harper & Row, 1951.

ZESKA, Major Von: *Das Buch vom Heer*. Berlin: Borg, 1940.

ZIEMKE, E. F.: *The German Northern Theatre of Operations, 1940–45*. Washington D.C.: Department of the Army, 1959.

    Stalingrad to Berlin. Washington D.C.: Department of the Army Historical Series, 1968.

Index

Aa, R., 107, 110.

Abbeville, 101.

Abwehr, 194.

Africa Corps see German Africa Corps.

Aire, 108.

Aisne, R., 97-8, 122, 125.

Albania, 143.

Allies, weakness of before war, 84-6; losses in campaign in west, 1940, 118; *et passim*; *see also under names of countries.*

Alpenveilchen, Operation, 143.

Altmark, 46.

Amiens, 88, 90, 121.

Antwerp, 86.

Ardennes, 58, 86, 91.

Armaments and equipment, 27, 77, 81, 184-9; in Operation Barbarossa, 270; *see also* Tanks.

Armeegruppe Guderian, 219.

Armoured idea, principles of, not used in Polish campaign, 19; nor in attack on west, 63-5, 70-4, 120.

Army *see under* German Army.

Army Ordnance Office, 183, 185.

Arras, 102, 104, 108, 111.

Balkans, 142-4, 189-93; *see also under names of countries.*

Barbarossa, Operation: plans for, 156-97; campaign, 198-300; situation August 1941, 238.

Beaulieu, General Charles de, 221.

Bechtolsheim, General von, 124.

Beck, General Ludwig, 36.

Belgium, 84, 85, 87-8; German plans for attack on, 53-63; *et passim.*

Berezina, R., 208, 211, 212, 215.

Bialystok, 206.

Blaskowitz, General Johannes, 10, 24.

Blitzkrieg see under Strategy and Tactics.

Blumentritt, General Gunther von, 92, 112, 177, 282.

Bobruysk, 208.

Bock, Field-Marshal Fedor von, 14, 20, 38, 56, 61, 63, 68, 91, 172; made Field-Marshal, 129; in Operation Barbarossa, 205, 207, 215, 219, 220, 243, 247, 250, 262, 264, 271-85 *passim*, 295.

Borisov, 210, 211.

Boulogne, 103, 104, 108.

Brauchitsch, Field-Marshal Walther von, 44, 48, 55, 62, 63, 112, 237, 297; opposition to attack on west, 33-6; made Field-Marshal, 129; and Operation Barbarossa, 237, 255, 259, 261, 273, 277, 280, 285; relieved of his command, 293-4; *et passim.*

Bredow, Major von, 250.

Brennecke, General Kurt, 163.

Brest-Litovsk, 204.

Britain and British Army, 84, 85; in France, 101-103, 107; proposed German invasion of, 134-38; German extension of war against, 139-142; in Greece, 191; *et passim.*

Brownshirts *see* SA.

Bug, R., 178.
Bulgaria, 142.
Busch, Field-Marshal Ernst, 172.
Bzura, 16.

Calais, 103, 104, 108.
Cauldron battles *see Kessel-
schlachten under* Strategy and
Tactics.
Churchill, Rt. Hon. W.S., 118.
Crete, 142, 193.

Denmark, 45.
Desna, R., 217, 265.
Dietl, General Eduard, 50.
Dnepr, R.: in plans for Operation
Barbarossa, 161, 169, 171,
175; in Operation Barbarossa,
208, 209, 211, 212, 215, 238.
Donets Basin, 158, 249, 254.
Dunkirk, 103, 106, 107, 115,
117.
Dvina, R., 167, 171, 208, 222,
223, 225.
Dvinsk, 222, 223.
Dyle, R., 86.

Egypt, 140, 141.
Engel, Captain Gerhard, 154,
168, 170.
Ersatzheer see Replacement
Army.
Estonia, 225, 227, 230.

Falkenhorst, General Nikolaus
von, 48, 49.
Felix, Operation, 141, 151.
Fellgiebel, General, 147.
Finland, 45.
France, 27–8, 84, 85, 87;
Maginot Line, 28, 55, 57, 58,
101, 120, 128; German plans
for attack on, 53–63; German
invasion of, 90–128; accepts

armistice terms, 128; Vichy
France, 141, 152; *et passim.*
Fritz, Operation, 166.
Fromm, General Fritz, 38, 48,
187, 273.
Fuller, Major-General J.F.C.,
89.

Gaulle, General Charles de, 102.
General Staff, the Polish
campaign, 13–20; status of at
beginning of Second World
War, 22–4; and plans for
destruction of France,
119–20; and plans for attack
on Soviet Union, 156–70;
*et passim; see also under names
of officers.*
German Army: moral responsibilities in relation to Hitler,
51; lack of resources and
equipment, 77–82; mobilisation, 11; the Polish campaign,
10–21; condition of on
invasion of Poland, 15; use of
mechanised units in Polish
campaign, 20; deficiencies
after Polish campaign, 27;
Hitler takes operational
control of, 42–5; condition of
before attack on west, 75–84;
numerical growth, 80; attack
on west begins, 88; the push
through France, 90–105;
advance on Dunkirk, 106; the
'halt order,' 107; failure to
achieve decisive victory in
west, 118–20; failure in
handling mechanised units in
Operation Red, 125–7; losses
in conquering France, Holland
and Belgium, 128; strength of
force for invasion of Soviet

Union, 173; condition of before invasion of Soviet Union, 180-93; the Generals' responsibility for failure in Soviet Union, 202; condition of, August 1941, 238-40; losses and shortages, November 1941, 277; losses March 1942, 280-2; Hitler becomes Commander-in-Chief, 294; other changes in leadership during Operation Barbarossa, 294-6; *et passim*; *see also under* Armaments and Equipment, Hitler, Rearmament, Strategy and Tactics, *and under Army branches and commands.*

Forces engaged

Army Group North (Polish Campaign): 14, 18, 20.

Army Group South (Polish Campaign): 18, 20.

Army Group A (In attack on west): 55, 56-63 *passim*, 70, 71, 75, 83, 86, 88, 90, 108, 110-4, *passim*, 119, 121, 125.

Army Group B (In attack on west): 55, 56-63 *passim*, 70, 83, 86, 90 *passim*, 112, 121, 122.

Army Group C (In attack on west): 56, 68, 83, 121, 128.

Army Group D, 182.

Army Group North (In Operation Barbarossa): 161, 167-72 *passim*, 175, 221, 223, 227-30 *passim*, 240, 245-50 *passim*, 255-60 *passim*, 268.

Army Group Centre (In Operation Barbarossa):

255-60 *passim*, 162-75 *passim*, 204, 212, 217, 220, 227, 230, 233, 238, 240, 245-64 *passim*, 268, 272, 277-81 *passim*, 289, 290.

Army Group South (In Operation Barbarossa): 161, 171, 173, 175, 193 *passim*, 227, 232-9, 247, 250, 254, 257, 269, 289, 290, 295.

2nd Army, 62, 121, 191, 211, 217, 264, 267-71 *passim*, 250, 275.

3rd Army, 14, 20.

4th Army, 14, 17, 69, 99, 109, 114, 122, 172-3, 177, 205, 208, 268, 282.

6th Army, 115, 122, 124, 173, 232, 233, 264, 290.

8th Army, 14, 24.

9th Army, 122, 173, 205, 207, 212, 269.

10th Army, 14, 17, 18, 20.

11th Army, 173, 240.

12th Army, 96, 122, 143, 191, 192.

14th Army, 14, 17.

16th Army, 122, 172, 220, 226-30.

17th Army, 173, 232, 290.

18th Army, 116, 122, 158, 172, 220, 223, 226-30.

II Corps, 74, 116.

XIV Corps, 17, 18, 75.

XV Corps, 17, 18, 74, 122.

XVI Corps, 17, 18.

XIX Corps, 17, 20, 61, 75, 102, 104, 117, 119.

XXI Corps, 20.

XXII Corps, 18.

XXVI Corps, 124.

XXXIX Corps, 108, 116.

XXXXI Corps, 75, 102, 116.
1st Light Division, 18.
4th Light Division, 18.
1st Mountain Division, 98.
3rd Mountain Division, 50.
see also under Panzer Forces.
Ghent, 55.
Gibralter, 141.
Goebbels, Reich Minister
  Joseph, 41, 290.
Goedeler, Carl, 32.
Gomel, 204, 217, 218.
Göring, Reich Marshal Herman,
  41, 49, 201; plans to destroy
  enemy in Flanders, 109–10;
  created *Reichsmarshall des
  Grossdeutschen Reiches*, 129;
  et passim.
Gort, Lord, 102.
Graf Spee, 46.
Greece, 142, 144, 151, 190.
Grieffenberg, Colonel Hans von,
  13, 112, 156, 191.
Groscurth, Lieutenant-Colonel
  Helmuth, 36.
Guderian, General Heinz, 18,
  20, 58, 61, 75: his strategic
  ideas, 70–4; in invasion of
  France, 93–127 *passim*; in
  Operation Barbarossa, 176,
  179, 205 *passim*, 207, 214–9,
  231 *passim*, 241, 250–2, 262–7
  passim, 270–81 *passim*, 292;
  dismissal, 281; *et passim*.

Halder, General Franz, 26, 55,
  61, 63, 111; as conspirator,
  34, 36–9; on plans for
  Operation Barbarossa, 158,
  178–80, 186; on Operation
  Barbarossa, 206–18 *passim*,
  223–7 *passim*, 231–55 *passim*,
  260–5 *passim*, 270–84 *passim*,
  292, 293.
Hammerstein-Equord, General
  Curt von, 36.
Heusinger, General Adolf, 242,
  255.
High Command of the Army,
  see under OKH.
High Command of the Luftwaffe,
  see under OKL.
High Command of the Navy, *see
  under* OKM.
High Command of the Wehr-
  macht, *see under* OKW.
Hitler, Führer Adolf: *Directives*:
  No. 1, 26; No. 6, 25–6, 53, 56;
  No. 8, 57, 61; No. 13, 111;
  No. 18, 141, 143, 150; No. 19,
  141; No. 20, 143; No. 21, 151,
  165, 175; No. 22, 57, 61; No.
  25, 61; No. 26, 61–2; No. 33,
  227, 246, 249; No. 33a, 230,
  246; No. 34, 230, 245; No. 35,
  267; No. 39, 278–83; con-
  spiracies against, 36–9; his
  intention to attack the west
  and destruction of Army's
  autonomy, 23–30; creates
  special weather reporting
  group, 41; takes operational
  control of Army, 42–7;
  weakness as military commander, 49–52; and plans for
  attack on west, 53–66; nervousness on French invasion,
  97; gives permission to
  advance on Dunkirk, 115; his
  triumph after victory in west,
  129–33; reverses objectives of
  Operation Barbarossa, 162–4;
  interference in military
  operations, 169–72; and
  Operation Barbarossa,

198–294 *passim*; his responsibility for failure of attack on Soviet Union, 201, 287; becomes Commander-in-Chief of Army, 294; *et passim*.

Hoepner, General Erich, 17, 19: and Operation Barbarossa, 224, 225, 227, 228, 232; dismissal, 281.

Holland, 84, 85, 87: German plan for attack on, 53–63.

Hossbach, General Friedrich, 295.

Hoth, General Hermann, 18, 42, 122, 176, 206: in Operation Barbarossa, 205, 212–6 *passim*, 220, 242, 255.

Hungary, 143, 159.

Indirect Approach *see* Armoured Idea.

Infiltration *see under* Strategy and Tactics.

Italy, 140, 143: entry to war, 128; in North Africa, 147.

Japan, 140, 150.

Jodl, General Alfred: increase in his power, 44; and Operation Barbarossa, 252, 298; *et passim*.

Keitel, Field-Marshal Wilhelm, 43, 44, 48: made Field-Marshal, 129; opposes plan for attack on Soviet Union, 200; and Operation Barbarossa, 251, 281, 293, 298; *et passim*.

Kesselring, Field-Marshal Albert, 288: becomes Commander in Chief, South, 299.

Kesselschlachten see under Strategy and Tactics.

Khan, Ghengis, 9.

Kharkov, 177, 254, 290.

Kiev: in plans for Operation Barbarossa, 158, 160, 169, 176, 178; and Operation Barbarossa, 232, 235, 236, 242, 262, 270.

Kinzel, Colonel Eberhardt, 157.

Kleist, Field-Marshal Ewald von, 75, 92, 94, 96, 103, 105, 121, 124, 173, 193; in Operation Barbarossa, 232, 233, 267.

Kluge, Field-Marshal Gunther von, 14, 172–3: character, 69; made Field-Marshal, 129; in Operation Barbarossa, 208–11, 215, 217, 219, 274, 295 *passim*; *et passim*.

Krasnogvardeisk, 230.

Küchler, Field-Marshal Georg von, 14, 172, 295.

Laon, 98.

Leeb, Field-Marshal Wilhelm von, 26, 38, 57, 167, 172, 221: character, 68; made Field-Marshal, 129; and Operation Barbarossa, 221–31 *passim*, 242, 292, 295.

Lemnos, 142.

Leningrad: in plans for Operation Barbarossa, 158, 162, 166, 171, 175, 177; in Operation Barbarossa, 220, 224–31 *passim*, 246, 248, 249, 254, 278, 291.

Ley, Reich Labour leader Robert, 41.

Libya, 142.

Liddell Hart, Sir Basil: quoted, 18, 90.
Liebenstein, General Kurt von, 274.
Liège, 55, 56.
Lille, 116.
Lindemann, Helmut, 51.
List, Field-Marshal Wilhelm, 96, 122, 125: made Field-Marshal, 129.
Lofoten Islands, 154.
Lossberg, Lieutenant-Colonel Bernhard von, 164.
Luftwaffe, 41, 46, 48, 57, 84, 201: strength before invasion of Soviet Union, 182, 188–90; supplies surrounded troops in Soviet Union, 292; *et passim*.
Luga, 226, 228.
Luga, R., 226, 227, 228.
Luxembourg, 53, 54, 91.

Mannerheim, Marshal Carl, 281.
Manstein, Field-Marshal Erich von, 59, 123, 186: opposition to plans for attack on west, 57–63; promoted to command Infantry Corps, 66; in Operation Barbarossa, 204, 220–9 *passim*; *et passim*.
Marcks, General Erich, 158.
Marita, Operation, 142, 151.
Marne, R., 126.
Mellenthin, General Joachim von, 124.
Meuse, R., 58, 67–8, 71–3, 88, 91: importance of, 92.
Minsk, 167, 175, 176, 206, 213, 216.
Moscow: in German plans for invasion of Soviet Union, 157, 158, 159, 161, 162, 166, 172, 175, 177; in Operation

Barbarossa, 202, 217, 220, 227, 238, 241, 245, 250, 252, 255, 267–72 *passim*, 287, 288; Operation Typhoon, 268–79; *et passim*.
Moulins, 124.
Murmansk, 154.
Mussolini, Benito, 142.

Nagel, Lieutenant-Colonel, 266.
Narva, 230.
Narvik, 50, 51.
Navy, 46, 182.
North Africa, 142; *see also under names of battles.*
Norway, 45, 154, 170; *see also under names of towns.*
Novgorod, 230.
Novorzhev, 224.

Oise, R., 223.
OKH, 24, 39, 96, 201: and Deployment Plan White, 13, 19; status at beginning of war, 22–4; attitude to attack on west, 24–36; decline in status of, 24–31; friction with OKW, 42; loss of status, 44–9, 51; plans for attack on west, 53–8, 64–6; disregarded in invasion of France, 112–4; and plans for destruction of France, 119–21; submission to Hitler after victory in west, 131–2; failure to press for invasion of Britain, 137–9; attitude to invasion of Soviet Union, 144–8, 151–5; and plans for invasion of Soviet Union, 156–94 *passim*; and Operation Barbarossa, 156, 233, 230–5 *passim*, 239–53 *passim*, 258–74 *passim*, 277, 278, 292,

294, 295; its power transferred
to Hitler, 294, 295; loses
influence to OKW, 296–300;
et passim; *see also* General
Staff.

OKW, 23, 41, 45, 49, 198–200:
announces attack on Poland,
10; report on Polish campaign,
17; opposition to OKH, 43;
begins to supplant OKH, 44;
plans for invasion of Britain,
136–8; lack of status in attack
on Soviet Union, 198–200;
and Operation Barbarossa,
237, 250, 252, 257; its
influence grows, 296–300;
et passim.

Ordnungspolizei, 82.

Orsha, 215.

Oster, Colonel Hans, 36, 39.

Ostrov, 224.

Otto, Operation, 166.

Panzer Forces: *Panzerverband
Kempf*, 14, 17; their role in
Polish campaign, 18–20; low
status in Operation Yellow
plans, 63–70; disposition and
command before attack on
west, 73–5; condition of
before attack on west, 75–6;
Hitler's concept of their use,
104–5; failure to use in
France, 119; leaders' discontent with proposed use in
Soviet Union, 176–80;
deficiencies before invasion
of Soviet Union, 181–6; in
Operation Barbarossa,
203–23 *passim*; 231–9 *passim*,
259–67 *passim*, 272, 274; *see
also* Tanks.

Forces engaged:

Panzer Group 1, 173, 232–6
passim, 247, 262, 289.

Panzer Group 2, 172, 177,
204, 205, 208, 212, 215, 247,
250, 262, 268, 271.

Panzer Group 3, 173, 205,
207, 212, 230, 242, 247–50,
268, 274, 276 *passim*.

Panzer Group 4, 172, 179, 221,
224–30 *passim*, 233, 247,
268, 292.

1st Panzer Army, 290.

2nd Panzer Army, 268, 274.

4th Panzer Army, 212–3, 219,
247.

XXIV Panzer Corps, 266.

XXXXI Panzer Corps,
224–30 *passim*.

LVI Panzer Corps, 204, 222–9
passim.

1st Panzer Division, 103, 107,
111, 122.

2nd Panzer Division, 18, 97,
101, 103, 122.

3rd Panzer Division, 267.

5th Panzer Division, 18.

7th Panzer Division, 102.

10th Panzer Division, 18, 20,
106.

17th Panzer Division, 211.

Panzerjäger, 77.

Paris, 88, 121, 128.

Paulus, Field-Marshal Friedrich
von: appointed Deputy Chief
of Staff, 162, 163; and
Operation Barbarossa, 228,
264.

Plateau de Langres, 121.

Poland: condition of Army on
German attack, 11–3; German
victory over, 11–21; *see also
next entry*.

Polish Corridor, 12, 14, 20.

Polotsk, 209, 213.
Portugal, 141.
Pripyat Marsh, 159–66 *passim*, 232, 233.
Pskov, 222, 225.

Raeder, Admiral Dr. Erich, 46, 139: and Operation Sea-Lion, 136; urges invasion of Britain, 152; critical of plans for attack on Soviet Union, 201.
Red, Operation, 120–8.
Reich Defence Council, 181.
Reich Defence Laws: 1939, 23.
Reich Labour Service, 41.
Reichenau, Field-Marshal Walter von, 32, 173: his opposition to attack on west, 32; made Field-Marshal, 129; and Operation Barbarossa, 233, 291; death, 295.
Reinhardt, General Hans, 116.
Replacement Army, 32, 118.
Reynaud, Paul, 128.
Rogachev, 212.
Romania, 142, 157, 169: oilfields, 157, 158, 160, 190.
Romilly, 124.
Rommel, Field-Marshal Erwin, 102.
Roslavl, 219, 220, 231, 263.
Rostov, 290.
Ruhr, 54, 55.
Rundstedt, Field-Marshal Gerd von, 38, 56, 58, 91, 173: opposition to plans for attack on west, 56–66; in invasion of France, 107–9; made Field-Marshal, 129; in Operation Barbarossa, 231, 232, 233, 236, 239, 288; relieved of his command, 290; *et passim*.
Russia *see under* Soviet Union.

Saarbrücken, 120.
Sabsk, 224.
St. Omer, 111.
St. Quentin, 97, 100.
Salmuth, General Hans von, 163.
Schlieffen, Alfred von, 54, 63.
Schmundt, Major Rudolf, 206, 293, 299.
Schobert, General Eugen Ritter von, 173.
Sea-Lion, Operation, 134–40, 147–9, 150.
Sedan, 95.
Seelöwe see Sea-Lion, Operation.
Seine, R., 124.
Sevastopol, 278.
Smolensk, 167, 172, 208, 210, 212, 214, 215, 216, 241, 244.
Sodenstern, General Georg von, 66–7, 68, 71, 163, 177, 234.
Somme, R., 98, 108, 120, 123.
Sonnenblume see Sunflower, Operation.
Soviet Union, 12, 16: attacks Finland, 45; proposed German attack on, 134, 139; the German decision to invade, 138–40, 144–56; the German plans for Operation Barbarossa, 156–97; Red Army strength (German estimate of), 1940, 159, 193–6; Operation Barbarossa, 198–300; *et passim: see also under names of towns and rivers.*
Spain, 141.
SS: *Leibstandarte* SS 'Adolf Hitler,' 82, 182; *Totenkopfverbände*, 82; Waffen SS, 182.
SS-VT: expansion of, 1939, 82; SS *Verfügungs Division* formed, 82.

335

Stalin, 231.
Stalingrad, 292.
Strategy and Tactics:
  Blitzkrieg, 11, 88–91;
  Kesselschlachten, 175;
  see also Armoured Idea and
  Vernichtungsgedanke.
Strauss, General Adolf, 172, 295.
Stülpnagel, General Karl-
  Heinrich, 13, 26, 173, 232: as
  conspirator against Hitler,
  36.
Sturmgeschütz, 186.
Sunflower, Operation, 142.
Sun Tzu, 86.

Tactics *see* Strategy and Tactics.
Taganrog, 290.
Tanks: production of before
  invasion of Soviet Union, 184.
  Types:
  PzKw I, 75, 184.
  PzKw II, 75, 184.
  PzKw III, 75, 184–5, 186.
  PzKw IV, 75, 184–5.
  PzKw 35(t), 75, 184.
  PzKw 38(t), 75.
  SdKt, 76, 143, 185.
Thoma, General Wilhelm von,
  19.
Thomas, General Georg, 33,
  186.
Timoshenko, Marshal Seměny,
  213.
Tippelskirch, General Kurt von,
  13.
Tripolitania, 142.
Trondheim, 50.
Twenty-Five, Operation, 143.
Typhoon, Operation, 268–79,
  287.

Uman, 204, 233, 237.

United States, 150.
USSR *see* Soviet Union.

Valdi, 230.
Verfügungstruppen see SS-VT.
Vernichtungsgedanke, 11, 13, 16,
  20, 117, 174.
Vistula, R., 12, 13, 16.
Vitebsk, 167, 209, 210, 215.
Volga, R., 219.

Wagner, General Eduard, 33,
  253, 277.
Warlimont, General Walter,
  298: on relations between
  Hitler and the Army, 28–30,
  43–4, 47, 132; on Operation
  Barbarossa, 166, 245, 252,
  261, 292; *et passim.*
Warsaw, 14, 16, 20.
Wavell, Field-Marshal Archi-
  bald, 50.
Wehrmacht High Command *see*
  OKW.
Weserübung, 46.
Weygand, General Maxime, 123,
  128.
Wietersheim, General Gustav
  von, 18, 73.
Witzleben, General Erwin von:
  as conspirator, 38; made
  Field-Marshal, 129.
Wodrig, General Albert, 124.
Wulfschanze, 298.

'X' Report, 40.

Yellow, Operation, 44, 53–66.
Yelnya, 212, 214, 215, 216, 269.
Yugoslavia, 141, 143, 154, 190,
  193.

Zossen, 39.

TRUE AND DOCUMENTED!
THE INCREDIBLE STRATEGIES, STUNNING VICTORIES, AND AGONIZING DEFEATS OF *THE SECOND WORLD WAR*

HITLER'S NAVAL WAR
by Cajus Bekker   (300, $2.25)
The incredible story of the undermanned Nazi naval force that nearly won WW II—Operation Underdog.

PACIFIC SWEEP   (332, $2.25)
by William N. Hess
They were a handful of heroes against a sky black with zeros spitting death!

HITLER'S GENERALS   (335, $2.25)
by Richard Humble
The incredible love-hate saga of the Fuhrer and his Commanders.

LINE OF DEPARTURE: TARAWA   (347, $2.25)
by Martin Russ
Man for man and inch for inch, the bloodiest battle ever fought in the Pacific War.

THE BOMBING OF NUREMBERG   (356, $2.25)
by James Campbell
The greatest single air battle of WW II—when the hunters became the hunted!

THE ADMIRAL'S WOLFPACK   (362, $2.25)
by Jean Noli
The spellbinding saga of Adm. Karl Doenitz's U-boats and the men who made these "gray wolves" the scourge of the seas.

THE LAST SIX MONTHS   (377, $2.25)
by General S. M. Shtemenko
The action-packed account of the Soviet Army's final drive into the heart of Hitler's Reich.

23 DAYS: THE FINAL COLLAPSE OF NAZI GERMANY (400, $2.25)
by Marlis G. Steinert
An hour-by-hour retelling of the death-throes of Hitler's Reich.

Available wherever paperbacks are sold, or order direct from the Publisher. Send cover price plus 40¢ per copy for mailing and handling to Zebra Books, 21 East 40th Street, New York, N.Y. 10016. DO NOT SEND CASH!